"John R. Corrigan accurately portrays life on the PGA Tour, and throws in a wonderful twist by adding a mystery and an interesting sleuth in Jack Austin. Anyone who likes golf and mysteries will find two here."

—PGA Tour player J. P. Hayes,
winner of the 2002 John Deere Classic and 1998 Buick Classic

"*Snap Hook* exposes its readers not only to the glamorous, slippery-putt tension of the PGA tour but to the fast-paced drama of crimes, high and low, local and international. A natural read for lovers of golf and suspense."

—Billy Collins

PRAISE FOR *CUT SHOT*

"*Cut Shot* is a riveting novel, with characters you care about, well conceived and gracefully presented."

—Robert B. Parker

"*Cut Shot* deftly combines life in professional golf's sunny top tiers with the dark world of life-or-death sleuthing. The first of a planned series, this debut novel is a fun, relaxing read. Beyond that, it's a fresh attempt to link a major sport to mystery in much the same way Dick Francis has linked mystery to horse racing . . . Corrigan is off to an impressive start . . . Good people, a good game and a good mystery add up to a score worth repeating. Let's hope Corrigan will repeat it soon."

—*Portland Sunday Telegram*

BAD LIE

OTHER BOOKS BY JOHN R. CORRIGAN

Cut Shot (Sleeping Bear Press, 2001)
Snap Hook (2004)
Center Cut (2004)

HARDSCRABBLE BOOKS—FICTION OF NEW ENGLAND

For a complete list of titles in the series,
please see WWW.UPNE.COM

BAD *LIE*

JOHN R. CORRIGAN

University Press of New England

HANOVER AND LONDON

Published by University Press of New England,
One Court Street, Lebanon, NH 03766
www.upne.com
© 2005 by John R. Corrigan
Printed in the United States of America
5 4 3 2 1

Library of Congress Cataloging-in-Publication Data
Corrigan, John R.
Bad lie / John R. Corrigan.
p.   cm.—(Hardscrabble books)
ISBN–13: 978–1–58465–454–4 (alk. paper)
ISBN–10: 1–58465–454–6 (alk. paper)
1. Golfers—Fiction. I. Title. II. Series.
PS3603.O773B33   2005
813'.6—dc22   2005016374

The author gratefully acknowledges permission to reprint the following lines of poetry:

pages 132 and 133: From NEW SELECTED POEMS by Philip Levine, copyright © 1991 by Philip Levine. Used by permission of Alfred A. Knopf, a division of Random House, Inc.

pages 34, 83, 221, 222, and 243: From WHAT WORK IS by Philip Levine, copyright © 1992 by Philip Levine. Used by permission of Alfred A. Knopf, a division of Random House, Inc.

page 79: From THEY FEED THEY LION AND THE NAMES OF THE LOST by Philip Levine, copyright They Feed They Lion, copyright © 1968, 1969, 1970, 1971, 1972 by Philip Levine   The Names of the Lost, copyright © 1976 by Philip Levine. Used by permission of Alfred A. Knopf, a division of Random House, Inc.

For my sister, Kelli

"For an instant I was the man in the mirror, the shadow-figure without a life of his own who peered with one large eye and one small eye through dirty glass at the dirty lives of people in a very dirty world."

—Ross MacDonald, *The Drowning Pool*

ACKNOWLEDGMENTS

Jack Austin tips his visor to the following: Deutsche Bank Championship Tournament Director Eric Baldwin, for providing a research opportunity like no other; Carl Bielstein of the Valero Texas Open; Dr. Lisa Leduc of the University of Maine at Presque Isle, for offering insights into various aspects of the criminal justice system and sex offenders; Presque Isle Police Chief Naldo Gagnon, who answers question after question (and plays great defense in front of an old goalie on Sunday nights); Adam Bernier, investigator with Allmerica Financial/Hanover Insurance Special Investigations Unit, for insight into handguns; Stacy Jandreau, M.D., emergency department physician at the Aroostook Medical Center in Presque Isle, Maine; Curt and Bethany Paterson, for their friendship, for providing information about Aroostook County, and for many great meals; and, as always, my cousin and former Secret Service agent Jon MacDonald, for sharing his knowledge of the criminal justice system. These people made the book better. Any blown putts within are the sole responsibility of the author.

Thanks, too, go to the people at the University Press of New England: Barbara Briggs, Hannah Fries, Sherri Strickland, Sarah Welsch, Susanna French, and always to John Landrigan, who champions the Jack Austin series.

Finally, thanks to my wife, Lisa, who makes it possible by offering me time and her endless support, and to my daughters, Delaney and Audrey, who always inspire.

AUTHOR'S NOTE

Although a golf course in northern Maine does in fact straddle the United States–Canada border, the events, characters, and scenarios in this book are totally and absolutely fictional and exist entirely in the author's (often overactive) imagination.

BAD LIE

In an uncertain universe, my vocation offers a black-and-white world. On the PGA Tour, either your score is low enough or it is not. The ball is in the hole or it isn't. You don't argue called strikes. Instant replay won't overrule decisions. In pro golf, results are final. So I trust my instincts and govern myself by the rules of the game. Unfortunately, life is rarely so straightforward.

On a Friday in late August, I was standing in the fairway on the par-four eighteenth at the Buick Championship, waiting for the group ahead of us to clear, when I spotted Nash Henley in the gallery.

From fifty yards, Nash looked like he always did—six-one, 225 rock-solid pounds, with legs thick as my waist. He wore a crisp white T-shirt that made his ebony skin look darker. The T-shirt had a black fist in the center and read POWER TO THE PEOPLE. His shaved head shone beneath the sunlight. I wondered why he had skipped football practice to be there.

The Buick Championship is played at the Tournament Players Club at River Highlands in Cromwell, Connecticut. Very few people had consistently followed my threesome—an occupational hazard when you're eighty-fifth on the PGA Tour's money list, ranked ninety-ninth in the world, and on the verge of missing another cut. However, the eighteenth fairway on any day at this venue near Hartford is shoulder to shoulder and three lines deep around the green.

"We're one-fifty-four from the pin," Tim Silver, my caddie, said and shook his head. "Got to hit a seven-iron, and we can't find level ground anywhere on this fairway."

We both knew the entire 156-man field faced the same condi-

1

tions. Silver was frustrated because we were two strokes over the projected cut line. After the second round, only the top seventy and ties play the weekend for the purse, which at this event was $4 million. I was on verge of being sent packing.

"I thought Nash couldn't come," Silver said. He was four inches shorter than me and built like a gymnast. His skin was lighter than Nash's, the color of creamed coffee, and his goatee made him look both angry and intellectual.

I shrugged, but stood looking at Nash, wondering what had brought him here. He appeared withdrawn, almost lost among the sea of faces at the fairway's edge as he stood staring off into the middle distance.

Across the fairway, from 160 yards, close friend Brian "Padre" Tarbuck selected an iron and stood behind his ball, aligning the shot. Brad Faxon, a fellow New Englander, stood to the other side of me, waiting patiently, having already stuck his approach shot six feet from the pin. Like me, he had a pair of red socks embroidered on his bag, a tribute to the Boston Red Sox. On occasion, we would watch a ballgame together.

Padre started moving to his ball, spotted a blade of grass on his white shoe, and bent to brush it off. Upset by the distraction, he began his entire preswing routine again—two practice swings, then he aligned the shot from behind the ball, checked the wind by tossing grass into the air—then he walked to the ball. This time a sound from the gallery bothered him—someone had crinkled a bag of chips. PGA Tour fairways are lined with marshals who hold large QUIET, PLEASE signs and stand near the players with raised hands to halt anyone from moving or talking while we hit. However, the occasional noise does not and certainly should not bother a player who has hit approximately three gazillion golf balls. Padre shook his head in frustration and backed off again. The marshal glared at the guy holding the chip bag. The guy stood breathlessly still.

"Never seen anything like this," Silver said. "Padre's not going to break ninety."

I knew he wasn't. Faxon did, too. Faxon and I had exchanged looks on several tee boxes but said nothing. The looks, however, spoke volumes: We were all witnessing something seen perhaps only a handful of times on the PGA Tour—a player unraveling for all the world to see. Ian Baker-Finch, now a commentator, won the 1991 British Open Championship, then, three years later, on the heels of thirty-one straight missed cuts and a ninety-two in the opening round of the 1994 Open Championship, retired from competitive golf. I had heard about Baker-Finch and that 1994 British Open from guys who had been there. Now I felt like I was witnessing it firsthand.

"I've never seen such a perfectionist," Silver said. "Any little noise throws Padre off his game. It's like he *thinks* everything needs to be perfect for him to hit a good shot. He's backed off eight or nine times today—retying his shoe, cleaning his clubs."

"I haven't noticed," I lied.

Padre made a beautiful practice swing—long, fluid, well balanced. It was identical to the other practice swings he'd made throughout the day. It was, however, antithesis to any swing he had used to hit a shot. He had pull-hooked several shots, sliced others, and even flat-out skulled two, causing the gallery to gasp. Although the score would no doubt be the worst of Padre's career, unfortunately, I knew this wasn't an isolated round for him this season. And anyone following the sport via print and television media knew that as well.

"At least he's swinging better than he's putting," Silver said, watching the practice swing. "He's made only two cuts this year. Christ, my five percent equals more than he's made. Maybe he can pull out of it."

"I hope so."

"So do I. The guy is gorgeous."

"Here we go again," I said.

"What? If you walked eighteen holes with Britney Spears, you wouldn't enjoy the view?"

"Britney Spears?"

"Whoever you're attracted to."

Faxon and his caddie had turned away each time Padre had made a swing. Likewise, Silver had made distracting comments to me. It was avoidance, PGA Tour style. Major League hitters don't like to watch eight consecutive teammates strike out, then face the same pitcher.

Padre moved to his ball again, carefully positioned the club-face behind the ball, then waggled the club. The waggle went on for close to thirty seconds. Then Padre shook his head and backed off once more.

"This is getting crazy," Silver said. "Say something to him, Jack. We're going to be timed."

The PGA Tour allows five minutes between shots. After a warning, the fines can mount to $20,000. Padre rechecked his alignment. Faxon's caddie glanced at his watch. Padre made another nice practice swing.

"I'm not saying a thing to Padre," I said. "He shot eighty-eight yesterday. A lot of guys would have withdrawn. He's gone twenty-seven events without making a cut. The guy's been a good friend. Besides, they're not going to give us a warning on the eighteenth hole."

Padre moved to the ball.

"Jesus," Silver said. "His knuckles are white. Looks like he's strangling the damned club."

We watched as Padre's caddie said something. I couldn't make out what it was, but the tone was soothing. Padre stepped away from the ball and bent over. He stayed hunched, shoulders trembling. The caddie moved to him and patted his back. Padre straightened and addressed the ball.

"Christ," Silver said, "this is tough to watch."

I called over to Padre and gave him a thumbs-up. He didn't acknowledge the gesture. With what he was going through, that was okay.

"He won two years ago," I said. "Finished in the top fifty on the money list last year."

"Missed that two-footer to get into a playoff at the U.S. Open last year," Silver said. "He's never been the same. This game can do that to you."

"Confidence is a strange thing," I said. "Padre's a good man. Like you said, this is tough to watch."

When Padre hit, he didn't bother to look up. The ball splashed into a greenside bunker. He started walking toward the green

4

immediately, as if hurrying a practice round to completion. As he walked ahead of us, I thought I saw Padre's right hand twitch.

Behind the rope lining the fairway, Nash looked oblivious to it all.

I sighed and drew a seven-iron from the big TaylorMade staff bag that stood between Silver and myself. I was trying to stay focused. Since I had been five years old, my father's mantra— "If you can control your mind, you can control your actions"— had aided me on the golf course. I'd won the Maine State Amateur Championship at nineteen, the New England Amateur at twenty-one. As a professional, I had waited more than a decade for my recent lone victory, which meant that year after year, to retain my Tour card, I had stood over a lot of must-make eight-foot putts to cash fiftieth-place checks. So the mantra had become religion.

I wasn't following it now. My focus jumped from Padre to Nash.

Five people to Nash's left, a white-haired older man leaned back and looked around the others to watch Nash. The guy stared at Nash, nodded to himself, then shifted from foot to foot as if nervous. He opened a manila folder, glanced down at it, then leaned back and looked at Nash again. He wore khaki shorts, a white golf shirt with a star-shaped logo on the left breast, and black Ray-Ban sunglasses, a decade past stylish. I'm no slave to fashion, but the white-haired man also wore navy blue dress socks with white tennis sneakers. *Ouch.*

The white-haired man looked out of place. I'd been around long enough to witness the socioeconomic changes of the average PGA Tour fan and thought I had seen every type—the Phoenix rowdies, the country-club set, the Ryder Cup drunks, the John Daly NASCAR types, and the English crumpets-and-tea gang. This man, his shock of white hair protruding like a briar patch from his straight-brimmed cap, fit none of those molds. And the guy wasn't even watching the golf. He was staring at Nash, noting his every move. Then he looked at me. Our eyes momentarily locked.

I turned away and put the seven-iron back in the bag. No

smooth seven here. This would be a fierce swing. I drew the eight-iron. The ball was above my feet, a hook lie.

"A birdie here," Silver said, "and maybe the field will come back to you."

That was Silver: Never say die.

At the top of my back-swing, sun flickered off the steel shaft like a camera pop. My back leg straightened, I paused for a split second, then began the down-swing, hips rotating, legs driving down and through impact. In my periphery, a divot danced end-over-end. My belt buckle pointed down the target line, and I held the follow-through.

I stole a glance at Nash. The white-haired man loomed nearby.

My ball descended slowly, right of the green, and plunged into the sand trap. I couldn't wait around wondering any longer. I walked to where Nash stood.

"Jack, I don't know what to do," he said. "Everything's gone now."

I leaned close to hear him over the cacophony of the gallery. "Calm down," I said. "What's wrong?"

"He's dead," Nash said. "My father is dead."

I stood slack-jawed. "Halle?" I said. "Your old coach? He's dead?"

"No. Owen Henley, my real father."

The answer caught in his throat and made my golf round seem insignificant. And Nash's face stated emotions his words didn't express: He was a twenty-year-old kid suffering a loss beyond simply the father he had never known. With his mother dead and gone since he was fourteen, that unknown and mysterious man, the one who abandoned him in inner-city Boston at age five, represented something I could never fully grasp. A year ago, Nash first mentioned finding his biological father, and I had told him that when he was ready, I would help look.

Now Owen Henley was gone—and with him, Nash's dream.

2

$\mathcal{A}$fter the golf round, we had driven to Milton, Massachusetts. Nash's apartment consisted of a main living room with attached kitchen, two bedrooms, and a bath and reminded me of where I had dwelled at UMaine twenty years earlier. The complex was a massive brick rectangle, each unit uniform in size and shape, although some windows displayed banners—Patriots, Red Sox, Curry College, and posters of rock bands I'd never heard of. No one hung posters of PGA Tour stars, but that didn't bother me. I wouldn't have been pictured if they had.

We were in Nash's room with the door closed. He sat next to me on his bed. The article he handed me was familiar. I recalled seeing the story covered in the Nation section of the *Hartford Courant*, "Beating and Execution in Milton, Massachusetts." The name of the victim was Owen Henley.

"He was my biological father," Nash said.

A year ago, Nash had explained his reasoning for wanting to find his father: to ask the man why he left, and if he ever thought about him. My response had been straightforward. I had warned Nash that he might not like the answers. But I told him I'd help when he was ready to look.

I glanced at the title again, "Execution." The word connoted instantaneous and remarkable images of cruelty and death, images that mixed with my sympathetic memory of a then-eighteen-year-old Nash telling me he was "stupid." Dyslexia is something I know, having struggled with the affliction since childhood. You can't be dyslexic and have a low I.Q. Doesn't work that way. And I'd repeatedly told Nash as much.

"*Owen Henley*," Nash said, "was my real father, the asshole who walked out on us. My mother used to say his name like a curse word. I never even met him." The anger faded from his voice, and he looked down. "Now I never will."

Through the window, the day's blue light was gone, and the night sky was a black field of velvet.

Nash leaned forward, elbows on knees, hands clasped. A computer was atop the disheveled desk we had built of plywood and two-by-fours when he moved in for preseason football weeks earlier. The computer's screensaver offered a picture of Hall-of-Fame running back Jim Brown frozen in the timeless Heisman pose.

"Remember the summer I caddied for you?" he said. "We went to Maine, and I played golf with you and your father?"

I remembered it well. I had missed a cut at a New England event, and we had met Dad at The Meadows in Litchfield, Maine, and played nine holes. Nash had connected with Dad immediately.

"I saw how you and your dad are. I was young when my father left, but I do remember him. I know my mother hated him, and she had her reasons. But I also remember holding his hand, how that felt. It was like nothing or no one could hurt me." His eyes left mine and fell to the floor.

I reached over and patted his back.

He bristled. "I'm not a kid anymore," he said. "I guess I just wanted . . . or I hoped I'd meet him, and he'd say something to make me understand." He turned his head to look up at me, forearms still on his thighs. "Jesus, the way he died . . ."

I didn't say anything.

"Police questioned me because of the photo albums."

"Photo albums?" I said.

"Yeah. They were all over his apartment. A hundred or so. Pictures of me from all ages, like he'd photographed my whole life. Some were really recent." He got up and went to the window, where he stood leaning against the frame, looking out at a starless sky. "Kind of freaks me out, you know?"

I could see why it would. Why would Owen Henley, who abandoned Nash fifteen years ago, have so many photos of him? And how had Owen taken or received recent pictures? It reminded me of something. "This article gives his address. He lived less than a mile from you."

"That's right," Nash said. "He always lived near me. Cops say he stayed close by my whole life. But all he did was take pictures. Everyplace I've gone—when my mother was still alive, when I lived with Halle after she died, even my year at prep school. Always close by . . ."

He let the words trail off, and I knew what he was thinking: Why only photos? He had always been so close. Why hadn't Owen Henley spoken to him?

Nash turned around and stood looking at the floor. He was twenty, still a kid. Confused. Hurt, too. Probably a little scared.

"Some of those pictures were of me walking around campus. There were newspapers clips going back to when I played Pop Warner."

"Clippings, too?"

"Articles and game results."

We were quiet for a long time. If I could've taken the burden for Nash, I would have. He had to be thinking the same things I was: Owen Henley had been murdered, brutally. Nash knew the man secretly photographed him—for years. What type of man photographs a boy from kindergarten-aged to adulthood? Was the murder in any way related to the photos? And this man was the father Nash had been desperate to meet.

I looked at Nash again. Outwardly stoic. Yet head down, eyes on the floor.

"I feel like I've been stalked."

"I understand," I said. "But photos are one thing—I don't let fans take my picture with Darcy because of the Internet—the press clippings, though, are like a written record of your life."

"Meaning what, he cared?"

"Maybe."

Nash turned to the window again and stood, back to me, leaning on the sill, staring out at darkness. "*Owen Henley.*" His head shook again. "Sometimes my mother would treat his leaving like it never happened, like I never had a father."

"Maybe she thought that was easier for you."

"It wasn't."

9

"I know."

"He never called. Not once. Never wrote. I remember every birthday, thinking, *This will be the year.* And every time I'd go to the park, I'd see kids with fathers. Even after my mother died, he never checked on me."

There wasn't a hell of a lot to say to that. Next to the computer stood a congratulatory card my wife, Lisa, and I sent when Nash boosted his G.P.A. from 2.0 to 2.5.

"Always close by. Why only take pictures?" His hand moved absently over his head, his face contorting with frustration as he scratched, as if the itch were a final straw. "Fuck," he said. "I never needed a father anyhow. Always looked out for myself."

Nash was working through things, and I sat by quietly. He looked at the five or six scars on his hands. They were like tiny pink worms and had been there when I had first met him. I never learned if they resulted from his childhood in Roxbury, Massachusetts, or from gridiron battles. At Curry College, Nash *was* the football team. Clemson recruited him, but dyslexia and SATs held him back. The result, at Division III Curry, was a man among boys. After only two seasons, he held the school's all-time rushing record and was on pace to break the national Division III record. More importantly to Lisa and me, he was halfway through a communications degree. His choice of major thrilled Lisa, a former television analyst and *Washington Post* reporter, to no end.

Lisa and I had met Nash two years earlier when he had written an error-filled yet heartfelt letter requesting work. My caddie, Tim Silver, had departed to put his journalism master's to work and write a book about life on Tour. Some players have salaried pro caddies. Some wives carry. Other players have celebrity friends loop. I had promised Nash a shot and had met his former football coach, Halle, the man who had taken him in, in the wake of his mother's death. And I had seen the pain on Nash's face when he realized Halle saw nothing more than NFL dollars in him. That left Lisa and me, and we had embraced Nash—he was that kind of kid. Now he was part of our family.

At twenty, Nash was in that gray zone between adolescence and adulthood. I remembered my first years of college well—

phone calls to my father after bad golf matches, his soothing, caring voice. Nash was a college All-American and a hard-working student, but still a kid. He had desperately needed love when Lisa and I first met him. And he still did. It explained his unique attachment to my two-year-old, Darcy. She represented a family.

"The Jake Place Apartments are just down the road," he said. "All those pictures. Cops say to take all those pictures, it must have been all he did outside of work."

"You never saw anyone follow you?"

He shook his head. "Cops asked that. I don't like being around cops. You grow up where I did and you just don't trust them. But I was honest with them. I never saw anyone follow me."

I heard the apartment's main door open and shut, then a guy's and a girl's voices.

"Cops also said they can tell from the photos he was getting closer to me all the time."

"What does that mean?" I said.

"They don't know. Maybe he was finally going to say something. Maybe he was going to check on me."

Nash was jumping back and forth from anger to hope to speculation. I had no idea who Owen Henley had been. The article had said he was thirty-seven when he died, so he was seventeen when he fathered Nash. And I didn't know what it felt like to have your old man abandon you before your sixth birthday. I did know Nash, though, and would do anything I could for him.

"You agree with that, Jack? That maybe he was getting closer and was about to reconnect with me?"

I had no idea. I was just mad at the guy for leaving. Yet Nash might need to believe his theory. "It's possible."

"He was working in the photo department at Wal-Mart. So he did stay close by."

"That's something."

"But it's not enough."

I got up. "I flew in and missed the cut. Pack an overnight bag, and we'll drive back to Maine for the weekend. We can be home by one A.M. Darcy'll be thrilled to wake up and have you there. So will Lisa."

11

Nash nodded and went to his closet, where clothes hung in disarray. "I told the cops I want the albums. I'm meeting with them again next week." He took a shirt off a hanger and turned around to face me. *"Murdered."* He shook his head. "They ransacked the place. Cops said it'll take a while to go through it."

Beyond Nash's closed bedroom door, I heard a fridge open and shut and the pop and spray of a can opening.

"It wasn't just a shooting, you know?"

"Yeah," I said. "I read that."

"They tortured him first."

I got up and moved closer. I was about to pat his back again.

"No," he said. "I'm fine. No problem."

He wanted space. I figured I'd give him a few minutes to collect himself before the drive to Maine.

I was reaching for the door when he called me back.

"Jack," he sighed and tossed the clothes he held into a duffle. Then he looked at me. "I want to know who my father was. It's all I've got now."

I looked at him and saw the pain in his eyes. His jaws were clenched. He was tense with anticipation. I nodded, and he smiled.

"Okay," I said. "We'll find out. But . . ."

He waited.

". . . it might not be what you want to hear, Nash. I think your best bet is to leave this alone. He was murdered."

"I spend time with you and your father and watch how you are with Darcy. I never got that. I keep going from angry to thinking he was about to contact me. Maybe I need to believe that, but maybe he really was coming back. All my life, when I'd be having trouble or a bad day, I'd remember holding his hand, how that felt. I need to know who he was, Jack."

"Are all your memories of him good?" I said.

"Of course," he said and looked away.

I waited but he didn't speak.

"We'll find out who he was," I said. "I'll help you look. I said I would."

"I'm ready for whatever comes," he said. "I know nobody

gets killed like that unless they're into something. But maybe he was a good person."

He needed to believe that.

"We'll find out," I said, and went to the living room.

. . .

When we'd arrived, Nash had parked his 1995 Jeep Wrangler next to a white Audi convertible. Now the Audi's owner was home.

"Jack," a blond kid said, rising from the couch where he was sitting, arm around an apparent girlfriend, "I'm Gregg Petroski. I keep telling Nash he didn't need the guy anyway."

Nash's former roommate graduated. I had never met Petroski. However, the kid's fatherly tone told me rooming with him probably wasn't much fun. First impressions can lead to generalizations, but I pegged the kid for a twerp.

"My father's excited to play a pro-am with you. I think it's next week or the week after."

"With me?"

Petroski was maybe Nash's height, but much heavier. It looked like the weight had come from the beer-and-pizza college diet, not the weight room. A big farm kid—beefy and wide, with blue eyes and freckles. Except the Audi didn't fit the farm image. And a spot in the pro-am had cost daddy at least $1,500. Petroski dressed weekend preppy—ripped khaki pants, faded Izod shirt, and a soiled and faded Red Sox hat.

"Dad's was the first name drawn," Petroski said. "And he selected you. It's some one-day fundraiser in Falmouth."

I nodded. It was for cancer research and slated for the Woodlands Club, my home venue. I had signed on months earlier, thinking the break would fit nicely in my schedule. My recent Tour win gave me a two-year exemption, but part of me wished I were playing every tournament before season's end because I was desperate to get back to the winner's circle and the feeling it had given me.

"I'm surprised your father drew the first pick and chose me," I said.

Petroski shrugged, walked past me to the fridge, and grabbed a can of Molson. He held a second one up for me. "Happy hour, Jack?"

"I'll take one," the girl on the couch said. She was thin with short black hair. She wore shorts, a T-shirt with "Please Recycle" on it, and hiking boots.

"No," I said. "Thanks." This wasn't happy hour for his roommate. "Does your father know Phil Mickelson and David Duval are in the field?" Getting them to weekend in Maine had been a coup and the news made all the papers.

He shrugged. "What can I get you? I get the drinks and Nash draws the people. That's how this place works. And this is *the* place to be on weekends."

I didn't like the sound of that and felt a parental ping in my stomach.

Nash emerged from the bedroom with a duffel over his shoulder, a cell phone to his ear. "Thanks, Coach," he was saying. "Definitely by Tuesday . . . Thanks for understanding."

When Nash hung up, Petroski walked over and patted his arm. "Hang in there, buddy. And remember, try to forget the guy. You never needed him. Never even knew him."

Nash made no reply.

Fortunately for Petroski, neither did I.

Outside, Nash and I got into his Jeep. As we backed up, then swung around, our headlights flashed across the windshield of an idling Lincoln. The white-haired man from the golf course sat behind the wheel.

3

At 7:30 Saturday morning, Nash was still asleep. Lisa and I were in the kitchen with Darcy. Lisa had the sports page open while she ate a bagel and sipped tea. I had eggs over easy, toast, ham, and hash browns. No one made coffee like Lisa. A cup of her newsroom-strength diesel and you were good to go for the day. I was working on my third cup.

Lisa looked at my plate and made a face. "That's a lot of carbs, you know?"

I smiled and chewed happily. Beside me, next to me, and on me, Darcy had milk-soaked Cheerios.

"They say a child's personality is formed at this age," I said.

"Like father, like daughter. Besides, table manners are genetic. Don't blame my sweet daughter for inheriting your genes." She turned to Darcy. "Sweetie, Nash is here to see you."

"Nash!" Darcy said. "Nash!"

Darcy wore a T-shirt that read "DAD (has no) RULES" and nylon Adidas shorts over a pull-up. Out of the corner of her eye, she looked at me, smiled to herself, and threw another Cheerio. She would be three in five months and had my blue eyes, but her dark hair and long lashes were all Lisa.

"So you told Nash you'd help him look?" Lisa said.

"And I'm keeping that promise." The strong scent of Tabasco rose from my eggs.

"You think he's really ready to learn about his father?"

"Would you be? Newspaper said he was tortured then shot, execution-style. That's not random violence. What we're going to learn about Owen Henley is not going to be good."

Lisa looked at Darcy for a long time. "Nash had a terrible childhood."

"He said he still remembers how it felt to hold his father's hand," I said. "He was five when the guy left."

"Nash told me he thinks what you and your father have is special and, had his father stayed, they'd have had the same thing."

"The guy walked out on him," I said. "Doesn't seem like the parenting type."

"It's easy for you to see that. Owen Henley wasn't your father, Jack."

"I know."

Darcy drank, spilling orange juice down her shirtfront. "Daddy, where Nash?"

"He's sleeping."

She reached into her cereal bowl and stuffed a handful of Cheerios into her mouth. Milk spilled on the table.

"Use your spoon, sweetie," I said.

Darcy looked at me and grabbed another handful of Cheerios. This time, she threw them on the floor.

"Darcy," I said. "No."

She did it again.

"Sweetie," I said, "we don't throw food."

When she reached for another handful, I pulled the bowl away. She screamed and kicked the table with her tiny Wee-Bok sneakers. Then she cried. And cried. And cried—long, loud sobs.

"Darcy," I said, "I know you can use your spoon. I've seen you do it."

The wailing continued.

"Do you need a timeout?" I said.

The question only incited her. The wailing grew louder.

"Darcy," I said, *"Nash is sleeping."* The comment was ludicrous. A two-year-old couldn't care less who slept and who didn't.

"Darcy," Lisa said, "would you like to play with Elmo?" She reached onto the chair beside her and picked up the red doll.

Darcy took Elmo and immediately fell silent, eating quietly. Worse, she was using her spoon.

I sat staring at Lisa. "You made that look easy."

She shrugged.

I shook my head and turned to Darcy, who took a bite and spoke softly to Elmo.

"A lot of good players missed the cut this week," Lisa said. "Mickelson, Els . . ."

"Trying to make me feel better?"

Lisa wore a pink sleeveless Oxford shirt, white shorts, and leather sandals with white straps. She ran five miles a day. In shorts, that regimen was obvious.

"Maybe," she said.

"Thanks, but it doesn't. I won last year. I proved something to myself. Now I expect to contend every week."

"Jack," she said, "I know that iron head of yours hears what it chooses to hear, but even Tiger Woods and Vijay Singh aren't in contention in every tournament."

I drank some coffee. "Feel any different about what we discussed last week?"

"No," she said. "I still want to go back to work. But I also still want to be a stay-at-home mother."

I drank some coffee. Through the window over the sink, the sun was an orange splash against a pale-blue sky.

"I watch Paul Staples sitting in my seat in the tower above the eighteenth green each week and I think, *He's not doing it right.* Or, *Why didn't he ask this?*"

"I appreciate your sacrifice," I said.

"I know. And you've said that three hundred times. But you don't know what it's like, Jack. I feel like I've worked just as hard as you to get where I am or was—anchoring a major network's golf telecast—and I have to walk away, at thirty-five. Just up and quit."

"It isn't fair."

"No, it's not. But that's how it is." She leaned over and kissed Darcy's forehead. Darcy was through eating. Lisa took her and walked out onto the deck.

The eggs sat before me. I wasn't hungry anymore.

By 9 A.M., Perkins and I were in my basement lifting weights. He hadn't driven up from New Hampshire to use my gym on a Saturday morning. The night before, I'd gone to my office, closed the door, and called him about Nash and Owen Henley. On a good day, Perkins—six-feet-five, 275 pounds, with white-blond hair and piecing blue eyes—looked like a cross between Hulk Hogan and Arnold Schwarzenegger. We were the same age, had grown up next door to one another in central Maine, and served as Godfather to each other's children. If he considered you family, he'd do anything for you. For me, that had once led Perkins to shoot a man to save my life. We named our only child in his honor.

Perkins bench pressed 305 pounds ten times and the bar clanged down.

"Winded, Darcy?"

"Don't call me that," he said.

I grinned and took a forty-five-pound plate off each side and began a set of twelve.

Lisa and I had bought the cedar-shake, 1928, oceanfront house and moved to Chandler, Maine, shortly before marrying. The house had what my father, a carpenter, called "character," meaning four-inch molding near the ceilings, hardwood floors, original baseboards, several stained-glass windows, and hand-crafted bookshelves built into the walls. "Character," in this case, also meant old and costly. Dad had done a lot of work to the outside of the home. Likewise, I'd put knowledge gained through many summers as Dad's sidekick to use—finishing the basement by creating a workout room with a practice putting surface made by laying a raised floor with indoor-outdoor carpeting.

"How's the job?" I said, pushing up and exhaling slowly.

"Boston office is busy, and Peter Barrett's a good guy to consult for. He listens to what I say, unlike the bunch in this house." He scowled. "Last summer, Nash talked to me about tracking down his father. I told him it was a bad idea. I've done that before for people, and it never turns out like in the movies."

"Nash asked you to look?" I was straining on my eighth rep.

"Yeah. I stalled him. I told him wait till he was out of college, so his father won't think he's after money."

"I never knew he went to you." I got off the bench.

Perkins added weight to the bar and leaned back again. "So Nash is pretty torn up?" Perkins didn't ask it coldly, but his voice held no inflection. It never did.

"Yeah. Doesn't say a hell of a lot. But I can tell he's hurting."

"Fuck." Perkins pushed the weight up slowly, exhaling as the bar moved. When the bar was at the top of the repetition, he inhaled. Then he shook his head. "I should've found Owen Henley for him when he first asked. Now he'll never be able to."

"Hindsight is a kick in the balls," I said.

At UMaine, I had played golf and Perkins starred as a lineman. He had played briefly for the Patriots and worked for Boston PD. His police career had ended when he and his partner had been called to a domestic dispute where they located a four-year-old rape victim. Perkins found the perpetrator—the girl's father—and had thrown the legal system out, seeing that justice, in his eyes, was served. The girl's father spent several days in the hospital. Now Perkins owned a Boston-based private investigations business and consulted for the PGA Tour Security Office, reporting directly to Tour Commissioner Peter Barrett.

"After you called," he said, "I didn't sleep a wink last night. I should've helped Nash. He's a good kid. With what the Tour's paying me, I can afford to do some pro bono. I should've found his old man, so now I'll find out who clipped him. I owe Nash that much."

I knew he and Linda had built a new home. I also knew that when Tiger Woods played his customary event in Dubai, the Tour sent Perkins with him in a bodyguard capacity.

My cell phone rang. When you're in a different city each week, a cell phone is the only way to go. Plus, AT&T gives Tour players cell phones and 1,000 minutes a month. So you get in the habit of taking it with you everywhere, even when home.

"Jack," a tired voice said, "it's Padre."

Perkins stood and waved his arms in large circles. Then he pointed to the bench and spread his hands. I waved that off, so he did another set. I walked to my putting green and shrugged the phone to my ear, setting an old 1965 Arnold Palmer blade behind a ball.

"Something's wrong," Padre said, "and I wanted you to hear it from me before it comes out in the press."

I didn't hit the putt. "Jesus, Padre, that sounds bad."

He didn't reply. Perkins finished a short set and let the bar down with a clang. The rectangular windows were open and the ocean's rich muddy odor, like damp leaves, wafted in. When I'd been injured one season, Padre flew to visit me. We spoke often, and he had been there when I had needed to talk about marriage. Likewise, he had always been there for me as a golfer, offering tips, making videos of my swing, and sharing information—which made his pause even more profound.

"I'm taking some time off," he said. "Got to figure some stuff out before I come back to golf."

"Your putting average is just higher than usual. That's all. You make some putts and everything will be fine. Stan Utley might be able to help. Or David Leadbetter. You've just got a kink in your stroke."

"I'm pretty sure my problems aren't mechanical anymore."

The silence now was mine. I knew his problems had little to do with mechanics. Overhead, shoes padded across the floor. I heard Darcy's giggle-scream. I went up the basement stairs and outside onto the back deck. Near the dock, gulls splashed down. One landed on the dock's railing and sat, as if confused, while his mates dove in search of fish.

In El Paso, Texas, Padre was facing some emotional and athletic crossroad. I didn't understand everything he was saying, but I'd been with him when he hit rock bottom.

"I'm just really tired, man."

"Of what?"

"I've got to go, Jack."

He hung up. Padre Tarbuck, the man who always had a different and stunning woman on his arm, was tired. Of golf? We were nearing forty together. Padre had won twice, but his last victory had come two years ago, meaning his exempt status was up at season's end. He was a well-liked veteran, respected for his community work as well as his game, which until this year had been solid. Unless you've won within the past two seasons (or have a major championship trophy on your mantel), you must finish among the top 125 on the money list to retain playing privileges the following season. With only two months left in the season, he needed several top-five finishes to secure his Tour card.

Padre and I had been rookies together, twelve years earlier. We had drunk beer together and watched a lot of ballgames. We had lifted weights together and closed a lot of driving ranges with Vijay Singh. I had worked with him on his putting this year. It hadn't helped. Now he was walking away. Golf was more than an occupation. It was what guys like he and I did.

What did Padre need to figure out? Could the bottom be so low that he had to go on without golf?

In the distance, a Boston Whaler sped past a lobster boat. Bad things play in threesomes: Padre's inner turmoil; Nash's lost dream; and the white-haired man who seemed disinterested in golf at the Buick Championship but had followed me to Nash's apartment.

"White hair, as in blond like me?" Perkins said. "Or as in gray and a geezer?"

"Geezer," I said. "Maybe sixty, sixty-five. A lot of bushy gray hair. Driving a dark Lincoln Continental. What *is* like you is the guy's fashion sense—he wears dark dress socks with shorts and white sneakers."

Perkins ignored me and took a vicious slash at a golf ball. Nash, Perkins, and I were at the Woodlands Club in Falmouth a half-hour from my home. The course plays to 6,848 yards from the back tees and was designed by renowned architects George and Jim Fazio. The venue has hosted four events on what is now the Nationwide Tour, the PGA Tour's top minor-league circuit. We were in the second fairway. Perkins and I were riding a cart. Nash was walking and stood across the fairway, out of earshot.

Perkins's ball started way right, cut back, and landed short of the green.

"The fifty-yard bend," I said. "If you had a curve ball that good, you'd be a rich man."

"I call it a calculated slice." Perkins slid his six-iron back into the bag. "I hate this fucking hole."

I knew he did. And I knew why: No. 2, a 349-yard, par-four dogleg, called for precision. For me, that meant a three-iron off the tee, leaving 130 yards to the green. The fairway turns left. So if you can draw the ball, you're golden. Perkins, however, doesn't own a draw. Indeed, the fifty-yard right-to-left bender is his routine ball flight, making a draw unthinkable. He was in the trees off the tee. Now he lay four.

"Get the plate number off that Lincoln?" he said.

"I did."

He looked surprised. "You thought to write the number down, even with Nash there?"

"No number. Vanity plate."

"In Massachusetts?"

"Massachusetts plate. *Stumpy twelve.*"

"That's the plate? Stumpy twelve?"

Nash had made par on our opening hole, and, to his credit, had done so hitting from the back tees with me. Now he was on the left edge of the fairway—safe, but a long way from the hole. Usually when we played, he often asked what club to hit. This day, he said nothing. In his apartment, when we'd first discussed his father's death, he asked that I treat him like a man. One's true colors always show up on the golf course. Nash wanted to be an adult, and that sentiment had carried over.

Nash hit his approach shot, the ball flying high and straight, landing on the green.

"Nice shot," I yelled to him. "Within ten feet."

"Nash, I want to revamp our wager," Perkins hollered. "I need a stroke a hole to play against you."

Nash smiled and shook his head. "No way. A bet is a bet."

"At least he's smiling," Perkins said to me.

"A long time coming."

"Fucking game doesn't make me smile."

"I don't think his mind is on golf."

"I know."

"I hate seeing him go through this."

"Well, if I find out who did it," Perkins said, "maybe he'll have closure."

Perkins and I were driving to where my tee shot landed, the electric cart humming quietly. The sun was bright overhead as the temperature neared ninety.

"Think this would be easier for Nash if he had known his father?" Perkins said.

"If Owen Henley had been there, at least Nash would have closure. Now he's only got questions." I shook my head. "But he's a tough kid. When I met him, his guidance counselor said he was one of two from his neighborhood not to join a gang."

"Nash's plan to find out who the old man was, well"— Perkins shook his head—"he might be better off not knowing about a guy who dies like that."

"That's not up to me and you," I said. "He's twenty and wants to work through this."

"I've got to ask Nash what he remembers about his old man," Perkins said. "Might give me a place to start."

"He only remembers good stuff."

"About a guy who goes out like that?"

"He was five," I said.

"Got a plan for looking into Owen Henley?" Perkins said.

"Nothing formal." We were at my ball. "We know where Owen worked. So we have a starting point. Other than that, I told him I'd help, so I will."

"Cops working the case might not like you running around asking questions. Try not to aggravate people too much."

At my ball, I got out of the cart and was swinging my nine-iron back and forth slowly. "What do you know about the murder?"

"Just what I read in the papers. Pretty brutal, a punishment killing or a message for someone." Perkins watched carefully as Nash approached us. "I know people don't randomly get beaten like that, then shot."

"The guy had a steady job. Worked in the photo lab at Wal-Mart."

"The killing wasn't random, Jack."

"Then what do you think Owen Henley was into?"

"No idea. But it won't be good, whatever we learn. And one more thing . . ."

I looked at him.

"You better watch your ass. Assuming it wasn't a random act of violence—hell, even if it was—someone won't want you asking questions."

"I know."

When Nash reached us, he opened the bag cooler Perkins had brought.

"Gatorade?" Nash held up the only Gatorade in the cooler.

"I'm a thoughtful guy," Perkins said.

"Then let me drink one of the beers."

"Are you twenty-one?"

"*Perkins*," Nash said.

"Sorry, my man."

I grinned. They'd had this debate often: Nash drank socially at college, and we all knew it. But Perkins, official or not, was a law officer. Moreover, for Perkins everything ended with his version of right and wrong. I guessed that Nash realized this because he took the Gatorade and stepped away.

"Hey, how's Michelle?" I said.

"Great," Nash said. "We're going to the semiformal in a couple weeks."

I nodded my approval.

"How long you been dating?" Perkins said. "Been a while, hasn't it?"

"Over a year."

My preswing routine never wavers, whether I'm playing Perkins for a beer and giving him two strokes a hole, or playing

Phil Mickelson for the Buick Classic title. I always align the shot from behind the ball, choose a target at which to aim, and take two practice swings. Finally, I execute.

"You've improved a hell of a lot, Nash," Perkins said. "What's your handicap?"

Nash shrugged. "I'm just playing more. Petro works at a country club. Gets us on a couple nights a week. I shot forty-nine last week. That's my best so far."

"'Petro'?" Perkins said.

I selected my target and stood over the Titleist, clubface waggling inches above it.

"Gregg Petroski," Nash said, "my roommate."

Nash fell silent, waiting for me to hit. I did, and the ball stopped within ten feet of the flagstick.

"What's Petroski play?" I said. "Line?"

Nash nodded. "He's a junior. Doesn't play very much, doesn't take football real seriously, you know."

"He get good grades?" I said, sliding my club back in the bag and sitting beside Perkins again.

"I don't know what Petro gets for grades. Why?"

"Must take something seriously. Kind of a waste to be on the team if you don't take the game seriously."

"I hadn't thought of it like that. His father's a lawyer, works in New York City, and they live in Connecticut. I think he just likes being known as being part of the team. Does that make sense?"

It did. It also explained why Petroski was living with Nash, the team's star.

.   .   .

At the green, Perkins was first to putt, from thirty-five feet. His ball ran four feet by, a distance I knew to give him fits. He marked his ball.

"Thanks again, Jack, for the golf balls you sent me," Nash said. "I saw them in a pro shop. Pro V1s are like forty-six bucks a dozen."

"I don't know exactly what they cost," I said. "Titleist gives me two dozen every week I play."

"Didn't give me any special goddamned golf balls," Perkins said, eyeing the X-out he held.

I grinned. "You'd lose them."

The Titleist Pro V1 had rocked the golf scene three years earlier. I had played Maxfli clubs, worn the Maxfli logo, and used a Maxfli ball. Then Maxfli had merged with TaylorMade and Adidas Golf and discontinued its club making, focusing on the TaylorMade line. So I had been forced to TaylorMade RAC irons and an r7 driver. Yet, with Maxfli still producing balls, I had broken contract to use the Titleist Pro V1—and had added nearly twelve yards off the tee by doing so.

I was next to putt, four feet farther than Nash. Ten feet for birdie.

"You can't putt without Silver here to read the green for you," Perkins said, smirking.

"Think so?"

"Ten bucks says you miss this."

"You're on."

I crouched behind the ball. It would break six inches, right to left. I selected a spot a foot in front of the ball over which to roll it. This assured me of at least starting the ball on-line.

I made two practice strokes, then pulled the trigger.

The ball fell, center cut.

"Damn," Perkins said. "Double or nothing?"

I shook my head. "Give Nash the ten bucks." Then to Nash: "Laundry money."

Nash shook his head, declining. He had requested help from me for the biggest event of his life—learning who Owen Henley had been. I realized now that if he could do it on his own, he would. This wasn't only about Owen Henley.

Nash replaced his ball. His line was nearly identical to the one I'd just followed.

"Learn anything?" I said.

"Oh, yeah."

He brought the putter back slowly, his wide shoulders rocking as the putter face moved straight back and through. He held the follow-through, head perfectly still. The ball fell, its Surlyn cover clicking against the bottom of the cup.

Nash pumped a fist. "Birdie!"

High-fives all around.

. . .

By the time we reached No. 18, the sky was clear, the course crowded. We were waiting for a foursome to clear the fairway. Eighteen is a 436-yard par four. A pond spans the entire left side. The green is angled, making the approach difficult, no matter how well you hit your tee shot.

Nash made several practice swings. He was a natural athlete. It may have been Ben Hogan who said your swing never changes much from the first time you take the club back. The first time I had seen Nash swing, he had made a long rhythmic motion, a wide shoulder turn, and a balanced follow-through. I had tweaked his address position, altered his grip, and widened his stance. But I hadn't taught him to bring the club back until it was parallel to the ground like Davis Love III. That was instinct, fitness, and the natural power and grace that allowed him to run forty yards in under 4.5 seconds and drag three would-be tacklers across the goal line.

This time, Nash's swing was well paced and taut, everything moving as one, the contact crisp. His ball found the heart of the fairway.

"Nice drive," I said. "Ego will drive you both crazy. Why don't you guys play the white tees? USGA has handicaps for a reason."

Nash and Perkins looked at each other.

"And let you think you can out-drive us?" Perkins said and smiled widely.

When he teed off, he swung hard enough to send himself to a chiropractor. This time the "calculated slice" failed him. The ball never turned back and found the pond.

"Goddamn it," he said, and tossed his driver toward the cart.

"Jack hasn't taught you golf etiquette?" Nash said, grinning.

"That wasn't a throw," Perkins said. "It was a toss. And etiquette this." He teed another ball. "I'm going to knock the cover off this goddamned ball."

At contact, Perkins looked startled. He'd caught it flush. Surprised, he watched the ball fly high and straight. It landed in the fairway.

"Any chance you'll actually count the first one?" I said. "Because you lay three."

"Mulligan."

"That's what I thought. And you still get two strokes a hole?"

"Nash and I both do," Perkins said.

"And the loser buys dinner?"

"Of course."

"Of course," I said.

We were playing "ready golf," meaning whoever was ready hit. I went last but cranked my drive over 300 yards, leaving only a short-iron to the green.

"Fuck," Perkins said.

"Etiquette," I said. "Etiquette."

.   .   .

Perkins hooked his second shot (fourth counting the mulligan) into the water.

"That's why Nash gets the Pro V1s," I said. "You'd have spent eight bucks on this hole alone."

"I hate this goddamned game."

"Then why play three times a week?" I said.

"Because God mocks me. That's why. He gives me an addiction I don't even enjoy. *Fuck.*"

I walked the rest of the hole with Nash.

"You told me you wanted to join the college paper," I said. "How's that going?"

"I was going to last semester but didn't get around to it."

As we strode, Nash looked at the ground. A lot on his mind. However, I didn't want Owen Henley, whose absence had yet to hold him back, to do so now.

"How come you didn't get around to it?"

"Busy semester."

We watched Perkins drop and hit a low shot up the fairway. When the ball landed on dry ground, he raised his arms to heaven in mock celebration.

Nash and I clapped.

"Screw you two."

Nash laughed. "Wow, golf gets to him."

"Be glad he hasn't broken a club today. He's actually toned it down. About ten years ago, I invited him to play a pro-am with me." I shook my head. "Never again."

"What happened?"

"He missed a three-foot putt and threw his whole bag into the pond."

"Jesus." Nash laughed.

"Then he remembered a three-hundred-dollar watch his wife had engraved for him was in the bag. Took him an hour and a half to get it."

Nash covered his face and laughed full out.

"What are you laughing at Nash?" Perkins said from across the fairway.

Nash tried to speak. Couldn't. Shook his head and held up his hand.

Perkins asked again. Nash tried to stop laughing, but couldn't.

"*Screw you two*," Perkins yelled again.

When Nash caught his breath, I said, "But Perkins would do anything in the world for you."

"I know."

We had reached Nash's ball. He pulled a five-wood, glanced at the pond to the left, then exchanged the five-wood for his four-iron, a wise choice.

"Perkins is going to investigate the murder," I said. "I'll help you look into the Owen's past."

"Awesome," Nash said. "But I've got to do most of it myself. I wanted to meet him, to show him that I made it—in spite of him."

"You've got nothing to prove, Nash."

"Yeah, I do. To him, wherever he is, but to me, too."

Nash hit his second shot. It landed short of the green.

"At least it's dry," he said.

5

$\mathcal{M}$onday, at 8:15 A.M., Nash should have been at Curry College taking handoffs and running pass routes. I had urged him to go—it would have been a reprieve since he was to meet with cops later that morning—but instead, we stood at the photo counter at the Wal-Mart where Owen Henley had worked. A woman, probably my age but who looked older, was filing packages of film into a large metal file cabinet. The skin under her eyes looked dark and puffy. She looked tired, the way people do when life comes at them at breakneck speed and they manage only to hold on as long as they can. She wore navy blue slacks and a blue Wal-Mart vest over a white cotton shirt. Her nametag read LEA.

"Oh," she said, walking to the counter. "Didn't see you there. Can I help you?"

She had shoulder-length blond hair and her narrow nose looked slightly askew, as if once it had been broken. When she neared us, I smelled cigarettes and coffee on her breath.

"I'm Jack Austin," I said. "We're not here for film."

"What then?"

"Did you know Owen Henley?"

Instinctively, she stepped back. "You cops?"

"No," Nash said. "I'm Owen Henley's son. I'm trying to learn a little about my father."

"Owen Henley had a *son?* You guys will do anything to get a quote, won't you? I said I worked with him. Then you put that shit in the paper after I said it was off the record. Now you try this? I ain't talking." She turned and walked back to the file cabinet.

"We're not cops," I said. "We can't make you talk to us. And we're not reporters. He really is Owen Henley's son. I'm just a golfer."

"Golfer?" she said. "Meaning what, you can't find a job?" She chuckled and continued filing the blue and white envelops of developed film. "I got a sister who says she's a sculptor, too."

"Ma'am." Nash's voice was near pleading. Lea heard it and looked at him. "My father was killed. I never got to meet him. I just want to know who he was."

Lea tilted her head and looked from Nash to me. "You look like a vice cop. Good haircut. Good clothes—wrinkled, though. But he's no cop. Too young."

I wondered how she knew what vice cops looked like, but I let it pass and just shook my head.

"You ain't a cop?" she said. "Well, I'm really sick of reporters." She had to be a Boston native. *Reporters* came out *reportahs.* "The *Globe* said I told them Owen had enemies. That was *off the record!* I ain't talking to any of them again, and my boss says I don't got to."

"My father worked here," Nash said.

"You got ID?"

We each showed wallets and she studied them closely, looking at Nash's driver's license. Then she focused on my PGA Tour card. "I'll be damned." She grinned. "I guess you ain't a cop." Then to Nash: "Owen Henley worked here, yeah. He worked the same shift as me. What do you want to know?"

For a moment, Nash didn't seem to know what to ask.

A customer came in to pick up film. It was a woman in her early forties wearing a business suit and just the right amount of makeup. She was thin and looked like she went to the gym, ate power breakfasts, and had business dinners. She had money, and I guessed she had no idea how vice cops dressed either. Lea gave the woman her film and change for a fifty and the woman left. I imagined nearly identical scenes played out like that day after day.

"I'm working overtime," Lea said. "I can't stand around. What do you need?"

"I don't know anything about my father," Nash said. "He left when I was little."

31

"That sounds about right for Owen. Why do you want to know about him? And why now?"

"I know it's too late," Nash said. "But I always wondered about him. I always wanted to know him. Never got the chance."

"If your old man was anyone else, I'd say that was sad." She looked down suddenly. "I'm sorry. I shouldn't have said that. It's just, Owen Henley wasn't right. You ain't missed much, kid."

"What do you mean by 'not right'?" I said.

She looked at me, then Nash. She looked at the clock on the wall and around the empty photo section. "I got two kids at home. And what happened to Owen makes me a little scared. I still remember the two guys who showed up here looking for him the morning he was killed. I don't like talking about it."

"You tell the cops about the two guys?" I said.

"Of course. The cops. The sketch artist. All those people. It's useless. Those guys are long gone."

"How do you know that?"

"'Cause I'd be gone."

As we spoke, top-forty music played over the PA system. The music was interrupted periodically by announcements offering deals. My father still bought tools and supplies from the hardware store on Main Street.

"Tell us about 'not right,'" I said.

"I got to stock the cabinet. Shift ends at nine. I can meet you in the grill at the front when I'm done."

I said okay and offered to buy her breakfast. Then Nash and I turned to go. To my left, in the automotive section, I saw a man at the counter pointing to a tire behind the employee. The employee reached for it, and the guy at the counter glanced quickly at me. When our eyes met, he looked down at the countertop, running his index finger over a glass-enclosed brochure. He wore a dark blue windbreaker, matching pants, and white sneakers. He had on a Red Sox cap. And a shock of thick white hair burst from beneath it.

He glanced over his shoulder at me again.

I started toward the white-haired man. He left the guy holding the tire and walked briskly to the automotive section's exit door. He pulled the handle, but the door had to be released from behind the counter.

He looked over his shoulder at me.

I broke into a sprint.

The kid set the tire down, and hit a button under the counter. The door opened. And the white-haired man walked out, turned left, then vanished from view.

When I reached the door, I watched through wire-meshed glass as the driver's door of a dark blue Lincoln closed and the car drove away.

.   .   .

We were waiting for Lea in the dining section of Wal-Mart. I was sipping coffee; Nash was drinking Gatorade.

"Put that stuff on your cereal?" I said.

I drank more coffee, which wasn't bad, and wondered who the white-haired man was. I had wondered that the moment I first saw him on the golf course. Now I wondered what the hell he wanted, too. Perkins was to run his license plate, so soon I'd know more about the guy.

When Lea approached, I stood and pulled a chair out for her.

"Wow. A gentleman. Didn't know there was any anymore." She sat across from Nash and me. "I've been thinking about why you're here, Nash. I shouldn't have said what I did about Owen in front of you. I'm sorry. My name is Lea Griffin. I worked with him for a year or so."

"I can hear everything," Nash said. "I *want* to hear it."

"Would you like coffee, Lea?" I said. "Eggs?"

"No, thanks. So you play golf on TV?"

"Yeah, the PGA Tour."

"No shit?"

"No shit."

She looked at me for a long moment. "Make a lot of money?"

"My father's a carpenter. Mother's an English teacher."

"So, compared to them, or me, you're rich."

"I'm lucky as hell, is what I am. You sure you don't want coffee?"

"Okay," she said. "Black."

I stood and went to get it. Nash and Lea sat in silence waiting for me. When you spend a lifetime traveling alone—hotels, planes, dinner tables—you seek solitary activities. And when your mother is an English teacher, you read. Lately, I was working through poet Philip Levine's *What Work Is*. "Burned" begins:

> I have to go back into the forge room
> at Chevy where Lonnie still calls
> out his commands to Sweet Pea and Packy
> and stare into the fire
> until my eyes are also fire
> and tear away some piece of my face
> because we're all burning

The poem was a good one. I'm more at home reading putts than reading poems, and I probably miss nuances. But I always enjoy Levine's poems. They are filled with people and voices from my childhood. My first round of golf was when I was ten— my father and I in blue jeans, his Chevy pickup with 180,000 miles on it, rattling into the dirt parking lot at Cobbossee Colony, a municipal nine-hole golf course in central Maine. That was where I'd come from. That was Lonnie, Sweet Pea, and Packy.

Now, unlike the people in the poem, and unlike Lea Griffin, I was no longer burning. If you get paid to hit a little white ball, if you do something for a living friends do on vacation, then you get paid a hell of a lot more than you should. And if you have any humility at all, you know damned well you're not burning. My old man was tacking shingles in Auburn, Maine, that morning. My mother was helping out at a day care. And Lea Griffin had just gotten off a night shift at Wal-Mart.

"Odd time for a shift to end," I said, putting coffee in front of Lea.

"Overtime. My husband . . ." She looked down at the table-top and absently wiped away a coffee spot with the tip of her index finger. "It's a long story. Let me tell you both about Owen Henley. It's less depressing."

That was a scary thought. I sipped some coffee and waited.

Nash had finished the Gatorade and sat very still, both hands holding the plastic bottle in front of him on the table. He wore his purple and gold sweat suit and a Nike visor.

"I know he was your dad, Nash, so I . . ."

"He left. I want to hear it all, Mrs. Griffin. Please tell me."

"Owen Henley is—was—the strangest person I ever met. No one else would work with him. The kids who stock shelves at night used to walk by him and sing 'Super Freak.' He was the kind of guy who laughed at stuff no one else did."

"How come you worked with him?" I said.

She shrugged. "I don't give a shit who I work with. I need money, and I need it bad."

She drank coffee then blew on it.

"Owen was mean to some customers and too friendly to others. One time we were working the counter. Old lady walks in, stumbles, trips ass over elbows. Lands—smack—on the floor. I rush out to help her. Owen starts laughing. Just . . . laughing. Other customers were pissed and a guy told Owen to shut up. Owen just laughed right through it. Well, the customer started toward Owen. Owen leaned toward the guy and whispered something—I never found out what. But the guy's face went white. He walked out, looking at Owen over his shoulder."

I drank some coffee and thought about that. Lea blew on her coffee again. Nash was looking at the parking lot through the window abutting our table. Outside, the sun shone brightly.

"And he must've spent three quarters of every paycheck on film development," Lea said. "I mean, Owen took more pictures than anyone I know."

"He didn't develop them?" Nash said, still looking outside.

"I know he knew how to. He talked about it once. But we send them out."

"Ever see his pictures?" I said.

"No. No way. That was another weird thing. He was crazy around his film. One time, I said, 'Think I'm going to steal your damned film, Owen?' He turned to me, pointed his finger, and said—and I'll never forget this as long as I live; scared the living shit out of me—he said, 'You ever touch my film, you no-good whore, I'll rip your guts out and feed them to you.'"

"Jesus Christ," I said.

Nash turned back to her. His face was deadpan, reminding me of when I had first met him. He had a mask he could hide behind, a self-preservation device that I assumed he had needed in Roxbury. He was wearing the mask now.

"I can see why you'd be scared," I said. "Were you two cordial most of the time?"

"Cordial?"

"Friendly."

She shrugged. "We worked together. I had to help him with some things, so he probably treated me better than other people."

"What did you help him with?" Nash said.

"He got stuff backwards a lot, numbers all the time. Had the cash register screwed up just about everyday. He wasn't dumb, just . . . I don't know." She spread her hands.

"Dyslexic," Nash said, nodding to me. "I get it from him." He turned and looked out the window. "When I read aloud in school, I'd always say *was* when the word was *saw*. Everyone would laugh. Probably happened to him, too."

Lea and I looked at Nash.

"Did Owen have friends?" I said to Lea.

"Not here anyway. Once in a while a couple guys would come by to see him."

"The same guys you described to the cops? The guys who came in the day he was killed?"

"No, different. They didn't come in together."

"What did they look like?"

She shrugged. "One was white. The other was black. They looked kinda dangerous."

"How so?"

"Like they had money and would do whatever they have to to keep it. I've seen the type before."

It wasn't much of a visual.

Lea looked at her watch. "I can't describe it. But thanks for the coffee," she smiled, "Jack Austin. But I got to get home. My husband gets mad when I'm late."

Nash was still staring out the window.

"Your husband's home now?" I said. "He work the night shift, too?"

"He don't work. He was in the Army. They sent him to Iraq. Car bomb took both his legs. We've got a two-year-old daughter and a six-year-old son. Sometimes I think they're all I have left. My husband's not the same anymore. He gets disability from the government, but it's shitty. And he's just . . . not ready to work. Not the same."

She drank the last of her coffee.

"Got pictures of your kids?" I said.

"Why?" She looked at me for several seconds.

I shrugged. "You said you had a two-year-old. I was going to show you mine." I reached for my wallet.

She took out a photo. A cute little girl was sitting on the lap of a black man wearing fatigues. A young boy with a scar on his cheek and wearing a faded Patriots T-shirt stood next to them. I held Darcy's picture out to her.

"My son is Leon; my daughter is Katindah," she said. Her daughter wore pink and had her mother's blue eyes, sandy-blond hair, and dark skin. "Thanks again for the coffee."

"Wait a sec," I said and went to the counter. I returned with a pen, wrote my name and number down on a napkin and slid it to her. "If you remember anymore about Owen, please call us."

She said she would.

"If it's okay," Nash said, "I might drop by again."

She looked at Nash for several seconds. Then she reached out and patted his hand in motherly fashion. He did not pull away.

"I hope your husband feels better," I said.

When she looked at me, I felt stupid for saying it and thought of the Levine poem. These people were burning.

"He won't," she said. "He sits on the couch all day. When he looks at our daughter, he says, 'They didn't have Nuks and I got like this.' He drinks and he cries. My son's trying to be a man. Probably senses what's happening to his old man. But he's a boy." Her eyes fell to the table. "He's my little boy."

I didn't know what to say.

She thought for a moment. "You a rich Republican?"

"Independent," I said.

Lea thought about that and nodded. "Good." She turned and left.

Nash and I sat silently, watching her through the window. Outside, she got into a rusted Honda Civic and drove away.

"You all right?" I said.

Nash nodded, still looking out the window as Lea's Civic grew small and faded from view.

The state cop was a burly guy with a thick brown beard and a small scar near his right eye. We were in the Norfolk County District Attorney's Office in Canton, Massachusetts. The nameplate on his desk read Martin Cronjagger. Cronjagger sat behind his cluttered desk as we spoke. Framed pictures of a woman with short blonde hair and three college-age kids stood between us.

"Thanks for coming," he said to Nash. Then to me: "You his lawyer?"

"Just a friend," I said. "I called my lawyer and was told there was no need to bring one. Is that not the case?"

"No. That's the case. Who are you?"

I told him.

Cronjagger looked at me. "The golfer?"

"Not many people recognize my name."

"I follow the PGA Tour. I know even the most obscure players."

"Thanks."

Cronjagger didn't get that. He turned back to Nash. "Like I said, thanks, again, for coming. I know you don't know much about your father, but I wanted to ask a few more questions."

A paper coffee cup sat on the desk, and the coffee smelled strong. The office was cluttered. Manila envelops. File cabinet. Straight chairs, which Nash and I sat in. The window was open behind Cronjagger, but the office was still hot. Beads of perspiration were on Cronjagger's brow.

"I want to help," Nash said. "I want to know who my father was."

"You don't know anything about him?" Cronjagger said.

"He left when I was five. I know he was dyslexic. I am, so that makes sense."

"Nash, some things have leaked to the media, so you might have read them already."

"I've read all the articles I could find," Nash said. "I've been reading the *Globe* every day."

"So you know your father was tied to a chair in his apartment, his mouth was taped, and he was beaten with something, probably a bat. Both forearms and one shin were broken. One of his ribs punctured a lung. Finally, they shot him in the chest. It was late at night, woke a lot of people up. But no one saw anything or anyone leaving."

Nash sat staring, motionless. He nodded once. Something in my stomach did a triple-toe-loop.

"You all right?" Cronjagger said.

"Yeah," Nash said. "It's just . . ."

"I know. Been doing this for twenty-two years and this is a bad one. I'm giving you the details because, with all those pictures of you in that apartment, I want you to know what he was into."

"Am I in danger?" Nash said.

"We don't know much of anything right now."

"Lea Griffin, from the Wal-Mart where Owen worked," I said, "told us she offered a description of two guys who showed up there the day he died."

"You've been busy," Cronjagger said. "Yeah, we talked to her. She didn't say much. Owen Henley was a loner. The descriptions of the two guys go nowhere. So far, it's been like sticking your head in a black hole." He reached in his desk, took out the sketches, and pushed them toward us.

One guy was white, the other black. One had a thin beard

and a full head of hair and a scar through his right eyebrow. The other was bald with no facial hair and bushy eyebrows.

"Ever seen them?" Cronjagger said.

Nash shook his head. So did I.

Cronjagger folded his hands on the desk. "Because of the, ah, extent of the murder, I want you to take a moment and try to remember if you ever saw anyone follow you, taking pictures."

"Never."

"That's what I thought. Ever hear the name Terrell Smith?"

"No," Nash said.

I sat silently, watching and listening to Nash. He'd grown a lot in the two years since we had met.

"Terrell Smith was an acquaintance of your father."

"Who is he?" Nash said.

I remembered Lea had said two guys with money had occasioned Wal-Mart to see Owen. Then I remembered someone else.

"He have white hair?" I said. "Guy in his sixties?"

Cronjagger turned to me, surprised. "No. Why?"

I shrugged.

He looked at me for a moment. Then he slid a photo of a black man about Nash's age with a pencil-thin Fu Manchu moustache and beard across the desk. Thick scar tissue ran horizontally through the man's left eyebrow, as if the brow had grown in two distinct halves. "Nash, you ever seen him?"

Nash looked at the photo for a long time. "Maybe. I can't place him."

"But you recognize him?" Cronjagger said.

"Maybe."

"This is Terrell Smith. We know but can't prove he killed four people." Cronjagger shook his head. "Hell of a start. He's only twenty-one."

"If you know it, why can't you prove it?" Nash said.

"You need witnesses willing to take the stand. What *you* need to know is this: Terrell Smith is dangerous. He's involved in the Boston crime scene. Terrell is a minor player right now, but aspires for more. We know he's peddled dope, pushed pills. And we found the remnants of a joint in your father's apartment, so that might be a connection between them. We're not sure. We don't know what Terrell's into right now, but we think your father might have worked with him."

"Doing what?" Nash said.

"That's what we'd like to know. You think you might have seen him?"

"I'm not sure."

"If you do," Cronjagger said, "call me immediately. What did your mother say to you about Owen?"

"Not much. Just that he abandoned us. She hated him."

"Did you?"

Nash shifted in his seat. "No. I'd like to kick his ass for him. His leaving made it awful tough for my mother. She died." Nash's eyes ran to the photo of the kids on Cronjagger's desk. A blond guy Nash's age was with Cronjagger, both men in softball uniforms, standing on a diamond. "I also remember the good things about the guy, though—like how he used to read to me."

"Do you know he taught high school for a time and lost that job?"

Nash shook his head.

"He was fired," Cronjagger said. "The report has only one vague accusation. Interpretations of the statements could range from a teacher just being gregarious to a teacher acting inappropriately with a male student. It was a long time ago. Owen was teaching gym. A kid claimed Owen touched him publicly. No one else saw it." Cronjagger spread his hands. "But he got canned. It was 1979."

"Touched him?" Nash said. The words left him like a whisper.

"In truth," Cronjagger said, "I don't know how much help you can be to us, Nash. But I can tell you some other things about your father."

Nash leaned closer. So did I.

"Did you know," Cronjagger said, "that you have a half-sister, Nash?"

*n*ash barely spoke two words on the drive from Cronjagger's office to D. Forbes Will Field, where I dropped him off for the Curry Colonels' afternoon practice. Sitting stoically in the passenger seat of my old Suburban, Nash said only that he wanted time to process it all. I would give him space, which was easy to do because I would be less than an hour away.

It was time for me to go back to work. At 1:45 P.M., I stood on the first tee with my caddie, Tim Silver. Second-year pro Kip Capers and I were playing a practice round.

Each year, my relatives, spread all over Maine, come out of the woodwork for the Deutsche Bank Championship because it is played at the Tournament Players Club in Norton, Massachusetts, deemed TPC Boston. The venue is less than three hours from Portland, Maine, and only thirty miles from Milton, Massachusetts, where Nash would be practicing football and pondering a father he never really knew and a half-sister he had yet to meet.

"We playing skins?" Capers said. "Twenty bucks a hole?"

"I'll feel bad taking money from a young guy like you," I said.

"You didn't last year."

"Or last week."

"I won last week," he said. "Got family coming down?"

I told him I did. As I'd done since the tournament was first played in 2003, I stocked relatives' rooms with snacks, soda, beer, suntan lotion, and week-long tournament passes. Lisa made dinner reservations for twenty, Wednesday through Saturday.

The first hole is a par four, 365 yards. TPC Boston gives you a

chance to get off to a fast start. No. 1 is a birdie hole, and I had taken advantage. With the pin cut in the front, I had put my approach shot ten feet to the right of the flagstick. I would face a left-to-right putt for my three. Capers, though, was struggling. He had twenty-five feet for par, having driven his tee shot into a fairway bunker.

"It's been that kind of season," he said.

Capers wore his trademark attire: short-sleeve turtleneck and slacks. Always black and white. Today the turtleneck was black, the pants white. The clothing, however, was only part of the overall image. From Capers's shirtsleeves to his wrists, tattoos lined his arms. When he swung, the black and blue ink beneath his ropy forearms moved like dancing snakes. A gold cross dangled on a chain from his left ear. Finally, a dark ponytail protruded from the opening at the back of his hat and hung down between his shoulder blades.

Capers's physical appearance belied his personality. Deeply religious, he'd told me he believed a successful PGA Tour career would offer a larger audience with which to share his spiritual beliefs than a single congregation would, should he have become a pastor. Consequently, he spent a lot of time on Tour away from the golf course—speaking at religious schools and meeting with church groups. I believed his rookie season would have been more successful had his sole focus been on golf. Yet I couldn't argue with his priorities.

"You'll turn it around," I said.

"Come on, kid," Capers's caddie, Mike Lorne, said. "You got all the talent in the world. Just focus."

I knew Capers was serious about his future when he hired Lorne, a sixty-something looper who once carried for Greg Norman. I heard Capers was paying him a salary and that the bill was six figures. If the locker-room rumor mill was accurate, Capers, who barely retained his card the previous season, would need all the money he could earn. He was 137th on the money list and winless, so he was year to year, fighting to crack the season-ending money list's top 125.

Capers leaned over the par putt and made a long sweeping stroke. It was a pretty stroke, but Phil Mickelson had a long flowing stroke, too, and it had taken him more than a decade to win a major. The longer the motion, the easier it is for the putter to get off line.

Capers's ball ran six feet past the cup.

Very few spectators walked the course mid-afternoon on a Monday. Near the green, two boys, maybe six or seven years old, stood. One wore a hat that read "Woodlands Club." The autograph area at PGA Tour events is definitely not the first green, but no one was behind us. I grabbed two golf gloves from my bag and brought them to the kids. They went nuts, jumping and clapping. The father winked at me. "Thanks," he said. "You made their whole week."

"Eight inches left to right," Silver said, when I returned.

I stood over my birdie attempt, made two concise practice strokes, accelerating through impact. Then I pulled the trigger.

Silver's read was dead on. The ball dropped.

I tossed the ball to the boys. They went wild again.

. . .

Three hours later, Capers and I came to the eighteenth, a par-five dogleg, a 543-yard world-class finishing hole. Your tee shot must carry wetlands. But the challenge lies with the choice you face: If you play to the right, cutting the corner and carrying the bunkers, you have a second shot with which you can reach the green. If you play straight off the tee, you are safe but can't reach the green in two. So, as one stands on the No. 18 tee, the question becomes, Do I need an eagle?

I didn't. I was up six skins on Capers, totaling $120. However, I wasn't completely focused on the victory and the money. This was a practice round, and Capers was a friend. And he was really struggling.

I played down the right side.

"Come on, Jack," Capers said. "I don't need you laying back. It's patronizing."

I shook my head. "It's the safe play. If I'm leading by two on Sunday, that's the play I'll make. This is practice. I'm supposed to simulate the real thing."

"And you're up a hundred and twenty bucks?"

"That, too."

"Shit," he said, and swung so hard he did a Chi Chi Rodriguez follow-through, "stepping through" with his right foot, his finishing pose like a pitcher's, the back foot coming forward.

His ball carried the bunkers on the right.

"Guys who swing hard tend to hit the ball straight," Lorne said. "It guarantees acceleration through the hitting area. Woods, Greg Norman—those guys take big cuts, and the ball goes straight."

"Your back has to hold up, though," I said.

Lorne shrugged.

"I need to try something," Capers said. "Or I'll be on the Nationwide Tour next season. You got a free ride this year and next, right?"

I nodded. My win at the previous season's Buick Classic carried a two-year exemption. But I knew what Capers was going through. I'd spent a decade hovering around the almighty 125th spot. Lose your status and you return to Q School, PGA Tour Qualifying Tournament or the "fifth major," where annually more than a thousand golfers pay roughly $4,000 to take a shot at thirty spots (and ties) on the PGA Tour. Capers survived Q School once and didn't want to return. No one did. The pressure there can make the United States Open seem like Sunday-morning five-dollar Nassau.

Capers and I started down the fairway. Silver and Lorne were behind us, talking about local eateries.

"Some days I think I should have stayed in divinity school, become an Episcopal priest," Capers said. "I talked to Padre yesterday. Told him I'm thinking of going back."

As we walked, I could see several hundred people around the eighteenth green. Ahead of us, Tiger Woods was just finishing. He hit three shots from the bunker, each to a different spot on the green, practicing for potential pin locations.

"Jack, you were going to teach high school, right?"

I nodded.

"But this game . . ." He shook his head. "Man, it just grabs you. Grabs your heart."

"And doesn't let go," I said. "I know. I went through a tough time last year. Everything was new—baby, marriage, house. I wanted to be home more."

"What did you do?"

"Talked to my father."

Capers nodded.

We diverged, and I went to my ball. I hit a lay-up that left just over 100 yards to the pin. Capers hit his second shot with what looked like a three-wood. The green is protected by wetlands and heavily bunkered. Capers's ball carried everything and hit the surface, settling within ten feet of the flagstick. He and Lorne exchanged a low-five.

"How do you want to play it, boss?" Silver said at my ball, where we lay two. "High and soft or low and skid it in there?"

"Low," I said. "Give me the wedge."

I played the ball back in my stance, hooded the clubface, and hit down on the ball. It amounted to a line drive, landing in front, skidding a couple times, and stopping thirty feet from where it originally touched down, leaving fifteen feet for birdie, not what I'd hoped for.

"This is a carryover," Capers reminded me.

I nodded. This hole was worth $40. I wanted to sink this birdie putt and make Capers win with an eagle. I was away and lined up my putt from several different angles. Finally, I stood over the fifteen-footer and made a smooth, slow stroke. The ball caught the right edge of the cup, did a 360, and spun harmlessly away. I tapped in for par.

"Let's make this one," Lorne said, "start the week off right."

Capers nodded. He set his putter blade behind the ball gently, exhaled slowly, and made his stroke. The ball missed and ran three feet past.

When he missed the come-back attempt, he settled for a par.

Capers's three-putt meant I had halved the hole, although I took no joy in it. His three-putt was tough to watch. I had been around almost fifteen years, had seen guys burst onto the Tour and flame out. Lose confidence. Get the yips. Develop a snap hook. A number of things can do it. They all equate to the same result: A stroke here, a stroke there, and you go from an average of seventy to seventy-one—and you're finished.

I didn't want Capers to go down in flames. For one thing, the kid had talent. I had seen that at the end of last season, when he'd made $300,000 in six weeks to retain his card. And I liked him.

"I'll square up in the locker room," he said.

I watched him walk away. His head was down.

Silver and I followed, moving off the eighteenth green toward the clubhouse. From behind, someone called my name. "*Mistah Austin.*" The Boston accent was pronounced.

I turned and looked squarely at the white-haired man.

"His uncle?" I said. "You?"

We were in the clubhouse dining room at 4:45 P.M. I had shown my credential, a PGA Tour money clip I wore on my belt, at the door and entered with my guest—the same one I had chased from Wal-Mart hours earlier. Perkins and Silver sat across the table from us. The room was rife with the scent of cologne and alcohol. Around us, people drank beer from sweating glasses and dark mixed drinks. I sat shaking my head at the white-haired man, who said his name was Sean O'Reilly.

O'Reilly looked as Irish as his name sounded: sixty-ish; pale watery eyes; a thick red nose with tiny capillary lines. He stared at the interior of the dining room the way I imagined Lea Griffin probably would. When I was young, my father stretched ends terribly far to make them meet, working carpentry ten hours a day and plowing driveways in winter, so I never take the lifestyle for granted.

"You're not Nash Henley's uncle," Perkins said to O'Reilly.

"No. 'Course not. He's black. I'm Irish." O'Reilly looked at me. "Can I have a whiskey?" He set his hands down on the table-top. They were ringless and scarred and marked with tiny liver spots. His right hand trembled slightly.

"You going to keep asking that?" I said. "We're not here to watch you drink." But the drink might help him relax, or at least allow him to stop shaking.

Exasperated, I held up a hand for the waitress. She came over, and I asked for three drafts and a whiskey. She went to get them. Around us, the room hummed with activity. It was only Monday, but many of the 156 players had arrived. Several players and their families were eating. I was to meet Lisa and Darcy here at 5:30.

"O'Reilly says he thinks of himself as Nash's uncle," I said to Perkins.

Silver sat beside Perkins. He was looking at O'Reilly.

"What the hell does that mean?" Perkins said.

"You see," O'Reilly's eyes scanned the room, "I was Owen's only real friend. Makes me feel kind of responsible for the kid, Nash." He seemed to relax deeper into his seat when he saw the waitress walking toward us with the drinks.

"What the hell are we doing here?" Perkins said. He shook his head annoyed, as if a fly had landed on his ear. "Tell us why you're following Jack."

The waitress set the drinks down. Accidentally, she put the whiskey in front of me. O'Reilly reached across and took it like a drowning man leaping for a life preserver. Through the window, I could see Kip Capers on the putting green. He missed a three- or four-footer, and his shoulders slumped.

"I'm worried about that kid," O'Reilly said.

I looked at him sharply. "Nash?"

"Yeah. So I was trying to get a line on him, checking him out." O'Reilly took a two-second pull from the whiskey, held it in his mouth briefly, then swallowed. He leaned back as the whiskey moved through him. "Owen was a strange guy."

"Strange how?" I said. I wanted to compare his remarks to Lea Griffin's description.

"A loner. Maybe even a hermit. I was literally Owen's only friend. I went to his apartment a lot. Saw the pictures he took of his son. I was the only one he ever let in the place." He pronounced *ever* like a real Bostonian, *evah*.

I thought of something Cronjagger had said. "You smoke dope?"

O'Reilly looked at me. "Huh? Why? It shouldn't be illegal to begin with. It's not bad for you. Doctors give it to people. How can it be bad for you?"

Cronjagger might not have established a clear connection between Terrell Smith and Owen Henley, but I could guess what the connection between O'Reilly and Owen had been.

"Tell us how Owen was strange," Perkins said.

O'Reilly shrugged. "I'm not saying he was nuts . . . just a little . . . you know, *strange*. The kind of guy who laughs when no one else does. Like he's in his own world most of the time. Not talking to his self or nothing like that—just—seeing things from his own view."

That was consistent with Lea Griffin.

"Poor Nash," Silver said, watching Capers putt. "Poor kid."

O'Reilly, Perkins, and I all turned to face him. Silver didn't look at us.

We were silent a few seconds.

"What's with the pictures?" I said to O'Reilly. "Why didn't Owen ever talk to Nash? Did he talk to his daughter?"

O'Reilly sat frozen. "Daughter? Whose daughter?"

All eyes were on me now. "State cop named Cronjagger told us Nash has a half-sister living in Maine. She goes to high school there."

"I know Cronjagger," Perkins said.

The waitress returned to check on us. O'Reilly immediately asked for a second whiskey. I shook my head. I had watched this guy follow me for days, wondering what it was all about. Now he sat next to me, ordering drinks on my tab.

"Owen never mentioned a daughter," O'Reilly said. "Did he know?"

"I asked Cronjagger the same thing. He must have. They found a few pictures of the daughter. When they went to talk to her, she knew nothing of him. She was adopted by a white family in Readfield, Maine, who own several stores in Augusta."

"Sounds like the daughter's life has been a hell of a lot easier than Nash's," Perkins said. "Who's the mother?"

"Not the same as Nash's," I said. "A woman in Portland."

"Maybe Owen felt guilty for being such a fucking coward and leaving one kid to fend for himself," Silver said, "while the daughter was taken care of, that he *needed* to smoke dope and take thousands of pictures. He didn't have the guts to talk to Nash—to admit what he'd done—so he thought pictures would show he cared. They don't show me a fucking thing." He said *fucking* with emphasis.

"Owen wasn't a coward," O'Reilly said. "He was trying. Those pictures were all he had. He couldn't have a son. Owen couldn't handle a family. It was sad. I felt terrible for the guy."

I didn't. But before I could say anything, Silver turned from the window to face O'Reilly. Silver's eyes were hard and small and locked on the old man's.

"Owen Henley had no family and no son by choice," Silver said. "He was a no-good coward. Lots of kids grow up with no old man, let alone a real father. And those kids have to fight for everything they get. Don't you ever defend an Owen Henley to me. It's easy to walk away. Real men stick it out."

O'Reilly looked from Silver to his whiskey. He looked at Silver again, couldn't hold Silver's stare, and looked back to the whiskey, this time clutching it and drinking deeply.

Perkins and I sat staring at Silver. We watched in silence as he stood, tossed his napkin on the table, and pointed a finger at O'Reilly. "Don't ever defend a guy who walked out on his kid to me, you son of a bitch." Silver turned and left, leaving us in the silent wake of his outburst.

Around us, the dining room crowd went on, no one noting the flare-up. I heard idle chatter and clinking silverware. The air-conditioned air was still and cool. O'Reilly's eyes followed Silver out of the room. So did mine. I had never witnessed Silver react like that. Silver wasn't a punch-you-in-the-mouth guy. He was contemplative—listen, take it in, evaluate, then say something to make you feel stupid.

"You know a guy named Terrell Smith?" I said to O'Reilly.

"Terrell Smith?" Perkins said. "That's a bad name. Cronjagger mentioned him?"

I nodded.

"Never heard of him," O'Reilly said, and blew out a long breath. "Your buddy, Silver, has Owen all wrong. Owen just didn't relate to people." He drank some whiskey. "Just couldn't do it. He frightened people."

"Then how'd he stay employed as a Wal-Mart cashier?" Perkins said.

O'Reilly shrugged. "Probably wouldn't have much longer. They switched him to mornings right off to get him away from the crowds. They were going to let him go. He told me so. He'd only been there a year."

"Fine," I said. "He didn't deal with people. No one knows that more than Nash. Now Nash is twenty and wants to find out what his father was like."

"I know," O'Reilly said. "I talked to Lea Griffin after you left."

I exhaled slowly. This was grating. "How did you meet Owen?"

O'Reilly shifted in his seat and drank the rest of his whiskey. "Spent a weekend with him once. I knew he needed a friend."

"What are you, a fucking social worker?" Perkins said. "Where and why?"

"Drunk tank. We both spent a weekend in city jail. I helped him get some work." He looked away. "And now he's dead."

It made me wonder about the job and its relationship to the murder. It also brought me back to the focal point. "Why are you concerned for Nash?"

"Owen made some real bad decisions in his last six months. I tried to help him, got him some work. But he couldn't handle it. I should have known that would happen. He just wanted to help Nash, to do something big for him, and it cost so much money. I tried to help him do it." O'Reilly finished the ramble as if making a confession. Then he sat back in his chair, staring at the empty whiskey glass.

Perkins watched his every move. "Tell us about the job."

"Ever hear of Jerome Pulchuck?"

I shook my head.

Perkins nodded. "Now we're getting somewhere."

"So you know him?" O'Reilly said.

"I know *of* him," Perkins said.

"Same difference. You know what he does."

"Yeah," Perkins said. "And what he is."

"Who is he?" I said.

"An unconvicted drug dealer. Pimp. He's maybe two players below the top guy. Runs a lot of stuff in Boston."

"He's not that bad," O'Reilly said. He looked as if he might continue to defend Pulchuck, but the look passed when the waitress came back. When I waved off another round of drinks, O'Reilly looked like I threatened to wean him.

"I'm doing you guys a favor coming here," O'Reilly said. "I was thinking this information might be worth something. Maybe a fee."

"You've got to be shitting me," Perkins said.

"You've been following me," I said. "Today you wanted to talk. Tell me why you're concerned about Nash Henley and I'll buy you drinks all night."

"I could use a little dough. I'm an old man."

"You're a hustler looking for a buck," I said, and leaned very close to him.

O'Reilly's eyes grew wide.

"I'm getting sick of sitting here watching you drink," I said. "Stop fucking around and tell me if Nash Henley is in danger."

"No, man. I didn't say that." His eyes ran to the empty glass before him. "I loved Owen Henley. You gotta know that. I'm alone. He's alone. We was friends. He needed money. I introduced him to Jerome."

"You work for Jerome Pulchuck?" Perkins said.

"Not like the guys he pays salary. I wish. I heard he gives some guys cars."

"What did Owen Henley do for him?" Perkins said.

"All I know is Owen was supposed to drive an SUV to Canada and back."

"Once?" I said.

"I don't know. But, after I introduced him to Pulchuck, Owen had money. And of course, he said he spent it all on the house he bought Nash."

"A house?" Perkins said. "In Nash's name?"

O'Reilly shrugged.

"Where is the house?" Perkins said.

"I don't know. Owen never went into details about *anything*. He just mentioned a house a couple times. Said he needed money for the house he wanted to buy Nash."

"Hold on," Perkins said, exasperated, "he *bought* the house or *was going to buy* the house?"

O'Reilly looked at him, confused.

Perkins blew out a long breath. "For Christ's sake."

My head was spinning: Job? House? Jerome Pulchuck? An SUV to Canada?

"All I know is Owen loved his son, Nash. And I was thinking whoever killed him tossed his apartment and saw the photos. What if they come for Nash?"

We were quiet, all of us sipping our drinks, thinking.

"Why would they do that?" Perkins said.

"I don't know. I was just thinking about it."

"That's the only reason?" I said. "There's nothing else?"

"No, man."

"You seen Pulchuck since Owen was killed?" I said.

O'Reilly nodded. "He didn't mention Owen, but he said something else. Can I have a drink?"

I waved the waitress over again. When she left for the whiskey, I said, "Tell me."

O'Reilly looked pained. He sighed. "Owen insulted Pulchuck when I introduced them. He didn't know how to talk to people. Pulchuck is short and stocky. Owen told him he should try that low-carb diet. Pulchuck's face got red and a couple guys who work for him laughed. The other day, Pulchuck said something about 'no one telling me to eat no fucking low-carbs again.' I just been thinking about that a lot now. A real lot." He stood. "I gotta go."

Neither Perkins nor I tried to stop him. We watched him walk out.

"He knows something," I said.

"He might know a lot," Perkins said, standing up. "I'll follow him and look into property owned by Owen Henley." He went out.

When the waitress arrived, I was alone. I took the whiskey and wished it were a double.

In the old days, Tour players gathered in the grillroom or the bar and workout regimens consisted of pumping twelve-ounce weights and eating health food like peanuts and chips. After a bad round, players sought counsel from cute waitresses with names like Dolly. Now it was sports psychiatrists. It was also the Tour's HealthSouth fitness van, a forty-eight-foot mobile gym complete with training staff and workout equipment. This was where Nash and I were Tuesday morning at 7:45.

I was on the bench. As I fought 225 pounds for an eighth rep, letting the bar down with a clang, I wished I had been born in that earlier era.

"Want to talk about your half-sister?" I said, sitting up.

The fitness van was designated for players. Nash, technically, was not allowed in; however, this morning my focus wasn't Tour policy. I would deal with the fine if it was levied.

Nash switched plates on the bar, killing my ego by adding thirty pounds. "No," he said simply. Then he lay back on the bench and did a rep with ease. By his fourth, he was straining, which gave me hope. Nash lifted weights with fierce concentration. His tongue protruded from his mouth as he concentrated, à la Michael Jordan, carefully exhaling as he pressed up, and inhaling as the weight moved slowly down. He appeared lost in each repetition.

The inside of the trailer was a mini health club—glass and chrome (unfortunately, no Spandex)—and it was busy. Most guys were stretching with assistance from trainers. A few players recognized Nash and waved. Jeff Sluman stopped by to ask how football was going.

Next, Emilio Rodriguez approached. Emilio was special assistant to PGA Tour Commissioner Peter Barrett. He wore pressed khaki pants, wing-tipped loafers, and a collared button-down shirt with "PGA Tour" on the breast. Like the trainers, his ID hung from his neck.

Emilio shook his head and smiled. "Didn't we fine you enough for bringing him in here when the guy caddied for you?" His voice carried the hint of an accent. I knew he had grown up in Modesto, California, and that his parents had been Spanish speaking. "How many times was it? Five? Six?"

"Eight," I said. "Consider it a charitable contribution."

He grinned.

"Somebody's got to give you headaches," I said. "Besides, right now I'm claiming Nash as my trainer."

"At least you're getting smarter. And at least Nash looks the part." Emilio turned to him. "You get bigger every time I see you. You do anything but lift weights?"

Nash got up and shook Emilio's hand. "Gained fifteen pounds and averaged seven yards a carry last year."

"And got a two-point-five G.P.A.," I said as I changed plates.

I got back on the bench, placed my hands on the bar precisely, and pushed the bar up. In an age where every other TV channel carries an infomercial promoting new fitness gear, free weights remain superior. You have to balance the weight, control it, while fighting gravity for the repetition. Balance and form are paramount. Nothing compares.

"Perkins is trying to reach you, Jack," Emilio said. "He wants you to call. He called your cell phone, then your hotel room, now the office."

"Makes me feel important."

"You're not," Emilio said, "but you are fined two hundred dollars." He smiled and walked out.

As always, I had left my cell phone in the locker room when I arrived and changed into shorts and cross-trainers, then headed to the fitness van. I hadn't spoken to Perkins since the night before, when he had left on the heels of Sean O'Reilly. After retrieving my cell phone, I chugged along on a Lifecycle and listened to Perkins begin the conversation with a chuckle.

"O'Reilly is a private investigator," he said. "That's what's stenciled on his office door in Milton. Shitty building in a nice town. Rent is probably cheap."

"I thought he met Owen in the drunk tank. He's licensed?"

"Yeah. Maybe he did meet him that way. I don't think he actually works. Not a hell of a need for PIs in Milton. Maybe divorce shit, stuff like that."

"A real peeper?"

"Maybe. Like I said, I don't think he's worked lately, maybe in years."

I watched Nash tighten the thick leather belt he wore around his waist. His pectoral muscles stretched the gray fabric of his Curry College football T-shirt. His arms looked swollen and tight. Veins protruded. Among the group of golfers, which included a young stud, Ricky Barnes, Nash *looked* like a football player. Tiger Woods is often described as having a defensive back's physique. Nash, though, is the real deal. He was no longer the big tough kid I had met two years ago. Now he was a man— 6 percent body fat, a thirty-two-inch waist, and twenty-nine-inch thighs.

"O'Reilly lives in his shitty office," Perkins said. "He slept there last night anyway. Which reminds me, I slept in my car, and I charge extra for that. It'll be on the expense account."

"What happened to pro bono?"

"That's for Nash. I'll still charge you."

Nash glanced over to see if I wanted to do military presses with him. I waved him off.

"Cute," I said. "Maybe I'll go see O'Reilly."

"Why?"

"So he can tell me how to see Jerome Pulchuck. You're a former Massachusetts cop and own a Boston private investigations business. You've worked on the wrong side of the law, according to Pulchuck. He'd probably know you, or one of his guys sure might. You wouldn't get within a hundred feet of him."

"So what are you going to do?"

"I don't know yet," I said.

We hung up, and I went back to Nash and started doing overhead triceps extensions with him.

Nash struggled with a fifty-pound dumbbell. Exhausted and frustrated, he set the weight down with a thud. "Shit," he said, breathing hard. He kicked the weight.

"What are you complaining about?" I said. "I'm struggling with thirty-five pounds."

"It's not that. I called Maureen Glenn last night."

I had an idea where this was headed.

"She's my half-sister. When I told her who I was, she said she didn't want to talk. I told her what had happened to my—our—father and there was this long pause. Then she said she didn't want to hear any of it and hung up."

I set the weight down and lay down on the floor. I started doing crunches. Nash was beside me, his torso moving effortlessly, two crunches for each of mine. I sensed this to be more than a routine workout for him. He went through his routine on this day the way Sean O'Reilly had drunk whiskey the night before.

Nash's call must have taken Maureen Glenn by surprise. She was a well-to-do high school student in a small town outside Augusta, Maine. Her adopted parents owned more than one store. Owen Henley's departure from her life hadn't left her destitute as it had Nash. In fact, his departure enabled the adoption that was her good fortune. I knew nothing of Maureen Glenn's biological mother. But Owen Henley's decision to leave Maureen Glenn had, seemingly, been the best thing to happen to her.

That was an easy observation. How did it make Nash feel?

"What do you want to do?" I said.

"I don't know. I don't really want to talk about it, Jack. I need to handle things myself."

"Before, you said you needed to show Owen Henley you made it, that you were a man. Don't forget something: Even men need help and people to talk to."

He nodded. We finished our workout in silence.

*Y*ou can't win a tournament on Thursday, but you sure as hell can lose it. As a rookie, I realized quickly you can post an opening-day score that leaves you no chance. Despite Tiger Woods occasionally testing my theory by opening with seventy-five and following with three consecutive rounds in the low sixties to win, I know my own abilities well enough to still believe each of the four tournament rounds is vital. This knowledge helps me to grind over every shot. At 10:25 A.M. Thursday at the TPC Boston, I was trying to grind it out during a rainy opening round of the Deutsche Bank Championship.

Yet I was struggling to focus. The weather was terrible, but that wasn't it. I had gone through a long stretch the year before—the only such period of my career—during which focus had been an issue, but I had been dealing with personal problems then. This was different. This time I was keeping a promise—to help a friend find his father or rather, now, information about whom that man had been.

My threesome had gone off early and we were on the seventh hole, a mammoth 600-yard par five. I was two over par, and this was no easy birdie hole. To play No. 7 successfully, you must hit a long straight tee shot, then typically lay up, avoiding right-side fairway bunkers, 120 yards from the green. With your third shot, you have to stay clear of sand traps guarding the left side of the green. I had never reached the putting surface in two. My playing partners, Jeff Sluman and J. P. Hayes, had already hit drives. They were −1 and even par respectively.

I swung the driver back and forth, making broad shoulder turns to loosen up, then made my ritual two practice swings before hitting a good drive to the center of the wet fairway. The ball only bounced twice but scooted past the two others, stopping 315 yards away.

"Finally," Silver said. "Nice swing."

A great thing about the PGA Tour is that, unlike other professional sports, in certain situations (like when a player finds the rough) a fan can stand literally feet from a player during competition. That's great for fans; it can be not so great for players, especially when things are going south and you feel like swearing. Or any time Silver opens his mouth.

Silver usually manages to control himself on the tee and did so here, taking care to whisper. "You see what Montel Williams wore yesterday? He looked incredible."

"I'm sure," I said.

Silver put the head cover on the driver and slid it into the bag. "You're going to have less than three hundred yards to the green. Think you can hit a three-wood two-eighty?"

"It's drizzling," I said, and shook my head. "Too risky."

We walked down the fairway toward my playing partners' balls. Hayes would be first to hit and took several practice swings.

I had a chance at birdie and tried to regroup, mentally. My thoughts, however, ran back to Nash Henley. I play a game for a living that demands autonomy and integrity. On the golf course, I once stood over a putt only to have the ball mysteriously move half an inch. I had ground my putter before the ball had moved, and therefore called a penalty on myself. I lost that tournament by a single stroke, and with it, a lot more. Victory on the PGA Tour can mean financial security via endorsements and appearance fees for clinics, corporate outings, and European Tour events. Yet we all live by a personal code that governs our actions.

Part of mine is that I keep my promises.

Nash Henley wasn't my son. Yet the more I learned of his biological father, the more I wished he were. His father had met Sean O'Reilly in the drunk tank, and they had smoked dope together. O'Reilly, who, according to Perkins, still had a private investigator's license, now worked small jobs for infamous Jerome Pulchuck, a major-league Boston low-life. What bothered me was that I sensed O'Reilly, grifter or not, had genuinely cared for Owen Henley and felt guilt over his demise. Worse, I thought O'Reilly was sincere in his concern for Nash—which meant Nash might be in danger. I was glad Perkins was sticking around Milton a few days to watch Nash practice.

Hayes hit a fine lay-up to 130 yards from the green. We moved to Sluman's ball. Behind the green, an electronic scoreboard flashed scores: Woods, -4; Garcia, -4; and a pack at three under.

Sluman is a little guy and had no choice but to lay up. The drizzle had seemed nonthreatening all morning, but was picking up. It tapped steady against my Gore-Tex rainsuit. My Taylor-Made hat was soaked. Dad and I had often played in rain on days when water would bead and steadily drip off my cap's bill. We would bundle in rainsuits and, as he would say, "Go for it." Those days, like all our golf rounds, provided time together, which always made it worth fighting the rain.

"All right, boss," Silver said, when we reached my ball. "In the bag room, a caddie said John Daly reached this green in two shots today." There was a hint of challenge in his voice.

"This isn't a pissing contest. I'm two over par."

"Eagle this hole and we're even." He pulled the three-wood out.

A Tour caddie has more roles than an octagon has sides, including swing coach, yardage guru, amateur psychologist, green reader, and, of course, club selector. My view has always been: The player is ultimately responsible for his score. So the final say is mine. That rationale originally allowed me to connect with Nash Henley. A player depending heavily on a caddie would never have hired Nash. However, guys like Steve Stricker, whose wife occasionally loops for him, and myself can go with an amateur. Indeed, I had even stooped to let Perkins carry.

"I think you can reach that green, Jack," Silver said, holding his pencil, reviewing his yardage book. "You've been killing the ball. Worst case, you pull it a little, dump it in a front trap. And you can get up and down from there."

Silver flipped the book shut and slid it into his poncho pocket. He was a pro. He had scouted the course, outlined various situations, and knew my tendencies: When I overswing, I pull the ball left.

I took the three-wood from him. It was humid and in the high eighties. The sleeves of the rain jacket stuck to my flesh. I made several practice swings to make sure my jacket wouldn't bind me.

Finally, I stood over the ball and brought the club back slowly, pausing just short of parallel to the ground. There was a half-second pause at the top, my body regrouping, preparing to change direction. I began the descent. My left arm pulled down. My right wrist turned over, snapping the ball airborne at the moment of contact. At finish, my belt buckle pointed down the target line, and I held the follow-through pose, not looking up until well after the fact.

"Pured it," Silver said.

I heard the gallery react and knew it wasn't the pitying sound I had heard the week before. This was the sound of gathering excitement. I heard it often when Woods was on the course. The sound said something happened and what would follow could be exciting. To have caused the sound gave me the feeling I play for.

.   .   .

At the green, Sluman and Hayes had eight and ten feet for birdie, respectively. My three-wood had come to rest twenty-five feet from the hole. I was putting for eagle. The drizzle was still coming, and I knew the wet green would be slow. The flag had been placed in the middle, where the green formed a valley, so my ball would go up before running down to the hole.

"Left to right," Silver said, "then really quick at the hole. Play it four balls off the left edge."

"To get it close, I have to almost stop the thing at the top of the peak and let it trickle down."

Silver shot me a look. I was glad he did. He had correctly interpreted my words: I was saying I didn't want to run the ball too far past the hole, if I missed. The result could be a three-putt. But you can't think like that. I had a chance at an eagle three. *Take one shot at a time.*

I stood over the ball and made two practice strokes, looking at the hole to gauge distance. I had the line. I had seen it exactly the same as Silver. I placed the putter face behind the ball and made my stroke.

The ball tracked and slowed at the crest. It looked as if four inches to the left would be too much. I thought it wouldn't come back. Six feet from the hole, though, the ball moved right—and died into the heart of the cup. I couldn't hear the change-into-a-tin-can rattle. The gallery was too loud. And I was even par.

. . .

By 2:30 P.M., I was at No. 17 and stood three under par. Woods, leading the event, was in the clubhouse with an opening-round sixty-six, −5. Sergio Garcia was −4 and Phil Mickelson had shot sixty-eight. The three of them would feed off each other and probably go low all week. I wanted to stay within striking distance. The drizzle was letting up and through an opening in the layer of clouds, the sun splashed golden. The forecast for the week predicted sunshine and temps in the nineties, which would mean lightning-fast, sun-baked greens. Most Tour players like to putt fast greens. Fast greens mean a shorter back-stroke and a shorter back-stroke means less chance to take the club off-line.

The seventeenth at TPC Boston is a dogleg left, par four, playing 420 yards. A collection of fairway bunkers guards the left side, catching wayward tee shots. The green, however, is unprotected by sand traps but guarded by a stream in front. I knew a safe tee shot would set up an approach shot that might yield a birdie chance. I had the three-wood out.

"Here we go," Silver said. "Keep it in the groove."

I made two practice swings, then set the club head behind the ball, carefully aiming the three-wood's face at a distant target. The world's best players simply hit fewer bad shots than anyone else. My world ranking was ninety-ninth. However, this time the contact was solid—not pure—but solid. The Titleist Pro V1 flew high and landed in the fairway, safely right of the fairway bunkers, leaving an eight-iron to the green.

"Be a nice day to shoot sixty-seven," Silver said.

"Most days would." We were moving down the fairway.

"Sorry about pulling my Norman Bates act with Sean O'Reilly," Silver said. "I guess there're some things I can't stand. Fathers who walk out on their kids fit the bill."

"Your mother raised you, huh?"

We paused at Sluman's tee shot. He had 165 yards to the green.

Silver looked at the gallery, then his eyes focused on something above the spectators in the distance. "My mother was everything—mother, father, teacher. When my old man left, she worked two jobs to make the rent. She told me every night of my life to stay in school, go to college. She died three days after I got my master's. Never saw my book published."

Sluman hit and we moved to my ball. Hayes had launched his drive well over 300 yards. I had 154 yards. The rain had stopped and there was no wind. The No. 17 green is large and always receptive. Today, being wet, it would allow me to go at the hole, which was cut in the center of the green. I brought the eight-iron back slowly, then down. The ball flew high and landed within six feet of the flagstick.

My birdie putt was dead straight. A common mistake I see among amateurs is over-reading the break in greens. It's why straight putts are often the most difficult. The clouds had once again sealed off the sun. I stood behind the ball making practice strokes. The eighteenth hole was 543 yards but, wet, would play much longer. I wanted a birdie here.

I got over the ball and made a good stroke. The putt fell, center cut.

When I looked up, Silver was not smiling at me. He was eyeing Sean O'Reilly, who stood in the greenside gallery.

11

"I was thinking maybe you could buy me a drink," O'Reilly said, when Silver and I walked off the eighteenth green.

"I bet you were," I said. "What do you want?"

"Jerome—remember that guy I told you about?"

"Jerome Pulchuck," I said. "Yeah, I remember. What about him?"

Silver took the clubs and headed to the bag room. It was late afternoon, which made me wonder if O'Reilly timed his appearances around happy hour. He stood before me wearing a rain-soaked white T-shirt with yellow sweat rings at the armpits and khaki pants. His pant cuffs were tattered, several strands of fabric hanging near scuffed shoes. He had no umbrella. His white hair was matted against his head.

"How long have you been out here?" I said.

"I followed you all the way."

"In the rain? Without an umbrella?"

He shrugged.

"Jesus Christ," I said. "Come with me before pneumonia sets in."

After I signed my scorecard, I led O'Reilly to the clubhouse again. Several golfers and a few Westchester Country Club members glanced over at O'Reilly, who sat with me at a table near the door. O'Reilly stood out. Everyone else either still had on a rainsuit or was dry enough to indicate they had worn one. I ordered O'Reilly a brandy and a pitcher of ice water for myself.

"Thought you were a beer drinker," O'Reilly said and smiled widely, as if we were long-time drinking buddies.

We weren't. I didn't smile back. "What did you come here for?"

The waitress returned with the drinks. O'Reilly took a long pull from his brandy. He had my father's sad Irish eyes, and they seemed to liven as the alcohol traversed through him.

"That guy's sandwich over there looks good," O'Reilly said.

I had finished at −4 with a sixty-seven. The rain had made the round seem longer than four and a half hours. I wanted to go back to the hotel, take a long hot shower, play with Darcy, and meet my extended family for dinner. The guy at the next table wore a blue blazer. He saw O'Reilly staring at his sandwich and turned away.

"For Christ's sake," I said, "I'm not getting you a sandwich. What are you doing here?"

"Jerome Pulchuck is going to see Nash," he said. "He's looking for him."

I set my glass down very slowly, staring at him. Nash was an hour away. I couldn't get there soon enough. Instinctively, I reached to my pant pocket for my cell phone, but it was still in my locker. Then I remembered Perkins was in Milton with Nash and sat back, folded my arms across my chest, and stared at O'Reilly.

"What does he want with Nash?"

"Wants to talk to him."

"How did you find this out?" I said.

"He called me in, asked me if I knew the kid in the pictures they got from Owen's apartment."

"And like an idiot, you said yes?"

"Jerome Pulchuck is not a guy you lie to."

"How does he even know about the pictures?"

"I don't know. I know Jerome knows a lot of people in a lot of places."

"Meaning cops?"

He shrugged.

"Why is Pulchuck interested in them?"

"I don't know," he said again.

I drank some ice water. The connection between Owen Henley and Jerome Pulchuck, according to O'Reilly, was a round-trip SUV ride to Canada.

"What's Jerome Pulchuck want with Nash?" I said.

"He said he needed to talk to him." O'Reilly finished his drink, set the glass down, and stared longingly at it. "That's what he told me, anyway. Can I get another brandy?"

I leaned across the table until I was very close to him, as I had the night before. I refrained from grabbing the old man's collar, but just barely. "You told me you were concerned for Nash. Did Pulchuck kill Owen Henley?"

"Look, man, don't get upset. I don't know anything about that. Jerome called me in, asked who's the kid in the pictures. I told him. I thought you'd want to know, so I came here. That's all."

O'Reilly started to lean back, but the conversation wasn't finished. I grabbed his shirt collar and pulled him close to me.

"What are you doing, man? I don't know anything."

"You gave Pulchuck Nash's name," I said. "If anything happens to Nash Henley I'll be looking for you."

"Jack, man, we're friends, right?"

I stood up. "Remember what I said."

I walked out, leaving O'Reilly with his empty brandy glass and my threat echoing in his ears.

.   .   .

Later that evening, I was at the other end of the universe. Sean O'Reilly was—almost—a distant memory. Nash was not. He was present. I was eating with Lisa, Darcy, Nash, Perkins, my parents, and a dozen or so other relatives who had driven south to see the tournament. The mood was festive—due to my sixty-seven—and my uncles drank beer with my father. The meal was steak and seafood. My tab.

Lisa spotted a former CBS colleague at a nearby table and went to talk. I had pushed back several feet from the table and sat bouncing Darcy on my knee. Perkins was beside me.

"Nash," Lisa called from the other table and waved him over. Nash got up and went to Lisa.

I turned to Perkins. "What happened with Jerome Pulchuck?"

"Pulchuck is the real deal." Perkins sipped some beer. "Just like I said before. He shows up at Nash's apartment in a Mercedes. His driver and another guy get out and come to Nash's place with Pulchuck."

"Bodyguards?"

"Daddy," Darcy said when I had stopped bouncing her, distracted by Perkins's tale. "Bouncy," she said. "Bouncy."

"Not in the traditional sense," Perkins said.

"Wow, UMaine really taught you a lot. Do other investigators say stuff like 'not in the traditional sense'?"

He rubbed his temple with his middle finger. "Pulchuck has a staff of tough guys. They knock and Nash lets them in. I'm on the sofa, watching. Pulchuck starts off by telling Nash how sorry he is about his father."

"Sorry?"

"Yeah. Says he read about it in the paper, that he knew Owen and is sorry." Perkins paused to drink from his bottle of Beck's. "Pulchuck went to Nash to see if he had any of Owen's photos. Nash told him he didn't."

"He will," I said. "He's next of kin. Cops will give Owen's possessions to Nash."

"Probably," Perkins said. "Maybe it'll remain murder evidence for a while. But Pulchuck's no dummy. Before he asks for the pictures, he asks who the hell I am. I tell him I'm Nash's big brother." Perkins smiled at the memory. "Pulchuck says he doesn't have a sense of humor. I told him not to drop by again then, because I'm a very funny guy. We stared at each other for a few seconds. Then he turns back to Nash and says he really likes his father's pictures and would be willing to pay for them."

"What did Nash say?"

"Nothing."

"So that's where things stand?" I said.

Perkins nodded. A stocky guy I recognized from television sat at the table Lisa and Nash were visiting. The guy was chuckling. Nash laughed full out, and Lisa stood, shaking her head.

"O'Reilly said Pulchuck gave Owen a job," I said, "driving. Then Owen is dead."

"That might speak to his job evaluation."

"It might."

"Or it might speak to the corporate culture at Pulchuck Enterprises."

"'Corporate culture'?" I said. "You're really something today."

Perkins smiled and drank some more beer. So did I. He could experiment; I was sticking with Heineken. The lobster and steak arrived and Lisa and Nash returned. Five pounds of steamed clams were put on the table. I opened one, stripped the neck, cleaned it in broth, then dipped it in butter. The belly was rich and gritty. Perfect.

Around us, the restaurant was busy. The sound of the Austin clan overtook the cacophony. There were bursts of laughter, silverware clicking against dishes, occasional fragments of my mother's voice talking softly to Darcy, and Nash's laughter as he talked to Dad.

Darcy was still on my knee. In a rare moment of silence, she looked at the lobster before me. "Do I going to eat one of those monsters, Daddy?"

The table exploded with laughter. I kissed her cheek and told her no. A plate of mac-and-cheese was placed before the booster seat. I set Darcy in her place between Perkins and me.

"Who was that?" Perkins said to Lisa. "Guy looks familiar."

"Paul Staples," Lisa said. "My replacement."

She said the last two words in a way that made everyone pause and look at her. There was an unmistakable longing in her voice. She realized it and looked down. I reached over and helped her with her lobster.

Perkins made faces at Darcy. She laughed and spit a mouthful of mac-and-cheese.

"Good going, uncle P," I said.

Nash continued to talk with my father. My father and mother often drove three hours south to watch Nash play football. They had gone to the Curry College Grandparents' Weekend as well. Mom, a devout reader, had arrived with the latest Robert B. Parker novel for Nash. Dad and Nash were talking about going to a Patriots game in the fall.

"What did Paul Staples say?" I said to Lisa.

We were eating casually. Lisa looked over and shrugged, dipped her lobster in butter, and ate.

"You know you're the only one at the table eating lobster with silverware?" I said. "Pretty obvious who's not from Maine."

"We have manners in Maryland." Lisa smiled. "I was trying to get Nash an internship, and Paul promised to look into it. He said something else, too."

I took the lobster's tail in both hands, cracked it, and pulled out the meat.

"Paul told CBS he's leaving to cover baseball for ESPN," she said. "He said CBS wants me back. Jack, they're going to call my agent and make an offer."

She stopped eating, awaiting my response.

"That's great," I said. "Congratulations."

Across from us, my mother got up and moved around the table. Darcy had spilled a cup of broth on Perkins. Lobster, for all of its flavor, has an aroma as strong as the beast is ugly, and the idea of Perkins going back to his room to scrub the scent away made me grin.

"I know this isn't the place for a family discussion," Lisa said, "but I'd like to get a sense of what you think. First impression?"

"Go for it," I said. "We can arrange something. Hell, Perkins is doing so well with Darcy maybe we can hire him as a full-time nanny."

Lisa grinned momentarily. Then she looked her plate. "Darcy is the X factor, isn't she? You can't really do TV work part-time."

"Some people can," I said.

Around us, the table buzzed with various conversations. My father's two brothers ran a logging operation in Aroostook County, Maine, and looked the part—jeans, work boots, and T-shirts. Uncle Bill wore a green and yellow John Deere cap; Mike wore a TaylorMade hat I had given him. Both were over six feet and weighed around 220.

"I know what you're saying," Lisa said. "I'd have to change to do part-time—not work so hard. I can do that, Jack. I really can tone it down."

I nodded and ate some lobster, remaining very consciously silent.

12

Friday's round had been mediocre, even par seventy-one. I had begun Saturday at −4, paired with friend Kip Capers. We were not among the leaders. Ernie Els and Phil Mickelson were deadlocked at −12. The weather was perfect for scoring. It was eighty-five, the sun burning golden overhead. The humidity, however, was brutal, and by the fourth hole I had sweat through my shirt. An infuriating bead of perspiration slithered down my spine just beyond reach.

The gallery following us Saturday afternoon was large, the most boisterous of fans none other than my family. In fact, a television network deemed our following "Austinites," and my relatives reveled in the newfound fame. Sunburns, beer, whooping, and hollering—you'd have thought Capers and I were waging war for the Ryder Cup.

"You've got it going pretty well," Capers said. "Nice birdie back there."

We were on the tee, waiting to hit, at No. 4, a 436-yard, par-four. Silver stood to the side of the tee box, drinking bottled water from a nearby cooler. The fourth hole doglegs right and the fairway is tree-lined. If that's not daunting in itself, fairway bunkers make precision off the tee even more crucial.

"Thanks," I said. "Your putting is on today."

Capers held a finger to his lips. "Shh. My putter will remember it hates me."

"You're stroking the ball with confidence today," Mike Lorne, Capers's caddie, said. He wore khaki shorts and a navy blue golf shirt, which sweat had turned black. Lorne had caddied on Tour for nearly three decades, and today the heat made him look his age. His brow was glazed with perspiration. "Keep it up." Lorne spoke like a seasoned coach.

Then a voice I recognized screamed, *"Come on, Jack! Rip One!"* It was Uncle Bill.

I looked over and tipped my cap, embarrassed.

Capers grinned. "Almost like playing with Tiger. I feel like I'm in Phoenix."

"Hey," I said, grinning, "my relatives aren't that rowdy."

Capers wore his trademark black and white. His white T-shirt was made out of some kind of fabric that looked like silk. The pants were black. The heat must have been oppressive in black. It pays not to be a fashion trendsetter.

I noticed a new tattoo, a purple cross, on the back of his right hand. "That one new?" The tattoo read "Jesus Saves."

He nodded. "Yeah. And it hurt like hell."

"Then why do it?"

"Self-expression, man. You ought to get one. People will think you're cool. I was watching a make-over show the other day, and the host told some guy he 'looked like a golfer.' It was the supreme insult."

"Why?"

Capers looked startled. "Why? Well, Jack, the guy wore khakis and collared shirts every day."

"That's what I wear."

"Yeah, like I said, maybe a tattoo would help."

Silver approached.

"Let's put it in play," Lorne said. "And keep stroking the ball with confidence." Lorne and Capers discussed club selection.

Silver held out my three-wood. When I took it, he moved the bag to the side of the tee box again. The group ahead of us was still in the fairway, so I took several practice swings. Capers did the same. He wore a leather bracelet on his left wrist. A one-inch cross dangled from his ear on a chain. I thought the bracelet fitting: On the PGA Tour, Capers was a leather bracelet in a gold Rolex world.

Capers made one final practice swing, then stood leaning on his three-wood. "You see the *USA Today* article about Padre this morning? It was written by Mitch Singleton."

Singleton, nearly seventy, had written for *USA Today* forever and was a journalist we all respected. He had begun when competition with other media outlets had not been at a premium, back when no story was slanted to sell papers. You could have a beer with him and watch a ballgame. As with Lisa, when you talked golf away from the course with Singleton, he would ask if the conversation was "on the record." If you wanted it "off," it stayed off, although he might push to use the material "as background only." If Padre had come forth about his sabbatical, Mitch Singleton would have been the reporter he called.

The group in front of us cleared, and Capers hit his three-wood to the heart of the fairway.

I addressed my ball, focused on positioning: I wanted to leave myself a short-iron to the green. My three-wood carries 285 yards, meaning this tee shot would leave a seven- or eight-iron to the green, which sat nestled behind two bunkers.

The Titleist landed safely in the fairway.

"What did the story say?" I said, bending to retrieve my tee.

"That Padre's decided to skip the rest of the season. The story gave no reason. I called his cell phone. He didn't return my call."

We started down the fairway.

"Padre helped me a lot last year," Capers said. "I don't know what I'd have done without him. I came out here"—he shook his head—"alone, with my beliefs . . . Padre had been a priest, so he understood. I wouldn't have made the top one twenty-five without his support. It's something I'll never forget."

The year before, Capers had struggled mightily, balancing his desire to use what he deemed his newfound "forum" to speak to people about religion, and his desire to play good golf. The first time I had played with Capers, he spent a lot of time working the gallery, shaking hands, telling people the Lord was with them. It had made me uncomfortable, and his game had suffered. Now Capers had found equilibrium. Padre had helped Capers locate the balance.

"Padre helped me through a rough patch, too," I said, "before I got married. It sounds ironic—Padre, the guy with a different woman each time I see him—but we went out for Mexican one night, and he offered great perspective."

Silver and Lorne walked in front of us. Neither spoke. Silver, his shaved head glistening with beads of sweat, was looking down. Days like this made me appreciate Silver's stamina. The guy could lug the heavy bag for hours.

"Padre's always had great perspective," Lorne said, staring off in the distance and nodding. "We had a drink in Tucson a couple months ago. He told me he's been thinking long and hard about Ian Baker-Finch."

I didn't like the sound of that. But I didn't have long to contemplate it. We had reached my ball. I had 150 yards, perfect distance to hit a full-throttle eight-iron. Like many of my contemporaries, I was hitting the ball farther than ever, even at thirty-eight years old. Weight lifting helped. My clubhead speed was 120 miles an hour at impact. And I wasn't alone. The added length of professional golfers, collectively, had made some classic golf courses obsolete, resulting in construction of new venues stretched until even Tiger, Hank Kuehne, and John Daly couldn't reach par fives in two. That was all fine and good. But that longer-is-better design philosophy made something else nearly obsolete, too: shot making. I had always enjoyed watching little guys like Justin Leonard and diminutive U.S. Open champion Corey Pavin maneuver the ball around a course, hitting fades and draws, sticking crisp approach shots, and draining fifteen-footers. Those guys could make the ball talk. Now rookies were spending hours in the weight room searching for ten extra yards. And pure shot making was a dying art, which was a shame.

I stood behind my ball and visualized my approach to the elevated green.

"Anywhere on the dance floor is great," Silver said.

I nodded. This was a hole where you take your par and run like hell.

I hit a high eight-iron that hit the green, bounced once, and spun six feet back. It had been a shot I did not always have. Contrary to today's rookies, who seem to step from college golf to the professional ranks capable of winning immediately, when I'd made the monumental leap from UMaine to the PGA Tour, I had come perilously close to missing the landing area and falling flat. I had golfed only six months a year and shoveled snow off fairways to hit wedge shots during winter. Predictably, as a rookie, I had been the equivalent of a pitcher with only a fast-ball—a power game but nothing else. Now I had finesse and touch enough to spin eight-irons like pulling a yo-yo back with a string.

Walking to the green, I saw Nash standing next to my father. Beside Nash, in the line of my family members, Sean O'Reilly drank beer next to Uncle Bill. To my astonishment, Uncle Bill nudged O'Reilly and pointed at me. O'Reilly gave a big friendly smile and waived. He hollered, "Great playing, Jack." Both men were drinking beer from paper cups. O'Reilly said something to Uncle Bill and they laughed. A guest pass hung around O'Reilly's neck.

I squinted to be sure I'd seen right. Then I shook my head. The consummate hustler had gotten someone to loan him a pass. My mother was suspiciously absent, and Lisa was standing next to my father, alone. So Mom had Darcy. It meant O'Reilly was drinking beer with my uncle and using my mother's pass. Next, he'd be in the tower above the eighteenth green, or have a seat next to Phil Mickelson in the clubhouse.

At the green, I glanced at O'Reilly again. Uncle Bill held up a cup and he and O'Reilly toasted me, arm-in-arm like lodge brothers. Uncle Bill waived me over. I neared the rope.

"What a great family," O'Reilly said. "You're shooting good, Jack."

"What are you doing here?"

"I can't believe this is your friend, Jackie," Uncle Bill said. "Sean O'Reilly and I played baseball at Husson College to-gether."

"Unbelievable," I said.

"Yeah," Uncle Bill said, "imagine running into him here."

"Imagine that," I said, looking at O'Reilly, who shrugged and spread his hands. A little beer spilled from his cup.

"Oops," he said, "don't want alcohol abuse."

Uncle Bill thought he was a riot. I had visions of O'Reilly at Christmas dinner next winter.

"You got a great family, Jack," O'Reilly said. "We'll see you tonight at dinner."

"Dinner?"

"Oh, Jackie," Uncle Bill said, "I told Sean to join us. That's okay, isn't it?"

"Unbelievable," I said again and went to the green, where Silver was waiting. A six-footer for birdie had to be easier than discussing Sean O'Reilly eating on my dinner tab. The last time I had seen O'Reilly, I'd threatened him. Apparently, he was quaking in his boots—not only was he back, he had my mother's pass and Uncle Bill buying him drinks.

And me buying him dinner.

.   .   .

"Glad we could spend some quality time together," O'Reilly said. "I think we got off on the wrong foot."

We were at the restaurant where we had eaten lobster the night before. It was 7:30 P.M. and the restaurant was bright and loud, alive with idle chatter and music from the bar. The scent of spices permeated the huge open room. O'Reilly told the waitress he'd have whatever I was eating—chicken parmesan and a Heineken. Of course, that had been nearly a half-hour ago, and O'Reilly had accepted the young waitress's offer for a fresh beer twice since ordering. At least tonight wasn't lobster.

Across the room, Phil Mickelson sat with his family. Food was on the table, but three people stood before him with paper and pens. Mickelson looked tired but pleasantly signed. Other players of lesser stature were dining, some alone, some with families, some in pairs and threesomes. All seemed to have on golf shirts. Most wore khaki pants. The commonality reminded me of Tim Silver's constant ribbing that "you can tell a pro golfer a thousand miles away."

"Too bad Bill couldn't be here," O'Reilly said.

"That's what happens when you drink a dozen beers in the sun."

O'Reilly looked at me like he didn't understand. "He told me to come tonight without him. I really feel guilty doing it, though."

"I'm sure."

"I went to the course to find you." O'Reilly spread his hands innocently. "And there was Bill. Boy we had good times in college."

"He doesn't drink much anymore," I said. "I've only seen him drunk two other times, at his sons' weddings."

"Yeah," O'Reilly said with a straight face, "I don't drink much either."

"What did you want to see me about?"

"Jerome Pulchuck heard you and I were friends—"

"Who told him that?"

"I might have mentioned it. Anyway, he wants to talk with you. I said I could set it up."

Jerome Pulchuck, a crook with a staff, was going through O'Reilly? Not likely. O'Reilly had figured a way to make a buck—by telling Pulchuck he and I were buddies. I looked at O'Reilly. He wore the same outfit he'd had on at the golf course: blue golf shirt, khaki shorts, and white athletic socks with black sneakers. He had taken his hat off when he'd come to the dinner table. His bird's nest of white hair looked like a thicket bush.

But he looked back at me with sad Irish eyes. They were the same watery, pale eyes the other men around the table had, including me. Part of me saw O'Reilly as a hustler, a grifter, a guy who didn't work and took what he could get from anyone he met. The other part of me viewed O'Reilly in a different light, the same light in which I had viewed Lea Griffin.

My father raised his glass. "Here's to Jack and another sixty-seven. Third place."

I had shot sixty-seven, even par (seventy-one), and sixty-seven. I was −8 heading into Sunday's round. Tiger was leading the event at −16; Mickelson was second, −15. I would play with Trip "General" Davis (−7) in the final round.

After the glasses had stopped clinking and conversations resumed, I said to O'Reilly, "Tell Pulchuck I can meet him here at ten tonight."

O'Reilly went, presumably, to make the phone call.

Lisa was next to me, Darcy beside her in a highchair. "He seems like a sweet old man."

"Maybe," I said, "but not likely."

"Is Perkins with Nash?"

"Yeah. Nash has practice," I said. "I saw you on the fifteenth hole."

She shrugged. "I was wondering if you did."

"Hard to miss. You were wearing headphones, holding a mic, standing in the first cut of rough."

"CBS asked me to do a little commentary. Your mom had Darcy." She shrugged. "It was fun."

"Did you praise my shot to the green?"

"I knew it was a mis-hit. I said you got away with a very poor swing."

I drank some Heineken and had to smile. "I hate it when you're objective."

She tilted her head to the side and grinned, her wide mouth slightly open, eyes dancing. Lisa had a variety of looks—beautiful (black sequined dress at a formal Tour dinner); adorable (shorts, T-shirt, and her pale blue GAP hat, short auburn ponytail bobbing through the opening in the back), and sexy (wearing my dress shirt as a nighty). Her smile was nice to see.

"You really enjoyed it," I said, "didn't you?"

"Immensely. I miss it more than I thought."

I nodded. We both knew what was coming. CBS was to call her agent and offer work. Journalism was part of who she was. We had met when she did a piece on putting—using my stroke as an example of what not to do, pointing out its flaws on national television. I had taken umbrage. She had shrugged and offered a lesson, infuriating me. Later, unable to get her out of my mind, I offered a truce in the form of a dinner invitation. I had fallen in love with her as my friend and as a serious journalist. But we both knew if she went back, Darcy would be in day care. We sat looking at each other.

Of course, it was O'Reilly who broke the silence. He returned and slapped me on the back and said the meeting was on for 10 P.M.

"Dinner's not here yet?" he said. "Place is kind of slow, isn't it?"

I shot him a look. Then I turned back to Lisa and looked beyond her at Darcy.

13

$\mathcal{A}$ lot of things in life remind me of Philip Levine's poetry, and Jerome Pulchuck certainly did. *Onomatopoeia.* That's what I thought when Pulchuck introduced himself at 10:05. He had three heavy hitters with him.

I was alone in a booth along the wall. The bar was to the left at the front of the restaurant, dimly lit with dark woodwork and lots of brass. Two well-built blondes in their twenties worked behind the bar. Each looked like she knew what she was doing. A rookie, who had barely made the cut, sat talking to the cuter of the two. However, the conversation between the pro golfer, who entered Boston like a sailor into a new port, and the cute bartender seemed to bother her partner since the place was busy.

Pulchuck motioned his three sluggers to the bar and sat across from me in the booth. The three tough guys wore suits, but the clothes didn't soften the image. They looked as much like business types as I looked like Bill Gates. One guy had a ponytail; one had a jagged scar on his chin. The third was a black guy with a shaved head and a goatee that partially hid the fact that his neck spilled over his tie. He sat with the other two, but apart. Goatee wasn't watching the Red Sox game. He was watching me in the mirror over the bar. Either loyal or well paid.

Pulchuck was short, squat, and thick, about five-ten and more than my 210 pounds. No neck; all shoulders and chest. He was built like a beer keg. He looked like his name sounded, and it made me think of "They Feed They Lion," by Levine. The poem was about race riots, and its repetition sounded heavy and ferocious.

Out of burlap sacks, out of bearing butter,
Out of black bean and wet slate bread,
Out of the acids of rage, the candor of tar,
Out of creosote, gasoline, drive shafts, wooden dollies,
They Lion grow.

Pulchuck sat down across from me and clasped his hands atop the table. He had a short ponytail, the length of a Doberman's stub, and wore a brown suit with a silk fawn-colored tie and gold cuff links. His gold rope bracelet made a tinkling sound as he shifted to look around the establishment. In his left ear, a tiny diamond stud glittered under the tract lighting. He put two thick fingers between the drawn shades and looked outside.

"Expecting someone?" I said.

He turned back to me, his stare flat and steady. "You know who I am, golf boy?"

"One hell of a dresser," I said. "You asked to see me. What do you want?"

In the bar mirror, my eyes met Goatee's. He held my look. A waitress came to the table and interrupted Pulchuck's iron stare. He ordered straight whiskey. I got a cup of decaf.

"Maybe you don't know me," Pulchuck said. "I'll tell you about myself."

I could tell he'd enjoy that; the line sounded rehearsed.

"I grew up in Brockton. Quit school and ran with some guys down there. They're all dead or in jail. I'm too smart for either."

"Used car business can be tough, huh?"

"You got a smart mouth, golf boy."

"You employed Owen Henley. What did he do?"

The waitress returned. Pulchuck sipped his whiskey at the same pace I drank the steaming coffee. The coffee was hazelnut. I hadn't asked for that and had wanted plain. Waitstaff was cute, but not efficient.

"You cut right to the fucking chase, don't you?" Pulchuck leaned back in the booth with his whiskey and smiled at me.

"Life is busy. No time to waste."

Pulchuck laughed. He waived Goatee over.

"You hear that, Terry? Golf boy says his life is busy. No time to waste." Pulchuck laughed hard at that. Terry, who didn't look accustomed to even the occasional smile, stood stonelike, glaring at me.

"You chase a white ball around all day," Pulchuck said.

"That's it. That's all I do. Sounds exhausting, huh?"

Terry looked like he couldn't believe I had even spoken much less mocked Pulchuck. Pulchuck had been avoiding my question. I knew the trick well. After all, I was married to golf's most serious journalist.

"What did Owen Henley do for you?" I said.

Pulchuck drank more whiskey and looked at Terry. The look must have said something because Terry went back to the bar.

"That's one bad-ass nig, isn't he?" Pulchuck said.

"Nice talk," I said. "What did Owen Henley do for you?"

"Owen Henley?" Pulchuck said.

"Name doesn't ring a bell?" I said.

"No."

"Of course," I said. "Might be hard to remember an employee who gets beaten to a pulp, then executed."

"Oh, that guy." Pulchuck finished the dark liquid. His eyes searched for the waitress. "I read something about him in the paper. What about him?"

"Am I talking too fast for you?" I said.

Pulchuck's eyes stopped searching for the waitress. His gaze swung to me again.

"What did he do for you?"

"That's not your business. And watch your fucking mouth."

Terry looked over. Pulchuck shook him off.

"What was in the truck Owen Henley drove to Canada?" I said.

That got Pulchuck's full attention. He put the empty whiskey glass down and looked hard at me.

"You got a smart fucking mouth on you, golf boy. Nash Henley has some photo albums. I'd like to see them. That's all. He'll get them back. I just want to take a look. I went to discuss it with him already."

"I heard something about that. How did the, ah, discussion go?" I finished my decaf and the waitress reappeared. I asked for ice water; Pulchuck got another whiskey. "I bet Perkins, the big blond guy with Nash, wasn't all that terrified by your three gorillas over there. And that probably created a problem for you, that and the fact that Nash doesn't have the albums. The cops do."

"I didn't bring all three guys."

"Your mistake."

Terry Goatee slid off his barstool and walked over again. "Jerome," he said, "how about I take preppy outside and teach him some manners."

"That's all we need," Pulchuck said and looked at me as if one of them had said too much.

I caught the look. Why would beating me up be "all we need"? Media attention? *Golfer Beaten After Friend's Father is Murdered.* "All we need" sounded as if something was going on already. Was Pulchuck expecting unwanted media attention? If so, what was in the photo albums?

"Cops have all the albums?" Pulchuck said.

"Yeah," I said. I didn't really know.

Pulchuck drank the rest of his whiskey. "I'll buy the albums when the kid gets them back."

"How much?" I was trying to see what they were worth, what might be at stake. A dollar figure might tell me how much danger, if any, Nash could be in. It didn't work.

Pulchuck said, "How much do you want?"

"Two hundred fifty thousand."

Terry Goatee made a sound like something was crawling up his esophagus. Pulchuck's eyes narrowed. "Are you fucking crazy?"

"Who killed the kid's father?"

"How the fuck should I know?" Pulchuck said.

"What was he doing in Canada?"

"I don't know nothing about no fucking Canada."

My watch read 10:25. I was in contention, and it was getting late. I stood and dropped $10 onto the table.

"Drinks are on me," I said. "Nice talking to you."

"This conversation ain't over," Pulchuck said.

"It is for tonight," I said and walked out.

In the elevator, I leaned against the wall and blew out a long, deep breath. Three-foot putts for six figures were easier than playing tough guy with Pulchuck.

Sunday morning, I woke early with Darcy. Lisa was still asleep, so I got the stroller and Darcy, took the elevator to the hotel lobby, and took Darcy for a walk. The temperature was pushing ninety a little before 7 A.M. It was humid already, and my black Power Bar T-shirt felt hot against my back under the bright sun.

We moved along the sidewalk, circling the parking lot. I wore running shoes, but the sound of patent-leather shoes clacking against the pavement seemed to echo. Men and women dressed for business walked to and from the hotel. Several players, who hadn't faired as well this week and had early tee times, walked to Buick courtesy cars. A Tour veteran in his forties got into a courtesy car, and I heard NPR on the radio. Two young guys, fresh from the college ranks, walked from the hotel and got into a Buick. When the driver rolled down the window, I heard Metallica blasting. My taste fell somewhere in between—Everclear, Creed, Springsteen.

Darcy was content in her stroller—wide awake, quietly sucking her thumb, and holding her blanket. Rich Lerner of the Golf Channel left the hotel and got into a car, heading to the course early. He didn't see me. Or maybe he did and failed to recognize me. Or, worse, maybe he had both seen and recognized me and just passed on the chance to get my expert opinion on the upcoming final round. Hard to imagine, but possible.

It was nice being on the road with Lisa and Darcy, despite Lisa being restless about her career. I had gone through a time, shortly after Darcy was born, when I had found traveling difficult. The result had been the worst slump of my career. Prior to Darcy's birth, for more than a decade, home had been my suitcase. The birth of my daughter created a traditional home, which meant I had a real home to leave each time I boarded a plane and headed to a tournament. I came out of that slump, and when my game finally showed signs of life, my father called to remind me that if I found it hard to leave to make a living playing a game others play on vacation, I could feel free to join him tacking shingles.

Point taken. I had rebounded with my first Tour win.

This year, despite not playing as well as I had hoped, at least Lisa and Darcy were with me. Darcy pointed to a pigeon and said, "Bird, Daddy. Bird." I tousled her hair. We continued on to the far end of the parking lot. Phillip Levine's poem "Among Children" reads:

> These are the children of Flint . . . You can see
> already how their backs have thickened,
> how their small hands, soiled by pig iron,
> leap and stutter even in dreams . . .
> I would like to arm each one
> with a quiver of arrows so that they might
> rush like wind where no battle rages . . .
> How dear the gift of laughter in the face
> of the 8 hour day, the cold winter mornings
> without coffee and oranges, the long lines
> of mothers in old coats waiting silently
> where the gates have closed.

The poem painted a bleak future for those kids, a future I knew Darcy wouldn't face. But I thought of Lea Griffin, of her kids—Leon, six, and Katindah, who was Darcy's age—in the photo Lea had shown me. I thought, too, of Nash, of his thickened back, of his hands soiled by a dream that could never come true. What had Nash said to his half-sister? Her dream had, in fact, come true. She had grown up affluent in a small town. Nash had grown up in Roxbury, Massachusetts. I would never truly understand what Nash had seen or experienced there. And I would forever wonder why and how Owen Henley, whoever the hell he had been, could abandon his kids, and why, as fate would have it, one child would be adopted into prosperity, while the other—Nash—had been left in the hands of a mother who would soon overdose.

Worse, if that question bothered me, what did it do to Nash?

Darcy and I were finishing our first circle around the parking lot when Mitch Singleton, the elderly *USA Today* reporter, exited the hotel. He smiled and walked over, wearing his trademark outfit—gray suit, tie hanging low, fedora, and a cigar dangling from his mouth. Old school. He held the cigar away from Darcy and bent to see the baby.

"Good thing she looks like her mother," he said.

"Got that right."

I knew two golf reporters who wore suits. Lisa was the other. They had more in common than their garb. Singleton was a diehard. I had seen and heard him scold young reporters once for getting drunk in a restaurant in New Orleans. He had spoken of reputation and responsibility.

"Talked to Peter Schultz yesterday," Singleton said. "He tells me you're putting better than ever and that you tightened your swing. True?"

"It's seven in the morning, and you're already at it?"

"Trying to keep up with your wife. Answer the question." He grinned and tickled Darcy, who giggle-screamed.

"Yeah. Schultz coaches me. We've tightened my back-swing a little. I'm in the fairway more consistently now."

It was all stuff Singleton already knew. Peter Schultz, eighty-four, was a Masters champion, a WWII hero, and a $500-an-hour swing guru, who worked with me for free. His wife and daughter had passed away, and Perkins had theorized that in Lisa and Darcy, Schultz had somehow regained them. I didn't know about that. But I knew I could talk golf with Schultz for hours.

"I also want to ask some questions about Nash," Singleton said. "*New York Times* is going to run something linking you and him and the murder of a Massachusetts guy named Owen Henley. You're in contention today, so it's timely and newsworthy."

"No one talked to me," I said. "I don't think anyone contacted Nash either."

"Welcome to my world," Singleton said. "Journalism in 2005. Can I buy you a cup of coffee, ask some questions?"

.   .   .

"Why would someone kill Owen Henley?" Singleton said.

We were in the hotel restaurant, sitting in a booth by the window. I was having coffee with cream and sugar. Singleton was drinking decaf. His face was slender, his narrow cheeks lined with wrinkles. A thin reporter's notebook lay on the table between us, the stub of a pencil resting in his hand, awaiting my response. I sat looking at Darcy, who stood beside me on the seat cushion. Sunlight entered through the window and highlighted her hair, turning it auburn.

"I have no idea," I said.

"What can you tell me about Nash's relationship with his father?"

"It was nonexistent."

"So you know nothing more than what the papers say?"

"I didn't say that."

Singleton smiled, shook his head, and set the pencil down. He drank some decaf. The waitress came by and topped off my coffee. I added another spoonful of sugar.

"Too much coffee will make you jumpy," he said. "Might hurt your putting stroke."

"I'll take my chances."

"So you're not willing to talk about the murder?"

"Not on the record."

"Off?"

I shrugged.

"You've got a reputation," he said. "Some people say trouble follows you, Jack. Personally, I don't see it that way. I think you just go out on a limb for people sometimes. And sometimes that bites you in the ass."

I drank some coffee. Darcy picked at a blueberry muffin Singleton had bought her. She had crumbs everywhere.

"Jack, Lea Griffin, from the Milton, Massachusetts, Wal-Mart, told me you went to see her."

"Nash wants to find out who his father was."

"So who was he, off the record?"

"Mitch," I said, "my wife's a journalist. She has dibs on anything I'm involved in."

"She's retired."

I didn't respond.

He raised his brows. "She going back to CBS or did someone else break the bank?"

"Look," I said, "I don't know a hell of a lot about Owen Henley. I know he was reclusive and strange and got in with some bad people."

He wrote that down. His notebook was tattered and three-fourths full. His shorthand was illegible.

"I knew Lisa couldn't stay away," he said. "She'd miss the chase too much."

"You're a smart old guy, you know that?"

"Yes, I do." He grinned, drank some decaf, and reached across the table to stroke Darcy's hair like a grandfather.

"Mind if I ask Nash some questions?" he said.

"Of course not."

"Will he talk to me?"

"Nope."

"Great."

"Sorry."

"Sure you are. At least you're looking out for Nash. You always have. Who told him not to talk to the media, you or Lisa?"

"Lisa. She told him how things might get."

"The business has changed," he said. "Wasn't a bunch of vultures when I started. Journalists are supposed to be public servants."

I nodded.

"So Lisa's giving Nash media-relations insight?" He shook his head. "And she's coming back. That'll make my life difficult.

Tough to compete with her—smart, beautiful, and she's got more energy than anyone I know."

He put $5 on the table and stood. "Good luck today. I need to get to the course. Mind if I get in touch about this again?"

I spread my hands.

"There's something there, Jack. I'd like to know what it is." He turned and walked out.

"I would, too," I said to Darcy.

She smiled and tossed part of the blueberry muffin at me.

Tournament leaders Tiger Woods (−16) and Ernie Els (−15) had not teed off when Trip "General" Davis (−7) and I (−8) stepped to the first tee under the mid-afternoon sun. On Tour, each member of the field (156 players; 144 before daylight savings) plays one morning tee time and one afternoon tee time prior to Friday's cut, which pares the field to roughly the top seventy and ties. Weekend tee times are played in descending order—first place plays last.

Our scores had not held up. The leaderboard still listed Woods alone at the top, but Chris DiMarco had played early and gone low. Now he was tied with Els. Moreover, Brad Faxon had shot sixty-two and was now tied with me. The winning total would probably be twenty or twenty-two under. That meant I needed to shoot sixty-six or better to have a chance to finish top-ten.

General looked like his nickname—close-cropped hair; a jaw you could split wood on. He was due to turn fifty soon, and most guys on the Champions Tour dreaded his birthday. His wife, Angela, was a long-distance runner. Whenever Lisa and I had dinner with them, I felt guilty if I ordered anything I couldn't burn off in a short workout. Self-discipline seemed to radiate from each of them.

I was standing to the side of the tee box, swinging my three-wood back and forth slowly, carefully rotating my torso, when I saw Jerome Pulchuck. He was in the first row of spectators, wearing khaki shorts and a pale blue golf shirt. His legs looked like he'd spent his entire adult life in a cave. Unlike O'Reilly, at least Pulchuck didn't wear dark socks and white sneakers. To the contrary—for some reason, Pulchuck had on golf shoes. Maybe he thought I'd let him hit a shot.

Pulchuck didn't wave. He didn't smile. When he knew I had seen him, he took his dark glasses off, folded them carefully, and hung them from his shirt collar. A diamond on his pinky shimmered in the sunlight. Then he looked at me. When we made eye contact, he gave me his toughest glare. It wasn't a look I wanted to see when I was alone.

"What're you staring at?" Silver said. "Big crowd today, huh? Beats the hell out of missing cuts, doesn't it?"

I nodded. Good things come with being in contention. Playing one group ahead of the leaders afforded me the attention of many of the anticipated 35,000 spectators. As many as 5,000 surrounded the first tee. I knew many would stay there to see Tiger and Ernie go off ten minutes after us. But I also knew at least at least several hundred would follow General and me down the first fairway. Pulchuck surely would be among them.

The problem was, Nash would be, too.

General hit his three-wood 265 yards to the center of the fairway.

"Been lifting weights, Jack?" he said, when I hit my three-wood twenty yards beyond his drive.

My ball avoided the fairway bunkers and set up an easy approach to the 365-yard, par-four first hole. It was a birdie hole, and, Pulchuck or not, I was trailing the leader by eight shots. I needed to make three.

"Jack?" General said.

I turned to face him. We were side by side walking down the first fairway.

"If you don't want to talk, just say so," he said. "I'll let you concentrate, but don't ignore me. I asked you how Darcy was three times."

"Shit," I said. "Sorry. A lot on my mind. Nothing personal, buddy."

General slapped my back. "No offense. It's what I like about you—your drive." He moved away and walked with his caddie. He had captained a recent United States Ryder Cup team. He knew the importance of concentration.

I only wished that was all there was to it. I had been scanning the gallery for Nash Henley. He waved to me. But I didn't wave back. That would draw the attention of Pulchuck. And Perkins wasn't around this time. Worse, Lisa was, and she was holding Darcy.

Nash waved again.

I looked away and moved down the fairway. After a few paces, I looked back at him. He looked hurt, and Lisa spread her hands as if to ask what I was doing. I made no return gesture, simply went to Silver who was waiting at my ball.

"Seventy yards to the front of the green," Silver said. "Pin's cut in the back, behind the front traps, so you've got to hit the ball about—What's wrong with you, man?"

"Nothing. Why?" I took the white towel off the golf bag, which stood between us, and wiped my brow. I took the sand wedge from the bag.

"Your head not into the round or something?" He took the sand wedge from me and handed me the pitching wedge. "You need to carry the ball a hundred yards, a nice choke-down wedge for you."

I nodded. He was right. I glanced at the gallery again. Pulchuck had his dark glasses on again. Now he was standing beside Lisa, talking casually. My father and Uncle Bill were not there. Neither was O'Reilly. Nash stood on the other side of Lisa. When he looked at me now, I saw fear in his eyes. Lisa said something to Pulchuck and pointed to me. Pulchuck nodded and smiled. I saw him reach up and tousle Darcy's hair.

A chill went down my spine.

Pulchuck looked at me and smiled widely. Then the smile

left. The glare I did not want to see in a dark alley returned. It was a look I had seen Perkins give people. It told them he was wired differently than the rest of us, that he could do something others could not—that he was willing to take a life. Not kill in self-defense. Simply eliminate a problem. No debating. No speculation. No regret.

"Jack," General said, "I don't mean to rush you, buddy. But we'll be timed if you don't hit."

I nodded. I didn't want to get our group warned for slow play and "put on the clock." I moved to my ball and hit. No practice swing. No alignment. The result was predictable.

"Never seen that before." Silver said it casually as he wiped the wedge clean.

"Never seen me dump one short into a sand trap?"

"Never seen you throw a fucking shot away, Jack. What the hell was that?"

It was hot, and I was trying to catch Tiger Woods and had eight strokes to make up to do it. I needed a clear head and would not withdraw. But the implied threat was to Darcy.

I swung wide on our way to my ball. At the ropes, I did something I had never done before.

"Hey, Jack," Pulchuck said. He held out his hand. "It's great to meet your family."

Nash was terrified of Pulchuck, and I could tell he knew who the two guys behind Pulchuck were—and what they were. Nash looked at me, his eyes asking what he should do.

"He told me you ran into him in the bar last night," Lisa said, "and had coffee."

Pulchuck put a hand out to touch Darcy again.

He didn't get that far. The sunlight was bright behind Pulchuck and seemed to burn my eyes as I watched his hand move in slow motion toward Darcy. I felt my chest get hot, my neck redden. Then I heard nothing.

My right fist exploded against Pulchuck's left cheek. As he went backward, on his way to the seat of his khaki shorts, his expression was not pain. It was shock. Maybe he thought I wouldn't react in front of my wife. However, she'd seen me hit people before. Or maybe he figured the gallery offered protection. But I wasn't in golf for PR.

His bodyguards helped him up. Security was there quickly.

"The guy said something," Silver said. "The guy's been bothering him since we teed off. I don't know what he said, but he's been distracting Jack."

I was silent, my chest pounding, my right hand throbbing. Lisa stood wide-eyed, taking it all in. She was too smart to say anything and knew she had missed whatever it had been that disturbed me. Nash stood slack-jawed.

"Daddy's just playing a game," Lisa said to Darcy. "He and that man are just playing a game."

As security escorted Pulchuck, and as the thugs followed, he gave me one final glare. "Fuck the pictures," he said. "This is personal. We'll settle up later." Then he looked at Nash and pointed his index finger. "You, too."

· · ·

After hitting Pulchuck, I played poorly, waiting every hole for a Tour official to arrive and tell me I was done. Like a pitcher who gives up back-to-back home runs, then looks apprehensively to the dugout to see if the manager is coming to pull him, I had scanned the crowd each hole. No one in shirt and tie approached.

I stepped to the par-five, 543-yard eighteenth tee with driver in hand. Woods was a hole behind me at −21; Els was hanging tough at −20. I had limped around the course at even par. On this course, in this field, even par was like driving fifty-five at the Indy 500. Eight strokes under par had me out of the top ten.

"How's your hand?" Silver said.

"Stop asking." The knuckles on my right hand were swollen and hurt like hell. "I'm a golfer, not a boxer. The hand feels like it looks." I took the driver from the bag and made several practice swings.

General had the honor, as he had for much of the day. He hit a long, high tee shot that carried the wetlands and the right-side fairway bunkers. He could go for the green in two.

"Nice swing," I said. General was −12 and swinging well. We had spoken very little since my run-in with Pulchuck.

I hit a drive that carried the bunkers and scooted past General's ball. We each reached the green in two. I had thirty-five feet for eagle.

Television cameras stared down at me. I saw the commentators in the tower above the green and guessed what they were saying. Many more reporters than my even-par performance warranted surrounded the green. At the 2004 United States Open, I had seen Steve Williams, Tiger Woods's caddie, take a spectator's camera after the fan snapped a picture during Woods's back-swing. I had never learned what disciplinary action the Tour had taken, but Williams wasn't a player. And he'd not punched a spectator.

I aligned the putt and stood squarely to the ball. I brought the putter back slowly. Muscle memory is a wonderful thing—it had to be the only reason the ball fell. My head wasn't into the round.

Silver pumped his fist and slapped my back. "I never doubt you, man. Let's get the hell out of here, and you can tell me what that was all about back there."

"Nice putt," General said. "You want to talk tonight, give me a call. You've got my cell number."

I nodded but knew I wouldn't call. I also knew I wouldn't field interview requests. This had begun with unseen photo albums. Now it had gotten personal. Head down, I pushed through the throngs of reporters toward the locker room. Things had escalated and were moving too fast.

16

"So that's why you hit him," Perkins said, nodding. "I would have, too. I told Peter Barrett who Jerome Pulchuck is, that he employed a murder victim who was the father of your former caddie, and that he might've had something to do with Owen Henley's death."

I had finished telling the whole story—about meeting with Pulchuck and him reaching to stroke Darcy's hair as if to say, *Wouldn't it be terrible if anything happened to her.*

Now I was sitting on the edge of a bed holding Darcy in a generic hotel room in Danvers, Massachusetts, about an hour from Portland, Maine. I was exhausted, not from the golf round, and not from the punch, but mentally drained. I had been surrounded by curious golfers in the locker room, had told them I was fine, and dodged all questions. Next, Emilio Rodriguez, special assistant to the Tour commissioner, appeared and said I could expect a call from Commissioner Peter Barrett. Finally, I battled reporters, upon exiting, all the way to my courtesy car.

And then there was the golf: When the dust settled, I had finished in a disappointing tie for nineteenth.

"What did Barrett say?" Silver said. "How much will the fine be?" Silver was still in his caddying garb, golf shirt and shorts, and held an attaché case, having waited to hear my explanation for hitting Pulchuck before heading to the shower.

"Might be more than just a fine," Perkins said, looking at me.

I nodded. Lisa stood next to me and reached down to rub my back. I had assumed a suspension was on the horizon. The situation was serious, from a variety of viewpoints. Perkins had dealt with the likes of Jerome Pulchuck previously and immediately had seen potential for retaliation. So he'd left a note in my locker—*I've taken Lisa, Darcy, & Nash to a new hotel. Call my cell.* Perkins had done what I expected from a guy hired by the PGA Tour Security Office. Tour Commissioner Peter Barrett's perspective, however, was different. Davis Love III once called a fan out when the guy heckled him during a head-to-head match-play event against Tiger Woods, but no Tour player had ever struck a fan. Barrett's job was to preside over and grow the game, and I had done the unthinkable—assaulted a spectator in front of other fans and a national television audience, no less.

But I hadn't been thinking about the game when I hit Pulchuck. I had thought only of my family. And I still was.

"Pulchuck was there to intimidate me," I said. "But the threat had been to Darcy. When will the cops give us the pictures?"

"I don't know," Perkins said.

Lisa took Darcy and sat next to me. Darcy quickly wiggled from her grasp and began jumping on the bed. "Bouncy. Bouncy!"

"What are the photos of?" Lisa said.

"That's the thing," Perkins said, "after Pulchuck came to Nash's apartment, I called Cronjagger. The State Police went through the pictures, and they can't figure out what Pulchuck's after. They didn't see anything."

"Maybe that's why Jerome Pulchuck said . . . screw . . . the pictures, Jack."

"Pictures or no pictures," Perkins said. "You punched the guy, and you did it in front of his people. He can't let you get away with that."

"I know."

"Why not?" Lisa said.

"He's a B-quality racketeer. He wants to move up to the big leagues, to be The Man in Boston. You don't get there by letting"—Perkins searched for a word, found none, and shrugged—"a rich, preppy dude punch you out in front of your people. Christ, Jack hit him on national TV. Pulchuck will have to even things up."

Perkins was right. Pulchuck had told me that he would come for me and Nash. Regardless, his initial threat had been to Darcy. "I'll pay to have someone from your office stay with Lisa and Darcy anytime I can't be with them."

"I have just the person," Perkins said and gave a sly grin.

I nodded, but I didn't feel much better. I had begun the day in contention and had been lapped by the field. I had disgraced the game and myself in front of thousands of fans and television viewers. Most importantly, Pulchuck had bared his teeth, showing me what the photo albums were worth: everything that really mattered to me. Elbows on my knees, my head fell to my hands.

"I'm sorry, Jack," Nash said, breaking the silence. "This is all my fault. I'm so sorry."

I looked over at him.

Nash was sitting on the other bed, leaning against the headboard, wearing an orange and brown T-shirt that had "Abercrombie" across his chest. "I should've let it go. It doesn't matter who Owen Henley was."

"This isn't your fault, Nash. I hit Pulchuck today because he put a slimy hand on my daughter. I'd do it again."

"Do you think Pulchuck killed my fa—Owen Henley?" Nash said.

"I don't know," I said.

Perkins was drinking coffee from a green and white Starbucks paper cup. He walked to the window and looked down at the parking lot.

"Why would Pulchuck draw this kind of attention to himself?" I said. "Like Nash just asked, he's made himself a murder suspect."

No one answered. We were quiet for a while, Darcy's chatter being the only sound.

"Jack, sweetie," Lisa said, "I've got to warn you: The punch will be big news. But I also think your reputation will help you. People know what you're like—that you give kids balls during practice rounds, that you've even let kids hit shots with your clubs during practice rounds."

"I'll be ready for whatever comes," I said, trying to sound stronger than I felt.

When my cell phone rang, I expected to hear Peter Barrett's voice. Instead, it was a gravelly deep voice, one I easily recognized.

"Son, what the hell was that about?" my father said. "Bill and Sean O'Reilly and your mother and I were waiting for you at the green. Never saw a thing. But I heard the fans talking about it. Then we watched the replay on *SportsCenter.*"

"It was already on TV?"

"Over and over. That's not why I'm calling. I'm calling because Sean O'Reilly went white when he saw it. He turned to your mother and me and said, 'Jack is in serious trouble now.'"

"That's probably true," I said. "Don't worry. We're going away for a few days."

Indeed, now it was personal.

$\mathcal{S}$unday night, I hadn't slept well, dreaming first worst-case scenarios of Peter Barrett fining and suspending me and of the kids who attend my clinics at the Woodlands Club having watched the punch on television, seeing me exhibit behavior that was the antithesis of that which I ask of them.

But it had been the second dream that caused me to lose sleep. I had dreamt of Pulchuck's hand on my daughter's fair head—and of the threat to my family it represented. I had gotten up after that dream and had sat staring out the window, thinking the situation over. What had begun as my attempt to help Nash, and to honor a promise, had gone further than I had anticipated. It had led to a threat, first against Darcy, and then, after I had defused that by punching Pulchuck, it led to a threat against me and Nash. Moreover, my family might still be in danger, and my decision to assist Nash had, unbeknownst to me, brought that upon them. Yet there was no turning back now. As Pulchuck had said, this was no longer about the pictures; this was about revenge for him now. Therefore, I was in it for the long haul, like it or not. So Perkins had promised a bodyguard for my family. However, if anything ever happened to Lisa or Darcy I would never forgive myself.

Now it was Monday, and we were about to land in El Paso, Texas. The desert terrain is so converse to anything seen on the East Coast that I thought we were landing on the moon—miles of brown sand, jagged ledge, and tumbling scrub brush. I had visited Padre once before and remembered having the same sensation. The sky was blue and clear for as far as I could see.

"Well, if we're going away to let things calm down," Lisa said, closing her laptop before brushing a line of hair from her eyes and looking out the window, "this is about as far from Chandler, Maine, as we can get."

She sat next to me on the plane. Darcy was asleep in her car seat in the window seat beside her.

"Is Perkins with Nash?" Lisa said.

I had the aisle seat, and my legs were stretched out before me, crossed at the ankles. I nodded. "Yeah. While Nash is practicing, he's going to talk to Lea Griffin about some guys she said went to see Owen."

"When do you meet with Peter Barrett?"

"The end of the week. When I said I wasn't scheduled to play this week anyway, he didn't seem to be in a big rush to meet with me, which I take as a good sign."

"No suspension? Just a fine?"

"That's how I read it. He said he'd call and let me know whether we're meeting Thursday or Friday. What are you working on?"

"Just typing some questions. I've got an interview with J. P. Hayes at nine tomorrow morning. I'll try to freelance the article."

"Do you ever rest?"

"You said you and Brian Tarbuck are playing golf." She shrugged. "Why are we here again? I mean, I know you wanted to get away, but wouldn't a cruise have been nice?"

"Padre's game has left him. He asked me for putting help in March. I think I just screwed him up worse. So I want to see if I can help him."

"He shot ninety-one in Hartford. That's not all putting. Besides, if you couldn't fix his putting problems in March, what makes you think you can fix them now?"

"I probably can't. He's lost his confidence."

"I hear he's taking the rest of the year off. How does a pro lose that much confidence? PGA Tour players, even present company, are the world's best golfers. How can one just lose it?"

"Confidence is a strange thing."

"You've never lost yours."

I shook my head, disagreeing. "Confidence is what you bring to the first tee. You carry it from the practice range like an egg, hoping if doesn't crack. Mine has chipped before, but never cracked. I believe in myself, that I can hit a shot when the time calls for it. That's toughness. My egg has chipped before—lots of times—but not cracked."

"And Padre's egg shattered?"

"That's what I think," I said. "But then, I'm no sports psychiatrist."

"What do you think went wrong?" Lisa said. "He had a chance to win a major last year but missed that two-footer to tie on the final hole."

"I don't know when it happened. I think I know how, though. The yips led to the shanks."

The plane touched down, hitting the runway like a bump-and-run shot—two hops, then coasting to a halt. We were in the middle of the plane, and Darcy was still asleep as we awaited our turn to deplane.

"I've heard a lot of things over the years," Lisa said. "But how can putting problems lead to swing trouble?"

"Padre started the season in a putting slump. Maybe that was because he missed that two-footer. I don't know. Probably no one really does. But when you putt badly, you do what the old saying says to fix your putting."

"To putt better, hit the ball closer to the pin?"

"Yeah. And, of course, that puts added pressure on your approach shots, your iron play, which eventually means you start feeling like you *absolutely must* hit every single fairway off the tee to have any chance to stick those approach shots close, which you must do to have any shot to make birdies. You see?"

"So his problems began on the green and worked their way back, all the way to the tee?"

"Yes."

"It must be incredibly frustrating."

We stood and got in the aisle. Lisa was carrying Darcy, whose eyes were flickering. I had the car seat and our two carry-on bags. We walked down the aisle, off the plane, and up the ramp to the waiting area.

"It goes beyond frustrating," I said. "It's damned near driven people crazy. Remember Ian Baker-Finch? Why do you think he went into broadcasting?"

She grinned. "I always assumed it was because broadcasting is clearly a step up."

I grinned.

"I know his story," Lisa said. "But why haven't you ever explained it like this to me before?"

"Race-car drivers don't talk about their friends' crashes," I said.

Lisa was in front of me riding the escalator down to baggage claim. She turned to look at me. "You're superstitious, Jack Austin."

"A little."

"Then you're taking a risk by coming here to help a friend." She rose up on her tiptoes and kissed my cheek. "That's sweet."

"It's probably dumb. But Padre's always been there for me."

. . .

El Paso, Texas, is one of the cheapest places to live in the United States and, if you like desert landscapes, one of the prettiest. El Paso is called "Sun City" because the weather is ideal just about every day. The city of 500,000 is nestled between the Rio Grande River and the rugged Franklin Mountains, a range that runs fifteen miles, from El Paso to the New Mexico border. Sun hits the Franklins from interchanging angles from morning to nightfall, highlighting the peaks of rock, cactus, and sand and offering spectacular shades of purples and browns as shade spots fall in different locales throughout the day.

Padre's five-bedroom, four-bath house faced the Franklin Mountains and had four garage bays. He lived alone. Monday afternoon, we were at the El Paso Country Club, where Tour veteran J. P. Hayes plays and Rich Beem once worked.

At 2:15 P.M., Padre and I were on the first tee. Late summer in Texas is like February in Maine: You suffer when you leave the house. It was 105 degrees and a breeze constantly pushed hot, dry wind against my face. We were playing the gold tees, from which the first hole plays 420 yards. The course spans 6,817 yards, a par seventy-one.

"You didn't have to come," Padre said.

"Lisa had an interview lined up with Hayes," I said. "I'm just along for the ride. Thought I'd get in a practice round while I'm here. You been beating range balls?"

"Not much. Like I said on the phone, I need some rest."

The guys at TaylorMade had sent me a new driver to try, a mammoth r7 beast that, coupled with my 120-miles-per-hour club-head speed, had me killing the ball. I took the club back slowly, made a wide shoulder turn, and started down. TaylorMade had my club specs on file, so anytime they sent a new driver, it came outfitted with a stiff shaft. When I snapped my right wrist over, I felt an extra little pop as the ball left the clubface.

"The ball just jumps off the face of this r7," I said. "It's like having a new toy." I watched the ball start down the right side and drift back, landing in the center of the fairway. "Hell of a job we have, huh? People send us new clubs all the time."

Padre moved to the tee, set his ball, and took a practice swing. "You know, you start playing the game for fun. Five, six years old, hitting it as far as you can, never reading a putt, just banging it at the hole."

"Hell, you still play that way, buddy."

Padre shook his head, almost annoyed. "No, I don't. Not anymore." He stood up to the ball and hit his drive.

Padre's ball began on the same line my tee shot had, except his did not cut back. It landed in the desert, right of the fairway. His reaction was atypical. No head-shake; no under-the-breath curse. Instead, nothing.

"Are you playing possum?" I said and slapped his back. "You told me you didn't want to wager. Now you'll bogey the first hole to set me up. Then we'll get to the second tee and you'll say, Twenty bucks a hole."

"I wish that were the case," he said, and smiled weakly.

I felt like I had when I'd watched Mike Tyson at the end—there was no fight left in him. Here, it was difficult to see. Padre looked tired. The game had gotten to him, beaten him. He simply slid the driver into the bag, got behind the wheel of the cart, and drove us toward our balls.

"I need a long rest, Jack."

"It's a ten-month season," I said. "Everyone's tired this time of year."

He shook his head. "You hear how the attendant found me after you and I missed the cut in Hartford?"

I shook my head. I hadn't heard a thing. I'd left that tournament quickly with Nash, my mind on the white-haired man.

"I don't know if any players heard about it. I know it never made the papers, thank God. But an attendant found me puking my guts out in a locker-room stall. He wanted to get a doctor. I told him, 'No. It's just food poisoning.'" He clutched the steering wheel hard, the leather of his gloved left hand quietly squeaking. "It wasn't food poisoning. It was nerves and stress."

"It's a frustrating game." It wasn't much, but it was all I could manage. He was worse off than I'd thought.

"It's gone beyond frustration. It's gotten pathetic, Jack. I don't know if I can play competitive golf again. You know, I look at David Duval. The guy won the British Open, went through this—and walked away."

"For a while," I said. "He came back."

"For a long while, Jack. Duval was the number-one player in the world. Game got to him. He went home. And I don't blame him. I know how he felt."

I had never fully understood why Duval had left and didn't know anyone who really did. We'd all read the same articles filled with speculation. But when Duval hit the skids, I had heard of no player asking him about it. It wasn't something any of us had talked about. It wasn't something I had wanted to think about, either.

"You're not thinking about retirement yet," I said. "I saw the new long putter in your bag."

"I've got three new putters in my bag—that broom, a belly, and a short, thirty-one-inch job to take my hands out of the stroke."

He stopped the cart in the center of the fairway. A gust of dusty, warm air blew a tumble weed across the fairway. The bush had needles the size of tees, and I made a mental note to avoid getting impaled as I stood over an approach shot. We were a hundred yards from either of our balls. When Padre turned to me, his vivid blue eyes were narrow slits. I hadn't noticed it before, but his eyes were bloodshot, too.

"I talked to Ian Baker-Finch, Jack. I had to ask him, 'If I can't turn this around, is there life after golf?' I'm looking for answers, anywhere I can find them. It's gone from me trying to hit every shot to within six inches of the cup, to where now I'm standing in the fairway thinking—and I know this is crazy— that I don't want to put the ball too close because I know from three feet, I'll miss. I'm *hoping* my approach shots land fifteen feet from the hole."

It was crazy, but I sure as hell didn't say that. Padre and I had been rookies together. When he'd won his first tournament, years before I'd won mine, we'd drunk champaign all night, missed our Monday flights, and had gone to the next event Tuesday, a day later than usual. When I had finally broken through to win, Padre was the third person on the green to congratulate me, after only Lisa and Darcy.

"Bernhard Langer reinvented his putting stroke two, three times in his career," I said. "He survived the yips and captained a European Ryder Cup team. We'll figure something out."

"It's not just my putting, Jack. I've got four drivers. I'm looking for one I can put the ball in play with."

. . .

On the first green, Padre had eight feet for birdie. His approach from the desert had been excellent. He had the short putter and stood behind the ball, his hands fully extended, hanging nearly to his knees. When his shoulders rocked, the putter face moved back and forth as if tied to a pendulum.

"Your stroke looks great," I said. "Nice play from the desert."

"I've had a lot of practice from there over the years." He grinned. It was the first time I'd seen him smile since we'd begun.

My approach shot had stopped ten feet from the hole, not very good from where I'd been off the tee. Yet my focus wasn't on my score. I brought the putter back slowly and through, never looking up, only listening. I didn't hear the rattle I was hoping for. The ball stopped inches to the right of the hole.

"Did I forget to tell you this one breaks left to right?" Padre said.

"I thought priests have a code of ethics?"

"That's why I'm a *former* priest."

Padre crouched behind his coin, replaced the ball, and viewed the line. He stood next to the ball, made two practice strokes, which looked perfect, then carefully set the putter-face behind his Nike ball. He blew out a long breath. His glove was tucked into his back pocket and sunlight glistened off the backs of his per-spiring hands. Just before he stroked the ball, his grip tightened.

He jerked the putter back and decelerated on the way through. The ball went right and stopped three feet short.

Padre made no reaction, simply walked to the ball, crouched and placed his coin behind it, aligned the logo, replaced the ball, and addressed it again.

This time the ball was off-line from the start. The back-stroke was quick, and he rammed the putter through, the ball stopping three feet beyond the hole this time. Padre shut his eyes tight and blew out a long breath.

I was embarrassed for him and knew why he didn't want to play on television anytime soon.

Padre went to the cart, replaced the short putter, and returned with the belly putter. "Can't control the takeaway with that little one," he said, and stood up to the three-footer, locked the butt end of the putter's shaft into his gut, positioned his hands, and rocked his shoulders.

This putt caught the right edge—a push—but fell.

"Hey," Padre said to me, "dead center for once, huh?"

"Yeah," I said. "Dead center."

.   .   .

The second hole plays 380 yards from the farthest tees and is also a par-four. As we stood on the tee, Padre didn't make practice swings or small talk. He locked the grip of his driver into his gut, as if it were the belly putter, and rocked his shoulders back and forth, practicing his putting stroke. Sometimes the best thing to do is to not think, just play. But I said nothing. Padre was somewhere I'd never been, and I was thankful to have only speculative knowledge of that place.

It was nearing 3 P.M. and, inexplicably, getting hotter. We had played one hole and rode, no less, yet I had sweat through my shirt. Ahead in the fairway, just before the dogleg left, I saw a small sand squall like a vertical wind tunnel shimmering from side to side. The squall was momentarily ferocious, then dissipated quickly, like a baby's tantrum. As I watched it, I wondered if Padre actually thought his last putt had gone into the heart of the hole. I also thought about what it must have taken to drive a guy—who not only plays a game for a living that requires great integrity but had also been a priest and was simply one of the most honest individuals I knew—to either see something that clearly wasn't there or to lie about it. Golf had left Padre face down in a bathroom stall. I felt like the proud owner of an exotic pet, who had been told the owner of a similar pet was found torn to shreds: I loved the animal but now knew what it was capable of.

I teed my ball and swung the r7 with everything I had. My typical swing is 80 percent of full throttle. That's the speed I can control and consistently stay down and through the shot.

"The hole plays three-eighty, Jack. You're not going to reach it. Safe play is three-wood." Padre showed me his Nike three-metal and teed his ball.

"I faded it into the dogleg," I said, "which was what I was trying to do."

"That you did."

Padre made a beautiful practice swing—well paced, rhythmic, and balanced. He moved closer to the ball, positioned the club behind it, and waggled the driver. He waggled the driver not once or twice, but close to twenty times, his grip going from light to white-knuckled. By the time he brought the club back, he was biting his tongue in concentration, and the muscles in his forearms were tensed. The ensuing results were predictable: The swing was quicker than Nick Price's and the ball snap hooked left, straight into the desert and made a *thwacking* sound as it leapt among the cacti and scrub bushes.

"Damn it," Padre said. "I was trying to leave myself one forty-five, the perfect eight-iron distance."

"You can't try to be perfect," I said. "Nothing about golf is perfect. Remember when Todd Hamilton won the Open Championship at Troon? He said he was 'good at playing ugly golf.' Remember that?"

Padre nodded, his eyes on mine for several beats.

"He was talking about missing fairways and saving par. Nailing an occasional birdie putt. The game won't allow perfection, Padre. That's the addiction. It's what drives the pursuit. You've got to let the idea of perfection go. You make a bogey and you can follow it up with two, three birdies. You're that good. You've got to believe that."

He didn't speak as we got into the golf cart and drove to search for his ball. But when we stopped at the side of the fairway, Padre looked at me. "And what if I'm not sure I believe that anymore?"

"Then the game wins, and it'll break you."

"Maybe it already has, Jack," he said and turned, squinting against the sun.

. . .

We were in the fairway of No. 18, a 388-yard par four. We hadn't kept a score card, but I knew where I stood: If I made birdie, I shot sixty-eight, three under par. The eighteenth has a fairway bunker guarding the right side and water in front of and to the right side of the green, which is also protected by a right-side sand trap. I wasn't into counting other players' strokes, especially given Padre's current state, but he had not played well. Worse, however, was his obvious lack of enjoyment. We had played hundreds of practice and tournament rounds together, but I'd never seen him like this. The round seemed to exhaust him. I knew it wasn't the eighteen holes; it was the game itself.

"Nice drive," I said. "You haven't mentioned the cancer event next week at my home course."

"I know I signed on to play," he said. "I'll honor the commitment. I was going to claim an injury and withdraw, but I can't do that to you."

"We'll have fun. It's a scramble—no individual scorecards. Lobster. A boat ride on the ocean."

At the green, Padre had ten feet for birdie. He had hit a well-positioned tee shot, a crisp approach, and now had a birdie chance. He had stuck with the belly putter and now carefully placed the putter's face behind the ball. He had read the putt from behind the ball and the side of the green. He brought the putter back slowly, a good takeaway. However, the forward stroke was much faster, out of sync, and ill paced. The ball ran by the hole, stopping four feet away.

Padre rubbed the back of his neck with his hand. "Just when I think . . ." He didn't finish, but I knew what he was thinking. He'd played the hole well but hadn't closed the deal. Now he faced a four-footer for par. The game is draining when you make unforced errors. After a birdie chance, what had seemed, at worse, a certain par would now be a struggle.

I went to my ball and stood over the fifteen-foot birdie putt. The ball would break maybe six inches, right to left. I made two practice strokes looking at the hole to get a feel for the speed. Then I focused on the ball and made a three-second stroke, back and through, never looking up. The ball didn't fall but stopped two inches away. I walked to it and tapped in for sixty-nine.

Padre replaced his ball, pocketed his coin, and addressed the Nike. Four feet. Just him and me; no fans; no TV cameras; no one around. But he inhaled deeply, then blew out a long breath. He repositioned his hands on the putter. Then he backed off the ball and read the green again. It looked straight to me.

Padre stood next to the ball and took two more practice strokes. Then he set the putter behind the ball, sucked in another gulp of air, and blew it out. Finally, he hit the putt. The ball missed four inches to the right and ran two and a half feet by.

Then Padre did something I'd never seen him do before. He walked to his ball, bent over, picked it up, and dropped it into his pocket.

"That's enough," he said. "That's more than enough."

I said nothing, only nodded.

"I can't go to Falmouth," he said. "I know it's for charity. But I hope you can understand."

"No problem."

Tuesday afternoon, Lisa, Darcy, and I arrived in Chandler, Maine, at 4:30 P.M. Perkins's forest green Toyota Camry was in the driveway, the garage doors were open, and lights were on in our house. Darcy had slept the two hours from Boston and hit the ground running. From the driveway, I could see Perkins on the dock. He waved. Beyond him, the ocean ran to the end of the earth. Twenty-four hours in the desert made me miss the sight. Late-afternoon sunlight still shone bright and hot overhead; it was eighty with scant humidity, one of those summer days for which you tolerate Maine's winters.

Lisa went inside, and I walked to the dock to see Perkins. Above us, a host of gulls circled and dove into the sea, emerging moments later, clutching silvery fish whose writhing bodies and flapping tails illustrated that life's final seconds often amount to an instinctive-yet-futile struggle. The flapping fish also reminded me of Jerome Pulchuck's final statement: "We'll settle up later." I was no longer a day away.

"Nash is inside," Perkins said. He raised a hand, halting my questions. "Everything's fine. But we've learned something about Pulchuck. I have a person who works for me coming by shortly. She found some information I want to hear more about. You'll want to hear it, too."

"You brought Nash with you?"

"Yeah. I talked to his coach. He agreed that I should bring Nash along." A thin line of perspiration glistened above Perkins's lip.

We both turned to look out at the ocean.

"How's Nash doing?" I said.

"Running over every guy who tries to tackle him."

"Off the field?"

Perkins shrugged. "That's not really my thing—being his counselor. I do better with the bodyguard assignments."

"I'm sure Lisa is giving him the third degree right now anyway," I said. "So this employee coming here is a she? Nice to know you're an equal-opportunity employer. Silver will be working for you next."

"I'm not that equal," he said. "Deirdre's a black-belt. Besides, Silver would get me shot talking about women's clothing or telling a thug they've got nice biceps. Deirdre will be with Lisa and Darcy when you or I am not."

Lisa came out of the house and walked toward us. I liked watching her walk. She had changed from her travel attire into shorts, and her tanned legs illustrated the results of her five-miles-a-day regimen. She had on a golf shirt with The Golf Channel logo on the front.

I took Darcy from her.

"Will you be around this evening, Jack?" she said.

"Sure. Why?"

"My agent called. CBS made the offer. I'd like to consider it." She looked at Perkins. He took the hint and walked toward the house. Lisa watched him until he was out of earshot. "It's a lot of money, Jack. More than that, though, I really miss my work."

There was a splash behind her as a gull hit the water with startling speed. "Birdie," Darcy said. "Birdie."

"Very good," I said.

Lisa touched Darcy's cheek.

"What would you be doing?" I said.

"Back in the tower. With Paul Staples going to ESPN, I'd get my job back. And I could start with a bang if Pulchuck was involved in Owen Henley's murder."

"What does Pulchuck have to do with golf analysis?"

The gull seemed to leave the water at nearly the speed at which he'd entered it, bursting through surface and rising toward to the sky.

She smiled and patted my cheek lightly. "Don't play coy. It's a chance to break a story. You know I love that."

"So you want me to tell you what we learn?"

"For starters," she said.

I didn't like the sound of that. I knew Reporter Lisa. She'd use any information we gave her and build on it—tracking down leads, chasing theories, and interviewing the type of people Pulchuck associated with, the types to whom I did not want the mother of my daughter talking. That was my gut instinct. However, I'd been with her long enough to know she was driven and tough enough and smart enough to look after herself.

I crouched and stuck Darcy's foot into the ocean. The water at the end of the dock was eight feet deep. Our frontage wasn't beach; rather, rocky shoreline, and the water temperature was only fifty-eight. Darcy giggle-screamed and kicked at the water.

I stood up and exhaled. "If you want to go back to work, I'll support you a hundred percent."

"A collaboration on the Pulchuck thing?"

"I'm not interested in news angles," I said. "This thing has spilled over onto my family."

She nodded and thought about that but didn't speak. We stood silently for a time. Boats moved in the distance, and waves slapped the shore.

"Jack, I love you, and I love Darcy. But this job offer . . . I need to be me, too. Do you understand?"

"And your job is part of who you are," I said.

"You're the same way, aren't you?"

In the distance, a small sailboat moved around the corner into our cove. The guy on the boat was young and wore a do-rag and a tank top. He waved, and I waved back absently.

"Yeah, I'm the same way," I said. "And that makes me feel guilty about your career."

"Because you love your job, but society doesn't expect you to give it up and care for Darcy?"

"It's more than that. I feel guilty because I really think you're the best choice to stay home with her. That probably doesn't sound right, I know. And financially, it's crazy—your money is guaranteed; mine sure as hell isn't. But Darcy is different with you than she is with me. You know?"

"That almost sounds chauvinistic and sexist."

"It's neither," I said. "The other day, when she was throwing cereal, you made it all look easy. All I know is, when Darcy is really upset, you're the one who can calm her."

Lisa turned and squinted into the sun, her lips pursed. "I need to give this a try, Jack."

"And I want you to."

.　.　.

To his credit, Perkins had not mentioned that his associate, Deirdre Hackney, looked a hell of a lot more like a Dallas Cowboys cheerleader than a black belt. She was in her late twenties with shoulder-length blonde hair streaked where the sun had lightened it, big violet eyes, a narrow nose, and a wide mouth. She wore very little makeup and, frankly, didn't need it. I tried my best not to notice.

Nash, though, couldn't keep his eyes off her. We were sitting around the kitchen table at dinner. Lisa and I took turns trying to get Darcy to eat. I had grilled salmon steaks seasoned with Cajun pepper.

"B. C. Budd is what they call it," Deirdre was saying. Her T-shirt read NEW YORK CITY JAZZ FESTIVAL 2003. She wore jeans and a shoulder holster, which was no longer hidden under the leather jacket she had on when she arrived. "It's a form of pot entering

New England from New Brunswick. It's very popular right now."

"Meaning," Perkins said, "it's very valuable right now. Street prices are through the roof."

I was coaxing Darcy to use her plastic fork instead of her hands, when I noticed how Lisa watched Deirdre. Lisa was studying her as she focused on anything or anyone she found interesting. Lisa wanted to know what made people tick. It was what had set her apart from other golf journalists and what would set her apart again. Her focus wasn't simply that someone missed a putt, but *why* they missed it. She found the internal struggles Tour pros face to be the most interesting aspect of her job.

I tried to give Darcy a spoonful of rice. She knocked it away, rice falling onto the floor. Lisa took the spoon and did the airplane-into-the-mouth trick. Darcy ate happily. I shook my head.

"Lisa decided amateur hour is over," Perkins said, and grinned at me. "Don't feel bad. I get that all the time. And my kid is five."

"That's supposed to make me feel better?"

Everyone laughed, but Lisa and I exchanged a look of recognition.

"This is what you were talking about on the dock?" she said. "Yeah."

She didn't say anything and went on feeding Darcy.

I took a dinner roll from the basket, buttered it, broke off a piece, and ate it. The table was crowded with the platter of salmon steaks, a bowl of Spanish rice, and a plate of corn-on-the-cob. There were dinner rolls, butter, and glasses of skim milk.

"B. C. Budd is also called Quebec Gold," Deirdre said.

"I've heard of that," Nash said, "it's big at college."

Deirdre nodded. "That's where the largest demand is. Jack, tell me a little about your meeting with Jerome Pulchuck—the coffee chat, not the fight."

I took a bite of salmon. It was perfect. The trick is to grill it on aluminum foil, skin down, then pry only the meat off using a spatula. You get everything but the skin, and, when cooked to perfection, the steak doesn't crumble.

111

"Pulchuck didn't strike me as particularly smart," I said. "I mean, when we met in the restaurant I knew right off he was trying to smooth-talk me."

Deirdre nodded, encouragingly.

"But then, again," I said, "I misread him. I didn't expect him to show up at the golf tournament. And I didn't think he was capable of the move with Darcy."

"Jerome Pulchuck is capable of a lot," Deirdre said. "He's known as a vicious man." She turned to Perkins. He nodded and she went on. "Pulchuck is suspected of at least four murders. His organization has certainly been involved in more than that. Two men who worked for him are serving twenty-five to life for conspiracy to murder. That means someone executed Pulchuck's plan, and when things fell apart, those two guys took the fall."

"They wouldn't talk?" I said. "They'd rather face twenty-five to life?"

"Tells you a little about Pulchuck's ability to persuade, huh?" Perkins said.

It did, and it made me recall the threat he'd made to me. The table fell silent as we ate, the only sound was Darcy's humming as she chewed.

"Did he kill my father?" Nash said.

For a second, no one answered. It was the money question, and it froze everyone.

"I know a few state troopers," Deirdre said to Nash. "They don't know. No one at Boston PD Homicide Division knows. What everyone does know is that Jerome Pulchuck has a lot more cash than usual."

"Extra cash was the telltale sign of drug dealing where I grew up," Nash said. "If someone had extra money to buy stuff, you knew he was dealing."

"Where'd you grow up?" Deirdre said.

"Roxbury." Nash looked at her for a long moment. Then he smiled shyly and looked down at his plate.

Deirdre smiled to herself, the way Lisa did when Nash pulled a chair out for her. "That would be my guess, too, Nash. And that's what my contacts at the DEA say as well. Ever consider a job in law enforcement?"

Nash smiled at her again, then shyly looked away. It made Lisa grin. It was one of those times when, despite Nash's NFL frame, you knew he was still a kid.

"The hottest thing coming from New Brunswick right now is this Canadian-grown pot," Deirdre said.

"They found a joint in Owen Henley's apartment," I said.

"That's right. The Hell's Angels are said to be going door-to-door in low-income areas, giving people the equipment to grow the stuff indoors, and saying, 'See you in six months. We'll pay you for anything you grow.'"

"Why is this B. C. Budd so hot?" I said.

Perkins was too busy working on his second salmon steak to answer.

"It's a very potent form of marijuana, right?" Lisa said. "I read an article somewhere. It originated in British Columbia."

"That's right," Deirdre said. "It's stronger than anything grown in the U.S., Columbia, or Mexico. A higher THC content."

"Owen Henley was paid to drive a sport utility to Canada, then back to Boston, before he died," I said.

"You think that's what my father was going up there for?" Nash said.

Each time he referred to Owen Henley as "my father" something tugged at my insides. We weren't going to learn anything good about the man.

"Possibly," Perkins said, chewing. "It's logical. But nothing else in this case is logical, so that may not mean anything."

"Where do the photos Pulchuck wants so badly tie into all this?" I said.

"I'm trying to have a nice dinner." Perkins grinned. "That's a loose end."

"Meaning you don't have a clue?" I said.

"Hey," he said, his grin widening, "I've got an employee here."

"Not a clue," Deirdre said.

. . .

That night, the windows of my corner office were black like darkened mirrors. My office was immaculate and possessed the kind of unparalleled organization that comes only from lack of use—I wasn't home often enough to mess the place up. My collection of poetry and drama books—some I'd owned since UMaine—lined the shelves. Beyond the murky windows, a single light bobbed up and down cutting the blackness like a flashlight's beam spearing a nighttime cave. A boat was moving slowly past our dock, but all I could make out was the light.

Nash and Perkins were in the basement lifting weights, Silver had arrived and was watching *Steel Magnolias* on satellite, Lisa and Deirdre were putting Darcy to bed, and I sat behind the closed office door, at my desk, alone in the silence and scattered dust of random thoughts.

A lot of things were bothering me: Padre, it seemed, had quit. The game had beaten him. Also, recent events regarding Owen Henley had happened so quickly everything had become blurred. I had been so busy with Jerome Pulchuck, the Deutsche Bank Championship, Lisa's desire to work again, and Nash—who wanted to conduct an investigation into his father and needed my help (but wanted to do a lot of it himself, which worried the hell out of me)—that I hadn't taken time to stop and consider it all. In spite of the distractions, the visit to Cronjagger's office tugged at me. Something was wrong, and whatever was bothering me stemmed from the conversation with Cronjagger.

Nash and I were trying to discover what type of man Owen Henley had been, and Cronjagger had told us Owen had two kids, thus, two families. Owen had had an entire second life, it would seem, that we'd not known about. Owen Henley's having two kids did not add up. But I couldn't put a finger on exactly what bothered me about his having two kids.

I did what I always did when I was confused: I took out a yellow legal pad, a Bic pen, and began listing thoughts and names, hoping one thing would clarify something else and that a picture would form.

As I scribbled, a floorboard creaked above me and I heard water running through pipes in the wall—a 1928 house tells you all.

All I knew about Owen Henley was what Lea Griffin and

Sean O'Reilly had told me. But Owen Henley had lived two lives. And Maureen Glenn, an adopted child, now residing in Readfield, Maine, represented Owen's second life, the life I knew nothing about.

I made a timeline, listing the year Nash was born, the year his half-sister was born, which had been six years later, then the month and year six months previous, when, according to O'Reilly, Owen had gone to Canada for Pulchuck. Finally, I wrote the date of Owen's death. A hole gaped between when Maureen Glenn was born and the trip to Canada.

Cronjagger said Owen Henley had been a schoolteacher. On the heels of what Lea Griffin and O'Reilly said, that was difficult to believe. Had Owen become the antisocial hermit after losing his teaching job? Had he always been like that, and been fired accordingly? When had Owen Henley taught? Where? How had he met Nash's mother? How had he met the woman who had his second child?

Owen Henley had gone to Canada, and when he got back to Milton, he was killed. Had he brought something back for Pulchuck and been killed when someone got to it—and him—before Pulchuck? Was that why Pulchuck wanted the pictures? What story would those photographs tell?

I listed names: Sean O'Reilly, Lea Griffin, Jerome Pulchuck, and Maureen Glenn, Nash's half-sister. Cronjagger had told us of Terrell Smith as well. Who was he?

I needed a place to start. I underlined Maureen Glenn three times.

19

$\mathcal{R}$eadfield, Maine, is a one-traffic-light town in the central part of the state, twenty minute from the state capital, Augusta, and near where Perkins and I grew up. We got off I-95 in Augusta, drove through Manchester, and at Readfield's lone traffic light, I turned left.

It was 9:35 Wednesday morning. Nash was in the second row of the Suburban wearing a grey T-shirt with 3EB BOSTON in small black letters across his chest and denim shorts. Perkins sat beside me in jeans and a blue sports jacket that hid his shoulder holster. I was off duty, so I wore khaki pants and a golf shirt with TaylorMade on the right breast. Admittedly, I'm a man of few looks.

"What's three E B?" Perkins said.

"Third Eye Blind, man."

"Third eye is blind?" I said. "What the hell does that mean?"

"You two are *old*," he said. "It's a band. I saw them in Boston."

"I've been playing Springsteen for you for years," I said. "When are you going to see the light?"

Nash grinned.

"Maureen Glenn's father didn't sound enthusiastic about this visit," Perkins said. "But I got the feeling he understands where we're coming from."

"Where are *we* coming from?" Nash said. "I didn't even know you called him. I wanted to do that. It's my half-sister."

"I'm sorry, Nash," Perkins said. "You can do all the talking when we get there. But let the phone call slide, man. I do this for a living. And I got us in."

"He's just trying to help," I said to Nash.

"I know," Nash said. "I know. But I'm twenty years old, Jack."

"And this is your deal. You take it once we get there." Truth was, this was no longer only Nash's deal. Pulchuck had dragged me into it as well. He was vengeful and had threatened my wife and daughter. Now I, too, had a stake in Owen Henley's past.

"Do you know anything about Maureen Glenn's mother?" I said. "Your father lived with her after he lived with you and your mother."

"Nothing," Nash said. "We can ask Maureen. I've been thinking about all those photos. I want to go through them, see where they were taken, and try to think back and remember if I ever saw him."

"I want a look at them, too," I said. "Maybe we can learn why Jerome Pulchuck wants them so badly."

"We'll all get our turn with the pictures," Perkins said. "Cronjagger called. He wants us to go back down. They have one they want us to see."

"What's that mean?" I said.

"It's of Pulchuck and Owen. That's all I know. The cops don't know where it was taken."

The road weaved as we traveled beneath a canopy of treetops. Sunlight filtered through, bright patches spotting the pavement. The speed limit was thirty-five. I had the window partially down and had offered Nash control of the CD player before we'd left the house. Two hours later, I needed an Excedrin. A boat launch sat vacant to our left. Beyond it, the lake sprawled, early morning whitecaps shimmering atop the dark blue water.

After crossing a tiny bridge, we took our first left onto Lakeview Drive. Maureen Glenn lived in a raised ranch across the street from the lake. The house was white. An old rope swing hung tattered from a tree. In the rearview mirror, I watched as Nash looked at the swing. The rope was worn from many years of use, and the tire hung motionless from an elm tree.

"This is where she grew up?" he said.

"This is the address," I said.

Nash nodded to himself and looked around, appraisingly. His front teeth pressed gently against his lower lip in concentration.

The Suburban climbed the steep driveway and we got out.

The garage doors were up and a Mercedes and a Buick Rendezvous were parked inside. A red Volkswagen Jetta was in the driveway. The Maine vanity plate read MGLENN.

We didn't make it to the door. A tall, red-haired man with clear blue eyes came out of the house. He wore a dark silk sweatsuit, the kind you see only in movies. He didn't smile as he stood before us. He didn't extend a hand, either. Beside him was a small brunette in apple-green Capri pants, a sleeveless matching sweater, and white sandals. She looked at Nash, then down to her feet, as if she couldn't bear to meet his eyes. Next to her stood Maureen Glenn.

Maureen bore a remarkable likeness to Nash. They stood looking at each other for a long time, and I wondered if each realized the resemblance. She had Nash's slate-grey eyes and stood maybe four inches shorter than him. She was thin with a wide mouth, and narrow nose, and a cover-girl's jaw. She wore her hair in black cornrows, her scalp showing palely beneath. Her white T-shirt made her hue seem darker. She looked defensively uninterested.

Beside me, Nash began to chuckle.

I turned to him. "What?" I looked around to see what I was missing. Maureen's expression lightened. Finally, she laughed, too.

"Nice shirt," Nash said to her.

Maureen's T-shirt read 3EB NYC in small black script.

"Great minds . . ." she said, and Nash nodded. "I heard the Boston show was killer."

"Totally," Nash said.

"I'm Timothy Glenn," the red-haired man said.

I told him who I was and introduced Perkins. We shook hands all around. His wife was named Tina. Her mood hadn't changed. She stood stoically aside, looking at Maureen, then back to Nash, and every so often her eyes fell to the ground.

. . .

It took some time, but we finally got inside. The living room was decorated artfully, and Norah Jones's silky voice rose softly from an unseen CD player. A flat-screen plasma television dominated one wall, and I guessed it to be fifty-two inches. Perkins, Nash, and I sat in a row on the huge L-shaped sofa, behind which stood a pool table, a pyramid of balls set neatly at one end. Pool sticks hung perfectly on the wall, each tip manicured. Brass lamps stood atop glass coffee tables. Wet bar. Plants of varying sizes and shapes. Burgundy carpeting. Teal pool water sparkled beyond the bay window. This was where Maureen Glenn had grown up.

And Nash took in every square inch of the place.

"I never even saw Owen Henley," Maureen said, and leaned back against the loveseat she shared with her mother and crossed her legs. Timothy Glenn, her adopted father, was on a chair to the side of them. Maureen wore shorts. Her toenails were rose colored. Her bearing expressed confidence and polish. She was the type of high school kid who, when I was young, would have intimidated the hell out of me—fourteen going on thirty-five.

"Did you ever look for him?" Nash said.

She shook her head.

"Maureen once spoke about that," Tina Glenn said, speaking for the first time. "I always thought that would be a bad idea. I think you should all just let it go, too." She looked from Nash to Perkins to me, then back to Nash.

Nash looked at me. I was letting him handle this. Nash, himself, had made a similar comment after the golf tournament in the hotel room in Danvers. Now he shook his head.

"I wish I could do that," Nash said. "I'm sorry to intrude, but I have questions about my—our—father."

"You're a college student and a football player," Tina said. "You, like Maureen, are successful. As I told my daughter, *Move forward. Let the past remain there.*"

"I didn't come to be lectured, Mrs. Glenn. But I appreciate your advice. Jack and his wife took me in a few years ago, and they've always said to go after what I want and never back down if I believe in something."

Tina looked from Nash to me with an expression that said I desperately needed parenting classes.

"And it's paid off," Nash said. "I had a professor tell me no football player ever got higher than a C+ in his class. I showed up every Tuesday for extra help and got a B."

"I need extra help all the time, too," Maureen said. "I've had private tutors every summer since seventh grade."

"Our father was dyslexic," Nash said. "I am, too."

Maureen nodded. "I have it. I always wondered about that. I asked Claire, but she didn't have anything to say." She looked at the wall above us. Behind her, the pool shimmered translucently.

"We conducted a similar search a while ago," Tina said. "It ended in pain for my daughter, and I won't have that again. Claire Henley ignored her."

"That's your mother?" Nash said.

Maureen shook her head. "She's my *biological parent*. This woman—" she motioned her chin toward Tina—"is my mother. Claire Henley got pregnant with me when she was nineteen. She gave me up immediately."

"It's natural for a kid to want to meet their biological parents," Timothy Glenn said, shaking his head sadly. "We know that, so we located Maureen's natural mother for her. The whole thing just did not go well."

"She wanted," Maureen paused and took a big gulp of air, "nothing to do with me." She blurted the final words as if they had to come out but were painful.

I imagined they had been.

"But you saw her?" Nash said.

Maureen nodded.

"She's in Portland, right?" Nash said.

Maureen tilted her head, quizzically. "How do you know that?"

"I've done some legwork already, talked to cops about the murder. I want to know who Owen Henley was."

"You went to the cops?" Maureen said. "You really did that?" She was fourteen and had grown up in a different world than Nash. His initiative impressed her. Me, too.

"They came to me first," Nash said.

"A homicide," Perkins said, looking at Tina and Timothy. He shrugged and spread his hands. "He's next of kin."

I looked at Perkins. He sat back, realizing what I meant: This was Nash's show.

"I'm next of kin, too," Maureen said. "The Massachusetts police called here."

We waited. She was looking at the floor. "I told them I'd never known him, never seen him, didn't know anything about him. That was it. It was upsetting. I mean, I knew I had a father. But I didn't want to know who it was because I knew that if I found out, it would be like when I learned about Claire. And that experience was so awful. She looked me in the eye and said, 'You were never supposed to come back.' I couldn't take that again. Then the police said he'd been murdered. And that he had a recent picture of me."

"Where was the picture taken?" Perkins said.

Again, I shot him the look.

"At school—walking into my high school. I thought, after meeting Claire, it couldn't get worse. But it could. And it did. I mean, how did he get a picture of me? Was he following me?"

"Probably," Nash said.

He told her about the albums.

"He took that many pictures of you?" Maureen said. "He stayed that close to you? Why would someone do that?"

"I hope it was because he cared," Nash said.

"I think he was nuts," Maureen said. "Sorry, but I can say it. I'm his child, too."

"Maybe," Nash said. "I don't know. But I need to find out."

"Why?" she said.

The conversation had moved away from the adults to Nash and Maureen, brother and sister talking alone. It was nice to see.

"I remember him," Nash said. "He left when I was five—"

"For my mother." She said it as if making a realization. The impact, though, was a factual statement, and the room fell silent.

"Even though he left when I was that young," Nash said, "I *do* remember him being there. I remember going around with him. What that was like. How it felt."

"How?" Maureen said. "I mean, shouldn't you just let it go, Nash?" She said his name for the first time, and it sounded natural. In fact, they seemed natural together. "After all, he's gone now."

"That's why. I can't get any of that back. I can only learn what he was like. And I can learn about him on my own, as a man."

Maureen's brows narrowed, her focus tightened on Nash. "You're out to prove something."

Nash glanced around the living room again. "My mother overdosed. I was on my own at fourteen. Part of me hates him, part of me misses him. I have to know what he was like."

"Your memories aren't enough?" Maureen said.

"No," Nash said and he looked down. "Those aren't good enough. They can't be all I have."

"Why?" Maureen said.

Nash shook his head.

.   .   .

Perkins and I went directly to the Suburban and sat with the tinted windows up. Nash walked out moments later with Maureen Glenn. They stood at the front door talking for a couple minutes.

"We're learning things," Perkins said to me inside the Suburban, "and we got Claire Henley's Portland address confirmed. I'm going to call her to let her know we'll be by." He flipped open his cell phone and dialed information.

"You mean to ask if we can drop by?"

"No," he said.

"Ever wonder why no one invites you any place?" I said.

He smiled.

A white Yukon drove into view and pulled to the curb near the Glenns' driveway. Perkins flipped the cell phone shut and looked at it. The Yukon had tinted windows like the Suburban.

Nash and Maureen hugged, and then Maureen went inside and shut the front door. Nash walked casually toward the Suburban, his youthful gait illustrating the exuberance I'd seen after he rushed for 200 yards and scored three touchdowns. It was a brittle confidence provided by a solitary success. He paused briefly and looked at the Yukon.

The Yukon's engine died, and a black guy with a Fu Manchu got out. He had a scar as thick as a nail running through one eyebrow. He was maybe Nash's age, but had a swagger that made him seem older. His was a confidence you don't see often, a self-assuredness that comes not from a solitary achievement but is earned and later worn as a badge. He was all of twenty-two, but this guy, wearing tear-away green and white sweatpants and a Paul Pierce Celtics warm-up jacket, was no kid.

Perkins and I were quickly out of the truck and beside Nash.

The kid had been about to speak and looked from Nash to us. "How's that line go? Even the best plans of mice . . ." His head shook back and forth and he chuckled softly. "I heard you were here alone, Nash."

"Well, he's not," Perkins said and stepped partially in front of Nash. "Terrell Smith, what do you want?"

"Easy, big fella." Terrell Smith grinned at Perkins. "Your office don't keep very good tabs on you. You're in Chandler today."

"Change in plans."

Terrell Smith looked past Perkins at Nash and smirked. "Hoping to catch you alone, so we could do some, ah, conversing. You always with your football buddies."

"I've seen you on campus," Nash said, and nodded as if he'd finally made the connection.

"I is an academic fool," Terrell said. He looked at me and Perkins again, shook his head. "Came too far to leave without talking, Nash. Got a minute?"

"Terrell," I said, "what do you want?"

He smiled. "You know me, too?" He grinned. "Guess lots of people know me. Even golfers."

"What do you want?" I said again.

"Like I said, I want to talk to my man. I'll make it worth his time."

Maureen Glenn came out of the house again. "Nash, is everything okay?"

"Nash, bro, you dog." Terrell clicked his tongue, a loud smacking sound. "That your ride, man?"

Nash sidestepped Perkins in a way that seemed almost easy.

I'd seen his quickness on the football field, but rarely off it. "That's my sister, man," he said softly.

"Hey, bro," Terrell said, grinning. Then he sized Nash up. "I heard you were a big motherfucker. Wouldn't want to meet you in a *weight room.*"

"Or out of it," Nash said.

Terrell leaned back and chuckled. The laughter faded quickly. "*Boy,*" Terrell said, leaning closer to Nash, "I nined a punk bigger than you last month. You a football player. I a man. Don't forget that."

"You want to talk," Perkins said, "get in your car and follow us."

etween Readfield and Augusta, Mulligan's Store sits adjacent to the four-way intersection of Western Avenue, Routes 17 and 202, and the Pond Road. At the intersection, we waited for the light to turn green and pulled into the parking lot. The store has a Dunkin' Donuts drive-through, and a little before noon, the place was busy.

Terrell pulled into the spot next to us and was quickly out of the Yukon. He stood leaning against the tailgate, waiting for us. "You guys know the hot spots, don't you?" he said when we had gotten out and stood near him. "Fucking Dunkin' Donuts." He grinned. "I feel like a yuppie. That how you feel, bro?" He looked at Nash. "You a yuppie?"

"Who told you I was in Chandler?" Perkins said. "Who at my office said that?"

"All I can tell you," Terrell said, "is that important people got connections." Terrell smiled widely.

"What're you here for?" Nash said. "Get to it."

"You sure your name be Nash? I was thinking maybe it be *Tom*."

The expression on Nash's face changed abruptly. Things had gotten out of hand once already—and I'd been front and center of that confrontation and now stood awaiting disciplinary action by the PGA Tour. However, this was different: There was no implied threat here. Schoolyard antics, an affront to pride. But why was Terrell Smith trying to rouse Nash Henley?

When Nash took a step closer, turning sideways, raising his left shoulder and tucking his chin in behind it, I grabbed him. Nash was eighteen years younger than me, ten pounds heavier, and bench pressed fifty pounds more than I could. He shoved me aside like he would a 170-pound safety.

Nash feigned a short left jab, which Terrell bought hook, line, and sinker. With Terrell dipping to his right, both hands raised, Nash came in under them and nailed him with all the right uppercut he had.

I'd met Nash after he'd left Roxbury, and he never spoke about his experiences there. But Nash knew what he was doing. The punch hadn't traveled a foot, and Terrell Smith was on his keester, bleeding from the mouth.

"I bit my fucking tongue, you motherfucker," Terrell said, the last word coming out *Moffer-fucker*. He spat. A string of saliva mixed with blood arced slowly and landed beside him on the pavement. "That was a mistake." He reached under his jacket.

"Terrell," Perkins said.

Terrell looked up, the fingers of his right hand beneath the "T" in Celtics. He paused when he saw Perkins's gun hanging loosely at his side.

"Put your hands flat on the ground, one on each side."

Terrell didn't move.

"Terrell," Perkins said raising his gun. Sunlight reflected off the stainless steel 9-mm semiautomatic.

Terrell had an amused grin as he did what he was told, putting his hands to his sides and reaching back. He leaned back and reclined, crossing his ankles leisurely. "You ain't gonna shoot me here, blondie."

"No. It's unfortunate for society. But I'm not," Perkins said and reached inside Terrell's warm-up jacket.

"Taking my gun?"

"Yup."

"Think that matters? Think I need my gun next time I see *Tom*? You know how many brothers I have?" A slow stream of blood oozed down his chin.

"I think it matters right now," Perkins said. "That's a nice jacket. Too bad your blood is staining the collar."

"Have the gun, blondie. Fucking piece cost me five hundred bucks. But I got a lot more money than that. And, who knows, you might just need it next time I see you."

Through it all, Nash stood staring at Terrell, motionless and silent.

A guy in a Saab had stopped to read the menu off the side of the building when the fight had started. He saw Perkins's drawn pistol and drove off, skipping the drive-through all together. Perkins reholstered his gun and dropped Terrell's through the open window onto the back seat of the Suburban.

I reached down and took Terrell by the arm and pulled him to his feet. "You're hurting business."

"Yeah," Perkins said. "Get off the ground, scumbag. You're making a scene." He shook his head sadly. "You street punks are all the same. Get in an argument, you shoot somebody. Never learn to fight doing that."

"I can fight, Face."

"Looks like it," Perkins said.

"Terrell Smith is a businessman. I came alone, motherfuckers. Just to talk. Left the posse home." Terrell turned suddenly to Nash and glared. "You made a mistake."

"I don't think so," Nash said.

"You their nigger?"

This time, Perkins caught Nash.

Terrell grinned. "Temper, temper, bro."

Nash stared at Terrell, a fierce, penetrating glare.

"Terrell," I said, "you sound like a fairy right now with that lisp. The show's over. What are you here for?"

"I came to talk to Nash, alone." Terrell spit again. Blood landed near his feet.

"You done bullshitting?" Nash said.

Terrell smiled. "I always bullshit, bro. Life ain't fun, so I amuse myself."

"Talk to Nash right here," Perkins said.

"No. Alone."

"So you can try to even things up for the cut on your tongue?" Perkins said.

"No. So we can talk business. And business is private."

"Okay," Nash said. "We'll go inside the store and sit in that booth in the window."

"We'll go in with you," Perkins said.

I shook my head. "No. We can wait out here. Nash can handle himself."

Nash looked at me and gave a solitary nod. Then he followed Terrell into the store. As I watched them go, my stomach began to knot.

. . .

We had no music playing in the Suburban when I pulled out of the parking lot at Mulligan's Store at 1:35 P.M.

"Terrell Smith is a head case," Nash said. "He kept telling me how much money he has. Said he didn't need college to get it either."

"That's what he wanted to talk to you for?" I said. "So he could one-up you?"

"He wanted to know if Wal-Mart contacted me."

"Wal-Mart?" Perkins turned in the passenger's seat to look at Nash in the second row. "Why Wal-Mart?"

"I don't know. He asked about Wal-Mart. Then he asked what the cops said."

"What did you say?" I said.

"I told him the cops asked what I knew about my father, and that was all. I didn't mention the other stuff, about Cronjagger warning us about Terrell."

127

"Cronjagger told us Owen Henley was involved with Terrell," I said. "Did Terrell give any hint as to what Owen was doing?"

"No. But he asked if the cops had mentioned Jerome Pulchuck," Nash said.

We were quiet a while, each of us thinking. In the rearview mirror, I saw Nash shake his head.

"I remember seeing Terrell on campus. I think I saw him a few times in the student center."

"What was he doing?" I said.

"Nothing I remember. Just hanging with some people, I think."

We had reached Augusta, and I turned onto the interstate, heading south. The Kennebec Ice Arena was on our right. On each side of the highway, farmland formed the landscape. Under the late-summer sun, the rolling fields were dark green.

Terrell Smith had driven three hours north to meet up with Nash, but had discovered Perkins and me with him. We sure as hell hadn't scared him off. What had Owen Henley done for Terrell, and what did Wal-Mart have to do with it?

"Terrell knows Owen Henley was involved with Jerome Pulchuck," I said. "How is that?"

"That's like asking how you know who Tiger Woods's caddie is," Perkins said. "These guys all have the same career paths. They know who works for who."

"But why ask Nash if the cops mentioned the other guys? To confirm the connection? Or is Terrell hoping Jerome goes down for the murder?"

Perkins shrugged. "Be one less guy to compete against."

"Or," I said, "maybe the word on the street is that Jerome did it."

We were quiet again. The road noise the old Suburban allowed was the only sound.

Finally, I shook my head. "I don't get it. Terrell is an arrogant punk. He wouldn't drive three hours to ask if the cops mentioned Jerome Pulchuck."

"The three-hour drive is what concerns me," Perkins said and dialed his cell phone. "David," he said, "tell Jimmy I need to meet with him—a special assignment—first thing tomorrow morning." Perkins hung up, leaned his head against the seat, closed his eyes, and rubbed his temples. "David has been with me five years. Top notch. A real pro, like Deirdre. This other guy, Jim Smythe, has been with me six months and gives me weekly migraines. Now he's done."

"How much you think Terrell paid him?" I said.

"Whatever it was, it's severance. What really worries me is that Terrell knew Maureen Glenn's address."

"What's that mean?" Nash said.

"It means Smythe was in my computer files. All my case notes are on my laptop and backed up on the network. He got by my password and in my files somehow—read my notes, got addresses. I can fire him, but he still has all that information. And there's no way of getting it from him. If he can break into my files, he sure as hell can hide the stuff."

My cell phone rang. It was Lisa.

"How's it going?" she said.

"All right."

"I wanted to give you a heads-up: Your run-in with Jerome Pulchuck is all over the news again today. And my first CBS feature assignment is on the state of security for players at PGA Tour events—because your caddie has crusaded for you, claiming over and over, to every reporter who'll listen, that you were threatened and simply defended yourself. Emilio from Peter Barrett's office is trying to reach you. So is Mitch Singleton and about a hundred other reporters."

"Fun stuff," I said. "I'll call Mitch. I have his number."

"I want to talk to Nash about the meeting."

"We'll be home soon," I said.

. . .

"I've been trying to reach you, Jack," Mitch Singleton's gravelly voice said through the phone's receiver. "Thanks for returning my call."

I was in my office at home in Chandler, Maine, at 4:45 P.M. Perkins and Deirdre were in the living room going through files on Pulchuck and Terrell. Outside, I could see Nash and Lisa on the lawn near the ocean. Lisa wore khaki shorts and a sleeveless white cotton top, her feet bare. Nash was dressed to lift weights, something I knew he'd do after the stressful day. Darcy was between them. Each time she began her two-year-old stagger toward the ocean, Nash jumped in front of her, his movement at once scaring and delighting her. Through the open office windows, I could hear Darcy's giggle-scream.

"Have you had your hearing yet?" Singleton said. "Not that it matters. I'll never know how much the fine is or if you're suspended. I love the Tour's confidentiality policy on disciplinary action."

"You want to sell the public on Tour players being 'gentlemen,'" I said. "You keep any and all behavioral issues as quiet as possible."

"Yeah, I understand why the Tour does it," he said. "Like when Jonathon Kaye didn't play for a month."

"He must've simply been on vacation."

"Sure. The guy was suspended. Every journalist knew it. No one could get it confirmed. I think we both know you'll be fined, Jack. I just want to know if it's exorbitant and if you're suspended."

"Me, too. I meet with Barrett tomorrow. But you can bet I won't be talking about it afterwards."

In the distance, a boat bobbed up and down, riding waves rhythmically. It was anchored about a hundred yards off our dock, a location where I'd never seen a boat stationed before.

"You want to tell me who the guy was?" Singleton said. "I tried to call you again, but your machine was full. And here I was, vain enough to think I was the only reporter you gave your number to."

"You are."

"Well, I guess people track you down when you're the talk of the town."

"No one did after I won last year."

"I did, Jack," Singleton said. "I spoke to Tim Silver for a half hour today. Silver says the guy threatened you. You want to comment on that?"

"I'll say this: I'll stand by my previous record when dealing with fans. I've always supported the Tour and promoted the game and will continue to do so. This was a very isolated incident."

"Were you threatened?"

I sighed. Four years ago, a kid named Hutch Gainer, a Stetson-wearing Texan, came to my hotel door late one night asking for help. He was being blackmailed to drop strokes, to bogey particular holes, all part of a gambling scheme. And dutifully I had tried to help. Not for Hutch Gainer. For the game. Thousands of kids come out each week to watch us play, believing they are seeing the best we have. No matter what the next day's hearing brought—fine and/or suspension—the fact that I had embarrassed the sport on national television was worse.

"Mitch," I said, "you've known me a long time."

"That's why I'm asking the question, Jack. I believe Silver. I'm giving you a chance to defend yourself. Yesterday, Michael Wilbon, on ESPN's *Pardon the Interruption* said the guy you punched got what he deserved. Wilbon was taking your side."

"Good to know. What did the other host say?"

"Tony Kornheiser? He said this was why you hadn't won more. 'Jack Austin is a guy who obviously can't control his emotions.'"

We were silent at that comment. On the anchored boat off our shore, I saw a black-haired man emerge from the cabin and walk to the stern. He stood looking at Lisa, Nash, and Darcy. Nash waved. The black-haired guy in a white T-shirt and a navy blue bathing suit didn't return the gesture. He stood staring at Nash. I saw Nash turn to Lisa and say something. Both looked at the guy on the boat, who retreated below deck.

"The people who know you will believe Silver," Mitch Singleton said. "The rest might not." I listened as he took a deep breath. "I'm not speaking as a reporter when I say, Goddamn it, Jack, defend yourself."

"I felt that my loved ones were in danger," I said. "That's all I can say right now."

"So there's more to come?"

"Maybe."

We hung up. I sat staring out the window at Nash, Lisa, and Darcy. The boat did not move.

Late that night, I was in my office, sipping instant coffee, made tolerable by three spoonfuls of sugar. I had pulled a book from the bookcases which lined my office and thumbed through, looking for a particular poem. The house was silent, save for the occasional creak and water moving through pipes behind the plaster walls. The next day, I was to meet with Cronjagger to discuss the photos and have my sit-down with PGA Tour Commissioner Peter Barrett—which had me feeling like a fourth grader sitting outside the principal's door.

Philip Levine's *New Selected Poems* offered one I knew well, one that seemed fitting. "Let Me Begin Again" starts out:

> Let me begin again as a speck
> of dust caught in the night winds
> sweeping out to sea. Let me begin
> this time knowing the world is
> salt water and dark clouds . . .
> Tonight I shall enter my life
> after being at sea for ages . . .
> The one child of millions of children
> who has flown alone by the stars
> above the black wastes of moonless waters
> that stretched forever . . .

I returned the book to the shelf and took an old Arnold Palmer blade putter that leaned against the wall. I had a few balls and a dime on scatter rug. Putting at a dime was an old drill that I had heard Ben Hogan used. The drill was good; my stroke wasn't. I hit a putt, and the ball ran off the carpet and clanked against the baseboard.

I had heard nothing of or from Jerome Pulchuck since punching him in the face. However, he had promised revenge. Terrell Smith hadn't expected to run into Perkins and me, but now he had stepped onto the scene—like a hot gust I'd experienced in El Paso. And the game I loved had broken one of my closest friends. On the home front, Lisa had accepted a CBS assignment, which meant Darcy's world would change. The PGA

Tour's day care would take Darcy while I played and Lisa worked. As an adult, I knew socialization with other two-year-olds was good for Darcy. As a father, though, especially on the heels of Jerome Pulchuck and Terrell Smith, I wanted Darcy to stay in this house with Lisa and me forever.

I thought of the poem again, then of Nash. Levine wrote, *knowing the world is/salt water and dark clouds.* Earlier that day, Nash's salt-water world had clashed with Maureen Glenn's glass-slipper life. For her, Roxbury had been conveniently replaced with a rope swing and a Jetta. The man who had left Nash to fend for himself at age five somehow had a daughter who was well cared for, a fact not lost on Nash. He had taken in everything about Maureen's Readfield, Maine, home, which no doubt, to Nash, represented her life.

It all led back to my relationship with Nash and his quest to know who Owen Henley had been. I had been raised in a working-class home—my father, a carpenter who worked twelve-hour days in season; my mother, a substitute teacher. Yet compared to Nash's upbringing, I was Beaver Cleaver. At thirty-eight, my relationship with Nash was more big brother–little brother than father–son. The irony was that Owen Henley had been about my age, so he had been only eighteen when he'd fathered Nash, and Nash had desperately wanted him to be a father. It would have meant a boy raising a boy. Maybe Owen Henley could never have served in the role of father, regardless of age. Lea Griffin and Sean O'Reilly hadn't described Owen in fatherly terms, which reminded me of Nash's comment to Maureen—about needing more than his memories, saying they weren't enough.

I didn't know what to make of that. And I couldn't do anything about the past. I could only keep my promise to help Nash learn the truth, no matter what the truth turned out to be. Aside from that, I couldn't turn back. Pulchuck had forced my hand when he had promised revenge.

The scent of salt air wafted in through a window I had cracked. I returned to the desk. The clock read 11:05. The thread running through Jerome Pulchuck, Terrell Smith, and Owen Henley was photography. Owen worked in a photo lab and was an amateur photographer. Cronjagger had a picture of Owen with Pulchuck that he didn't know what to do with, so he wanted Nash, Perkins, and me to look at it. But Pulchuck was willing to pay Nash for Owen's pictures. The picture meant something to somebody. I was eager to have a look. And Terrell had asked if Wal-Mart had entered the scene. Why would Owen's employer, for whom Owen worked in a photo lab, do that? Photography again.

I snapped off my desk lamp. Through the window, I saw a light in the cabin of the boat anchored beyond our dock. No one had anchored there since we moved in two years earlier.

Lea Griffin had told me Owen spent a fortune on film development at Wal-Mart, that Wal-Mart sent the film out for development, and that Owen threatened her life, should she look at his pictures. Were they of Nash, and Owen feared being viewed as a stalker? But I didn't think pictures of Nash would have Pulchuck threatening my family. There had to be more to the photos than that.

"You're still awake?" Lisa said, opening the office door. "What are you doing?"

The anchored boat's cabin light went out.

I turned to face her. "Just looking out."

"It's a full moon. Beautiful night. Come to bed." She turned and went upstairs.

I returned my coffee cup to the kitchen and went upstairs. The bedroom was dark when I slid into bed beside her.

"Are you nervous about tomorrow's meeting?" Lisa said.

"Yes. I returned the call to the TaylorMade people. They're not dropping me."

"I didn't think they would."

I moved closer to her, realizing at once she wore no nightgown.

"You've had a hard week," she said and kissed me, a long kiss, one meant to lead to more.

It did. When we made love, Owen Henley, Terrell Smith, and Jerome Pulchuck were finally out of my mind. Only the steady, rhythmic pounding of waves against the shoreline was present.

$\mathcal{W}$ednesday morning, Perkins, Nash, and I were back at the Norfolk County DA's Office in Canton, Massachusetts, seated in Cronjagger's office, looking through every picture the cops had taken from Owen Henley's apartment. There were over 300, and I now knew why Cronjagger was willing to call us in. I had expected him to have Nash look at the photos (maybe Nash could make a connection), but asking Perkins and me to look had come as a surprise. However, the cops had 300 pictures and 299 seemed alike and insignificant. If that wasn't enough, the photo of Jerome Pulchuck and Owen Henley seemed insignificant as well, although we all knew it couldn't be.

The pictures lay on Cronjagger's desk. Many of them were of Nash on the football field. Cronjagger quickly set those aside, moving with the efficiency of a Las Vegas card dealer.

"Gone through these before?" I said.

"Once or twice," he said, shaking his head. "I was here last night until eleven."

After excluding the football pictures, nearly 200 remained. It took a few minutes, but Cronjagger arranged them in three piles: Nash's elementary school years, his high school days, and the recent ones.

I held up the photo of Jerome Pulchuck and Owen Henley. Owen Henley wore a soiled and faded Red Sox cap, the kind with plastic mesh in the back. He wore a white T-shirt that said CURRY FOOTBALL and blue jeans with a hole in the left knee. On the T-shirt and jeans there was what looked like grease or engine oil.

"You know where he got the T-shirt?" Cronjagger said to Nash.

"No. Probably went to the bookstore and bought it."

"Curry College Bookstore has no credit card record for your father. And he was big into credit cards. He had three—all maxed out. See anything at all, Nash?"

"No. Nothing."

"There must have been at least one other person with Owen and Pulchuck," I said.

Cronjagger nodded. "Whoever took the picture."

Converse to Owen's workman's garb, in the photo, Pulchuck was dressed casually—khaki shorts and a windbreaker. I couldn't see his feet. He wore a Red Sox hat. It didn't have plastic mesh. It was fitted, the kind that cost $30. On his left thigh, there was a smudge of the oil-like substance as well.

"What is that?" I said and pointed to the oil.

"We can't tell," Cronjagger said. "We have the shirt Owen had on, but it's clean now. We don't know how old the picture is. But the shirt was made two years ago, so the picture must have been taken within the last twenty-four months."

Owen and Pulchuck stood alone. Thick woods lay behind them. On a tree, over Pulchuck's right shoulder, was a huge circular bull's-eye target, maybe the size of a garbage can lid, white with a red center.

"We've looked for that thing at every goddamned target range in the state," Cronjagger said, "including archery ranges. Nothing."

I leaned closer.

"See something, Jack?" Perkins said.

"I don't know."

"I didn't bring you in here for I-don't-knows," Cronjagger said. "What is it?"

"Just looks familiar, that's all. I can't place it. It's a shooting target?"

"I'm assuming it's for shooting," Cronjagger said. "It sure as hell isn't to steer a car at." His voice sounded tired, frustrated. "Pulchuck says he can't remember when or where the picture was taken or by whom. He said only that he and Owen were acquaintances, that he hired Owen to 'sweep the yard once in a while.'"

"You talk to Sean O'Reilly?" I said.

Cronjagger nodded. "Perkins gave me his name. We picked him up, brought him in. He said nothing. His memory, apparently, is worse than Pulchuck's. And he was drunk."

"Which probably didn't help," I said. "O'Reilly mention a house?"

"A house?"

"O'Reilly told us Owen bought or was about to buy a house for Nash."

"No record of any Massachusetts properties under Owen Henley's name."

I turned back to the picture. Both men were smiling. Although facing forward, Owen was not looking at the camera. His eyes had run to Pulchuck, and he was looking at him the way a boy would a trusted adult—there was joy and even need and longing in his eyes.

I leaned back in my straight chair. My head hurt, and I had yet to meet with PGA Tour Commissioner Peter Barrett.

Cronjagger sifted through the photos again, removing all the pictures of Nash with other people. I saw photos of Nash with his old football coach, Halle Basker. There were pictures of Nash in uniform with other football players at the Horizons School, the boarding school where he'd gone prior to Curry College.

I stopped Cronjagger when he reached pictures that included me with Nash and those of Nash with Lisa and Darcy. There were seven. All had been taken at Curry College.

"You said you saw no one taking your picture," Cronjagger said.

"That's right," I said. The pictures made me feel uneasy, vulnerable.

"How the hell did he do that?" Perkins said.

A smiled crossed Nash's face, a rare and inexplicable moment of pride. It reminded me that we were discussing Nash's father—and that, like any kid, there was an attachment (maybe love, maybe something else) that existed there and could not be broken.

Several other photos were of Nash with his girlfriend, Michelle, and one, a fuzzy shot of Nash, although I couldn't make out the facial details, with a little kid. They stood on asphalt in what looked like a parking lot. The photo was badly blurred, but I could tell the child was not Darcy—too tall—and the picture was in color, so I could tell the kid was dark-skinned and wore a Red Sox T-shirt. But the shot was too distorted to see much more. Were they looking at one another? They were maybe five feet apart. Had they simply been crossing the parking lot at the same time? As luck would have it, it was the only blurred picture in the bunch. On the back a large question mark had been written.

I looked at Cronjagger. He spread his hands.

"Nothing?" Perkins said.

"A parking lot somewhere. Nash, you recognize the kid?"

Nash held the photo a long time. He moved it closer, then farther away, squinting. "No way, officer. I can't make it out. Looks like we're just passing each other. The only little kid I really know is Jack's daughter."

"That's par for the course," Cronjagger said; then to me: "Pardon the expression."

There was also a picture taken in a bar—Nash, his roommate Greg Petroski, and a man whom I did not recognize. The man was shorter than Nash by probably four inches, putting him around five-nine, and he had a thin beard, the kind for which you have to buy a special electric razor and trim daily. The back of this picture read "roommate & roommate's father." Apparently, I was looking at the man I would partner with at the Woodland's cancer charity event.

"A house?" Cronjagger said, staring out the window.

"O'Reilly was pretty vague on that," I said.

"Sounds like him," Cronjagger said, turning back to us. He shook his head. "And I was hoping you guys could clear things up. Nash, anything strike you? You see anything?"

"You can tell my dad liked that guy Pulchuck, that he trusted him. You can see it in his eyes."

"If so," Cronjagger said, "he trusted the wrong guy."

138

22

*C*onstruction in Boston, known as "The Big Dig," has been going on since the beginning of mankind. For a guy who grew up in rural Maine, even one who is now in his late-thirties and has traveled all over the continent, it makes Logan Airport the most excruciating destination in all of New England. In fact, if I were a politician instead of a golfer, my suggestion would be to have Massachusetts drunk drivers forgo the weekend in jail that Maine drunks face and make them circle in and out of Logan for forty-eight consecutive hours. Then, of course, seek counseling for road rage.

By an act of God, I made it from Cronjagger's office to the Hilton at Logan and was sitting across from Peter Barrett at 11 A.M.

"Mr. Austin," Barrett said, shaking his head, "didn't we have a similar situation—and meeting—last year?"

"No," I said, "last year the guy I punched was only a reporter."

Somehow Barrett managed not to smile. "Odd humor, coming from a guy married to a journalist."

Barrett looked down at a yellow legal pad. We were alone in a conference room the size of Fenway, and he sat in a high-backed leather chair behind a large cherry desk. I felt like I had in third grade when I pushed Perkins off the jungle gym and had to sit across from the principal, awaiting my father. Barrett made you feel like you were in the principal's office. As Tour players, we all knew the buck stopped with him—and he was the kind of guy you wanted running the Tour: forthright, direct, and exuding confidence. The man with the answers. Except right now, I didn't want to know the answers.

"The man's name," Barrett said, "is Jerome Pulchuck, a spectator, a guy who drove out from Boston, paid his forty-five dollars for a day's pass to watch golf."

"He's a little more than that."

Barrett held up his hand. "I know, I know. Mr. Perkins has made that point repeatedly. What I don't like is that a year ago, you hit a reporter from *USA Today*. I can't have a renegade golfer running amuck, punching people's lights out, Jack."

This was not going well. On the ride down, I had been thinking *small fine with no suspension*. Barrett clearly wasn't into telepathy.

"Mr. Perkins put me in touch with Boston police officials," Barrett said. "So I know all about Jerome Pulchuck's past. However, he says he was simply a fan at the event."

"Perkins must have told you that isn't true."

He nodded. "And I called Tim Silver, and he said the same thing. Tripp Davis, your playing partner the day you hit Pulchuck, though, said he didn't notice you being heckled. Perkins tells me this is part of something larger, Jack, involving the Nash Henley kid."

"Pulchuck was at the tournament to threaten, so I'd get some photos from Nash."

"Photos of what?"

"I don't know."

Barrett blew out a long breath, shook his head, and leaned back. "You don't know?"

"No."

"Perfect." He steepled his fingers on his chest and tapped the tips together. His eyes were closed, and he inhaled deeply through his nose, seemed to hold it, then exhaled through flaring nostrils. My case was making the guy meditate.

"Jack," he said finally, "do you know how many people *volunteered* at the Deutsche Bank Championship?"

I shook my head. This was turning into a lecture.

"Thirteen hundred people *paid* seventy bucks to volunteer. Of course, they received shirts, jackets, some other items, and free admission, but consider that for a moment. Those people quite literally make the PGA Tour go. My job is to protect the good of the game. And to grow it so that people want to watch and be involved. You know that, right?"

I said I did.

"When you originally hired Nash Henley, the differences—and similarities—between you two brought the Tour a great deal of positive media attention, something I enjoyed."

He was headed somewhere.

"However," he said, "you have assaulted two people in two years. I see no other players with these issues. How do you account for that?"

"I can't."

"That's what I thought." He leaned back again and did the breathing routine. "You know what I do when I have a migraine coming on?" he said, eyes still closed, continuing the breathing scheme.

"I hope not much more than what you're doing now."

He sat up straight. "You think this is funny, Jack?"

"No," I said, "but I hope you realize that any headaches I've caused over the years have been from trying to protect the game or the people close to me."

"Part of me has thought of that. Hell, part of me might even believe it. But I'm still sick of seeing your name in the paper for stuff like this instead of low scores."

"So am I."

"So what can we do about that?" he said. "I know what I can do. Tell me what you're going to do about it."

I knew what he wanted to hear. In third grade, the principal had said something remarkably similar. Then, I had told the principal Perkins had grabbed my leg, so I pushed him off the jungle gym. I had said I'd do it again, too.

"I work out two hours a day," I said. "I hit four hundred practice balls some days. When they close the course, I putt in my hotel hallway. I'm not going to do anything differently. Nash Henley came to me for help. I love the kid like a younger brother. I'm going to help him. As for the USA Today guy, he pushed my wife. I'd punch him in the mouth again."

"I see." He straightened and ran a hand over his face, his thumb and forefinger meeting at the point of his chin. He was staring hard at me.

Barrett was no Jerome Pulchuck. I held his gaze.

"Last year, I fined you ten thousand dollars. That figure didn't seem to deter you in this incident. You are fined fifty thousand dollars, Jack, and you will begin counseling."

"Counseling for what?"

"Anger management."

"Jesus."

Barrett looked at me with raised brows. "Your next incident will lead to a lengthy suspension."

"Lengthy?" I said.

"Have you ever considered the European Tour, Jack?"

"No."

We looked at each other through a long pause.

"That's all," he said.

I got up and walked out.

. . .

I had little time to stew about Barrett's remarks, as Nash, Perkins, and I arrived at Claire Henley's fifth-floor Congress Street apartment later that afternoon. She had kept Owen's name after divorcing him following a year of marriage. Dark-skinned with dreadlocks, and a lot of light-blue eyeliner, she wore cut-off blue jeans and a tie-dyed T-shirt that read PORTLAND PLAYERS — SUMMER 2005. She was holding a paperback copy of *Hamlet* when she answered the door.

"Can I help you?" she said.

"I called last night," Perkins said.

She looked at him, puzzled. The door was on a security chain, but her voice was soft, and her tone expressed genuine confusion. Apparently, Maureen Glenn had gotten a much different reception. Maybe this wasn't going to be as difficult as I'd anticipated.

"I'm Nash Henley," Nash said.

She looked from Perkins to Nash.

"You were married to my father," Nash said, his eyes wide, his expression one of desperate hope. "I'm looking for answers about Owen Henley's life."

Claire's placid face became an instant scowl, and the door began to swing shut.

Perkins put a foot in the way.

"What are you doing?" she said from behind the door, her voice straining as she pushed. "Let me close this door."

"We won't bother you," Perkins said. "Just ten minutes of your time. Please."

"No. That was a long time ago. Thank God it's over."

"Ma'am," Perkins said, "you can't close the door."

"Then I'll call the goddamn police."

"You want to borrow my cell phone?" Perkins said. "Or are you going to leave the door unguarded while you get yours?"

"Very cute."

Perkins looked at me and shrugged.

"Claire," Nash said in a calm voice, "I just want to ask you about my father. I never got the chance to know him."

"Tough shit. But be glad for that, kid."

"How about I take a different approach?" Perkins said. He reached into the breast pocket of his sports jacket and held his license through the door. "I make one phone call and Portland PD hauls your ass downtown, and you answer our questions in a holding cell. That sound appealing?"

"You a Portland cop?" she said.

"Yeah. And this is my friend. Here or downtown? I'll count to five. ONE . . . TWO."

"Hold on," she said.

Perkins stopped. I heard footsteps—she was running—then something clanged and a door slammed shut. When she returned, she was panting. The door closed, the chain slid off, and the door opened.

We entered, and Claire Henley led us to a tiny living room. There was a beaten sofa, a scarred coffee table, and a lamp, its shade askew. A small television with rabbit-ear antenna played a soap opera or the like. I couldn't make out the details through the snowy screen. A half-drunk cup of tea was on the coffee table.

Perkins, Nash, and I sat on the sofa behind the coffee table as we had upon meeting Maureen Glenn. Claire took the Lazy-Boy. The chair was tilted to one side and forced her to lean to the right. Maybe the chair hadn't survived the trip up five flights of stairs.

There was a residue like oregano on the coffee table. I knew why she had been running around before letting us in and why she didn't recall Perkins's phone call. All the windows I could see were wide open. A fan hummed in one.

"I have to go over my lines," she said, waving the copy of *Hamlet*. "Our production begins in two days."

"You act?" I said. She was maybe Lisa's age and height, but a lot heavier. Her figure looked block-shaped beneath the tie-dye.

"Among other things. I'm an artist. I have assumed the persona of Ophelia for this role. So anything I say may be tinged."

"From the smell of this place," Perkins said, "you've assumed the persona of Bob Marley. We came for straight answers. We get tinged and you go out of here with blue lights flashing."

"You don't have to be so . . ." she looked at Perkins, exasperated, ". . . threatening. God, you're a difficult human being."

"Yeah," Perkins said.

"How did you meet my father?" Nash said, reeling her back in.

"My God," she said, "way back, at Boston University. I was seeking alternative forms of self-expression then. We were in a photography class together. The most gifted student was Owen Henley." Her eyes drifted, and she looked out the window as if seeing her old classroom. "He had such a beautiful physique and his photos were startling—vivid and captured the human condition so well—but he was failing the class."

"Failing?" Nash said.

"He couldn't pass the written exams. It was sad. The professor used Owen's photos every week as examples, citing artistic qualities none of us other students had, then Owen failed the mid-term, and the professor accused Owen of having cheated all along, of having someone else take his photos. Owen never talked much about it. But I always thought that was why he quit college. I don't think he ever got over that accusation."

Nash sat on the edge of the sofa as Claire spoke. Owen Henley was coming into focus, and Nash was taking in every inch of the picture.

Claire stood up. I figured she was going to ask if we'd like something to drink. Instead, she stole a quick glance at the copy of *Hamlet* she held, and then looked up at us, smiling. Inexplicably, she broke into song: "How should I your true love know / From another one? / By his cockle hat and staff, / And his sandal shoon." She stood before us, her grin now a smirk. "None of you know that, do you?"

"It's the scene where Ophelia goes to the king," I said. "Before the brother shows up all pissed off because the silly long-winded guy got killed."

"Polonius," she said. "Very good. *Very* good."

"I'm thrilled you approve," I said.

She frowned and sat down again. "Was I patronizing? Owen used to accuse me of that all the time."

He probably hadn't been alone.

"You see," she said, "Owen was not an eloquent speaker, by any means. But I, on the other hand, have always been articulate. My father is an architect in San Francisco, and I went to private schools before leaving home."

"How old were you when you ran away?" Perkins said.

"I didn't *run away*. I needed to find my spiritual center, so I moved on. My spiritual and artistic selves were being stifled. I was seventeen when my father and I had a fight, and I left for good to prove to him I could do all I ever dreamed of. And I will yet."

Perkins said nothing, his face void of expression. I hoped mine was, too: Claire Henley was in her late thirties, still out to prove her old man wrong. There was something ugly in that, which made me see the importance of this quest Nash, at twenty, was undertaking.

"Back to Owen," Claire said. "He struggled socially at times. He couldn't explain the photos he took very well, only in rough terms." Her head shook slightly, as she thought about the past. "But if those pictures were Owen's, there was something in them—a talent our professor probably didn't even possess."

"Did you doubt they were his?" I said.

"No. Not really. It was just that I never saw him take pictures, even after we married. I knew he did. He would bring them home. And he went out a lot, alone. I guess, looking back on it, that was what he was doing. But I never saw him take them."

"They must've been personal to him," Nash said, "private."

She looked at Nash, her body leaning in the tilted chair. "You've learned about him already, haven't you?"

"Some. He was dyslexic. So am I. A lot of times taking information in is hard for me. Putting it out is easier. In journalism class, my professor read my feature assignment and asked me why I had asked a certain question. I couldn't explain it. He said I had a great *feel* for interviewing. I got B's on all my articles." He smiled and shrugged. "Grammar kills me. But I got only C minuses on my two exams."

She sat looking at Nash. Perkins was leaning back on the sofa. I said nothing.

"When Owen quit BU, we became active in other things. How much do you want to know?" She looked hard at Perkins. "And what stays confidential?"

"All of it," Nash said, "on both counts."

Claire sighed and leaned back in the tilted chair. "Some of those activities, ridiculously, are not accepted by society."

"Drugs?" Perkins said.

"Marijuana is used medicinally. It also increases my sensitivity, helping me enter into my most primal state. It allows me to fully experience the roles I play."

"Sure," Perkins said.

"Owen had a life before I met him that he never spoke of. I never knew about you, Nash. I have a daughter who came back last year, but it was all too much to handle."

"So you used your medicinal marijuana?" I said.

"You're wearing a gold watch worth more than all my possessions," she said. "You don't know what it's like to need an escape. Go to hell."

"Money has nothing to do with Maureen Glenn coming here and having a door slammed in her face. She's your kid."

"How do you know what happened when she came here? I couldn't handle it when she was born. I was nineteen."

"Tell us about you and Owen," Perkins said. "Everything goes no farther than this room."

Outside, a horn sounded on Congress Street. The scent of marijuana was gone. The fan now served only to blow in hot air.

"God, when I read the articles in the paper, I wondered if that was him." She blew out a long breath and looked at Nash for a moment. "We were together only two years. BU was the first year. Then we both left college. I don't say dropped out because at that age, you don't quit, per se, you move in another direction. I was discovering myself in an artistic way college theater classes forbade me to."

"Meaning you found a theater that allowed you to act while high as a kite," I said.

She ignored me completely.

"Owen had a little job in a laundry, and I was making a name for myself in local theater projects. And then the bottom fell out. I got pregnant." She turned to stare out the window again. "I was thinking of Owen this morning when I read the lines that reminded me of him: *He is dead and gone, lady,/He is dead and gone;/At his head a grass-green turf,/At his heels a stone.*"

There wasn't much to say to that, and the three of us were silent across from her. Perkins was shaking his head, but Claire didn't see it.

"Our relationship was dead by then," she said. "But I was pregnant. I knew Owen didn't want anything to do with the baby. Hell, at that point, he didn't want anything to do with me." She paused and looked at Nash. "Aside from dyslexia, what do you know about your father?"

There was something in her eyes. She knew something. The way she leaned forward made me think she was even anxious to say it. Yet at the same time, the woman who had just leaped up to recite *Hamlet* looked uncomfortable under the weight of our collective gaze.

"That's about all I know," Nash said.

Claire put her hands on the armrests and pushed back. She sat slumped in the chair, chin nearly to her chest for almost thirty seconds. Her face held no hint of eagerness now. She was contemplating.

"Your father," she said, and broke off.

We waited.

She started again and stopped.

"It doesn't leave the room," Perkins said.

Claire nodded and looked at Nash. "Your father liked little boys." She shook her head. "Built like a granite sculpture, just like you. But he liked little boys." Her eyes fell accusingly upon Nash.

"You have evidence for that accusation?" I said, trying to help Nash move from beneath the weight of her stare. It worked. She looked at me. Her eyes were wet.

"Evidence? I was sleeping—or trying to sleep—with the man. I caught him in a mall bathroom with a little boy. I hit Owen with my purse over and over—'*What are you doing? What's* WRONG *with you?*'—and took him home. He left the next morning. I never saw him again."

I felt like we were inside a deflating balloon. It was hot. Beads of perspiration lined Nash's brow. No one said a word. Below us, Congress Street traffic battled, voices shouted. The smell of cooking food entered.

"I never told anyone that." Claire sniffled and went to the window. She stood looking down. "I should have. I know how those people are. One victim means more. But I didn't. He left, and I tried to forget."

Standing back to us, her block figure seemed smaller. Her shoulders shook, and her chin sagged to her chest. I got up and steered Nash to the door. Perkins shut it behind us.

.   .   .

By 8:45 P.M., I was pretty sure Darcy was the only one who had things under control. I sure as hell didn't. Claire Henley had opened a door I didn't want to walk through. And to go with her comments, the commissioner of the PGA Tour suggested I go to Europe.

Nash, no doubt reeling, had insisted on returning to Curry College and his football career, although he was to return shortly. Perkins was in New Hampshire for a night with wife Linda and son Jackie before continuing the investigations of Terrell Smith and Jerome Pulchuck. Likewise, I was home in Chandler, where Lisa was readying for a second run at network golf coverage and Darcy was continuing (and succeeding) with her all-encompassing mission of wrapping me more tightly around her finger. She lay on her back in my bed beside me wearing the PJs she seemed to wear three out of every four nights, the purple Disney Princesses pajamas my mother had gotten her. She was sucking her thumb, rubbing her "silky," which had begun life as one of Lisa's slips.

Lisa moved from her closet with several outfits on hangers and set them into a large suitcase at the foot of our bed.

"The Canadian Open," she was saying. "CBS takes over coverage of the event from ESPN this weekend. The CBS people presented it as a trial run, for both parties. I'm going to bring Darcy, and we're going to see how the whole situation works—me in the tower and Darcy in the PGA Tour's day care. She's two. I think socializing with other two-year-olds will be good for her."

"What will they talk about?" I said.

She looked at me, started to answer, and caught herself. "Cute."

"How long have we been together, five years? And I can still get you to answer those."

"I didn't answer," she said.

"Almost."

She put pale blue Nike running shoes, a CD player, headset, and Sheryl Crow's *The Very Best of Sheryl Crow* CD into the suitcase.

"Did you ask Nash about his time with Owen Henley?" she said.

"I asked if all his memories were good. He said, 'Of course.'"

"That's all?"

"His step-sister asked why his memories of Owen aren't enough, which I thought was a damned good question."

"And?"

"And Nash said, 'Those aren't good enough. They can't be all I have.'"

"'Those aren't good enough'?" she said. "As in memories aren't *enough*? Or his specific ones aren't *good enough* to be all?"

I shrugged. "That'll probably come out when I ask him about his time with Owen, specifically regarding what Claire said. But I wanted to let things settle down a little. He was devastated." I tickled Darcy's stomach, and she squirmed. "Besides, I wanted to run the whole thing by you, first."

"Run the afternoon's events by me before talking to him?"

"Is that a display of confidence or what?"

"It's an awful lot of pressure is what it is," she said. "I'm no therapist."

Darcy grabbed my finger and bent it back. I pulled it away, and she reached for it again.

"But you know him," I said. "And you question people for a living. It won't be a pleasant discussion, but I have to ask. I just want to make sure he's okay. I mean, we're all the family Nash has."

"And the more we learn, the better that fact seems to be." Lisa took running shorts and a T-shirt that said REAL MEN MARRY ATH-LETES from a drawer and put them in the suitcase.

"Cops told us Owen Henley was fired for alleged inappropriate behavior with a high school male."

"One act?"

"Allegedly."

"Maybe only one victim had the courage to come forth."

"Very possible," I said. "Owen's ex-wife insists he was a child molester."

Lisa closed the suitcase, zipped it, and hung the bag from the doorknob. Then she moved to the edge of the bed and stood quietly. Somewhere in the house, John Mayer's CD *Heavier Things* played. Silences between Lisa and I were usually comfortable. The tension now was nearly tangible.

"Nash lived with Owen until he was five," I said. "When we left today, he could barely walk down from Claire Henley's apartment."

"That doesn't necessarily mean he was a victim, Jack. He learned something awful today, if it's true."

"Why would she make it up? To hurt Nash? And it goes with

Cronjagger's story about losing the teaching job." I shook my head. "I don't see Claire Henley as cruel. That's not in her. She's selfish and self-centered. But that's all. We asked about Owen, and she told us what she knew. Hell, she was upset she hadn't reported the incident."

"She felt guilty?"

"Yeah."

A layer of fog had crept in on the heels of a thundershower. A strong ocean breeze puffed the white cotton window treatments. In the distance, I heard the rumble of thunder.

"If Owen hurt Nash," I said, "we need to make sure Nash gets help. I have to ask about it. Nash said he wanted to play football tomorrow, so he drove back to school. I think he wanted to be alone. He's coming back tomorrow night or Saturday because this weekend, he's carrying for me at the Woodlands's cancer charity event. Ironically, I'm paired with his roommate's father."

"You'll have the whole house to yourselves. I don't mean to sound selfish, but I'm glad I'll be in British Columbia. That's one conversation I don't envy." She picked Darcy up and rocked her. "Fifty thousand dollars is an awful lot of money, Jack. Are you going to appeal the fine?"

"The guy suggested I go play the Euro Tour. I'm going to keep my mouth shut and pay."

"He suggested what?"

I detailed my conversation with Barrett.

When I finished, she was quiet for a while, considering. Her tongue ran along her upper lip—something she did only when she was angry.

"As your wife, I'm furious that he would threaten you. As a journalist, I think I'll look into it. The PGA Tour commissioner cannot ask players to give up their livelihood."

"Lisa," I said, "you calling Barrett on this won't help me."

"I have a job to do. The public needs to know if Peter Barrett is running the Tour like a dictator."

"He's always run it like a dictator," I said. "You know that. The only difference being that right now I'm in his doghouse. Other guys have survived it. I will, too. I'm exempt through next season, but I'd like to win again this year—tack another year onto that exemption. And besides," I smiled broadly, "how could anyone stay mad at *Moi?*"

"How could anyone stay mad at you, huh?" Lisa stopped rocking Darcy. "You better win soon, Jack."

23

$\mathcal{F}$rom the black tees, the Woodlands Club in Falmouth, Maine, plays 6,848 yards and gives you all the golf course you can handle. I had spent Friday there practicing—400 range balls, eighteen holes, and an hour on the putting green. Shortly before 8 A.M. Saturday, Nash and I shook hands with Martin Petroski and his annoying son, Nash's roommate, Gregg, on the first tee. Martin was smallish with a thin beard—the man in the barroom photos with Nash and Gregg.

The tee box was surrounded by area golf fans, who had been asked to make a "charitable contribution" of $35 upon entering. It was a chance to watch Tour players for the day, and the cost of admission to the Deutsche Bank Championship in Norton, Massachusetts, was $45. A member of the Woodlands Club had organized the event, and I had helped out by recruiting Phil Mickelson, Brad Faxon, David Duval, and eleven other Tour players, all of whom I lured to Maine with the promise of lobsters and steamed clams at a dinner party at my home. Padre Tarbuck was to have captained a sixteenth team. We had anticipated anywhere from 300 spectators to 3,000. This was the first year of the event, and judging by the people waiting to see me hit my first shot, I guessed the actual attendance figure to be at the high end of the estimation, because I was certain Mickelson's gallery would double mine.

"I've been looking forward to this," Martin Petroski said. "I'm sure you'll be impressed by my game."

"I'm sure I will," I said.

Wednesdays on Tour are pro-am days. Local amateurs pay around $1,500 to play typically a one-day team event with a Tour player. The pinnacle of the pro-am circuit is the AT&T Pebble Beach National Pro-Am, where annually Bill Murray does stand-up while pros and amateurs alike try to hit golf shots and Ray Romano takes a month to play eighteen holes. None of it bothers Tour pro Mark O'Meara, who seems to thrive in that atmosphere, having made a fortune by winning five times.

I've always liked Wednesdays; I've played with bigwigs from Charles Schwab, who gave stock tips, and guys like Ken Griffey, Jr., who gave me an autographed glove that hangs in my TV room. Wednesdays are for promoting the game and making sure your amateur partner has a good time. When the amateur is easy-going and takes neither himself nor the game too seriously, it's enjoyable. I have, however, heard tales from colleagues paired with that one dreaded amateur, the twenty-eight handicapper who insists he understands the golf swing better than guru David Leadbetter and wants to explain how to cure his pro's flawed swing. Fortunately, I'd never had such a partner. Apparently, though, Martin Petroski was going to change that.

"You playing the black tees?" Petroski said.

I told him I was.

"I should be playing from back there, too," he said. "They have me listed as a twenty-three handicap, but I'm a very accomplished athlete. I was on the crew team at Yale."

"Crew team, huh?" I said.

The sun was bright overhead. It was hot in Falmouth, and listening to Martin Petroski made me long for the ocean breeze I could have been enjoying at home. But the guy had paid his $1,500, and the money was for cancer research. Nash and I headed back to the black tees. Petroski stayed at the whites.

The first hole plays 391 yards from the black tees, and Doug Van Wickler, director of golf at the Woodlands Club, had pushed the tees to the back quadrant of the last tee boxes. A lake is left of the fairway while bunkers and trees line the right side.

Nash chuckled. "Let's see you try to hit an iron from back here."

I took the three-wood from the bag. "Cute. How was football practice?"

"It felt good to hit people," he said.

That statement said a lot, and I let it hang between us momentarily.

"You've missed some practices," I said. "They add any new plays while you were gone?"

He shook his head. "Almost the whole offense returned, and we averaged forty-one points a game last year. But we gave up almost as many. The coaches are focusing on defense."

"Sounds logical." I swung my three-wood back and forth, loosening my shoulder muscles. "How long have you known Petroski?"

Nash shrugged. "Six months."

A small group of people had followed Nash and I to the back tee box, so I whispered, "Is he a pain in the ass?" I knew what I thought; I wanted to get Nash's take.

"You mean *like his father?*"

I smiled.

"Yeah," Nash said. "He kind of is."

I made two practice swings. Then I tried to visualize the ball flying down the right side and landing in the fairway. I moved to the ball and made solid contact. The ball settled in the fairway 110 yards from the green. Nash and I walked to the white tee box, where Martin was preparing to hit.

"Jack, my man," Martin Petroski said. "Give me five for that drive."

I slapped his hand.

"Now just don't choke on the next shot," he said.

I glanced at Nash, who turned away, shoulders trembling as he laughed.

"What's funny?" Martin said.

"Nothing, Dad," Gregg Petroski said. "Just hit the damned ball."

"Hey, I'll hit when I'm ready. I can shoot seventy-two on this course, but I need to focus. Focus is something you could add to your football game, son."

"Sure, Dad. I'll get right on that."

Martin Petroski shot Gregg a look. Then he shook his head, as if a fly were bothering him, and stepped up to the ball. To say Martin swung hard would be like saying Shaquille O'Neal is a "good-sized man." The club moved so fast down and around that his follow-through wasn't one: The club never appeared to stop, and he spun full around trying to catch up so he wouldn't fall over. He finished nearly facing the opposite direction. I had never seen anything like it and stood in stunned silence.

The ball landed in the water, left of the fairway.

"Why's your mouth open like that?" Martin said to me. "That was actually a great swing. I stumbled on this damned tee box."

"The tee box?" I said.

"Yeah. If I didn't have great balance, I'd have fallen over. Don't you have greens keepers to fix these? It slopes. You'd think this place could afford to fix that, but I guess all of Maine is back-woods."

"Mr. Petroski," Nash said, "there's nothing wrong with the tee box."

I bit my tongue. On the heels of a $50,000 fine and the threat of suspension, you tend to do that. There were no ropes lining the fairways, so fans could walk the course with us. I could tell from various facial expressions that Martin's "backwoods" comment had not gone unheard, nor had it gone over well.

"Dad," Gregg Petroski said, "Nash is right. You just pull-hooked that one."

"Son, it's the tee box. I'm telling you."

.   .   .

We were in the second fairway. I had 130 yards to the elevated green. Martin had hit three shots already. Now his ball lay in the greenside bunker.

The tournament format was Best Ball, so Martin and I each

played a ball, while the lowest individual score on each hole (using handicaps) served as the team score. I had parred the opening hole, so our team was even. Martin had taken a seven (net six) on No. 1—if you want to call it that. It had taken him six shots to reach the green, and since I had been putting for birdie, he was out of the hole. What he had decided, though, was to give himself a "gimme"—from eight feet. "I'm money in the bank from this distance, Jack," he had said. I had bit my tongue and two-putted.

"Let's go, Jack," Martin was saying now, as I made a practice swing and tried to visualize the 130-yard nine-iron carrying the bunker that protected the front-left portion of the green. "Put this one close, Jack. Make up for that birdie putt you missed on number one."

"Make up for it?"

"Yeah, you kind of let down the team, missing that putt."

"I see."

Martin and Gregg moved down the fairway. Nash and I stood twenty feet in front of a handful of spectators. I made my customary second practice swing. I had hit three-wood off the tee, and the swing had produced a payoff for Friday's hard work: The ball had moved right to left, a draw. I'd spent Friday working on the shot. A draw always produces more distance than a fade (or, worse, a slice), so I had dropped my back foot slightly, aimed down the right side of the fairway, and smiled when the ball drifted left, bending around the dogleg as planned. The view had been almost nice enough to make playing with Martin tolerable.

I carefully set the clubface behind the ball, aligning the clubface with the target, and positioned my feet. I made one final check—shoulder toward the target—then swung. The contact was crisp, and I stared the ball down, watching the Pro V1 carry the sand trap and fade toward the pin location.

"You love it, don't you?" Nash said.

I turned to him. "Love what?"

"Golf. I mean, even here, in this charity tournament, you're lining everything up, concentrating."

"You play like you practice. And, yeah, I like to compete."

"Yeah, I know that, but sometimes it surprises me—like the smile on your face just now, after you hit the nine-iron. It's probably the same smile you had when you were ten."

"I love that feeling—hitting a pure shot. It's what I spend hours on the range looking for."

"When you're done playing, think you'll coach the University of Maine golf team?" Nash said.

Ahead of us, near the green, Martin Petroski looked crestfallen, and I saw a nearby spectator offer encouragement. The guy was short and squat and wore a large straw hat and dark wraparound glasses. He said something, and Martin laughed.

"No," I said, "I won't coach. It's not my thing."

"You could still compete that way."

"That's not why I love the game. I like to compete, but it's not only that. Golf offers you the truth," I said. "And I like learning the truth."

"The truth?"

We started walking down the fairway, in front of my diminished gallery. Duval had just teed off.

"Sure," I said. "You're all alone. And you're either good enough or you're not. You've worked hard enough or you haven't. The game gives you instant feedback, daily."

"That's why you love it?"

"Mostly. And the feeling of hitting a pure shot, stroking a pure putt."

"Football is such a team sport," Nash said, "that I guess I don't get that kind of feedback." He grinned. "And I've never hit a pure shot, so I haven't gotten a feeling worth all the hours you put in on the range."

I held out my hand. He gave a low-five. As we got closer to the green, I saw that my nine-iron had stopped fifteen feet from the pin, farther than I'd anticipated.

Martin saw my ball and looked as if I'd put one in the water. "No problem, buddy. Fifteen feet isn't very good. But I'll carry you this hole."

My father's words of wisdom—"If you can control your mind,

you can control your actions"—helped in that I didn't strangle Martin. Instead, I walked to my ball, marked it, and stood waiting for Martin to hit his bunker shot. I thought a little more about Nash's question and subsequently about the game. I had grown up learning disabled. School had been a place of humiliation. Golf became a positive outlet, a venue that allowed my name to appear in the newspaper. Yet golf was also more than an ego stroke. As I had told Padre, the game won't allow for perfection, but it teases you with that rare "pure" shot, a moment of total autonomy, a moment where everything comes together, and you almost believe perfection to be possible. Maybe Padre had believed it. Fortunately, I never had. At age ten, I hit a five-iron that flew 130 yards. I had brought the club back slowly, then down, the contact crisp, the sensation running up the club's shaft, through my hands, up my forearms, shoulders, and into my chest had been stunning. I watched in glory as the ball flew straight, bounced short of the green, and rolled on. Then I had leaped into the air. One hole later, I had put one in the lake. The game lied to you. If golf offered a moment of perfection, it brought you to your knees the very next instant. Maybe Padre had believed the lie.

Martin's bunker shot barely reached the lip of the sand trap. Now, he'd have to chip on. It would be his fifth shot.

Nash handed me my putter. "Try not to let Mr. Petroski down, huh." He smirked and went to chat with Gregg.

.   .   .

The eighteenth hole at the Woodlands is called "Home," a place my five-hour round with Martin Petroski had me longing to go. No. 18 plays 436 yards from my tees. It's a par four with a pond down the left side. I aimed for the last tree on the right and hit driver. The ball started left, then drew back, stopping 121 yards from the green, and drawing applause from my small gallery.

"Killed that one," Nash said. "Was that 'pure'?" He held his palm out as we walked to the white tees, where Martin was preparing to hit.

"No." I slapped him five. "That's my new r7 driver."

I had shot even par on the front and was two under on the back. Seventy was nothing spectacular, a fact not lost on Martin.

"Faxon's team is eleven under par," Martin said. He made a slow practice swing. I had seen him rubbing his back after his tee shot on No. 17. "Gregg tells me you're having the pros to your house for dinner tonight."

"And their families, if the families are here. They're skipping an event to come here and play for nothing. I appreciate the support."

"Are the amateurs invited?" Martin said.

"No."

He stopped mid-swing. "No. What the hell kind of answer is that? That's offensive."

"Martin," I said, "hit your tee shot."

"Well, what about having your teammate come, buddy? I gave Faxon my card. I just bought a miniature golf place. I want him to go in on it with me. He could be the spokesperson."

I knew Faxon designed golf courses. "Miniature golf, huh?"

"Yeah. I defended two pharmaceutical companies this year. Four hundred bucks an hour, and the cases lasted four months each. I needed a tax write-off."

I exhaled and smiled.

Martin swung his driver—also a TaylorMade r7—almost as hard as my 120 miles an hour. But without the tempo and balance. The ball moved like a Greg Maddux slider—starting low and straight, then diving to the right, and dropping fast.

"Ever heard of Moe Norman?" I said.

"No." Martin slammed the driver into his bag. "Who's he?"

"A Canadian golf legend. He was reclusive, but they brought him to a golf equipment testing facility in Massachusetts. His swing produced a rating of zero spin on the ball. Perfect contact. No one could believe it. Zero is basically impossible. He did it over and over."

"What's that got to do with anything?"

"If you brought the club back more to the inside, you wouldn't cut across it and produced that sidespin, which gives the slice."

"Hey, you're ranked ninety-ninth in the world. Christ, I could do that."

"I was trying to help," I said. "Let's just finish this round. Then you go your way and I'll go mine."

"Fine. I don't want to go to your damned house tonight anyway."

. . .

On the eighteenth green, I had a tricky side-hill putt for birdie. I don't usually lack for motivation, but I wanted badly to sink this putt. Sixty-nine was a good score, and it sounded better than seventy. Besides, I wanted to give Martin something to chew on.

Martin had chipped his fourth shot to ten feet and had marked his ball. I reviewed my putt from all angles. I'd hit this putt probably a hundred times previously, so I knew what it would do.

I made two practice strokes and pulled the trigger. The ball caught the high edge of the cup, ran around the rim, and spun off at the bottom, feeding down the slope, and stopping six feet below.

"What were you thinking?" Martin said.

"Dad," Gregg Petroski said, "you're totally obnoxious."

Martin was over his ball, about to putt. He straightened. "Don't you talk to me like that. I'm paying for your schooling."

"So what? I can't take it anymore. Look at how you act. Jack is a pro. You've embarrassed me all day long. Don't you ever wonder why mom left us?"

Martin pointed his finger at Gregg. The finger shook. "Don't you—"

"No. Don't you tell me to stop. I've had it. You've been a jerk for years, but today is the worst. Mom left us because of you, of how you treated her. Think she didn't know about you and your secretary?"

Martin's face fell ashen. "No," he said. "Not here. Not in front of them." He quickly hit his putt. The ball stopped two feet short. He walked to it and hit it into the cup. Then he walked off the green and kept walking.

Nash, Gregg, and I stood in shocked silence for several seconds. Then I went to my putt and hit the six-footer in. A few seconds after the ball fell, I heard applause—a singular, slow, clap. One fan stood to the side of the eighteenth green, as the gallery dispersed.

I tipped my hat to the stocky man, who wore a wide-brimmed straw hat and dark glasses. Then I walked off the green.

It was one of the biggest mistakes of my life.

*n*ash and Gregg Petroski were in the clubhouse having something to eat. I had turned in my team's scorecard and stood outside the pro shop for fifteen minutes, smiling and chatting casually as I scribbled my name on hats, flags from golf holes at nearby courses, and programs from past PGA Tour events. On Tour, I signed only the occasional autograph. In Maine, however, and especially at the Woodlands Club, I felt like Tiger Woods.

Finished signing, I rounded the clubhouse and entered the parking lot. Blue sky was layered amid white puffy clouds, which emitted scattered shafts of sunlight. The temperature was seventy-five. In northern Maine, patches of leaves would already have changed. This was southern Maine, though, and it was a perfect early fall day. My mind was on the upcoming party. Lisa and Darcy were at the Canadian Open. Had the caterer arrived at my house as scheduled? Was everything set for my fourteen guests and families? The amateur turnout for the tournament was small but encouraging. Fifteen people had spent $1,500 to play with a pro. I had to return to the clubhouse and make a brief speech, thanking all participants before the tournament director conducted the award ceremony, after which I'd dash home to check on things. Nash was to catch a ride with Faxon.

Thinking of what I'd say and who I'd thank, I stopped at my Suburban, popped the back door, and changed into sneakers. I put my spikes in the truck, shut the door, and turned to go back to the clubhouse. When I did, something exploded into my stomach.

I doubled over.

"We got to talk, Jack." The voice was Pulchuck's. Either he was lucky or his timing was perfect: No one was in sight. He steered me to the side of the Suburban, out of view from the clubhouse, between two rows of vehicles. He tossed the straw hat and sunglasses aside. The glasses clicked and skittered along the pavement.

"Why leave town?" he said. "Why bother? I mean, I knew you had to be here. *Boston Globe* gave your tournament a lot of press. Or did you think I ain't gonna do what I say?"

I didn't answer. I hadn't vomited, but it had been close. I stood and faced him.

"Where'd you go?" he said.

"What do you want?"

"Sorry about the punch," he said. "Just wanted to get your attention. You have four inches on me, but that don't mean much, now does it?"

"Not when you sucker-punch me. What do you want?"

"Wednesday, a cop came to see me, a guy named Cronjagger. I got the impression that he knew I was interested in the pictures. Any idea how he knew that?" He lunged, attempting to hit me in the stomach again.

I got a forearm down. His fist felt like a sledgehammer. I put out a straight left.

He deflected it and looked at me as if amused. "Want some of this, golf boy?" He threw a straight left, which I moved away from—and directly into his right cross.

It caught me on the right check, and I went down, amid a bright white flash and chimes sounding in my ear. It was only a few seconds later, but I came to—to the sound of Pulchuck's laughter.

He was standing above me. "Jesus Christ," he said, "if I knew you can't take a punch, I'd just slap your wrist. We need to talk about Cronjagger."

I got up and flailed at him, a lunging, over-the-top right that he easily sidestepped. Then he hit me on the back of my shoulder, knocking me down again.

"You're outmatched, golf boy."

I didn't have any legs, but I wasn't staying down. I climbed to my feet and stood, wobbly, looking at him.

"Cronjagger can make my life difficult," he said. "Have you seen the pictures?"

"Yeah."

"And?"

I'd been sucker-punched and beaten. I was pissed, and Pulchuck was offering a speck of daylight. I ran for it. From what, and into what, I didn't know. "I've seen the pictures," I said. "And you're fucked."

"You're full of shit, asshole."

Like a gambler with only a single low pair, who'd already bet everything, I kept the bluff going. "Cronjagger knows about New Brunswick. He knows what Owen Henley was doing up there and who sent him. And who killed him."

Pulchuck's eyes narrowed. He looked at me for a long time, appraisingly. "You're still alive because Cronjagger is on my back. When this blows over, he won't be, and you won't be."

Then he turned on his heel and walked away.

I leaned over and vomited. Then I walked into the clubhouse with a red golf ball on my cheek and knots in my stomach.

25

"*Y*ou throw a good party," Nash said. "That guy on your cheek looks like it hurts."

"It does," I said, and sat across from him at the breakfast table Sunday morning with a throbbing head and a sore stomach.

The day before, after my Pulchuck field trip, I had returned to the clubhouse and told people I slipped in the parking lot, accounting for the red lump on my cheek. Later, at my house, the lobster had been fought with and eaten on the back deck, the deck hosed off, and the house picked up after the last guest left late Saturday night. Cleaning up after sixteen Tour players is not like cleaning up after a fraternity party. It had taken less than two hours. Head pounding, I had gotten to bed around 2 A.M.

Nash had the *Maine Sunday Telegram* spread across the kitchen table, amid a gallon of milk, a box of Cheerios, a plate of pancakes, syrup, butter, a bottle of orange Gatorade, toast, and a bowl of hard-boiled eggs. I needed a top-ten finish just to feed the kid. The *Sunday Telegram's* sports section's front page had an article titled "Woodlands' 'Pros Against Cancer' Event Raises $27,000." Next to the article, was a picture of Phil Mickelson embracing his amateur partner on the eighteenth green. I was envious of his pairing. The article quoted me talking about the "fun had for a good cause" and praising my colleagues, who had given up a potential payday. I had made a similar toast at the beginning and conclusion of the dinner party.

"You're up early," I said.

"I was online looking for shelving. You know those white wire shelves that go in closets? I found a good deal on eBay, and

I'll pay for them." He drank his Gatorade. "Your dad said he'd help me hang them. Can I put some upstairs in my room?"

"Of course. It's your room."

"Cool," he said, nodding. "Thanks. You look like a train wreck. Want coffee?"

"Please."

The kitchen smelled of hazelnut. Sunshine streamed through the window over the sink. Nash got up and poured a cup, spooned in my customary two sugars, and returned. I thanked him. My head was pounding, but only partially because I'd stepped into Jerome Pulchuck's right cross.

"I want to talk to you about Owen Henley," I said, "and the time you spent with him."

Nash was eating Cheerios, scanning the box scores. He set his spoon down slowly, swallowed, and looked up. "What's there to talk about?"

I exhaled. "Claire Henley made some serious accusations, Nash. They concern me."

"What do you mean, 'concern' you?"

"It's been few days," I said. "We've all had time to digest what she said."

He nodded. "And I think she was making it up to hurt me."

"Why would she do that?"

Nash shrugged and dipped his spoon in the bowl for another mouthful of Cheerios but inexplicably spilled the cereal on the table. "Shit," he said and stood and got paper towels to clean the spill.

"Nash, you know my only concern in this whole thing is you."

He stopped wiping the table. "Where are you going with this?" His voice carried the hint of the shut-down street toughness I'd seen occasionally from him. He would go inside and peer out through a hard exterior shell. His eyes now looked distant.

"You lived with Owen Henley until you were five," I said. "Cronjagger, the cop, told us Owen was fired from a teaching job for alleged inappropriate behavior with a male student. I want you to know that if Owen hurt you, I'm here, and I'll figure out a way to help."

The spill was dry, but Nash continued to wipe the area. As with weight lifting, his tongue protruded from his mouth as he concentrated. The silence between us was unlike any we'd ever shared. He scrubbed for another thirty seconds, lost in his activity, wiping the table the way he moved from exercise to exercise in the gym. And I realized why he had 6 percent body fat: Weight lifting was his means of escape. I needed to know from what.

"Nash," I said, "the table is dry."

He looked up at me as if he'd forgotten I was there.

"Did you hear me?" I said.

"Yeah, I heard you insinuate that my father was a pedophile. I ever call your father something like that? You think you're the only one with a good relationship with your father, Jack?" He walked to the sink, opened the cupboard beneath it, and tossed the paper towel away. "Gregg Petroski is coming to get me in twenty minutes. We have practice at one. I'm taking a shower."

Nash walked out of the kitchen, leaving me in weighty silence—alone with my thoughts, my apparently ill-chosen words, and the lump on my cheek, which I had decided to name Jerry after the man who'd given it to me.

onday's forecast called for rain, and for once, the weatherman was right. Raindrops speared the windshield of Perkins's Chevy Malibu like tiny icicles. We were sitting in the parking lot of a strip mall in North Attleboro, Massachusetts, drinking coffee and eating Egg McMuffins.

"Why'd you buy the coffee at McDonald's?" I said. "The stuff always tastes bitter."

"Jesus Christ," Perkins said, shaking his head. "You preppy golfers are so spoiled. Add more sugar, if it's too strong. I'm not dropping ten bucks at Starbucks so you can have fancy-boy coffee."

"You have an expense account."

"Not for this job."

I looked at him.

He nodded. "This really is pro bono, buddy. Peter Barrett says, since the cops are looking into Jerome Pulchuck, I don't need to."

"The guy threatened my family," I said, "and my life."

Perkins looked at me.

"So I'm on my own as far as the Tour is concerned?"

"Sort of."

"What's sort of on your own?"

"I'm sitting here, aren't I?" Then he sighed. "When I told Barrett that Pulchuck jumped you Saturday and threatened you, Barrett called Cronjagger to report it. He said that was all he could do."

"In the past, he's done more."

"I think you pissed Barrett off this time. I told him Pulchuck is the real deal, a legitimate threat. Barrett says the Tour is not for fighting crime. It's for promoting golf."

I took a deep breath, blew it out, and slid deeper in my seat. Rain beaded on my window and rolled slowly down in stringy rivulets.

"Barrett's right," I said. "The Tour is about golf. And I'm as sick of this thing as he is. I want to finish the season strong. I want to just play golf. This Owen Henley thing has gotten way out of hand."

"But it isn't your doing. When Jerome Pulchuck says someone's going down, they usually go down. Pulchuck dragged you into this."

"And, apparently, he dragged *you* into it, too. I didn't know this was pro bono. Thanks. I apologize for the crack about the coffee."

"Shit." He shrugged it off. "I can't let you get killed. Who would I pick on?"

We were parked three rows from the nondescript strip mall, which housed a bookstore-greeting card shop; a pet store; a Chinese restaurant, the door to which advertised an all-you-can-eat $5.99 lunch buffet; and a dry-cleaner. Each business had a large glass door. Only one had metal bars lining the inside of the door and windows, the place on the end—Pulchuck Consulting. Apparently, Jerome Pulchuck didn't consult early. At 8:45 A.M. no one was there.

"You know what I was thinking about on the drive down here?" I said.

"That if you gave me my legitimate handicap, thirty-six, and a decent fucking ball to use—like, I might add, the ones you give Nash—that I could beat you?"

"I was thinking about Darcy, about how you and I went from being five years old, fishing together in a canoe and playing Little League, to this—trying to find a Boston low-life before he finds us."

Perkins drank some coffee. The radio was on, and his favorite, John Coltrane, played.

"Life isn't simple," he said. "Sometimes you've got to stick your neck out there. Most people won't do it. They do what serves them, and everything else comes second. But you're not hitting golf balls today. You're sitting here, looking at an empty office, partially because Pulchuck was right—this will all blow over and Pulchuck's the type who would shoot you in the back two years from now—but you're also sitting here because you told Nash you'd help."

Dyslexics often see the world in black and white. Maybe it had made me one-dimensional. Like I had told Nash, I would never coach. Perkins had known me forever. He understood that. His outlook was similar but stemmed from his no-nonsense disposition and rigid moral code, which led him, on occasion, to take legal matters into his own hands.

"You gave Nash your word," he said, staring at the dark windows of Pulchuck Consulting. "And sometimes that's all there is."

I drank more coffee. It didn't taste so bitter after all.

Shortly before noon, I picked up my cell phone, dialed information, got the number for the Wal-Mart in Milton, and found out Lea Griffin was working.

"Let's go back to where we started," I said.

"Giving up on Pulchuck?"

"No. But this is a waste. And Lea Griffin spent forty hours a week with Owen Henley in the months before he died."

"Cronjagger says she gave a description of two guys who came in looking for Owen on the day he got killed. The description went nowhere, though."

"Cronjagger's a cop," I said. "People don't like talking to cops."

"But someone like Lea Griffin likes talking to you—a rich pro golfer?"

"I'm not that rich," I said.

"Compared to her you are. Hell, compared to me you are."

"I don't like talking about money," I said. "You know that."

"I know. But you get my point. Also, I went to see her, and she also mentioned two others who came to see him. A white guy and a black guy. She said they were 'scary' looking. That's not much to go on. Her descriptive skills are for shit."

"Yeah. But she's all we have right now. And the first time I went to see her, Nash was with me. Let's go to Milton. I'll go see her alone this time."

"It's a forty-five-minute ride."

"We'll be back here by four. I'll even spring for lunch and dinner."

"You know the way to a man's heart," Perkins said.

"Don't tell Silver," I said. "He'll be all over me."

. . .

It continued to rain, so the drive from North Attleboro to Milton took an hour. But I didn't mind the rain. Rain meant I couldn't have been practicing, and I had worked out Sunday—for two hours on heels of Nash's departure—so I didn't feel guilty sitting in a car half the day, eating Dunkin' Donuts and drinking coffee. What I was missing out on wasn't career-related: I could have caught a morning flight to San Antonio for the Texas Valero Open, which began Thursday, and been with Darcy and Lisa. I hadn't seen Darcy in three days and missed her terribly.

It was 1:15 when we arrived at the Milton Wal-Mart. The lunch crowd had departed to resume the workday. Stay-at-home moms, retirees, and the odd vagrant walked the aisles. Perkins entered the small dining section of the store, where the only other customer was an unkempt man with a green garbage bag filled with empty cans at his feet. The man was eating a hotdog, which, according to the sign behind the counter, he'd gotten for fifty cents.

The photo lab was empty. Lea Griffin was the only employee. A boy sat on her lap. He had a small scar on his cheek and wore faded dungarees and a Sponge Bob Square Pants T-shirt. Lea looked tired, and when she saw me, forced a smile.

"Wait here, Leon. Daddy's shopping with Katindah. He'll be right back." She put the boy down and he stood quietly. I remembered she had told me she had a six-year-old son. "Can I help you?" she said to me.

"I was here with Owen Henley's kid a while back."

She nodded. "I'm sorry. I forgot."

"No problem. Long shift?"

She nodded. She wore Old Glory blue jeans—Wal-Mart brand—and a plain white sweatshirt under her blue vest. Her white sneakers looked new. They were made by Spaulding but had an emblem on the side that looked a lot like the Nike swoosh. I thought of her husband—disabled in Iraq, home now, and depressed. She had two young kids, too, a girl Darcy's age and the six-year-old son. Lea Griffin hadn't bought the sneakers because they looked like Nikes. Life didn't afford her those kinds of choices. I knew that when I arrived in San Antonio, I would find two new pairs of $150 Adidas golf shoes and three new shirts with matching slacks hanging in my locker. Something wasn't right about that.

"How are things at home?" I said.

"Some of it's good." She looked at Leon. "Some isn't. I like coming to work, but thanks for asking. What can I do for you?"

"I was wondering if there was anything else you can tell me about Owen. The last time I was here, his son was with me. If you held back so you wouldn't hurt Nash's feelings, you can tell me now. I'm still trying to figure this all out."

"Figure what out? Who killed him?" She spotted a blue and white envelope of film on the counter, read the name, and moved to a large filing cabinet. The drawer whined as it opened. Leon stood quietly, watching her every move. Lea filed the film and turned back to me.

"Maybe," I said. "You ever see him with a short, stocky guy named Jerome?"

Her eyes fell momentarily to the floor. Then she looked up again, her stare now steady.

A customer entered the photo department and moved behind me.

"Can I help you?" Lea said. I thought she relaxed a bit.

The woman gave her name, Lea retrieved her film, and the lady paid.

"How's the golf going?" Lea said, when the woman was gone.

"Fine. Before we were interrupted, I asked if you had seen Owen with a guy."

"You said his name was Jerome Smith, huh?" she said. "No, I never heard of him."

I nodded. I hadn't said Jerome's last name. But Terrell's last name was Smith. Although Smith was a common name.

"The last time we talked, you said Owen spent a ton on film development and was protective of his pictures."

"That's an understatement." She tousled Leon's hair, and he put his arm around her leg. "I think he was like those artists who don't relate to people, so they stand off by themselves and just watch."

"He was a loner?"

"Oh, big time."

She seemed to relax again. These questions let her direct the conversation.

"You ever see Owen Henley with a young black guy with a Fu Manchu. Kid is about twenty, named Terrell. Thinks he's hot shit."

"You just described half our clientele."

I wished Perkins were here. He was better at this than I was. If Lea knew of Terrell Smith, and didn't want to say, my questions had put her on call. Now she was giving nothing away.

"How's Nash doing?" she said. "I like that name, Nash."

I didn't really know. I hadn't talked to Nash since he'd stormed out of the kitchen the day before and didn't know if his reaction validated my questions or had simply been a fit of jealousy over my own father–son relationship, one he would never have.

"As good as can be expected."

"I always feel bad for the kids," she said and tousled Leon's hair again.

"Is that your son?" I said. "You told me he's six, right?"

Dance music I'd never heard before played over the PA system. An advertisement cut in, announcing deals on fall sweatshirts and fleece jackets.

She nodded.

"Anything else you can tell me about Owen Henley?" I said. "The guy wasn't a saint but he was killed brutally."

"Like I told Nash, he didn't miss much by not having Owen around."

"Why do you say that? You're a parent."

"That's why I say it," she said. "And I knew the guy."

"Nothing new?" I said.

She spread her hands.

She hadn't introduced me to her son, so I waved. "I'm Jack," I said.

He smiled and nodded.

"He looks like you," I said.

"Yeah," she said. "Everyone tells me."

"It's Leon, right. And your daughter is Katindah. I really like that name. It's unique."

She looked down again at her son. "Thanks. I love those kids more than life itself. You have a daughter. You understand that?"

"Yeah, I do."

She looked around and made an inclusive gesture with her hand. "You'd do anything for them."

"Tough job," I said, "working here?"

"Bad hours. Sometimes my husband will bring the kids here, so I could spend a little more time with them."

"Not for a while," Leon said.

"No, you haven't been here for a while. Anyway, Ronny can't work anymore and his disability pay ain't good."

"So it all kind of falls to you."

"No 'kind of' about it." A faint smile crossed her face and she shook her head. "You understand a lot for a guy with money."

"Didn't always have it," I said. "And I don't have all that much."

"More than most."

"Probably."

The conversation had swung to money and ended abruptly. As we stood silently, I felt as though we were looking at each other from different ends of life, and that bothered me.

"I'll be by again," I said.

"I'll still be here," she said.

.   .   .

Discarded Subway sandwich wrappers were strewn on the floor of the Malibu. The radio had gone from Perkins's jazz to my choice, retro rock. We were listening to Springsteen's "Born to Run," acoustic version—just the man and his guitar and harmonica—as we passed Gillette Stadium, home of the New England Patriots. We were headed back to North Attleboro, and Perkins commented that the Red Sox had finally taken a page from Patriots owner Bob Kraft's playbook and "started doing things right."

At 4:25 P.M., we arrived back at the strip mall. It was still raining. Now a red Mercedes convertible was parked in front of the Pulchuck Consulting, its black canvas top up. It had a Massachusetts vanity plate that read *Stumpy 1.*

"Sean O'Reilly drove a car with a 'Stumpy' license plate," I said.

"O'Reilly made it sound like only Jerome Pulchuck's salaried guys got cars," Perkins said. "So maybe we've just learned something."

"That Jerome Pulchuck has twelve cars?"

"Cute," he said, and reached in back for a second twelve-inch turkey-on-wheat. "When are you going to San Antonio?"

I shrugged. "All I know is I'm playing the Valero Texas Open this week and it starts Thursday. Usually I'd head out today or tomorrow. But we'll see how this goes."

"Lisa already there?"

"With Darcy." I told him about the PGA Tour day care and our arrangement.

"Jack, the bachelor."

"It sucks," I said.

"When Barrett sent me to Dubai with Tiger, it was a two-week deal. I missed the kid more than anything. You can talk on the phone with your wife. But a lot of stuff with a kid is unspoken."

"At least this weekend is an exception. I had that charity event, and I had to talk with Nash about what Claire said. Had to ask some tough questions."

"How'd that go?"

"Nash walked out."

Perkins's eyes left Pulchuck Consulting for the first time. He was chewing. After he swallowed, he said, "Not a good sign."

There wasn't anything to say. I blew out a long breath and was quiet.

"Show time," Perkins said.

I looked up and saw Jerome Pulchuck, all five-feet-ten, 210 pounds of him, dressed to impress in pleated khaki pants, black loafers with tassels, and a thin white sweater that looked too tight. He walked from the office to his car, which was parked fifty yards away. Perkins had the windshield wipers on "intermittent," but the rain didn't seem to bother Pulchuck. He paused at his car and quickly scanned the lot, stopping to look at our vehicle, which was running. He didn't squint or react.

"Fuck," Perkins said. "Keeping the car running so we can use the wipers makes us stand out."

Pulchuck got a manila folder from the Mercedes and returned to his office.

"Think he made us?" I said.

"I don't know. Watch the windows. If he says something,

174

someone will probably look out." Perkins was wearing a navy blue blazer over a white T-shirt and jeans. He reached inside the blazer, retrieved a 9-mm handgun, checked the load, and set the gun on the seat between us.

"Is that loaded?"

"Yeah, Jack. Pointing your finger at them doesn't work real well."

"Sorry. Not used to sitting in cars with loaded weapons."

He shrugged. "You and I spent half our childhood in the woods behind my house shooting twenty-two pistols. Christ, you're actually not a bad shot." He turned back toward the office. "Jerome's loafers are cute. You got beat up by a guy who wears tassels?"

"I got sucker-punched."

"Which is why I have the gun out and ready."

I sipped some coffee from a Styrofoam Dunkin' Donuts cup. We had filled up and gotten donuts and coffee for the trip home. Perkins checked rearview and side mirrors.

"I want to pay your daily fee and expenses," I said.

He shook his head.

"No?"

He shook his head again and sat staring straight at Pulchuck's office. "This is for Nash. I want to get the killer. It's on me."

A plain white Explorer pulled around from the back of the strip mall and stopped in front of the Pulchuck's office. The driver was a young guy with a shaved head. He left the Explorer running and went inside. Jerome Pulchuck walked out of the office. Sean O'Reilly was with him.

"I'll be damned," I said.

Both men got in the Explorer, which pulled out of the lot and turned left, with O'Reilly driving. Perkins seemed relaxed as he gave them a head start.

"Stop adjusting the radio," I said. "Let's go."

"Jack, Pulchuck is arrogant enough to have a vanity plate. Tailing them won't be hard."

27

$\mathcal{P}$erkins was right. Tailing Jerome Pulchuck and Sean O'Reilly wasn't hard, but it was time-consuming—seven hours, in fact. North on I-95, past Portland, beyond Augusta, and three hours farther than Bangor, where most people, Mainers included, believe the world ends. It's easy to see how the misconception occurs. Aroostook County, Maine, has only 74,000 people but consists of a land mass the size of Connecticut and Rhode Island combined.

All of this made the tail job more complicated after Bangor, because Pulchuck's white SUV and our Chevy Malibu were the only cars on I-95 North. As far as we knew, O'Reilly was still driving, even after a stop to refuel. Perkins fell a mile behind him and occasionally accelerated to regain sight of the Explorer. Finally, we arrived on Main Street in Presque Isle just before 11 P.M. A Red Sox–Yankees game had ended, and we were listening to the post-game show. The ballgame had been the finale to a long rainy day, so the Yankees, of course, had won.

"We've gone from New Hampshire, all over Massachusetts, to the fucking Canadian border," Perkins said.

"New Hampshire?" I said. "My day began in the Portland area at five this morning."

"They got hotels up here?"

"No," I said. "Igloos. What kind of question is that?"

"I haven't seen anything but trees for three hours. And you have a camp up here." He shrugged. "I figured you'd know."

"Yes," I said, "hotels exist in Aroostook County."

"Well, let's hope these assholes find one. And fast."

They didn't, and downtown Presque Isle, at 11 P.M. on a weeknight, offered little traffic, which made staying incognito difficult. The Explorer made a right onto State Street. As it turned, I saw Pulchuck slumped in the passenger's seat, sound asleep.

"I followed O'Reilly around Milton to find out what he did and where his office was," Perkins said. "With Pulchuck asleep, this becomes a hell of a lot easier. O'Reilly couldn't spot an elephant following him. But we'll still play it safe." Perkins pulled to the curb near the Northeastland Hotel and let the Explorer get ahead of us.

"I'm just surprised he's been sober for eight hours. Don't lose them. We've spent half a day to get this far."

"Trust me." Perkins pulled back onto Main Street and turned onto State. Behind the Explorer, we drove out State Street, onto U.S.-1A, and headed northeast. We drove for another hour.

"Christ," I said, "my camp is in Garrett."

"That the next town?"

"Yeah."

The radio was off now. There was a border crossing in Garrett that led to Mitchell, New Brunswick. Was Pulchuck crossing the border? It was nearly midnight. Crossing the border in Garrett, Maine, is low-key compared to crossing the border in a place like El Paso, Texas. Still, trying to cross in the middle of the night— with Massachusetts plates, no less—would likely send up red flags. What was Pulchuck's plan? They had the SUV for a reason. Pulchuck wasn't a truck type. If he was going to ride seven hours, it would be in a luxury automobile. So what, exactly, were he and O'Reilly up to? What was in the Explorer? Or were they bringing something back? I thought of Perkins's colleague, Deirdre. Was Pulchuck here to get a load of infamous B.C. Budd? Marijuana had been found in Owen Henley's apartment.

The white Explorer moved through the one-light town of Garrett, over the Crystal View River, and turned right. I had been here before. We were on River's Edge Road, which led to the Garrett Golf Club. My fishing cabin was a par five from GGC, a quarter mile down a dirt road, along the Crystal View River.

River's Edge Road weaved along the Crystal View River, and O'Reilly drove slowly. We climbed a hill. Ahead and to the right lay two potato fields separated by a potato house. The potato house looked as if it had been dropped from the sky and had sunk until earth reached nearly to its metal roof. Farmers built the storage facilities deep in the ground to keep the potatoes temperate. Pulchuck's Explorer was a quarter-mile ahead of us when it turned right, just before the first potato field, and went down a dirt road. Moments later, we drove past the road.

"You know where we are?" I said.

"East bumfuck?" Perkins said.

"My cabin is three miles ahead, down a dirt road, on the right."

"Well, shit," Perkins said, "you and Pulchuck are neighbors. Let's invite him over to play cards."

Perkins pulled to the side, and we both got out. In the trunk, he had a Winchester twelve-gauge pump-action shotgun. He put several rounds in the chamber. Then he handed me the 9-mm handgun he had set on the front seat in North Attleboro. It was late September. Overhead the sky was layered with white streaks of cloud cover, which made the moon, beyond, look hazy. I'd been awake nearly twenty hours, and the evening's events and our surroundings now had a surreal quality. I stood looking at the handgun like a kid dared to hold a snake. Moonlight reflected off the stainless-steel barrel. The grip was black and felt tacky. The gun felt heavy in my hand.

"You got pockets?" Perkins said, rummaging through a large black duffle bag in the trunk.

"Why?"

"Here." Without looking up, he handed me a clip. "Ten-round clip, plus one in the chamber. It's a slide-action. When was the last time you fired a handgun?"

"Came up here to bird hunt last fall," I said. "My father's got a nine-millimeter. We shot some cans."

"Then you know what you're doing. So don't look at it like you're afraid of the goddamned thing. Christ, we hunted together every fall since we were nine. Once you put one in the chamber, it's ready. Just squeeze the trigger until whatever you're aiming at falls." He paused and looked at me. "And I know you've used one in a situation like this before."

I had. Years earlier, I'd been forced to defend myself in a life-or-death situation.

"I've got a kid now," I said.

Perkins stopped pawing through the bag and looked up. "Changes everything, doesn't it?"

"Absolutely."

"So load the damned gun and jack a round into the chamber."

"That wasn't exactly what I meant," I said.

Perkins ignored me. He was in business mode. He stuck a flashlight in his belt, pumped a shell into the twelve-gauge's chamber, and took inventory of our surroundings.

Comprehending my meaning or not, Perkins had been right. Fatherhood did change everything. Often, it made things more complex, as with Lisa's desire to return to TV journalism. Now, however, fatherhood simplified things: Pulchuck said he'd wait this out, and then kill me. He'd have ample time and opportunity. Worse, his threat had spilled over onto Lisa and Darcy at the Deutsche Bank Championship, where Pulchuck made it clear that family was neither beyond his reach nor outside his moral boundaries.

"You ready?" Perkins said.

"Can't look over my shoulder forever," I said. "And my wife travels with our baby, sometimes alone."

"And your occupation makes you a standing target, in an open area, with thousands of people there to cause havoc in the aftermath of a gunshot while someone simply slips off into nearby woods."

"You rehearse that?"

"Let's just say I've discussed the fact that PGA Tour Security is an oxymoron with Peter Barrett."

Perkins closed the trunk quietly, and we moved across a ditch, into a potato field. The potatoes had sprouted blossoms already. They would be harvested and hauled off well before Thanksgiving. Under the moonlight, the field was long and wide. If Jerome Pulchuck saw us, there would be nowhere to go. Finally, we reached the edge of the woods. Through a thick layer of pines, I saw lights. About a hundred yards below us, Pulchuck's cabin sat at the edge of the Crystal View River.

We continued down the embankment and swung wide of the cabin, staying in the woods outside the perimeter of the porch light. From about twenty yards, I saw a single light glowing in a corner inside the cabin. Neither Pulchuck nor O'Reilly was in view, and I presumed both asleep. I tapped Perkins's shoulder as I would if we were hunting and I'd seen something move. He froze. I reached around him, took the flashlight from his belt, and motioned him to stay.

"No way," he whispered. "I'll check out the Explorer."

"Then we both go," I said.

The Explorer was parked nose-in and at an angle. We kept its body between ourselves and the camp. I had the light; Perkins had the shotgun raised. First, I tried to look inside the truck without the light. That was no use. I set the 9-mm on the ground and pressed the flashlight's bulb against my torso and flicked it on. Only a tiny ring of light glowed against my chest. I moved to the passenger's-side window and shined the light through. A map lay on the floor, a steel thermos beside it. Nothing more. A red light pulsated on the dashboard. The SUV had an alarm. There was no way I was trying the back door. I clicked off the light, retrieved my gun, and we retreated back to tree cover.

. . .

We arrived at my camp—which, as irony would have it, was no more than a forty-five-minute canoe paddle from Pulchuck's outpost—before 1 A.M. There was no use sleeping in the woods. We knew where Pulchuck and O'Reilly were, and it was highly unlikely they'd go anywhere in the middle of the night. For one thing, there was nothing to do in Garrett at night. Additionally, they wouldn't try the border at night. Traffic would be busiest there in the morning with commuters. Perkins called his office and left a message telling Deirdre (only) where he was. I cracked the bedroom window, allowing the cool night air in, and fell asleep before my head hit the pillow.

We woke before 5 A.M., checked on Pulchuck's white Explorer, and went to downtown Garrett for breakfast—which was a plastic grocery bag of orange juice, donuts, sandwiches, chips, and milk to go with four large coffees—at the only twenty-four-hour convenience store in town. We were back on the hill above Pulchuck's camp before 5:15 A.M. There was no movement below.

"You've been inviting me up here for years," Perkins said.

"Look at the fun you've been missing."

"Yeah. Not even October yet, and I'm freezing my ass off."

We both wore jeans, baseball caps, and sunglasses. I had on a gray T-shirt beneath a navy-blue sweatshirt that had smudges of white paint from when I'd painted the cabin's small front porch the summer before. I wore an old Maxfli cap I'd left at camp the summer before. Perkins looked like a native in my uncle's green and yellow John Deere cap. Of course, his ever-present scowl, coupled with his wraparound sunglasses, skewed the effect. Perkins had brought only a nylon windbreaker but had said it made too much noise, so he'd taken one of my uncle's sweatshirts that had been left at the camp. Along with the sweatshirt, Perkins had also grabbed a box of twelve-gauge birdshot from my uncle's dresser.

"You leave the guns and ammo right in the camp?" he said, leaning against a tree, eating a donut.

I was sitting on the ground, against the base of the same tree. Perkins had the shotgun folded across his forearms, as if waiting for a deer to cross. I sipped some coffee. There was no way the convenience store drew a coffee crowd. "We leave a lot of stuff there," I said. "Garrett isn't exactly a high-crime zone."

"If you think that, then you don't know your neighbors very well."

"That camp doesn't belong to Pulchuck," I said.

"You know that?"

"Our camp has been in the family for years. I called my father while you were in the store. He said he met an old lady living there last summer."

"Where is she now? You get a name?"

I shook my head.

We were about a hundred yards away, but the forest was still. In the silence, I heard several loud clicks and a chain release. Then the front door of the cabin opened inward, and the screen door screeched as it was pushed out. Jerome Pulchuck stepped onto the porch, wearing only white briefs. In a suit, his short squat physique was intimidating. It wasn't now. His 210 pounds were not chiseled. Worse, about 90 percent of his torso was covered with hair.

"Good God," Perkins whispered. "Tassels yesterday. His gut hanging over his dick today. I'm going to puke."

Pulchuck yawned and patted his stomach.

"Usually," I said, "I get up to watch fish jump or try to catch a glimpse of deer coming down to the river."

"Come out here, jackass," Pulchuck called over his shoulder. He breathed deeply and stretched his hands over his head. "Air is clean up here, ain't it? Ever smelt air this clean before?"

Sean O'Reilly came out of the cabin and stood beside his employer. O'Reilly looked worse than usual. His khaki shorts and white golf shirt looked as though he'd slept in them. He wore what I had come to consider his trademark, navy blue dress socks, pulled to nearly his knees, and white tennis shoes.

Pulchuck nudged him in the ribs. "Ever smelt anything like this air?"

"We got good air in Milton."

"Milton? You think that's good air? You wouldn't know good air if it bit you in the ass."

"There any of that scotch left?"

"It ain't even six in the morning. You drank half the goddamned fifth before you went to bed. You don't need no more scotch. We're busy today."

"Throat's dry," O'Reilly said, "that's all. I'm kind of hungry, too. I was thinking maybe you could buy us some breakfast, seeing as I drove up."

Pulchuck cuffed O'Reilly on the back of the head, a hard enough slap to make the sixty-year-old man stumble forward.

"And who's paying for the gas, asshole? I'm paying you for your fucking time, too. The first fuck who came up here didn't do so well. Just worry about doing better."

I looked at Perkins. He looked back with raised brows.

"What do you think?" I whispered.

"Let's watch this play out. Then I'll go see Cronjagger."

I nodded. Pulchuck stretched again. Perkins turned away

from the sight, cursing under his breath. Finally, Pulchuck returned to the camp; O'Reilly followed like an obedient dog.

Perkins sat beside me, reached into the bag, and retrieved another plain donut. He sipped some coffee. I stood up and shook out my legs. The 9-mm had been beside me on the ground. When I stood, I tucked it into my belt.

. . .

At 8:55 A.M. Pulchuck and O'Reilly emerged from the camp fully dressed. Pulchuck now wore a white golf shirt and fawn-colored slacks. Again, he wore the tasseled loafers. "Fairy," Perkins mumbled. O'Reilly was right behind Pulchuck, and both men carried coffee travel mugs. O'Reilly wore the outfit he'd slept in.

The wooded area was thirty yards wide and ran from the river to the road. Our car was a good quarter-mile away, parked near someone's driveway. Pulchuck went to the Explorer and started it up; O'Reilly climbed in the passenger's side. When they started up the long dirt drive, Perkins and I hit the ground. Through the trees, we watched as they turned right at the end of the driveway.

"Border is to the right," I said.

We moved quickly toward the road and sprinted to our car.

28

"This guy drove eight hours to play golf?" Perkins said.

We were at the Garrett Golf Club. The clubhouse is a large two-story building, the north side of which is nearly all glass, and inside which is the golf shop, dining room, and locker rooms. Pulchuck's white Explorer was parked near the end of the third (and last) row. The lot was full, and Perkins and I were forced to park curbside along the street. Cars and pickups with both U.S. and Canadian license plates had spilled over from the parking lot and parked along the road. A large sign announced SPUD OPEN — COURSE CLOSED 7 TO 9 A.M. It was 9:10.

The Garrett Golf Club straddled the U.S.–Canada border. Americans and Canadians parked facing one another, separated by a four-foot strip of tar and gravel. The parking lot was mobbed. Many people, mostly elderly men, walked from the clubhouse to cars. Some, like us, had arrived after all the participants had begun. Perkins and I, both wearing dark glasses, stepped over the barrier, and into Canada.

Beyond the clubhouse, past a group of guys standing around talking, Pulchuck stood on the first tee waiting to hit with O'Reilly and two other golfers. Hat pulled low and wraparound shades firmly in place, Perkins went in the golf shop to rent clubs and a cart. I knew the club's pro and didn't want to be recognized. But waiting outside wasn't much better—Pulchuck and O'Reilly stood maybe thirty yards away. I hoped to simply blend in with the masses.

The Garrett Golf Club is not a hotbed of golf pretension. It's a blue-jeans-and-T-shirt golf course. This day, Aroostook County humility served Perkins and me well because in jeans, sneakers, and oversized sweatshirts—which hid the 9-mm Perkins had tucked in his belt—neither of us had dressed for golf, yet we managed to fit in. As I waited for Perkins, I pulled my hat down to my dark glasses and tried to be a weekend hacker distracted by the foliage as I stood among the high roofs and windshields of the rental carts clustered near the golf shop door. I nodded to two guys who were walking toward their carts. Jack Austin, one of the boys.

Pulchuck and O'Reilly shook hands with two other guys on the first tee. O'Reilly was the only man on the tee box without a club, although there were four large staff bags on two carts. Apparently, he hadn't driven seven hours north to play golf. When Pulchuck took a practice swing, I hoped he hadn't either.

The two guys with them wore blue jeans, golf shoes, and red poor-boy hats that read "Roots Canada." Both men were dark-skinned and looked Native American. I knew there was a Canadian reservation nearby. The taller man had a ponytail that hung to his mid-back. He wore a flannel shirt unbuttoned. His shirt-tails flapped as he swung the club awkwardly. The second guy was shorter with neatly trimmed hair and a hawk-like nose, pronounced and hooked. He wore a windbreaker that had the Deutsche Bank Championship logo. I wondered if he'd seen my fairway exchange with Pulchuck live.

Perkins came to the golf shop door.

I held up my hand for him to wait. Crowd or not, Perkins was hard to miss, and we were next on the tee. We had to let them get ahead of us. The real trick would be keeping them far enough away so neither Perkins nor I was recognized, while trying to get close enough to see why Pulchuck and O'Reilly had driven nearly half a day.

.   .   .

"Those two guys are Canadian," Perkins said, as we took warm-up swings on the first tee.

"You know that?" I said.

Pulchuck's group had just hit to the first green. Two large TaylorMade staff bags were on the back of Pulchuck's cart. O'Reilly still wasn't playing. He sat in the cart, looking at the scenery, like a guy from downtown Chicago who'd just stepped onto the set of *The Sound of Music*. It had taken Pulchuck and his poor-boy-hat-wearing counterparts three shots each to reach the green. Perkins and I were stalling to keep our distance. A foursome in carts sat waiting behind us.

"I tossed the kid in the golf shop a softball," Perkins said. "'Looks like a high roller on the tee.' Kid looks out the window at Pulchuck and sort of rolls his eyes. 'If those other guys are playing for high stakes,' he says, 'they'd better be getting strokes. They come across the border once a month or so and lose at least ten balls. I mentioned lessons, but they're not interested.'"

"You're one to talk," I said. "I've offered you lessons for years."

"Too much pride to take lessons from you."

"I doubt they come over here every month," I said, "just to lose golf balls."

"Sounds reasonable to a guy who plays like me," Perkins said.

The Garrett Golf Club is known for its water hazards. Water is piped in from the nearby Crystal View River, and twenty-one water hazards exist among the eighteen holes. The opening tee shot requires you to hit over a large pond—a 200-yard carry— and the hole stretches 385 yards with out-of-bounds to the left. Although there were no Customs offices, the golf course was technically in Canada. The border runs parallel to the out-of-bounds stakes on the first hole. Rumor has it, the clubhouse had been strategically placed in Canada during Prohibition to make life back then a little more tolerable.

Perkins had purchased eight used balls and rented two sets of Callaway clubs. He slashed, and his ball started forty yards left and seemed headed O.B., before bending right and barely clearing the pond.

I shook my head.

"Calculated fade," he said.

"More like a hard slice."

I hit a three-iron over the water to the center of the fairway, leaving a five-iron to the green.

"We're not going to stay four hundred yards away from them the whole time," Perkins said. "We have to get closer, take some chances, if we're going to learn anything."

"This place is busy as hell," I said. "People are hitting into groups and playing near one another. There might be other ways to do that."

As we drove to our balls, I saw Pulchuck motion O'Reilly to get out of the cart near the green and hold the flagstick. A ball flew just over the top of Pulchuck's cart, and two guys holding cans of beers drove a cart next to Pulchuck's cart. One guy got out, took two abbreviated practice swings, and slashed his ball down the fairway—directly at us, before it cut back to the eighteenth fairway.

"Place is a fucking zoo," Perkins said.

We parked near our tee shots and waited for the green to clear. Pulchuck was putting from twenty paces below the cup.

He lined the putt up from every conceivable angle—at one point lying on his stomach on the green—then took about seventy-five practice strokes. And missed. Ponytail went next; he two-putted. Hooknose was closer and made his putt. When he whooped and hollered, Pulchuck spoke loudly, telling him to shut up. Hooknose slid his putter into the red and white Wilson staff bag on his cart.

"And you think my golf etiquette is bad," Perkins said.

I hit a lay-up with a six-iron, ten yards short of the green.

When Perkins hit his second shot, I was once again reminded that you never know what will happen in this game. Miraculously, he hit the first green—from 175 yards away and using a four-iron, no less. I had better odds of getting a hit off Curt Shilling than Perkins did of reaching that green with a four-iron. But there it was—his used golf ball sitting four feet from the pin.

"I'm looking at the second birdie of my life." Perkins's grin grew to a broad smile. "Oh, and I forgot to tell you this hole is for a hundred bucks. Good luck with your chip."

It reminded me of who he was and what he did: He acted as if he was truly unaware that the four men in front of us might have been responsible for Owen Henley's violent death.

Perkins had yet to put the four-iron back in the bag. He looked at the Callaway iron. "Might have to get me some of these."

We drove to the side of the green and parked. Thirty yards away, Pulchuck, the two Canadians, and O'Reilly stood on the second tee. Pulchuck was washing his ball and never looked up.

Perkins got his putter from the back of the cart and moved to the green. I walked to my ball. It was a typical fall morning in Aroostook County—mid-fifties, sun bright overhead, with low, puffy clouds. The foliage was two weeks from peak, but a smattering of oranges and reds danced on distant hills. I had to face the second tee to hit my bump-and-run and did so quickly, without looking up to check my alignment. The ball raced ten feet beyond and right of the cup.

"Shit brains," Pulchuck said and, momentarily, I thought he was mocking me. "Wipe my driver off, like I told you. See what I have to put up with? Can't find anyone in Boston with two brain cells to rub together."

I heard the Canadians laugh. A ball from an adjoining fairway rolled to within ten feet of the second tee box. Two men in Nike caps, creased khaki pants, and leather golf shoes drove up. One man set his Styrofoam coffee cup down, politely excused himself, then hit his ball back to the fairway.

"This course is never this busy," Pulchuck said. "The first guys were drunk—at nine A.M.—now these guys just can't play. I can't concentrate with people hitting into us."

"I've always 1 hated this course," Hooknose said. "There's water everywhere."

"I'm just saying it's too busy today," Pulchuck said. "Don't blame the course if you can't hit it straight. But this is the place. The other border course has cameras and sensors in the parking lot."

"That reminds me," Hooknose said. "You see the pictures yet?"

Head down, I proceeded to my ball. I heard someone hit a tee shot and curse.

"Marty," Pulchuck said, "Marty, slow your swing down. Christ, you think you're Tiger Woods? I saw one picture. Cops called me in, showed me one of me and Owen. If that's all they got, they got shit."

"Shouldn't have let that shit-bird bring his camera." Hooknosed Marty slid his driver into his red and white Wilson bag on his cart.

"Don't worry, Marty. My lawyer says if the cops had more pictures, they'd have done more."

"Maybe."

"Hey," Pulchuck said, getting agitated, "if I say the cops don't have shit, they don't have shit. Besides, unless they come here, it's all on Terrell Smith."

I putted my ball toward the hole. It ran two feet by. I walked to it slowly. Perkins crouched behind his four-footer. He made four or five practice strokes and hit the putt. Lo and behold, it fell, for birdie. He looked at me and winked. I only shook my head and glanced over at the second tee. Jerome had his back to us, gesturing with his hands, and speaking quietly to Marty.

Ponytail hit and swore. He tossed his club into a blue and yellow Dunlop bag on the back of his cart. Then they climbed into carts and drove to their balls.

. . .

We had reached a wooded stretch of holes. Numbers four through eight had been carved among dense forest. The Pulchuck foursome had reached the fifth tee. High above them, Perkins and I stood on the elevated tee at the par-three fourth, which called for a nine-iron over water to an island green. I wasn't thinking swing thoughts. I could see Pulchuck, O'Reilly, Marty, and Ponytail preparing to tee off to my right. But I knew that once they hit, they'd be gone from view for the next twenty minutes, maybe longer judging from Pulchuck's tee shot—which, according to the *thunk* and *clap* of a his ball striking trees, certainly had not benefitted from the narrow fairway.

"After they hit, you play this hole," I said to Perkins. "I'm going to walk through the woods a while, following them up to the green, so we don't lose sight of them."

"I'm the guy carrying the gun. And I'm the private cop, Jack."

"But I know the golf course," I said. Perkins continued to protest, but I finally convinced him.

And I knew the fifth hole to be deceiving. The scorecard listed No. 5 as a dogleg par-five, only 465 yards. Unless you can fade a driver, which Pulchuck had not done successfully, the smart play is to hit over the fifty-yard pond toward the target hanging from a tree 220 yards from the tee box. Next, play to the green or lay up with a wood or long-iron. The dogleg right is severe, and both sides of the fairway are tree-lined. There is no bailout area for Perkins's slice—water in front, woods to both sides.

I had once played the fifth hole with three amateurs and had been the only one not to lose a ball off the tee. Two of the three amateurs had lost two balls that day before finally putting their drivers away. Pulchuck's group seemed to have a similar course-management philosophy. I was in the woods between the fourth tee and the fifth fairway. Fifty yards below, Pulchuck had apparently pull-hooked his tee shot and was now searching, left of the tee. Marty must have sliced because he took an iron from the bag on his cart and started into the woods toward me.

I moved behind a tree and watched Marty look at the base of the hill. The terrain there was nearly hard-panned from golfer after golfer combing the area. Marty's observation skills put me at ease—he walked past his ball twice before swearing and giving up.

"I can play it." Pulchuck's holler echoed from across the fairway.

I heard him thrash. No ball emerged.

I heard another swing—it sounded like a machete cutting thickets. Still no ball. "Fuck" was the only other sound, and finally, Pulchuck walked to the fairway. "I'll take a drop. So I'm hitting three."

"Three?" Ponytail said. "You're hitting five. You lay four when you picked up."

"I never touched the ball on those swings."

Ponytail got out of his cart, shaking his head. "The fucking rule is anytime you swing, you count a stroke."

"If that's right," Pulchuck said, "then why don't they count practice swings, asshole?"

It was almost hard to remember these people were dangerous. From a golf perspective, it was like watching a *Three Stooges* rerun. Yet Pulchcuk had stumped Ponytail, who apparently knew nothing of grounding your club or addressing the ball.

"Yeah." Pulchuck was nodding, gaining confidence in his theory. "See, it don't count unless you hit it. Fucking Indians."

"What was that?" Ponytail said.

"Nothing."

"What did you say?" Ponytail stepped closer. "You hear that, Marty?"

Marty had taken a ball from his Wilson bag, dropped it, and had stopped in mid-practice swing. "He just make an Indian crack?"

"Yeah," Ponytail said.

I was still behind a large white birch tree. Maybe they'd shoot each other, and my problems would be solved.

"Just kidding around, you guys."

"We don't like those kind of jokes, Jerome," Ponytail said.

"Hey," Pulchuck said, "don't give me your fucking tough-guy attitude. You don't scare me. You want to know what I can do, ask O'Reilly."

"Fuck O'Reilly," Marty said, "and fuck you. Let's get this over with. Should've just sent the delivery boy again. We don't like dealing with you directly."

"Hey, same here. I thought I could train the last guy, so I rode up here, showed him how things work. Fucking guy turns out to be a freak. Starts telling me shit I don't want to hear. He's out, so I'm training a new guy." He motioned to O'Reilly.

Marty shook his head and hit an iron shot. His ball cut the corner of the dogleg and landed near the white 150-yard marker. Pulchuck took his illegal drop and hit his so-called third shot into the woods with a three-wood.

"What did you hit it there for?" O'Reilly said.

"Shut the fuck up," Pulchuck said, and they all drove down the fairway to Ponytail's ball, which, apparently, had been the lone straight tee shot.

The carts stopped at the landing area, near the target hanging high on the tree.

Behind me, Perkins was on the green. His ball was ten feet from the hole, and he was spending a lot of time lining up his putt. He had birdied the par-five third hole and was one over so far, a career day.

I moved quickly down the hill to where Marty had searched unsuccessfully for his ball, staying thirty feet from the edge of the fairway. The landing area was at the base of a slope, 220 yards from the tee, and just in front of the target at which players on the tee box aim—a large white circle with a red bull's-eye in the center.

Then something clicked for me.

29

I followed the Pulchuck foursome to the sixth tee and tried to add everything up. The photo of Owen Henley and Jerome Pulchuck I'd seen in Cronjagger's office—the one of the two men standing beneath the red bull's-eye dot—had been taken on the fifth hole at the Garrett Golf Club. Was that why Marty and Ponytail were interested in Cronjagger's photos? But why should they care? The photo of Owen and Pulchuck hadn't allowed Cronjagger to pin anything on Pulchuck. And Marty and company didn't seem the types who sweat small stuff.

Pulchuck said "everything" would fall to Terrell Smith anyway. That explained Terrell's willingness to drive to find Nash in Readfield, Maine. So Terrell had a lot at stake. Why had he asked about Wal-Mart? What could be going on here, on the Canadian border that could have severe consequences for Terrell Smith in Boston?

With Perkins on the fifth green, I had to return. But the fifth green was only fifty yards from the sixth tee, which was too close for comfort. I high-stepped, as if deer hunting, to the fairway's edge and walked to the fifth green—with my hand pulling up my zipper. No one on the sixth tee was watching. I went casually to the cart, grabbed my putter, and went to the green. Perkins had been crouched behind his ball, reading the putt.

When he straightened, there was a second ball behind him.

"Clever," I whispered and addressed the second ball as if I'd hit it there. I had my hat pulled low, and my dark glasses were still on. I glanced up and saw Jerome Pulchuck looking toward us. O'Reilly went to Pulchuck and said something.

I had met Pulchuck once in a bar, and then he had met me at

the Woodlands Club. Both times I had been dressed for golf. Perkins had met him once at Nash's apartment wearing professional attire—jeans and a blazer. Now we both wore fall farm clothes. And the dark glasses and caps covered much of our faces.

I putted the ball Perkins had dropped. It ran toward the hole then darted, missing on the low side.

The Pulchuck group hit their tee shots and moved on.

.   .   .

The sixth hole was wide open, so Perkins, sitting in the cart, and I watched team Pulchuck from the tee. I finished telling him what I'd overheard and about Cronjagger's photo.

"So Owen was replaced by O'Reilly," Perkins said, "because Owen was a 'freak'?"

"He made a few trips up here six months before his death. I think he was fired."

"Why would Jerome wait six months to kill him?"

"I don't know," I said. "But don't forget, Jerome told me he'd wait for me."

"There's that," Perkins said, and shook his head. "I've got a good round going. I'm three over par."

"You're supposed to be worrying about protecting me."

"Protecting you?" Perkins grinned. "I'm the one with the good score."

.   .   .

We were in the middle of the eighteenth fairway, watching Pulchuck and his Canadian associates finish their rounds. It was 1:45 now, and the golf shop kid's estimation was off: Ponytail and Marty had lost well over a dozen balls. Pulchuck had not broken a hundred. And nothing noticeable had taken place. Could they have actually driven seven hours to play golf?

"This is the first time I've seen you miss a meal and not complain," I said.

"You know what I shoot if I par this?"

"Eighty-eight. Got to be your all-time low."

"You weren't going to mention it?"

"Nope."

He looked at me, head titled. "You're not going to break my balls? You're going to let me try to shoot my score?"

"Correct."

Two hundred yards ahead, Pulchuck made a putt and pumped his fist. Marty rubbed his head. I heard Ponytail tell Pulchuck to shut up. Either the Canadians had forgotten Pulchuck's "Indian" comment, or they were letting it ride. Maybe the business arrangement was so large they had to overlook the comment. But nothing at all had occurred. Maybe they were gambling. I thought about Terrell Smith wanting to know about Wal-Mart. Two guys had gone to see Owen the day he died. Two others—a black guy and a white guy—had stopped by Wal-Mart several times to see Owen, according to Lea. Pulchuck was white; Terrell Smith was black.

Perkins hit when they cleared the green. I was next to play and shot for the greenside trap.

"I'm giving you your two-putt," I said. "We need to follow them."

"I know that, and it sucks. I'd have made that for birdie."

"You're thirty feet away," I said. "Take your two-putt and run like hell."

I drove the cart to the green. Near the clubhouse, Pulchuck parked his cart and sat looking at us again. Had Pulchuck made us? Perkins took the cue and went to his ball. The gimme two-putt was off now. He crouched behind the ball and lined the putt up. I went to the sand trap, where my ball lay, and hit a crisp bunker shot to within three feet. I cleaned up my par putt and waited for Perkins. Pulchuck was still watching. Marty and Ponytail came out of the golf shop, each carrying a box of balls. Pulchuck got off his cart, and they prepared to get their clubs.

I motioned to Perkins, who quickly slapped his ball toward the hole. I watched in disbelief as the used ball disappeared for a birdie, eighty-seven.

" 'Take my two-putt and run,'?" Perkins said as we got into

the cart. "Take your two-putt and shove it up your ass, Mr. PGA Tour."

"Jesus Christ," I said.

We got back on the cart, and I pulled away from the green, but stopped well short of the clubhouse.

Ahead of us, Pulchuck, O'Reilly, Ponytail, and Marty shook hands. They had parked their respective carts near the clubhouse and were maybe forty paces from us. Their parting gestures complete, all four turned their backs to us. O'Reilly reached to take his untouched TaylorMade clubs off the cart, but Pulchuck nudged him, and O'Reilly did a quick *Oh, yeah* gesture. Instead, Ponytail and Marty took the two TaylorMade staff bags off Pulchuck's cart and walked to their red Pontiac Grand Am, popped the truck, loaded the bags, and drove off. O'Reilly took the yellow and blue Dunlop bag and Pulchuck grabbed the red and white Wilson bag Marty had used. They walked to the far end of the third row of the parking lot, where the Explorer was parked, and loaded the bags.

Perkins and I pulled our cart to the clubhouse, left the rental clubs on the cart, and began walking across the parking lot to the Malibu.

But then Pulchuck and O'Reilly did the unexpected: Pulchuck set the alarm, and they walked back toward the clubhouse.

Perkins and I were caught between the clubhouse and Pulchuck.

Twenty paces away, O'Reilly stopped. He leaned close to Pulchuck and said something. Pulchuck looked around. Tournament over, the parking lot had thinned out. Through the clubhouse window, I saw three old men eating a late lunch. Pulchuck glanced at them, then at me. In the distance, the Grand Am had pulled to the side. Ponytail was leaning out the passenger-side window, watching.

"Yeah," O'Reilly said. "I told you it was him."

Pulchuck said nothing. He stood looking at me, a penetrating stare.

"I've got to hand it to you," Pulchuck finally said. "You're a pretty bad golfer when you want to be. Threw me off. But I've had enough of you." He patted his windbreaker pocket. "This ends, up here. You're coming with us."

"I don't think so," Perkins said.

"You sold me out," I said to O'Reilly. "My uncle, my family dinner. And now you sell me out."

O'Reilly looked like he was going to protest. But he didn't get the chance. The red Grand Am came roaring into the parking lot. It made a U-turn and stopped behind Perkins and me. Pulchuck hollered, "No!" when Ponytail jumped out, but by then it was too late.

Everything happened in slow motion. Perkins turned and saw Ponytail's handgun beginning to rise, then Perkins's hand flashed from beneath his sweatshirt. He squeezed off two rounds before Ponytail fired. Even before the pistol's report was heard, Perkins had whirled toward Pulchuck. The shots knocked Ponytail against the Grand Am. He slid to the ground, a red smear streaking the backdoor. The Grand Am floored it out of the parking lot. Ponytail lay on the ground, blood pooling around his body. There was a dark spot the size of a basketball in the center of his chest. His eyes were wide open, and his final facial expression was one of disbelief.

Perkins stood with the 9-mm leveled on Jerome Pulchuck. But Pulchuck was holding a handgun pointed at Perkins.

30

*n*o one spoke for what seemed a long time.

"If it ends here," Perkins said slowly to Pulchuck, "Jack and I will be the ones walking away."

"What are you, fucking stupid? I'm watching your finger, asshole. It even wiggles and you're gone."

They stood maybe twenty feet apart. If one fired, the other's reaction would be instantaneous and the result nearly simultaneous—mutual homicide. In the distance, I heard sirens. Beside me, Perkins's breath seemed to rasp in and out. A bead of sweat ran down his forehead. O'Reilly and I existed only peripherally. This was now a two-man show—Perkins and Pulchuck. Either both men would walk away or both would fall. The sirens grew louder.

"They're coming," Pulchuck said.

"Yeah," Perkins said, "they are."

"Jerome," O'Reilly said. "We got to—"

"Shut the fuck up, old man. *Shut up.*" Pulchuck took a small step backward.

Perkins did the same. They proceeded like that. When they were thirty yards apart, Pulchuck said, "Another time, another place."

"Looking forward to it," Perkins said.

"Better enjoy the time you got," Pulchuck said, and his gaze swung to include me, "because you ain't got much left. And one more thing, mother fuckers. Those guys were brothers. That short guy? He's a vindictive sonofabitch."

Pulchuck dropped his gun to his side. Perkins did the same. We stood watching as Pulchuck and O'Reilly climbed into the Explorer and drove off.

.   .   .

We were in a tiny meeting room in the Garrett Police Station, which was at the back of the Garrett Town Hall. Perkins and I had given independent statements. Then we'd waited three hours. Now, it was nearly 6 P.M., and four law-enforcement officials were across a conference table from us.

"Cronjagger vouched for him," Garrett Police Chief Randy Miner said, pointing to Perkins. He stood casually, glancing down at a yellow legal pad with notes on it. "He says you're a golfer who, a few weeks back, wanted to know about a murder victim."

"That's true," I said. "Did Cronjagger vouch for me?"

"Makes no difference if a Massachusetts cop vouches for anyone," a small red-headed guy said. He sat stiffly across the table from us. When he shifted, his metal folding chair scraped on the linoleum floor. His nametag read Lemieux, and he was with the Royal Canadian Mounted Police. "We're not in Massachusetts."

"We've been through that issue once," a guy nearly as big as Perkins said. "No, we are not in Massachusetts, but we have Mr. Perkins and Mr. Austin in the room with us, so why don't you let it go." His nametag read Shirley. He was a Maine State Trooper with a shaved head and a five-o'clock shadow. "And Cronjagger's word is good with me." Then to Miner: "Thanks for securing the scene, Randy. Sorry I couldn't get here sooner. I was in Ashland."

Miner nodded. He was in his sixties with a full head of white hair and a big beard. He had watery pale-blue eyes and thick hands with dirt beneath his fingernails. There was no contempt in the nod. He was a local cop, following protocol.

"Cronjagger tells us you helped him with an ongoing murder investigation," Shirley said.

I nodded.

"And he says a suspect in that murder is the same guy you two followed here."

"Yeah," Perkins said.

Lemieux started to speak, but Shirley raised a finger for him to wait.

"Three eyewitnesses to today's shooting confirmed Austin's and Perkins's stories. That's five people who say the same thing, Claude: That Robert Pike pulled his gun and pointed it at Mr. Perkins, and that Perkins somehow got his gun out and shot Pike first. Self-defense." He glanced at Perkins. "Quick for a big guy."

Perkins made no reply.

"Plus," Shirley went on, "the three old guys in the window at the golf course gave descriptions that match the picture of Jerome Pulchuck that Cronjagger faxed over."

"I don't need a police academy lecture," Lemieux said. "All I'm saying is this: A Canadian citizen went to the U.S., played golf, and was shot before reentering Canada."

"Come on, Claude," Miner said. "You know there's a hell of a lot more to it than that."

Lemieux sighed audibly. "I'm not saying Robert Pike was a saint. But the guy is dead. And we're taking a Massachusetts cop's word on the shooter, so he walks."

"Three eyewitnesses saw it," I said.

Lemieux glared at me.

Miner jumped in before Lemieux could say anything. "Maybe Mr. Austin and Mr. Perkins should sit in the other room. I thought everything was agreed upon when we brought them in here."

"It was," Shirley said. "And it is. You worked homicide for Boston PD and are a private license now, right?"

Perkins was leaning back in his chair, arms folded across his chest, legs before him, ankles crossed. He looked calm enough to doze. "Yeah. My biggest client is the PGA Tour Security Office. Pulchuck assaulted Jack and threatened him. That's why I came up here."

"Not for the foliage?" Shirley grinned.

"Not really a foliage type," Perkins said.

"Who can I call at the PGA Tour for more background on you two?"

Perkins gave Peter Barrett's number. This latest event would not help my image with Barrett. I was headed to San Antonio, where the Tour was stationed, and was to attend my first anger-management session at the end of the week.

"Want coffee?" Miner said.

We both nodded. Neither of us had eaten since the bag of junk food that morning. Miner walked across the room, pulled two Styrofoam cups from a stack in a clear plastic bag, and poured two cups. He didn't offer cream and sugar. He brought the cups over and set them before us.

After the shooting, Perkins had checked Ponytail, a.k.a. Robert Pike, for a pulse, found none, and carefully set his gun on the ground. We had waited in silence for a couple minutes as the sirens drew nearer. It turned out to be a single cop car, and Miner had stepped from the car, pistol leveled on us. We had been cuffed and taken to the Garrett Police Station, which had, as far as I could tell, a total of three rooms, including one cell.

The young cop who'd been at the crime scene with Miner, a kid named Mickey Spree, was not present. Instead a U.S. Border Patrol agent sat quietly at the head of the conference table. He was tall and thin with olive-colored skin and dark eyes. His name tag read Jimenez.

Miner was drinking his coffee with ease. It was one of the three worst cups I'd ever had. But it was hot, so it hit my empty stomach like a blowtorch.

"I'm not trying to be difficult," Lemieux said, "and I know Pike has a record fifteen feet long. But he was a Canadian citizen, and the guy is dead. So I have a hard time letting these guys walk."

"Mr. Austin is no risk of flight," Shirley said. "He plays golf on TV, for Christ's sake."

Lemieux chewed on that.

"Are you charging Mr. Perkins?" Jimenez said to Lemieux. If Jimenez was tired of listening to them go in circles, he gave nothing away. He was expressionless.

"I don't know," Lemieux said. "Where do you stand in this?"

"I just want those golf bags." Jimenez shrugged as if apologizing for not taking Pike's death more seriously. "They exchanged something out there. When the victim saw the deal going sour—maybe Pike thought Perkins and Austin were about to steal whatever he had just given Pulchuck; maybe he thought they were cops or FBI or DEA or Border Patrol—he got worried and went back. Witnesses said he tore back into the lot and jumped out, gun in hand. To me, that kind of reaction speaks volumes. Whatever is in those golf bags is valuable."

"Bottom line here," Shirley said to me and Perkins, "is that your story checks out: The shooting was legit, and Cronjagger says this guy, Pulchuck, is a thug, an ambitious one—that he's basically a second-tier player in Boston, but he's growing and has more cash than usual. That's the same story Mr. Perkins told us when he came in." He turned to Jimenez. "Anything on the camp?"

"They're not at that cabin," Jimenez said. "Although someone has obviously been there recently. We checked into it. Place is owned by a lady from southern Maine, who, interestingly, is now in a condo in Clearwater Beach, Florida. Bought the Florida place last year. Said she lives down there full time and rents her cabin—and this is a direct quote—'to a nice man from Boston who loves to fish.' Name she gave us is a lawyer in Boston. We've got a call in to him. I'd bet my next paycheck that he represents Pulchuck. Of course, the old lady in Florida has no idea when the cabin is being used or for what, besides fishing."

Shirley nodded and looked at his watch. "You Border Patrol guys really do never sleep, huh?"

Jimenez was still deadpan. "Not since nine-eleven."

The room was quiet. Somewhere a door opened and shut, and I heard a muffled voice. Miner slurped some coffee, and everyone looked at him.

Shirley looked at Perkins and me. "Where will you two be?"

"My camp tonight, back in Chandler for me and New Hampshire for him tomorrow. And we both head to San Antonio after that."

"Got cell phones and addresses?"

We gave him the information.

"Everyone satisfied?" Shirley looked around the room. Lemieux was staring at the table. "Hope your tournament goes better than today's round."

Perkins and I stood to leave.

"I've got one more question," Lemieux said. "It's been almost six hours. The APB went out a long time ago, and traffic between Houlton and Bangor is not exactly bumper to bumper. So where the hell is this white Explorer you said was headed to Boston?"

Shirley looked from Lemieux to Perkins and me again. I had no answer. Shirley motioned to the door, and Perkins and I walked out.

. . .

Perkins entered the cabin and slumped into the big Lazy-Boy my father had picked up at a yard sale. A huge fireplace with a woodstove insert dominated the far wall, and Perkins sat staring at it. I went over and poured some pellets into the stove. Six hours earlier, Perkins had shot Robert Pike dead, and for all his toughness, his face now looked like he had indeed killed a man. The invisible barrier he put up was down now. I knew his wife Linda and I were the only ones who saw him without it.

"I'm going outside," he said, getting up. "I need to call home." He took the cell phone off the counter and went out. He closed the front door, and the screen door slammed shut.

From the kitchen window, I watched as he walked back and forth on the dirt drive, talking passionately, his empty hand waving as he spoke. After nearly five minutes, his demeanor changed. I knew his five-year-old son, Jackie, was on the phone.

Perkins clicked off the phone and hung up and came back inside. I took two bottles of Molson from the fridge and handed him one.

"You had to do it," was all I said.

The journeys of our lives were so deeply intertwined that it was all I needed to say. I had been there when he and Linda had lost their first baby, a girl, Suzanne. We had called her Suzy for three days, before Perkins and Linda had made the toughest decision they would ever make—and told doctors to take her off the machines, that machines were no way for a baby girl to live. Suzy had died in her mother's arms, Perkins's big arm around Linda's shoulder the whole time. It had been before I'd known Lisa, and I had sat in the waiting room, crying for their loss. My subsequent experiences as a father only illustrated even more how incomprehensible their pain must have been and indeed must remain.

"That's what Linda said." He drank from the bottle, shook his head, and looked out the window. Darkness was falling. The river looked black and cold. "Three times now. The feeling never gets better. I don't know who Pike was, but a kid might go home tonight to learn that his old man is gone forever."

"I named my daughter after you because I respect you. I still do."

He nodded, looking at me.

I was glad the phone rang.

31

"Is this . . ." The voice paused, a woman's voice, one I had heard before but couldn't place. "Is this Jack—Mr. Austin?"

I said it was.

"This is Lea Griffin . . ." Again the pause; then: "You probably meet a lot of people. Probably, you don't remember someone like me."

"I remember you well. How are your children and your husband?"

The pause was longer this time. I listened to her faint breathing.

Across the room, Perkins lay reclined in the Lazy-Boy, his feet hanging over the footrest, sipping his second Molson, and staring out at the black river. Darkness was coming fast now. I was at the breakfast bar in the kitchenette, which separated the living-room area from the stove and refrigerator.

"My kids are fine," she said. "My husband, Ronny—well, he's the same."

"I'm sorry to hear that."

"Yeah, well, you said you wanted to know if I remembered anything about Owen Henley or anything like that, right?"

"Yes. I still do."

"Well, there's something happened today—I don't know if it means anything, or nothing, but something happened."

I sipped some Molson and waited. There was no sense rushing her. She had called to talk. It was going on 7 P.M., we had yet to eat dinner, and Perkins showed no signs of starting the grill. But the beer was cold.

"The store manager called me in today. A cop was in his

office, and the cop asked how well I knew Owen," she said. Her words came faster now. They didn't sound rehearsed, and she didn't seem confident in what she was saying. Rather, the pace indicated a need to get them out. "I told him I didn't know Owen real good. But he showed me a picture from the last roll Owen had developed at Wal-Mart."

Something in my stomach moved. The events of the day had offered the unexpected already—and I sensed Lea would add something new. "Was the cop's name Cronjagger?"

"I don't know. A big guy with a brown beard."

That description fit Cronjagger.

"The picture was of Owen with a guy who came in now and then to talk to Owen. I said, 'Sure, I seen that guy.' He was a black guy, pretty young, with a Fu Manchu and a big scar through one eyebrow. Looked like he got in a knife fight or something."

"Terrell Smith."

"The cop never said his name. You know him?"

"We've met."

"Well, I told the cop and my manager that I didn't know nothing about him. Just that I'd seen him. And the manager told me to call if the guy came around again."

"You see any other pictures from that final roll?"

"No. Just the one they showed me. But the manager said something after the cop left about him, something that made me think to call you. He said the guy was 'young and crazy.' I said, 'So he must be the one who killed Owen Henley.'"

"What did the cop say?"

"He said they're still investigating."

"He mention the two guys who came in the morning Owen was killed?"

"What two guys?"

"The ones you described to the sketch artist. The two the cops are looking for."

"Oh, those guys. No nothing about them. Like I said, they probably did it and now they're long gone."

Perkins grabbed the lever on the side of the Lazy-Boy and retracted the footrest. He got up, walked past me to the freezer, and took two plastic bags out. "VENISON" was written on each.

He tossed the packages in the microwave and defrosted them. The microwave would kill a lot of the meat's flavor, but if we put a little butter on the steaks while we grilled them, we could get some of it back.

"How long did you talk to the cop?" I said.

"Half an hour."

"What else did he say?"

"He just asked how often the guy dropped by."

"I told him five or six times. Owen would go on break. They'd go out to the guy's car for a while. Then Owen would come back in, alone."

"What do you think they were doing?"

"I don't know. A lot of the kids working here have friends that come around. Sometimes they go out in the cars—especially the nightshift—and smoke a joint, or drink a little beer. You know?"

"Sure."

"But not Owen and the Fu-Manchu guy. I don't see that happening. The Fu-Manchu guy looked busy. He looked like a guy with plans."

"So what was he doing with Owen Henley, a guy with zero going for him?"

"Maybe Owen dealt dope."

The microwave buzzed three times. Perkins took the meat out and went outside onto the deck. I watched as he pulled the cover off the grill, reached beneath it to start the gas, and clicked the starter. The starter button had been broken for years. I got a book of matches from a counter drawer, walked to the screen door, and tossed the book to him. The night air was much warmer than it had been that morning. Hovering above the slow-moving river was a low layer of fog.

"You think Owen had a little side business?" I said.

If what Pulchuck had gotten from the Canadians today was drugs, that scenario made sense: Owen Henley drove whatever Pulchuck was getting back to Boston. Was he stopping at Terrell Smith's before delivering the goods? But Pulchuck told Marty and Robert Pike that, if the cops put the heat on them, everything would fall to Terrell Smith anyway. Did that mean the murder of Owen Henley? Or was that the smuggling scheme, whatever was being smuggled? Either way, what was there to incriminate Terrell Smith? Photos? The picture of Jerome Pulchuck and Owen hadn't made much difference. Was there one of Terrell that was much more incriminating?

"Owen was smarter than most people gave him credit for," Lea said. "He could be a smooth talker. That much I know."

"You know?" I said. "I thought you said he was strange and quiet."

"I mean, he was like that with me. But I seen him smooth-talk other people. Guy had the gift for gab, you know?"

"Sure. A lot of people do."

I wanted to keep Lea Griffin on the line. A different picture of Owen Henley was emerging from this conversation. But it wasn't to be.

"Got to go," she said. "Katindah and Leon are fighting."

I heard only silence in the background, but she hung up.

32

At least the company was great and the food was Tex-Mex. That was about all I could say after shooting seventy-two in the opening round of the Valero Texas Open at the La Cantera Golf Club and Resort in San Antonio. It was 7 P.M., and Lisa, Perkins, my caddie Tim Silver, and I were eating dinner in the hotel restaurant. Darcy was on my lap, eating a dinner roll.

The Valero Texas Open had a $3.5 million purse that year, and I had a $50,000 fine to pay. So I wasn't pleased with my seventy-two, especially considering par is seventy and the track plays less than 7,000 yards. In 2004, winner Bart Bryant shot a third-round sixty, and on this day, Brad Faxon tossed a sixty-five on the leaderboard. I had to get under par in a hurry.

"You haven't put Darcy down since you got here," Lisa said. The empty highchair stood beside her.

We were sitting at a circular table. The scent of hot spices was present, as was the clatter of silverware. Across the room, Fred Couples was having dinner with a guy in a conservative suit. At the table near them, Skip Kendall ate a pasta dish, alone.

"I played eighteen holes this afternoon," I said. "And I didn't carry Darcy with me."

"Probably should have," Silver said. He was next to me and reached for Darcy. The two-year-old's face lit up, and she went to him easily. "Darcy might have made some putts."

"Now, boys," Lisa said.

"No, it's all right," I said. "I didn't make one. Nothing all day. But I worked on that for an hour after the round."

"The face of your putter was open," Lisa said. She sipped some iced tea, set the glass down, and spread her hands. Before her, lay a plate of enchiladas. "You pushed everything."

"Everyone's an analyst," I said, and grinned.

"Literally," she said. "What are you going to do about the interview requests? The shooting in Maine has gotten out."

"Nothing," I said. "I'll no-comment everyone."

I ate part of a fajita. It wasn't as hot as you'd get in Guadalajara—I wasn't in physical pain—but it was spicy. I could feel my forehead perspire. A waitress moved quickly past, carrying a tray of sizzling fajitas. At the bar, an old man sat alone, a short, dark glass before him, a draft chaser next to it. I thought of Sean O'Reilly.

"Have you talked to Nash?" Lisa said.

"I left four messages."

"Nash is a resilient young man," Lisa said. "He'll talk when he's ready."

"I offended him, I guess. I tried to help, but it probably came out wrong."

Lisa turned to Perkins. "Anything new on the whereabouts of Jerome Pulchuck?"

"I knew you people invited me to dinner for a reason," Perkins said. "We on the record?"

Lisa made a *tss* sound. Then she smiled warmly.

"Stupid question," Perkins said. "We're always on the record."

"Hey," Lisa said.

"The answer is no. Cronjagger doesn't know where Pulchuck is. No one does."

"Someone does," Lisa said. "It's just a matter of finding that person."

"Go for it, Little Lady." Perkins drank some Tecate I had ordered us.

"Hey," I said, "she doesn't need to be chasing down crime lords."

"Anyway," Lisa said, shooting me a look, then turning back to Perkins, "I'm surprised to see you here so soon."

"I don't like it," Perkins said. "I had three employees. I fired one. Deidre is with you and Darcy, and my other guy is with Linda and Jackie. I was going to have them come here, but I want them far away from me and Jack, in case Pike takes a run at us here."

Perkins spoke of things in black and white, and Lisa stiffened a little.

I knew Perkins didn't want to be there. He hadn't been home much lately. The ability to maintain family life while on Tour was something I cherished. It hadn't always been that way— when Darcy was an infant, Lisa had stayed behind with her. I'd traveled alone for a long half-season. Now two years old, Darcy was able to fly and traveled well. That might change once she began school; however, some Tour families make travel a way of life, home-schooling their kids, so the family can remain together. By contrast, through Lisa, I'd met many golf journalists who worked schedules similar to mine—on the road twenty or more weeks a year—but without the luxury of having their families with them. Now I was seeing my best friend, Perkins, face that same dilemma.

"Any word on Pulchuck's white Explorer?" I said.

"No. He probably dumped it. Pulchuck hasn't been to his office, either."

"That's odd," Lisa said. "He can't just up and leave, can he?"

Perkins shook his head. Next to him, Silver lifted Darcy, who'd been sitting on his lap, and turned her to face him. She stood on his knees and smiled. He held her hands, and she weaved back and forth, smiling and giggling.

"Come here, beautiful," Silver said. "Uncle Tim will teach you all about fashion and accessorizing. You'll wear Baby Gap, then Abercrombie, then Talbot's."

"Jesus," Perkins said. "The kid will be a cross-dresser."

"That's offensive," Silver said. "I don't cross-dress. I just know style." Silver had ordered a taco salad and had been the first to finish. He was still working on his drink—something called "The Gringo Surprise," a margarita the size of my golf bag.

"Pulchuck wouldn't pack up and go," Perkins said. He took a dinner roll from a basket, cut it, took a piece of butter wrapped in gold tinfoil, and spread it on the roll. He took a bite and swallowed. "A guy like Pulchuck can't go anywhere. He'd have to begin all over, and he's worked too hard to do that."

"Plus, he's moving up the ladder," I said, and drank some Tecate. It certainly wasn't Beck's; it wasn't even Bud. But we were in Texas, so I was drinking it.

"That's right. And what that means is Pulchuck has his hands in several cookie jars—the smuggling thing in Canada might die down for now, so he'll focus on something else. He's going to seek additional revenue, stockpile capital, so he can continue to grow all his ventures."

"You think he'll go back to Garrett?" I said.

"If the Canada thing was big enough, he'll go back," Perkins said. "Or he'll figure out a new way to continue whatever he was doing." He took Darcy from Silver and tickled her.

"Mac-a-cheese," Darcy said, giggling, "more mac-a-cheese."

"Just like your father," Perkins said. "All you think about is your stomach."

"You describe Pulchuck like this is Wall Street," Lisa said.

"He's a businessman," Perkins said.

"I realize that, but you talk like he's got a legitimate enterprise."

"He's an enterprise, all right," Perkins said. "And it's growing."

I drank some more Tecate and thought about that. The principals that applied to Pulchuck's criminal ventures—gain capital and branch out to increase revenue—were the same as those used by valid businesses. There was something odd about that.

"So what do you think he's into?" I said.

Perkins drank some Tecate and made a face. "This stuff is awful. Why did you order it?"

"We're in Texas."

"We're Mainers in Texas, Jack. That means we can order Bud Light." He pushed the beer away. "All I know is Pulchuck is obviously smuggling something into or out of Canada. Other than that, I don't know any specifics. Cronjagger says they think Pulchuck probably runs a gambling operation, and some vice guys say Pulchuck is probably behind two or more pimps. Christ, he's probably at Gillette Stadium right now trying to fix Patriots games."

"It's interesting, though," Lisa said. "He's a criminal, but he's also a large enterprise."

"You're not that naive," Perkins said. "You knew that."

"Yes, I know it happens. But I've never heard it spoken of like that—several smaller ventures continually growing and adding sources of revenue like an entrepreneur."

Perkins shrugged. "You don't want all of your money coming from one area or going into one area. Too easy to track that way. But Cronjagger said the same thing Deirdre did: Pulchuck has a lot more cash suddenly. And Owen Henley was driving a van to and from New Brunswick. And B. C. Budd is being grown in New Brunswick."

"You still think that's it?" Lisa said.

Perkins shrugged. "If I had to bet right now, I'd put my money on that. But nothing's certain until we get a golf bag."

Something occurred to me, something that had been lost in the shuffle of Pulchuck, the photos, the Canadians, my punch, Pulchuck's Woodlands visit, and Padre's struggles.

"When this thing started," I said, "O'Reilly mentioned a house. He said Owen made money from Pulchuck and either wanted to buy or had bought Nash a house."

"A house?" Lisa said.

Perkins nodded slowly. "Yeah. We were in the bar, in Westchester. Silver, you were there, too."

Silver shook his head. "I don't remember any house."

"Is Cronjagger still looking for the house?" I said.

Perkins held up his hand to signal the waitress. She came over, and he asked for a Bud Light. I loaded some sour cream and lettuce on a tortilla and made a fajita. For three hours that afternoon, I had not thought of Owen Henley, Jerome Pulchuck, Terrell Smith, or Marty Pike. I had thought of golf, drinking in the distraction. Now it was all back.

"I get soda, Mommy?" Darcy said.

"Soy milk, sweetie."

"I get Daddy's soda?" Darcy reached for my bottle of Tecate. I grabbed it. Everyone laughed.

The waitress returned with Perkins's Bud Light.

"The house," Perkins said, shaking his head, drinking the Bud Light like it was champagne. "That goddamned house. Cronjagger said they looked—must have been in Massachusetts—for any properties owned by Owen Henley. I wonder if they looked throughout New England or even nationwide. If Owen did buy it, we would finally have something that would leave a paper trail."

33

The reason Texans fair well at the British Open Championship is because they can play in the wind. If you grow up playing golf in "The Big State," you learn to play the game on the ground. Case in point, short-hitting Justin Leonard's lone major championship had not been earned hitting high, long shots at a

United States Open, but rather by controlling trajectory and rolling the ball onto greens at Great Britain's Open Championship. Growing up in Maine, I'd learned to maneuver around tight, tree-lined venues, but the three-quarter knockdown shot was not second nature to me. Friday, at 10:30 A.M., the wind was gusting, and I was pleased to be two under par on the day.

"Padre would enjoy a day like this," Tim Silver said, setting the bag down in the fairway of the par-four fifth hole.

No. 5 was a 494-yard beauty, a dogleg right, requiring a mid- to long-iron approach on even benign days. This day, I had hit driver 265 yards into the wind. Now I was toying with the idea of hitting five-wood to the green, but bunkers surrounded the putting surface.

"He won this event a couple years back," I said. "I thought he might show up."

Silver moved away from the bag and held both arms out like a scarecrow to gauge the speed and direction of the wind. "It's letting up a little," he said. "But we still have two twenty-five to get home from here."

I took the head cover off the three-wood and swung it back and forth, slowly. I visualized the shot—a low-flying line drive, landing on the front of the green, and running to the flagstick. Out-of-bounds loomed behind the putting surface. When I had the shot locked into my mind's eye, I focused on the necessary mechanics: I made several abbreviated swings, my follow-through curtailed, right arm stopping just below my left shoulder, the club pointed skyward rather than around the back of my neck, as with a full swing.

I addressed the ball, widened my stance, and tried to make a swing identical to the practice motions.

The Titleist Pro V1 stayed low, maybe twenty feet off the ground, landed on the front edge and stopped thirty feet below the hole.

"Never released," I said.

"But you just drained a thirty-five-footer," Silver said. "You can do it again."

My playing partners this day were Kip Capers and an old friend, Tripp "General" Davis, a former Ryder Cup captain. General owned one of the most distinguished playing records of all my contemporaries, and Kip Capers seemed to always play well in his company, as if trying to earn a spot on a future Ryder Cup team. General had begun the day −5 but now stood −2; Capers had shot sixty-seven Thursday and was −2 on this day, −5 for the event. I was even for the tournament but putting for birdie.

"Had dinner with a friend of yours last night," General said, walking with me to the green. "Padre flew in. Angela and I ate with him."

"How's he doing?"

"Said he hasn't picked up a club since he played with you in El Paso."

"That doesn't sound good."

"You know Ian Baker-Finch never made it back." General wore a windbreaker over a white Izod golf shirt. The breeze made his nylon jacket slap against his body.

"Baker-Finch hasn't come back *yet*," I said. "He still might. You think Padre is done?"

"I know he didn't drive out here just to eat with me," General said. As we walked, he brought an imaginary club back and paused at the top, moving his right arm closer to his body; he had come over the top of several shots. "Padre came up here to see Finchy and David Duval."

"Duval took some time off," I said. "Now he's back, playing well."

"That's what I told Padre."

"What's your sense of the whole thing?" I said.

The early fall wind blew hot and dry against my skin. The air was dusty. It was like sitting near a New England campfire, midday, in July. The temperature was close to ninety, but on this day, San Antonio was not humid and perspiration seemed to dry as quickly as it formed.

"Padre might be done, Jack." General shook his head as if sadly admitting the truth. "That's what I think. He told me he's planning a trip to Europe in March."

"He usually gets off to a fast start. Both his wins came in March."

"Well, his next win won't. Not this March, anyway."

Across the fairway, Kip Capers prepared to pitch from thirty yards. General and I paused to watch him. The wind had turned the hole into a par-five for Capers. The air carried the scent of suntan lotion and cooking spices, as if a barbecue was taking place inside the hospitality tents.

When Capers was safely on the green, I went to my ball and marked it. Silver took the cover off my putter and handed the club to me.

"Back to that old thing?" Silver said. "All the technological advances—three-ball putters, inserts, offsets—and you're back to the old Bull's Eye?"

"Yesterday, I couldn't hit the ocean from the end of a pier. I needed a change."

"Well, it's working."

I had picked up the Bull's Eye for $5 at an Orlando yard sale, back when I'd wintered there. I had been offered good money for the thing once, as a collector had deemed it an original, but I'd declined and was glad. I often found myself coming back to the Bull's Eye the way a lost sailor wanders back to a well-known port.

I crouched behind my marker and looked at the line to the hole. Silver stood behind me.

"I see it three feet, left to right," he said, behind tinted Oakley shades. He walked half the distance to the cup and stopped, examining the topography again, nodding to himself. Then he came back. "Into the grain and over a little swale, Jack. Hit it firmly."

I nodded, looking at the hole. I had not played well this season, a bitter disappointment on the heels of my lone Tour victory. The difference between wins and losses on Tour is usually found in putting statistics. It was true for me. I was still driving the ball well—fourth in driving distance behind John Daly, Hank Kuehne, and Tiger Woods—and ranked in the top fifty in overall driving, meaning I was hitting plenty of fairways. But the season before, when I had won, my putting numbers had been at an all-time best. I had ranked in the top fifty in putts per green. Now I was 112th. I had used the best putters money could buy—$400 jobs—and had putted inconsistently since January. I had been around long enough to know it hadn't been faulty equipment. Yet a change was needed, a fresh start. So I had brought the archaic Bull's Eye to the practice green early that morning, and my stroke had reappeared like a lost friend.

I made two practice strokes, looking at the cup to gain a feel for speed. Finally, I set the copper-colored clubface, pocked with battle scars, behind the ball, exhaled slowly, and made the stroke, not looking up until the ball was well on its way to the hole.

The ball stopped two feet short. I looked at Silver.

"Good roll," he said. "Par on this hole, playing into the wind, will be like picking up a birdie on the field."

I shrugged and walked toward my ball, reaching into my pocket for my coin. The gallery applauded my lag, and I scanned the faces as I tipped my hat. Standing behind the green, near the out-of-bounds stake, was a short, thick man with the stub of a ponytail protruding from the back of his cap. He wore a white golf shirt and spikeless golf shoes like a teaching pro. Sunlight flashed off his gold bracelet. I couldn't see his eyes beneath his wraparound sunglasses.

"Jack," General said, "you all right?" He was waiting for me to mark my ball. "Tap it in, if you want."

I shook my head, realizing I had stopped, mid-motion. I resumed, bending and sliding the coin beneath my ball. I tossed the ball to Silver, who wiped it with a white towel.

When I looked for Jerome Pulchuck again, he was gone.

. . .

When we got to the tenth hole, I was −5 on the day, −3 for the event. The sun was bright overhead, and the wind was gaining ferocity. Gusts whipped dust against my face. I didn't usually wear shades, but I unzipped the front pocket of my big Taylor-Made staff bag and pawed through. There were three new gloves; three sleeves of balls and a felt-tipped pen to mark them; sun block; extra socks; my rain suit; a plastic bag with nearly a thousand tees; pencils; the tape recorder I used to note swing thoughts; Power Bars; Gatorade packets; one item that set me apart from probably every other professional golfer, a lucky book, *The Simple Truth* by Philip Levine; and, finally, Oakley sunglasses in a protective case. I put them on.

"Christ," Silver said. "I hardly recognize you."

I remembered Perkins's comment about golfers being standing targets and saw my name in large block letters beneath the Red Sox logo when I zipped the pocket closed again.

"You're quiet today," Silver said.

"Faxon shot sixty-four," I said and pointed to an electronic leaderboard that read Faxon −11; Leonard −10; Woods −8; Garcia −8. My name was at the bottom of board.

"Jack, three, four guys are going low today," Silver said. "You're one of them. Everybody else is just trying to hold on and shoot par. It's miserable out here."

"Be a good day to go low," I said.

I took the three-wood from the bag and aimed down the left-hand side of the 460-yard tenth fairway. It was a par four, and in different weather, I might play a driver, in hopes of hitting only a wedge to the green. But the wind was with me. And the shorter the club, the more control you have. Capers was four over on the day, walking the narrow cut line like a tightrope artist weaving back and forth, high above a crowd. General was coming off a bogey and was −1. I had the honor.

I brought the three-metal back slowly, making a wide arc, a big shoulder turn. At the top, I paused ever so slightly, then began my downswing. My weight transfer was smooth, my right hip firing through as the clubface stuck the ball. I finished with the abbreviated follow-through I had used all day.

The wind-aided three-wood carried 295 yards, leaving 165 to the middle of the green, a six- or seven-iron to get home.

Capers hit next. He was rail-thin and needed to play a driver on this hole. He pushed it into the rough.

"Pays to be an ox," he said to me.

I shrugged. "You can get home from there."

"Yeah," he said, "but it helps like hell to be able to bomb it. My driver is short of your three-wood—and I lift weights five days a week."

"In Maine they feed them raw meat until age five," General said.

Silver laughed.

I winked at General. "Aren't you fifty yet? When are you going to the senior Tour?"

"They call it the *Champions* Tour now." He grinned. "'Cause of guys like me."

He hit a driver into the heart of the fairway, and we all walked toward Capers's ball.

Capers's Nike ball was a speck of white in the three-inch rough. I stood next to General, waiting for Capers to play to the green, and scanned our small gallery. Angela Davis stood near the yellow rope lining the fairway. She waved to General; he waved back. There were a couple kids standing next to a woman who looked disinterested—a mother, perhaps, braving the wind and dust so her boys could see a Tour event. It made me think of my mother, who would've done the same. Most of the spectators had left because of the wind and sandstorms. Or maybe they had just all gone to watch Tiger.

"There's Lisa," Silver said and pointed to her walking down the cart path.

Lisa wore khakis, tennis shoes, and a white golf shirt with "CBS Golf" embroidered on the collar. A press credential hung in clear plastic from a navy blue strap around her neck. She wasn't on-air until 3 P.M. and had done interviews on the range all morning. Now she had Darcy in the back carrier. She smiled and gave me thumbs-up. Then she held up her open hand, indicating the number four.

Silver quickly shook his head and held up an open hand—five. Lisa smiled broadly, continuing to walk toward me.

Pulchuck fell in, ten feet behind her.

My face must have given me away because he smiled widely at me. My throat felt dry. The wind circumnavigated the Oakleys and stung my eyes. I took the six-iron from the bag and moved toward Lisa, who stopped near the rope, beside Angela.

When I got to her, Lisa kissed me on the cheek. Pulchuck was standing six feet to Lisa's right, alone.

"That's sweet," he said.

"Do I know you?" Lisa said.

Angela didn't speak, but I could feel her tense. PGA Tour

217

wives are easy to spot in a gallery. For one thing, their plastic-enclosed credentials, worn around the neck, don't resemble the glossy-paper day-pass, the average fan ties to a belt loop. Typically, the worst thing a player might fear is his wife hearing some twenty-eight handicapper criticize a bad swing. Maybe a drunk might say something obnoxious. After more than two decades, Angela Davis had no doubt seen and heard it all. So when she moved away from Lisa, I knew the tone of Pulchuck's voice had registered.

"I played golf with Jack in northern Maine a few days ago," Pulchuck said. "Except I didn't know it until we were done. And by then it was too late."

"What do you want?" I said.

General had come over. So had Silver.

"I'm just a fan here to watch a professional play." Pulchuck pointed to his ticket dangling from his shirt buttonhole. "Just here to see my favorite golfer."

"Bull shit," I said.

"Don't be so vain, Jack. Tiger's over there," he said and turned on his heel and walked away.

"What the hell was all that about?" General said. "Guy looks familiar."

"You saw him in Boston," I said. "And you saw him flying, ass over elbows, on *SportsCenter* about nine hundred times."

"My God," Lisa said. "That was Jerome Pulchuck?"

"Yeah, where is Perkins?"

34

I grabbed my cell phone off the nightstand before the second ring. Darcy was sleeping soundly at the foot of the bed in the porta-crib. Lisa, beside me, always slept like the dead and didn't stir. The clock read 3:24 A.M.

"Jack," the voice on the phone said, "sorry for storming out of the kitchen. That wasn't right. I shouldn't have done it."

"Hold on, Nash."

The air in the hotel room felt thick and heavy; motionless, the way air-conditioned hotel rooms often feel. It took a moment to get my bearings. Nash didn't sound frightened or in pain, but there was something different, something I hadn't heard in his voice before. I took the cell phone and rolled out of bed, slowly. With one hand, I pulled a pair of athletic shorts up and moved to the hall, careful to slide the deadbolt out so I could gently prop the door against the frame, leaving it ajar.

"Nash," I said, "no problem. I'm not upset about that. Where are you?"

I leaned against the hallway wall. The carpet felt thick under my bare feet. The only noise was the monotone drone of an unseen television.

"School. Well, actually, at a pay phone downtown." *Downtown* was stretched to three syllables.

"You okay?"

"Sure. Happy. Real happy."

"Drunk?"

"A little."

"I thought you don't drink."

"Never have before," he said. "But I kind of like it."

219

"You're twenty years old."

"Telling me you never had a drink at twenty?"

"I admit to underage drinking," I said. "Is Michelle there with you?" I didn't want him wandering around alone if he was drunk.

"I broke up with her."

"When?"

"When I got back."

"Why?" I said.

He belched.

I realized what was happening. He had called to let me know he was drunk. I had a two-year-old daughter; I knew about kids pushing adults' buttons. Yet Nash had never before done something like this. There was more going on than him getting drunk and calling to apologize. The call was for a different reason, one I didn't fully comprehend yet. And the breakup was something I hadn't seen coming. They had dated for more than a year.

The elevator was at the far end of the hall, along the opposite wall. I heard a clang, and then the doors opened with a low groan. A man and woman stepped from the elevator shaft into view and walked toward and past me. The woman looked covertly at me standing shirtless in the hall, a quick sidelong glance. Her fragrance smelled briefly of lilac before being overtaken by the heavy odor of smoke. The man wore a dark blue sports jacket, his tie at half-mast.

"Did you scrimmage yesterday?" I said.

Nash said they had and that he had scored twice.

"How come you're drinking?" I said. "You're out past curfew, Nash. What's going on?"

"You're not my father," he said. "You can't ask me that."

"Nash, we never finished our conversation in the kitchen."

"Yeah, we did."

"Claire Henley made some serious accusations. Cronjagger all but confirmed them. All I'm saying is I'm here for you, if you need to talk or if your father—"

"If he what?"

"If he hurt you."

"I was five years old, Jack."

"I know. And I'm not trying to pry, but you're part of my family now. And that's what family does."

"Pry?"

"If that's what it takes."

"You know, you can be belligerent."

"Yeah, I know that. Stubborn, single-minded, probably a little self-righteous. I know all that. But I help people who mean a lot to me."

We were quiet for a while. I heard the elevator open again. I turned to see who it was. No one got off.

"Jack," Nash said, "I got to go. But guess who I saw today at a house party?"

I waited.

"Terrell Smith. He never saw me, but he was across the room. I left."

"Smart move. You sure he didn't see you?"

"Yes."

"Nash, why'd you break up with Michelle?"

"I gotta go."

He hung up, and I closed the cell phone and stood in the corridor, staring absently toward the elevator. Still no one got off. I heard someone hit a button, and the doors whirred closed.

.   .   .

I couldn't go back to sleep. So at 3:55 A.M., wearing jeans, a gray Curry College Football T-shirt, and running shoes, I was in the hotel lobby, drinking leftover coffee from the courtesy counter, and reading Philip Levine's *What Work Is*. I found a poem called "Among Children" and reread it slowly.

> I walk among the rows of bowed heads—
> the children are sleeping through fourth grade
> so as to be ready for what is ahead,
> the monumental boredom of junior high
> and the rush foreword tearing their wings
> loose and turning their eyes forever inward.
> These are the children of Flint, their fathers

work at the spark plug factory or truck
bottled water in 5 gallon sea-blue jugs
to the widows of the suburbs. You can see
already how their backs have thickened,
how their small hands, soiled by pig iron,
leap and stutter even in dreams. I would like
to sit down among them and read from *The Book of Job* . . .
I would like to arm each one
with a quiver of arrows so that they might
rush like wind where no battle rages . . .

The lobby was empty. No one manned the front desk at this hour; a young employee sat in a back office, reading a Harry Potter book, his door open to steal glances at the counter and lobby. I leaned back on the sofa and put my feet up on the coffee table and crossed my ankles. I stared at the book's glossy cover. On it was a black-and-white photo of a girl who looked frightened, no older than ten, with long braided pigtails, wearing a soiled cotton dress; behind her, the view of a factory.

I thought of Nash, of his reaction in my kitchen when I'd mentioned his toddler years with the late Owen Henley. Nash had instantly retreated inside himself and scrubbed the tabletop endlessly before leaving the room. I hadn't kept up very much on his love life, but Lisa loved Michelle and said they were "sweet together," Nash holding Michelle's hand when we walked around campus. Nash had broken up with Michelle, and now he was in Milton and drunk—an emotional retreat. I needed to know from what.

To top it off, Terrell Smith was at Curry College parties.

Beyond the black windows of the hotel lobby, the vacant parking lot was lit by street lamps. Buick courtesy cars, white magnetized signs marking Valero Open participants, dominated the lot. I remembered Jerome Pulchuck's words before the balloon had burst in northern Maine. He had called Owen Henley a "freak" and told the brothers Pike he wouldn't have freaks working for him, and that Owen was now out of the picture. Was that a confession to Owen's murder? Not one that would hold up in court.

I wondered, again, how Owen was connected to Terrell Smith. Cronjagger had said Terrell was just a minor-league dope peddler and pill pusher. Was that what he had been doing at Curry? Yet Terrell had driven nearly three hours to meet up with Nash, pick a fight, and ask about Wal-Mart. Additionally, Pulchuck had told the Pikes not to worry, that if things went south, Terrell was the fall guy.

None of it made sense.

I drank more cold coffee. Two sugars hadn't sweetened it, the taste a sharp metallic. I thought of my own image—a man in his late thirties sitting alone in a hotel lobby in the wee hours, sipping coffee, staring off into space, searching for answers to a string of endless and seemingly unrelated questions. I had come to San Antonio to play golf, to compete against a field that included Tiger Woods, Brad Faxon, General Davis, and others among the world's best. I had played well and, at -5 after two rounds, was only six shots off the lead with thirty-six holes to play. Moreover, if the gusts maintained their ferocity, the leaderboard could change in a hurry. After a season of mediocrity, I had reason to be encouraged and excited about the next two days.

But it was hard to make golf my top priority. Drunk and trying to agitate me, Nash had called for a reason. He had hung up abruptly, apparently not finding whatever he had called in search of. And without Michelle, he was alone. Part of me wanted to drive to the airport, board the next plane north, and find him. But that wouldn't work. Something unspoken was going on, and for now, he was moving slowly.

I had been staring at the coffee table, but now felt the presence of another and looked up.

"Where's Perkins?"

He was alone this time. His face seemed to contort as he spoke, perhaps illustrating a physical pain I couldn't see. He stood looking at me, narrow eyes puffy, encircled with purple rings.

I didn't answer.

He spotted the kid in the office behind the counter and nodded to himself. Then Jerome Pulchuck went to the coffee dispenser, filled a Styrofoam cup, added two sugars, stirred, and sat beside me on the sofa. He was dressed like he had been when we'd first met—a crisp white shirt, buttoned to the top; creased gray slacks; and the gold bracelet that chimed each time he moved his hand. The clothes were the same; but, somehow, the man was not. He was tired now. I waited for his muscle to arrive; no one entered.

"You know Perkins's name," I said.

"Of course."

"You looked into him after the standoff."

"He was lucky."

"He'd say you were," I said. "What do you want?"

"What did you see in Garrett, Maine?"

"I played the same golf course you did. So I saw a hell of a lot of water." I shifted and recrossed my feet. "I hear they've got twenty-one water hazards over eighteen holes."

"Cut the shit."

I sipped some coffee.

"You know the only reason you're alive right now?"

A question like that doesn't offer a lot, but I made do: "Because you put money on me to win this week."

"You got balls," Pulchuck said. "I'll give you that." He almost smiled, but settled for a sip of coffee. "Because of who you are. That fucking sucker-punch was on TV about eight million times. I clip you, and it makes every paper in the country and every goddamned TV news show."

I hadn't pegged him for rational and didn't trust him one bit. If he knew what I saw, I was dead.

He was leaning forward, forearms on thighs, and put his coffee on the table. "Fucking coffee's terrible. What did you see?" he said, again.

I looked outside. A lone car had headlights on. Two guys stood near it. A telephone rang, and I heard the kid in the back office answer it, giving the hotel's five-second slogan.

"I'm a businessman," Pulchuck said. "My business requires more confidentiality than some others. So we've got ourselves a little problem."

"Only problem I've got is figuring out how to birdie number fifteen."

"Jack, you're smarter than that. I just told you your job has bought you some time. But I've thought over different scenarios—accidents, disappearances." He paused to look at me.

I sat motionless, my expression deadpan.

"I'm willing to work something out," he said.

"Wow. If I was Tiger or Phil, you'd probably make me a partner."

Pulchuck's jaws flexed; his narrow eyes became pinpoints. "I'm not unreasonable. I came here to talk business."

"Owen Henley might call you unreasonable."

"What are you talking about?"

"Owen Henley," I said. "You don't recognize the name?"

"I know the name. What are you talking about?"

"I'm talking about how you tied the poor bastard to a chair, hit him with a bat or something, then shot him in the chest."

Pulchuck shook his head and reached for his coffee.

"Not in the head," I said. "You shot him in the chest, probably so he'd suffer a little longer before he died."

He set the cup down without drinking. "I thought golf was a clean sport, but you're on something, asshole. I didn't kill Owen Henley. But the guy was a fucking pervert. I'm glad he's gone. I don't have all night. What did you see in Garrett, Maine?"

"As I was leaving, I saw you walking toward the clubhouse, probably to play golf."

"You played right behind us, Jack. You followed me around the course. Cut the bullshit." He glanced over the counter at the kid sitting behind the desk.

"He's still there," I said.

"Fuck the kid," Pulchuck said. "I told you, if I wanted you gone, you'd already be in the ground. You've bought time. Perkins is a different story."

"What's that mean?"

He shook his head.

Outside, the skyline was going from ink to gray. The two guys near the car were coming into focus. One looked black and had a goatee. I'd seen him in the bar, the first time I'd met Pulchuck.

"You know why I'm interested in Owen Henley's death?" I said.

"The kid with the pictures. Whatshisname—Nash."

"That's right. He's Owen's son. He's a friend of mine. He wanted to know his old man."

Pulchuck exhaled and leaned back on the couch. "I didn't kill the pervert. Got that?"

"I don't believe you."

"Tell me what you saw in Maine, or I tell Marty Pike that Perkins isn't the only one who needs his ticket punched."

"I told you, I saw you walking toward the clubhouse. I've got a fishing camp up there."

Pulchuck sighed dramatically and stood. "Fuck you. We could've settled this like businessman, asshole. All you had to do was give me a reasonable price."

I didn't believe him for a second. "Nash Henley wanted to know his old man," I said. "You took that away. There's no price on that."

He looked at me for several moments, and I could see a realization taking shape before him. "There might be a price on something else, though."

My eyes narrowed. He didn't continue.

"Anyway," he said, "from what I hear, your friend is better off not knowing his old man."

"That wasn't for you to decide."

He turned and walked out the lobby doors. When Pulchuck got in, Goatee closed the back door behind him, and they drove off into the darkness.

I sat staring at the little girl with ponytails on the cover of *What Work Is.* Her eyes were opened wide, as if caught in a headlight, her arms outstretched. On one side, she braced herself against factory equipment; on the other side, there was a gray wall, just below a window. The window was closed.

35

"What time did you get here?" Tim Silver said. "I went to the bag room. The stall was empty."

"I got the bag myself," I said.

We were on the driving range. It was 10:30 Saturday morning. I made a full swing, hitting my seven-iron at the 150-yard marker. The ball started low and rose against the crystalline sky, leveling out the way a plane raises into flight; then it reacted as if hitting a wall: It dropped down, falling thirty or more yards short of the target.

"I thought you said we'd meet here at eleven?" Silver said.

"Couldn't sleep. I came over with Lisa, played with Darcy in the day care center, then worked out. I putted for a half-hour and come here around nine-thirty. I've hit three bags of knockdown shots."

"You look like it. You'll need a fresh shirt before we play."

I knew I would. Three bags of range balls represented practice, not a warmup. According to the locker-room television, gusts were expected blow a minimum of fifteen miles an hour all day.

"I need to talk to you about something," I said, and was about to speak when I saw Perkins approaching. He wore a white golf shirt with the PGA Tour logo on the left breast, khakis, his wraparound sunglasses, and his typical scowl. His credential hung around his neck.

Jeff Sluman looked like a fifth grader next to him and quickly got out of Perkins's way.

"Quite a goddamned phone message you left me," Perkins said to me. He spit and crossed his arms, his biceps stretching the fabric of the XXL shirt. "You called at five-fifteen A.M.?" he said. "I was running."

"Where have you been?"

"Looking for Sean O'Reilly. Figured Pulchuck wouldn't show up here. Not with everyone looking for him. Guess I misjudged him. I don't usually do that." He took his sunglasses off. His face was flushed, and he squinted, his eyes adjusting to the sunlight. Crow's feet lined the corners of his eyes. "People can get killed if I misjudge somebody."

"What's going on?" Silver said.

I took the five-iron from the bag and addressed a Titleist Pro V1 range ball. I positioned the ball back in my stance, just below my left instep, waggled the clubface a couple times, and brought the iron back, an imperceptible pause at the top as my weight shifted. Then I began the down-swing. The contact was crisp, and I accelerated through the ball but finished low, my right hand never going higher than my left shoulder.

"Did Pulchuck say where he's going?" Perkins said.

I shook my head.

"You spoke to him?" Silver said.

"Yeah. He wanted to know if I saw them switch the bags. I didn't admit it, but that's what I need to talk to you about. I came out early to line up somebody else—a local cop—if you don't want to carry. And I wouldn't blame you one bit."

Silver pushed his sunglasses up and left them resting on his forehead. Sunlight shone down on his shaved skull, reflecting off it as it would a bright penny. "I'm in," he said.

"Tim, I won't think less of you. Reading greens is in the job description; death threats are not."

"It's never been dull carrying for you," he said. "Missed cuts, a win, punching people, now this. Just another chapter for my next book."

"Well, leave me out of it," Perkins said. "Lisa know about Pulchuck?"

"I told her," I said. "If I'm in danger, she might be, too. I tried to get her to take Darcy and go to Maryland, stay with her parents for a while. She won't do it. At least Deirdre is with her."

"Is she breaking the story?" Perkins said.

"What story?" I said. "That we followed a guy around northern Maine and now he's here? The Robert Pike shooting has been covered already."

"So Pulchuck is coming for me?" Perkins said.

"I think so. He wanted me to tell him what we saw in Maine. I wouldn't do it."

"Smart," Perkins said. "If he finds out you know about the smuggling, he would think he has to . . ." He made a gun with his right hand and let his thumb fall to his forefinger.

"I know," I said. "But I don't think he believed me. I think he'll be after us both."

"Let him come," Perkins said. "Let him come." He turned and walked away.

"He's not speaking for all of us, is he?" Silver said.

.   .   .

The wind had changed directions, making knowledge gained the previous day obsolete. But the old Bull's Eye was still rolling the ball well. I stepped to the tee at the par-four, 446-yard fifteenth, −10, five under par on my third round. I'd needed only twenty putts through fourteen holes.

The uphill fifteenth requires a drive down the right side of the fairway. After that, the green is protected by a deep trap to the left, a rock outcropping to the right, and a lateral hazard in back. It's a "TV hole," meaning the networks know fates will ascend or perish on this hole, so they station a camera behind the green and an on-course commentator in the fairway. Lisa was manning the tower behind the eighteenth green; the on-course commentator on No. 15 was Dan Ferrin, a former Tour player from Ireland.

"Got the flat stick going today, pardner," he said.

"I brought her out of retirement. Never heard an Irish guy say *pardner* before."

"This is Texas, Jack."

"Ahh," I said. "With that brogue, no one will guess you're not local."

The autumn Texas air felt cool as I swung the driver back and forth, keeping my back loose. My windbreaker flapped against my sides in the stiff breeze. The hole was playing into the wind, so three-wood was out of the question. When I was hitting it straight, driver was my wild-card against the field, and I would need it here.

I brought the TaylorMade r7 back slowly, making a wide arc and a big shoulder turn. When my back was to the target, I started my down-swing, striking the ball solidly, and finishing low, trying to keep the ball below the wind.

It landed in the fairway, 156 yards from the hole.

"ShotLink says that one was two-ninety," Ferrin said.

"Any birdies on this hole today?" I said.

He held up two fingers.

The leaderboard had changed dramatically. Faxon had slid down to −5, on pace for a seventy-six. J. P. Hayes had moved to −11 and was now the leader. Tiger was still hanging around at −9, which made me nervous. And, at ten under, I had played myself into solo second.

"Got time for a ten-second interview?" Ferrin said.

"If I say no, will you tell my wife?"

Silver chuckled.

"Of course I will," Ferrin said.

I gave a dramatic sigh and Ferrin smiled. The cameraman took his place.

"Jack, after struggling much of the summer, you're in contention. How does that feel?"

I had often complained to Lisa about the questions some of her colleagues asked. This one reminded me why.

"It feels great," I said, forcing a smile. "After my first Tour win and putting so well last year, I had very high expectations coming into this season."

"Is that why you've struggled a little bit, additional pressure on yourself?"

"I haven't analyzed the situation," I said. "I don't do that. I just work harder."

"Well, you're in great position off the tee. Ladies and Gentleman, we might see our third birdie of the day here, at number fifteen. Good luck, Jack. Thanks for taking the time."

"It's always good to talk to you, Dan."

The light on the camera dimmed. My playing partner, Jeff Sluman, was nearing his ball in the fairway. Silver and I moved toward him. The size of our gallery was to be expected. Whether I was in contention or not, Tiger Woods was in the field—and people paid to see Tiger, not Jack Austin. There were not more than 300 spectators following us. But that beat playing in front of only my family and the spectators who arrive at 6:30, lawn chairs in hand, and stake out a spot near the ropes, waiting to catch a glimpse of Phil, Tiger, Ernie, or Vijay. After nearly fifteen years on Tour and ranked inside the world's top 100 for the first time, I gladly take what I can get.

Sluman hit a rescue wood that ran onto the front of the green, leaving a long birdie putt. The pin had been cut at the back of the green.

At my ball, Silver and I each took yardage books out and did the respective math, trying to predict how many clubs the wind would equate to.

"One fifty-six to the middle," Silver said. "A hundred seventy yards to the back. But it's a two-club wind. I'd hit a five."

"Six-iron is my one-sixty club," I said.

"But four-iron is too much," Silver said. "There's a hazard in back. Short is safe. Long is dead."

We were one shot off the lead. My gut said six-iron, but Silver, who said he only caddied to write books about life on Tour, was rarely wrong. The big TaylorMade staff bag stood between us. I took the five-iron.

Silver hoisted the bag, iron heads clinking as he slung it over his shoulder, and moved to the side.

I brought the five-iron back and made crisp contact on my down-swing. As I looked up at the low-flying Titleist, I saw a foxtail of sod leap and dance, an end-over-end tumble, before the divot fell to the ground. The ball landed near Sluman's on the front of the green but ran up the putting surface, stopping fifteen feet to the right of the flagstick.

I pointed at Silver and winked.

"You know what Tiger pays Steve Williams?" he said.

"No."

"Well, neither do I, but it's a lot more than I make," he said. "And we both know I'm the best caddie on Tour."

I grinned. "Are you asking for a raise, right here? One good call doesn't make a career."

"One?!"

I grabbed the divot and threw it at him. It made a brown streak on his white poncho before falling to the ground.

.   .   .

At the green, Perkins stood alone, outside the rope at the back of the putting surface. The mid-afternoon sun burned a golden layer above the gray dust-swept sky. With his wraparound glasses, Perkins now wore a TaylorMade visor a rep had given him. But he looked like neither a golf fan nor a Tour official. He shifted from side to side and glanced around, his arms folded across his chest, his forearms the width of footballs and striped with thick cords of muscle.

Four college-aged kids were ten feet to Perkins's left. They wore Izod shirts and looked drunk. One kid said something to another and pointed at Perkins. He whispered something to his buddies. They all laughed. One of the friends made a *try-it* gesture. The second kid shook his head—*No Way.*

Perkins looked at them, a steady, heavy glare. The college kids weren't too drunk to catch the look or what it told them. They walked toward the sixteenth tee.

I didn't go to the back of the green. Silver set the bag on its side on the fringe, pulled the Bull's Eye out of it as if removing a sword from its sheath, and handed me the putter. I marked my ball and tossed it to Silver, who wiped it with the towel draped over his shoulder.

Sluman's ball was outside mine. He'd putt first.

"Let's go to school," Silver said. "He's got the same line."

I nodded. Sluman faced a putt identical to mine, only longer. I would gauge the break and speed by how his ball reacted. Sluman was not a long hitter but had an efficient game, meaning he made very few mistakes—fairways and greens. And he made a lot of putts. On this one, he'd have to navigate nearly fifty feet of green, but I knew he wouldn't three-putt. I watched carefully as his ball traversed over a ridge and gained speed, moving left and stopping two feet from the hole. I acknowledged the effort and gave Sluman a pat on the back as he moved past me to tap in.

I replaced my ball and crouched behind it. As always, I set the Titleist logo so that if struck solidly, the word would spiral, blurring into a single black line.

"Play two inches more break than Slu did," Silver said. "Aim just a little higher." He moved off the green like a voice coach offering a final tip and clearing the stage for the protégé.

I only nodded. I moved behind the ball and made several practice strokes while looking at the cup, an effort to gauge the speed. Then I looked down and made two more practice strokes, watching the copper putter face move back, then forward, swinging slightly open when it reached my back toe, squaring at the point of impact, and shutting on the follow-through—a perfect pendulum.

I moved to the ball and carefully positioned the blade behind it. Then I made my stroke, not looking up until the ball was fifteen feet away.

At six feet, it was dead center. I had my left hand raised, the putter pointing to the sky.

At two feet, I pumped my fist in the air.

The ball caught the right edge and spun out, ending my celebration. I tapped in for par.

"Thought you were going to grab the trophy before the ball even reached the cup," Perkins said, after I had given Silver my putter and walked to him. "That's what you get for celebrating early. Vanity will get you."

"You came back to say that?"

"No. I put something in your locker. You got a sports jacket?"

"Yeah. Why?"

He shook his head. "Got to go. You'll see. Have a good round."

36

"Funny meeting you here," Reporter Lisa said and grinned as she always did when she interviewed me.

I had signed my scorecard for a five-under-par sixty-five and was −10 overall. Now I wore headphones and sat in a high director's chair beside Lisa in the CBS tower behind the eighteenth green. In the years I had known her, we'd discussed every imaginable topic. Yet live television interviews with her still made me uncomfortable. They certainly didn't bother her. But then, she was the one asking the questions.

"Embattled Tour veteran Jack Austin has joined me," Lisa said, looking into the camera. "Austin is now the tournament's leader, on the heels of J. P. Hayes's double-bogey finish." Then to me: "Jack, you're ten under par this week, and playing well, but you've struggled this year. Why?"

"It's been an up-and-down season. I've shot a bunch of low scores, but never consecutively."

"How much does concentration have to do with that? Is it hard to concentrate with what took place between you and the fan in Boston?"

"No," I said. "I grind it out—every shot, every round."

Behind me, a clear plastic backdrop offered a view of the eighteenth green. On a nearby monitor, I saw Tiger Woods crouched behind his ball on the eighteenth green, hands on both sides of his cap's bill, forming a tunnel, so he could focus. I wondered if that image had prompted her question. A cameraman and a young redheaded woman stood in front of us. Both were dressed in jeans and T-shirts. The redhead wore a headset and held a stack of papers.

"But you've experienced some controversy this season," Lisa was saying. "That can't be easy to deal with. To push that aside or even overcome it and play this well takes focus. Viewers would be interested to know how you've done it."

I exhaled. She was known for asking tough questions. Players had always known that, and CBS certainly did when it brought her back to network coverage. She had a master's in journalism, had guest lectured at Georgetown, and had reported for the *Washington Post*. But I had been up half the night; I was still waiting to discover Perkins's mystery gift; and I had fought the wind—and beaten it—for the past thirty-six holes. I wanted a steak, a bottle of Beck's, and my two-year-old jumping on my hotel bed. Not a reporter dredging up my season's low points, especially those involving Jerome Pulchuck, who had again threatened me—especially when the reporter was my better half.

"Putts just haven't fallen this year," I said, and shrugged.

"Golf is a mental game," she said. "Millions of viewers struggle with that aspect every weekend. How can a recreational player put personal issues aside and focus, as you've done on golf's largest stage this week?"

She had an angle and wasn't letting go. "Like I said, the putts are starting to fall. If I knew why or how, I'd be ranked number one in the world."

I saw her eyebrows rise slightly. Then she ran her tongue along her upper lip, something she did only when she was angry.

"I changed putters this week," I said, trying to make up ground and hoping my TaylorMade sponsors weren't watching. "That's one difference. I'm using an old Bull's Eye."

"To your credit," she said, "the golf course doesn't usually play this hard. What are the conditions like?"

"The wind seems to change direction every day. All you can do is try to keep the ball low and play by feel. And putt well."

"Well, you are certainly doing that right now. Thanks for your time, Jack."

The light went off on the camera. The redhead brought Lisa a bottle of water.

"'Embattled Tour player'?" I said. "Jesus, Lisa, did you have to bring up Boston?"

"It takes strength to put that behind you."

I shook my head. "I'm surprised you didn't mention the shooting in Garrett."

"That's part of an ongoing investigation. You'd have no-commented me."

I stood up. "'Embattled Tour player,'" I said again.

"You don't consider yourself embattled, Jack? Peter Barrett sent me an e-mail today asking me to remind you of your meeting tonight."

"What meeting?" I said.

She shook her head. "I told him it was between you and him."

The girl in the T-shirt said, "Lisa, back in five . . . and four . . . and . . ."

"I'll get Darcy and meet you at the hotel," I said and left the tower.

. . .

The daycare center, like the Tour's fitness facility, was mobile. The PGA Tour moved circuslike, in forty-eight-foot trailers, city to city. The day care center was superb with three teachers and soundless pagers so players' wives could watch the action while maintaining contact with the daycare providers in case they were needed. Before heading to the locker room, I swung by to get Darcy.

As always, I went to her "cubby," a tiny locker in which Lisa or I would leave a backpack with a change of clothes for Darcy and one of my old T-shirts Darcy could wear as a smock on days when the kids painted. The backpack was pink and had come from LL Bean. *Darcy* was stitched on the outside with a friendly owl next to the name. Darcy's extra sneakers lay beside the backpack. I grabbed the sneakers and opened the backpack to put them inside.

There was a handwritten note on hotel stationary.

If you told me what you saw, we could have settled this like businessmen. Are you too good for my money? I grew up with people like you. You should forget Garrett, ME, *because everything has a price and your daughter is a lovely child.*

I couldn't focus on the note. The words were bouncing, as my hand shook. I stuffed the small sheet into my pants pocket just before I heard, "Daddy!" and felt Darcy's arms wrap around my legs. I scooped her up and took her to the locker room with me.

. . .

"Jack."

I had just left the locker room and was in the parking lot. I nearly jumped at the sound and whirled.

"You're on edge, Jack," PGA Tour Commissioner Peter Barrett said, walking toward me, his patent leather shoes clicking on the pavement, the cuffs of his dark slacks dancing with each step. "I sent your wife an e-mail. She wrote back, saying she was here this week as a journalist and didn't agree with my decision to begin with and therefore wouldn't pass my message on to you."

"What's the message, Commissioner?"

I had foregone the sports jacket Perkins had recommended. Instead, I'd tossed it along with his gift in a duffle and zipped it tightly. The duffle was on one shoulder, Darcy on the other.

The parking lot in front of the clubhouse was roped off, allowing access to only players and Tour staff. The lot looked like a Buick dealership. J. P. Hayes, wife Laura, and their two kids walked from the clubhouse to a Rendezvous. Hayes waived, and I returned the gesture. It was nearly 6 P.M. The huge Texas sun was setting. The wind was dying, but I smelled the sweet scent of the desert landscape. The aroma reminded me of eucalyptus. It might have been sagebrush or cactus. I was more comfortable naming pine, maple, and birch trees than I was the Texas landscape, but had always enjoyed the terrain.

Darcy's carseat was strapped into the courtesy car, a Buick Rendezvous. I popped the trunk and set my shoulder bag gently inside.

"Doing laundry?" Barrett said, and pointed at the duffle.

I stepped back and closed the hatch. If I were to put what was inside the bag in the washer, Perkins would be out $400.

"Yeah," I said. "I'm doing laundry at the hotel. Can you believe the prices for that?" I moved to the side of the vehicle, opened the back door, and set Darcy in her seat.

"Where's Mommy?" she said.

"Working, sweetie. She'll meet us for dinner."

"Jack," Barrett said and extended his hand. In it was a business card. "You're to be at this woman's office at seven-thirty tonight."

"This the anger-management program?"

"This is an evaluation."

"Did Daly have to do this?"

"Tour personnel issues and disciplinary actions are confidential."

"You sent him to a counselor. Is it the same one?"

"Tour personnel issues and disciplinary actions are confidential, Jack. You don't know John Daly was *sent* anywhere."

"Just like Jonathon Kaye's suspension."

Barrett's brows furrowed. They were brown and seemed to clash with his silver hair. Brass-framed glasses were neatly folded in the breast pocket of his crisp white shirt. I was surprised to see him without his suit jacket. It was almost difficult to be mad at the guy. He had grown the PGA Tour to the point where a player of my stature—one win in more than a decade—could have career earnings beyond his wildest dreams. But he hadn't done that by being a Boy Scout. He was a tough negotiator. And he would protect the game, his tour, and its reputation at all cost.

"The media speculated on Mr. Kaye's situation," Barrett said, "as it did with Mr. Daly's. I suggest you focus on yourself, Jack. On getting your emotions in check. This woman can help you."

"I'll go see her. But consider my emotions this week when judging me. Everything is in check here. Boston was an isolated incident."

"You were involved in a shooting at a golf course in Maine, Jack. Some people say trouble follows you." He turned and reached into the car to pat Darcy's head. She grabbed his hand and pulled his finger. "I think maybe it's the other way around."

"Perkins must have explained what happened in Garrett, Maine."

"And I told Mr. Perkins that he is employed by the Tour, not as your personal bodyguard. As I said before, I'm tired of these situations. And they seem to always involve the same player."

"I'm doing the best I can," I said.

"Go talk to Dr. Chavez tonight. If you need help, I want to know."

Barrett turned and walked away. I took the bag from the trunk and set it gently on the passenger's seat. I wanted the 9-mm beside me.

$\mathcal{I}$ was trying to be rational—Lisa was a CBS journalist, her face splashed across televisions every week; I was a Tour veteran, not famous, not in TV commercials, but known by many. Would Jerome Pulchuck abduct our child? A few years ago, Brian Taylor, an associate of mine at Tour Headquarters in Ponte Vedra Beach, Florida, had asked himself similar questions and had, apparently, answered no. His little girl had been kidnapped. Maybe I had learned from Brian Taylor. Or maybe I was just a different man. Regardless, I was running on instinct, and I wouldn't let Darcy out of my sight.

The 9-mm was a Smith & Wesson. It had a four-inch barrel and held ten rounds in the clip, one in the chamber. It was loaded. And it no longer felt heavy in my palm.

A knock on the hotel room door shook the room.

"Let me see the note," was all Perkins said when he entered with Lisa, whose mascara had streaked her face. She set her bag down and went to Darcy without a word. Lisa sat rocking Darcy on the edge of the bed, crying softly.

"Mommy," Darcy said, pushing away from Lisa, twisting to reach toward the floor, "my Raggedy Ann." Lisa put Darcy on the floor. The two-year-old waddled happily toward her doll, picked it up, examined it, and hugged it, mumbling, "My baby. My baby."

"No one at the day care saw anyone," I said. "They told me no one came to visit Darcy. So he just left the note and took off."

"But he got in there," Perkins said. "Pack everything up. I've arranged for a room change."

"Pack up?" Lisa said.

Perkins nodded. "Pulchuck is much better than we, or I, thought, Lisa. I'm not taking chances. He got past the front desk at the day care. It's not exactly the Pentagon. And maybe he timed it just right—a shift change or when someone was in the restroom—or maybe he got lucky. I don't know. But I know when I go in the day care, I have to show ID."

Lisa's face was pale, her bottom lip started to tremble. I had seen her put Earl Woods on the spot about his Jesus-like world-changing predictions of greatness for Tiger. I knew she had approached Tiger himself about death threats he reportedly received, saying she wanted to track the threats back to the sender. Woods had declined comment, but her inclination had made him smile. Lisa was tough, determined, and strong. But Darcy had been put in danger, and now Lisa was badly shaken.

I put my arm around her. "Everything's going to be fine," I whispered. "It's going to be okay."

She looked at me, black lines staining her cheeks. "Say it again."

I did.

.   .   .

"You've looked at your watch four times since you arrived, Mr. Austin," Denise Chavez said. Her head shook back and forth sadly.

I didn't deny it. I was well aware of the time: 7:45 P.M. Exactly fifteen minutes had crawled by like wounded soldiers.

I had arrived on time. Deirdre was still around, and Perkins agreed to stay with Lisa and Darcy until I got back. Lisa was staying in San Antonio, declining, again, to visit her parents in Maryland, saying she wanted to know Perkins and I were nearby. Sunday, we would all fly back to Maine. The USA network had Thursday and Friday coverage of the next event, the 84 Lumber Classic of Pennsylvania. So we could take a three-day breather in Maine.

"Now, tell me how you feel when you are angry."

I looked at her. "Angry."

"I see," she said. Chavez's Spanish accent lost some of its elegance because her voice was a rusted gate. "Let's delve into your psychological state, shall we? What do you *see?*"

"'See'?" I said.

"Yes. What do you visualize when you're angry. For instance, tell me what you saw when you struck the fan in Boston?"

"I saw a threat to my child. So I dropped the guy."

"That's what you *perceived,* Jack. Tell me what you *saw.* Tell me about the images—colors, shapes—your mental landscape."

"Excuse me?"

She managed not to sigh, but she did recross her legs and jot something on the small white pad resting on her lap. Dr. Denise Chavez wore a navy blue business suit. Her slacks exposed a thin ankle bracelet, which surprised me. Maybe she had more personality than I'd given her credit for. She wore her thick black hair in a long braid. Huge hoop earrings hung to the collar of her suit jacket. Her eyeliner was pronounced, and when she looked out at me from behind thick, wide spectacles, I felt like the struggling English major I had been at UMaine.

The office was small and faced the River Walk. The outer wall was glass. Chest-high bookshelves lined the sides of the room and above them hung photos that I imagined had been selected to soothe—a chocolate Lab standing near the edge of a pond; a boy and girl Darcy's age holding hands; and one—blatantly— of a woman in a hammock, a Caribbean sunset in the distance.

"When you are angry, Jack, really angry, do you remember all of the events that take place?"

"Yeah."

"Why are you grinning?"

"Because I'm not nuts. Did you talk to Daly?" If the Tour could schedule Saturday night appointments, I guessed her to be the Tour's first choice.

"Who?"

"John Daly. Did Barrett make him do this, too?"

"Tell me what you remember about hitting the man in Boston," she said.

"He was standing next to my wife and reached over and touched my child. He did it as a threat."

She waited.

"The guy has a long criminal history," I said. "He touched my daughter's head. It was a message. So I sent him one back."

"Is that how you deal with all conflicts?"

"Of course not."

"What makes you certain it was meant as a threat?"

"I met with the guy the night before," I said. "He wanted some photos a friend of mine had."

"What were the photos of?"

"Turns out nothing much. But he thought they might jeopardize his illegal enterprises. Look, Dr. Chavez, I don't have anger issues. This same guy got into my daughter's day care facility today. He left me a note. I'm not overreacting."

She chewed on that. It was 7:55 P.M. now. My appointment ran until 8:15.

"I have helped many people deal with personal problems, Jack. I can help you as well."

"I don't have problems," I said, the irony apparent even to me—the guy who had driven to his hotel with a 9-mm on the car seat next to him.

"You have no personal problems? Come now, Jack."

"Peter Barrett might be one. He wants me to join the Euro Tour. He thinks bad luck follows me, or I follow it. Either way, it's bad for his tour."

"Which is it? Do you follow bad luck or does it follow you?"

Outside the Texas night was clear and bright. Stars lined the sky like bright rocks in a riverbed. The moon was nearly full.

"Quite a view," I said. "The sun sets late here."

"You don't like my question?"

"Sorry," I said. "I'm married to a journalist. I don't follow bad luck, Doctor. This began with a kid asking for help. The kid means a lot to me. He's all but adopted by my wife and me. And I won't let him down."

"Meaning what?"

"Meaning I tried to help him, and this thing spilled all over me and my family. Now I'll do whatever is required."

"What will Peter Barrett think of that?"

"Not much. And I don't care. I do the best I can. Sometimes that gets me in trouble."

She wrote some more. Her face gave nothing away.

. . .

Saturday night, as Lisa and Darcy slept, I lay awake thinking about my conversation with Denise Chavez, recalling her question: Did trouble follow me, or did I follow it? As I listened to Lisa's rhythmic breath and saw Darcy's tiny features in the moonlight, the question seemed reasonable.

The first time I had met Pulchuck, that night in the bar, I could have promised to have Nash get Owen Henley's photos and agreed to turn them over to Pulchuck. None of this would have happened. Darcy would not have been threatened. Lisa wouldn't have been terrorized in a way only a mother could be. Richard Pike would still be alive, and thus Perkins would not suffer the guilt of Pike's death.

But that train of thought felt all wrong.

Finally, at 1:33 A.M., still awake, I sighed and got up. I sat by the window, reading Philip Levine's book by the light of a tiny book lamp. The poem "Fire" begins:

> A fire burns along the eastern rim
> of mountains. In the valley we
> see it as a celestial prank, for
> in the summer haze the mountains
> themselves are lost, but as the night
> deepens the fire grows more golden
> and dense . . . I know my son
> is there . . .

This fire was no celestial prank. Never before had I felt so conflicted. I had made the people closest to me fearful and vulnerable. But Nash had asked for help, and Lisa, Perkins, and I would all do whatever we could to assist him. However, no one had seen Pulchuck's day care threat coming.

I snapped off the small lamp, closed the book, and looked at Darcy, her moonlit face angelic. Again, she wore the purple Disney Princesses pajamas. She slept in a posture fit for dreams of flight—arms cast out to her sides, a faint smile on her lips. Her small hands quivered, and I noticed the pale skin of her palms—unblemished, uncallused, pure. I had once read a quote by Daryl Stingley, a paralyzed former NFL player, who said a man should never do anything that jeopardized dancing with his daughter on her wedding day. I noticed the tiny roadmaps lining the smooth flesh of Darcy's hands and thought of the future.

.   .   .

Sunday morning, I did not feel like the tournament leader. For consistent contenders, sleeping with the fifty-four-hole lead is probably easy. I had led going into the weekend only a handful of times and had held on to win only once. I never slept soundly with the lead, knowing full well what a Tour win would mean—exemption, financial gain, respect among my peers, and, more than anything, self-respect, knowing that for one week I had beaten the world's best. As was typical when I played with the lead, on this day, I arrived at the course tired from fitful sleep. The difference was that in the past, I'd always spent the night thinking golf and strategy. This day, I arrived tired, my mind cluttered with thoughts of Jerome Pulchuck.

At 9:45 A.M., I entered the locker room with Darcy. I was dressed in jeans, a gray T-shirt that said VACATIONLAND, and loafers on my bare feet. After lifting weights, I would change into my "uniform"—a collared shirt, khaki pants, a Concho belt with my PGA Tour money clip attached, Adidas shoes, and a TaylorMade cap—before heading to the range. I set Darcy down on the carpet.

At the beginning of the week, my locker had contained four

outfits. Now it was down to two. Both shirts were striped. One was red, the other black. Tiger was known for his "Sunday red"— wearing a red shirt on Sundays when he was in the hunt. I'd wear black. It had been that kind of week.

General Davis sat down beside me and picked up Darcy. "Better than finding Tim Silver in here."

I grinned. The handbook states only participants and players' sons are allowed in the locker room during tournaments, with a $100 fine for a player who violates the rule. Darcy wasn't a son, but I was keeping her with me, which probably wouldn't help my image with Peter Barrett. But a hundred bucks was worth peace of mind.

"Let's hit the buffet, Darcy," General said. He picked her up and walked across the room.

The locker room smelled of ham and fried onions. I'd always enjoyed the golf course but would come back each year for the breakfast buffet alone: orange juice, fruit, flavored coffees, eggs, omelets, breakfast burritos, and plenty of peppers, Tabasco, and salsa.

J. P. Hayes and I were slated to play together in the day's final afternoon pairing. Hayes had not arrived yet. I was five hours early, but Darcy was safer in a crowded and secure locker room than in a hotel. Across the room, Fred Funk was kidding Billy Andrade about something. A group of players seated before lockers laughed. Skip Kendall was sitting in front of the television, watching *SportsCenter*. In the buffet line, General held Darcy and one plate and told Justin Leonard what to put on a second plate. They walked to a card table in the corner and sat down, Leonard holding his plate and Darcy's. I got a coffee and joined them.

On a second television, CNN updated the Iraq War. Three more soldiers had been killed, the Middle East reporter said. I thought of Lea Griffin and her husband. I was seated among millionaires. I was eating a gourmet breakfast, graciously provided to me free of charge because I could hit a golf ball. I looked at the television again. It showed the carnage of the Hummer, which a suicide bomber had driven into, armed with explosives.

"Mr. Austin," a locker room attendant said.

I turned from the television. The man was my father's age, short, with olive skin and dark eyes.

"There is a man outside," the attendant said. "He would like to see you. He does not look . . ." He paused, his eyes moving from mine to the General and Leonard. His gaze came back to me. "He does not look like, well, like someone you would know, sir."

"What do you mean?"

"He seems rather . . ." Again he paused. "Well, unkempt, sir."

"A short guy? Stocky? Ponytail?"

"Ponytail? No, sir."

My description fit Pulchuck. If not him, who? I thought about it. "Keep Darcy," I said to General. "If I'm not back in ten minutes, call Perkins."

"Perkins the security guy?"

"Yeah."

"What are you talking about?" General said.

I kissed Darcy, stood, and headed out the door.

"I'm here to say I'm sorry." His appearance certainly fit that of a man who had not been seen or heard from in almost a week. And Sean O'Reilly hadn't changed a bit. He spread his hands and smiled warmly. "I was thinking maybe you could buy me a drink, and we could be friends again."

"You sold me out once," I said, looking over my shoulder. "I wouldn't mind punching your lights out."

"Would you hit an old guy like me?"

"No. But I don't trust you."

"I'm friends with your uncle Bill. We went to college together. Sort of drifted apart after that. Things went different for him than for me." He looked down.

Behind me, the locker room door opened, and Mike Weir walked past, glancing covertly at O'Reilly. O'Reilly was still looking at the ground. He was unshaven, his hair was matted and greasy, and his clothing more soiled than usual—faded jeans and a white T-shirt with yellow rings at the armpits. Spectators also walked by, fans who had paid around fifty bucks to attend. It made me wonder how O'Reilly had gotten in.

But many passersby glanced at O'Reilly and turned away with expressions of distaste. O'Reilly saw one woman do it, and his eyes fell to the pavement again. It had been an affront to his dignity. He was about sixty—my father's age—but unlike my father, he was ashamed.

"I came to apologize," he said, not looking up. "Do you accept it?"

"Shit," I said, exasperated. "Wait here."

I went back to the locker room, nodded to General that all was fine, made a trip through the buffet, and went outside again.

"Here," I said, handing the plate to O'Reilly. "You look like you haven't eaten since Garrett."

He took the plate. "Thanks, man. It's been along trip. I caught a cab and the homo driver tried to get me."

I held up a hand. "I don't want to hear it. Where is Jerome Pulchuck?"

"Don't know, man," he said, chewing a burrito. I had brought three.

"O'Reilly," I said, "my best friend had to kill a man because of you. You're wanted as a witness in that shooting and, probably, as a suspect in what most likely is an international smuggling ring. *Where is Jerome Pulchuck?*"

O'Reilly swallowed the last of the first burrito. His eyes danced up to meet mine, then returned to his food the way a hungry dog looks at you when you try to interrupt a feeding—the command had been heard, yet the instinct to eat had him torn.

I reached for the plate.

He turned sideways. "What are you doing, man? What's this about witness and suspect?"

247

"Robert Pike was shot dead. You saw that. You guys switched golf bags. Something was in them. Probably money and pot. Don't you think some federal agents, FBI and Border Patrol types, would like to sit down with you?"

"I didn't do anything." Egg yoke fell down his chin and streaked the front of his shirt before hitting the ground. He kept eating.

"You were there. Guilt by association. Tell me where Jerome is. The guy is crazy, Sean. He threatened my daughter. He threatened Bill's niece."

O'Reilly had finished. He didn't know what to do with the plate. I took it and set it atop a gray-hooded garbage receptacle near the door. O'Reilly was nervous. He had nothing to do with his hands now and clasped them before him, then suddenly thrust them in his pant pockets. His head was down again—a sixty-year-old man standing like a scolded fourth grader.

"Man, I was *just driving*." His head shook back and forth. "Just like Owen. I knew he'd run his mouth and lost the job. So I wasn't going to do that. I was *just driving*."

"Didn't work out that way, did it? Things went sour, and a guy got shot. Perkins and I could have been shot. Where is Jerome Pulchuck?"

"Last time I saw him was up in Maine. We stopped for gas in Presque Isle. He sent me into a store, and when I came out, he was gone."

"How'd you get here?"

"Jerome paid me fifteen hundred up front. I flew. Cost most of it."

"Why'd you come?"

"To say I was sorry," he said. "To tell you that, man. You bought me some drinks, took me to dinner. Not many people have done that."

I heard myself exhale and looked at my watch: 10:35. I didn't tee off until 2:20. "You sit your ass right here. I'll be back in five minutes. This time, you're going to help me."

"Help how?"

"I'm going to get some people who want to find Pulchuck

and who want to know what's going on along the border. If you talk honestly, you can help me and yourself, too."

"Okay," he said. "Can you bring me another burrito?"

I said I would and went back to the locker room. I dug my cell phone out of my locker and called Perkins's cell phone. Then I got Darcy from General and took her to the bathroom to change a soggy diaper. When we reappeared from the changing table, Perkins entered the locker room from the clubhouse, his PGA Tour credentials hanging from his neck, his wraparound Oakleys still on. Two uniformed cops were with him. I led them outside.

"Where is he?" Perkins said.

"He was right here," I said.

People moved to and fro, heading one direction toward the first tee and going the other way to walk the back nine. Sean O'Reilly wasn't among them. The plate he'd eaten burritos from had fallen off the garbage can. It lay in pieces on the ground.

J. P. Hayes (−9) and I (−10) made up the tournament's final pairing at 2:20. I had spent time on the range and putting green and had fielded several interview requests—all of which were less stressful than Lisa's embattled-Tour-player angle, although her interview and our ensuing disagreement now seemed long ago. Sean O'Reilly had not been found, which concerned me, but I felt comfortable as I swung the club back and forth, keeping my back loose on the first tee. Hayes and I were waiting for the twosome in front of us—Brad Faxon and Sergio Garcia—to clear.

The final round had begun early that morning, with me clutching a one-stroke lead. The lead had held up. None of the big guns had made significant charges, although Woods was on the fourth hole at −9. Justin Leonard had shot the day's low round and was in the clubhouse at −9, tied with Woods and Hayes. The morning had seen sporadic gusts, which might have accounted for the lack of movement on the leaderboard. Now, however, the air was still and dry.

My mind was nearly clear for the first time in almost twenty-four hours. I had shoved thoughts of Sean O'Reilly aside, and Perkins had put me at ease when Deirdre Hackney, his blonde associate, had turned heads when she walked onto the driving range at 11:30 with PGA Tour credentials and said she would spend the day in the day care with Darcy. Two rookies had approached me not long after she departed. I'd told them she was my sister and to back off.

"Well, boss, let's run and gun," Tim Silver said. "Kick all the bullshit aside. We've got a tournament to win."

Just hearing it gave me goose flesh. *Winning.* It was why I played. If I could hold on, I could turn around the season. A strong four-hour stretch of golf could make up for eight months of missed putts and missed cuts. The winner took home $630,000, but money was secondary.

I took my Titleist Pro V1 from my pocket and tossed it casually into the air. Players have gimmicks to relax. Lee Trevino used to yawn, making opponents think he was calm enough to doze off, while taking in extra oxygen. I had always tossed a ball, keeping my hands soft and shoulders and arms loose.

In the first row of spectators beside the tee box, Padre Tarbuck stood wedged between an older couple and a young boy who wore a visor with signatures scribbled in black felt-tipped marker. In the fairway, Faxon was standing with a yardage book open, discussing something with his caddie. I had time. I walked across the tee box to Padre.

We shook hands. I looked at the kid beside him. The boy was nine or ten. "You know who this guy is? This is Brian Tarbuck. He's won a bunch of tournaments, but he's on vacation this week."

The kid held up his visor and pen. Padre signed it.

"Just wanted you to know I'm pulling for you, buddy," Padre

said, handing the visor back to the boy. "I've been putting better. Left hand low. Shot sixty-nine last week."

"Good to hear. So when are you coming back?"

"Don't know if I am."

The older couple beside us appeared interested.

"Duval is playing well," I said, "isn't he?"

Padre looked at me. I said nothing, but held his gaze.

Finally, he shook his head and grinned. "You're a clever guy, Jack Austin, and a good friend, but I'm not sure what I'll do."

I smiled and went back to Silver.

The first hole played downhill and was playing downwind, a 665-yard par five. The slight breeze from behind carried the sweet scent of sage. After contact, I held the follow-through pose and watched my Titleist fly long and straight, landing short of the fairway bunker I used as my target. I still had a long way to reach the undulating green, yet with water behind the putting surface and the flag tucked in the back quadrant, my second shot would be a lay-up, leaving 115 yards—a full pitching wedge—to the pin.

At the green, Hayes and I both lay three. He had four feet for birdie. I was six paces from the hole.

"That ridge makes this putt a bitch," Silver said.

My "perfect" 115-yard wedge shot had been adrenaline-jacked and carried 122—long and left—resulting in a side-hill putt that would feed across a slope, then down, to the hole. If I let the speed get away from me, the ball could run eight or ten feet by.

I selected the line. I didn't want to miss on the low side—it would gain speed and run way by. On the other hand, if I played too much break, and the ball missed above the hole, it might run even farther past the cup. But I hated missing low on side-hill putts. It meant you'd left it short, and short putts have no chance. Moreover, I was leading the event. I didn't want to take my foot off the pedal.

The scoreboard near the green showed that Woods had bogeyed the fifth hole, dropping to −8. My lead was one over Hayes and Leonard, who was in the clubhouse no doubt waiting to see if I'd hand him the trophy.

I vowed not to.

I addressed the putt and made two practice strokes, looking at the cup to gauge the speed. Then I positioned the Bull's Eye, setting the toe of the blade behind the ball, rather than the blade's sweet spot, to deaden the blow.

I squeezed the putter once, turning my knuckles white, then released, blew out a long breath, and made my stroke, never looking up until the ball was four feet away.

It tracked too high and ran past the far edge of the hole, down the slope, and stopped six feet below the hole—not the start for which I'd hoped.

Hayes was next to putt and buried his, to go to −10 and a share of the lead.

I went back to work, grinding over my six-footer. I didn't want to drop a shot and start the day playing catch up. I wanted to finish what I had begun. If you enter a final round with the lead, you have to be able to hold it. Great players close the deal.

"Straight in," Silver said. "Just make your stroke. You know the line—aim right for the heart."

I had been crouched behind the ball and straightened. Silver walked to the fringe, clearing the stage. Golf tournaments are usually lost, not won. And every tournament hinges on two or three momentum-changing events. I had been around long enough to sense those moments when they were at hand.

I looked over at Hayes. He looked back, deadpan—no encouragement, no outward desire to see me fail.

I set the blade behind the ball and made my stroke. The "Titleist" logo blurred to a black line, and the ball fell into the heart of the cup. I was still −10. But now I shared the lead.

.   .   .

Hayes and I came to No. 7 still deadlocked. The hole is a par four, the tee box sits eighty yards higher than the landing area, and the layout is only 316 yards long—reachable, on paper, for long hitters. However, water runs right of the fairway, and a bunker called "Rattlesnake" makes all tee shots dangerous. On this day, no doubt to add drama, the pin was cut in the front, on the left, a placement that would surely tempt many to swing for the green.

Hayes had the honor, and I saw him take what looked like a three-iron out. He made a rhythmic pass at the ball, leaving himself optimal sand-wedge distance to the flagstick—a smart play, a safe play.

I pulled the head cover off the big r7. Several spectators around the tee box murmured. They knew I was going for it.

"You sure about that, hoss?" Silver said. "Wind is at us a little. Three-sixteen might play three-thirty."

"It's downhill," I said, "and we haven't been in this position all year."

"We've got eleven more holes today, Jack."

But I handed him the head cover and pulled the driver from the bag. The sun was warm on my back. The weatherman promised high eighties and had delivered. A slight breeze blew dry against my face. Nearby, a leaderboard showed Woods still at −8, alone in third. For him, three birdies were not unlikely. Since the fifth hole, in fact, his scorecard showed three birdies, offset by three bogeys. But he still had eight holes to play.

It was a four-man race, and I knew Leonard sat safely at −9. I couldn't see what Woods was doing ahead of me, only listen for the "Tiger roars" and wait to see the score board change. But I did know what Hayes had just done—played safe—and I knew that opened the door for me. If I could drive the green, I could make birdie easily and eagle possibly.

Silver was placid as he took the bag and moved to the side.

I made two practice swings that felt well paced and solid. Then I addressed the ball, the big 400-cubic-centimeter titanium head of the r7 brushing the grass behind it. I brought the club back, pausing just short of parallel at the top. Then my hips began shifting to my left, my weight transferring, my left hand pulling the stiff graphite shaft down. At the moment of impact, everything was square again—my hips, the clubface, and my hands—then the right wrist rolled over the left, and I felt the crisp sensation of contact. The ball was airborne.

As if someone had momentarily hit "mute" then restored the volume, the sound of the surrounding crowd came back to me. But when I looked up, I knew instantly why the cheers had faded to a unified sigh. The ball had carried the left greenside bunker but kicked hard to the left when it landed. I would face a difficult chip from the left side to get up and down for birdie.

Next, Hayes hit an approach shot that, from our vantage point in the fairway, looked no more than eight feet from the hole—for birdie.

When we reached my ball, things went from bad to worse. The Titleist had nestled in an old divot, fifteen yards from the green. Silver went to the putting surface and paced off the yardage, figuring how far I needed the ball to carry.

"It isn't good," he said when he came back. "Got to fly it over the trap, and there's only ten paces from the edge of the green to the hole."

I had read somewhere that Chi Chi Rodriguez could hit six different clubs (six different shots) from any greenside lie. I looked down at my ball and shook my head. This shot selection wasn't one that offered choices. I had to get the ball high and stop it on a dime. The ball sat in the depression, half of it below the turf like a fried egg. I had one thing going for me: The divot pointed down my target line. Someone had played this shot already. I wondered how they had fared and decided it was probably better not to know.

The real problem wouldn't be hitting it out of the divot; that was why I lifted weights. I could muscle the clubface through the dirt. The problem would be judging *how* the ball would come out. Easy, like a bunker shot, or difficult like gnarly rough?

"What do you think?" Silver said.

"You seen guys have to do crazy things in tournaments, like hit left-handed from behind a tree?"

He nodded.

"It's like that," I said.

I took the sixty-degree wedge from the bag and swung it back and forth, taking long, hard swings. Then I addressed the ball and took a monstrous cut, hitting well behind the ball, nearly sending the entire divot in which the ball sat airborne.

I heard Silver yelling for the ball to go. When I looked up, I saw a divot larger than one of my size tens fall short of the green, but watched as the ball landed near the flagstick. The gallery cheered wildly.

"Damned near perfect," Silver said.

Hayes slapped my back in appreciation.

But when I got to the green, I saw my birdie putt was nearly ten feet. I had needed to land the ball short of the pin, with backspin, to have it stop close. I hadn't been able to do that. Advantage: Hayes.

I was still away and would putt first. Straight and slightly uphill. I could be aggressive.

I set up to the ball, made two practice strokes, and pulled the trigger. The birdie attempt ran three feet by. Silver said nothing. I marked the ball and watched Hayes drop his birdie putt into the heart of the cup.

I replaced my ball and checked the line—straight in. As I addressed the ball again, a "Tiger roar" went up ahead of us. Woods had done something positive—birdie or eagle. I looked at the hole again. A standard golf hole is four and one-quarter inches wide. This one suddenly looked no bigger than a dime. I backed off the putt. There was no leaderboard nearby, but Hayes was −11 and Woods surely was −9, if not −10. We had reached one of those momentum-swinging moments again.

I exhaled slowly. Three feet. I had made hundreds of thousands of three-footers in my lifetime. My father used to say three footers were where you saved strokes and made up ground.

I brought the Bull's Eye back slowly and made a solid stroke, never peaking, waiting to hear the tapping of the Surlyn cover against the plastic cup. That music didn't come. The gallery sighed.

I saw my ball sitting to the left of the hole. It had caught the right edge and spun out. Bogey. I had fallen to −9.

.   .   .

When Hayes and I reached the tee at the 186-yard par-three seventeenth, we were tied at −9, with Woods in the clubhouse at −11, having finished with a flurry. Neither Hayes nor I spoke on the tee. Each of us knew what needed to be done.

Par is usually a great score on this hole. The green is protected front-right and back-left by bunkers and has a lot of subtle un-dulations. But I knew par wouldn't be good enough. I needed a birdie–birdie finish.

I took a step in the right direction, hitting a laser to within six feet of the pin.

"Best swing of the day," Silver said. "No fat lady singing yet." He handed me my putter and gave me a high-five.

Hayes hit next, sending his ball ten feet past the flag, still a makeable birdie putt.

At the green, Silver and I went to work, reading the breaks between my ball and the cup. Hayes was first to putt and when his ball died just short of the cup, he hunched, hands on knees. Par wasn't good enough. Both of us needed to make up two shots with two holes to play. Hayes's reaction told me he knew he had inadvertently conceded.

I replaced my ball and made two practice strokes. The ball would move four inches, right to left. I had played the course each year since the tournament moved to La Cantera Golf Club in 1995, so I had faced this same putt before. And I had missed it before—by not playing enough break. I had only six feet. I would play five inches. If I missed, it would be on the high side, not short.

I made my stroke and never looked up. I didn't hear the ball click against the bottom of the cup this time either. The gallery's cheer was too loud. I was −10, one off Woods's lead with one hole—and one final birdie opportunity—left.

.   .   .

The eighteenth is a par four and plays tougher than its 426 yards might indicate. I was reviewing the yardage book, trying to de-cide where to position my drive to leave the best angle to the flag. I was contemplating the right-side fairway bunker. I could try to fly the bunker, which would leave a short-iron to the green, or I could hit my three-wood short and not worry about the bunker at all. Except three-wood would leave a long-iron to the green, and I needed a birdie.

In the distance, I heard a siren. San Antonio is a large city. But the siren seemed to grow louder, as if getting closer. Ahead, near the clubhouse, I spotted blue lights from a police cruiser. Near it, I saw the green flashers of an ambulance.

A murmur went through the gallery. Faxon and Garcia were in the eighteenth fairway. Garcia had been preparing to hit his approach shot to the green when he had backed off his ball. I watched as he said something to Faxon and pointed toward the clubhouse.

"What the hell's going on up there?" Silver said. "We're trying to win a golf tournament here."

Police, serving as security, are at every PGA Tour event, but not with lights flashing and sirens. Like a gust of hot desert air, a thought struck me and my mind broke into fifty-yard sprints: Jerome Pulchuck had threatened my family. I looked around the tee box and counted eight uniformed cops. Why the cops? What was an ambulance doing at the clubhouse?

I saw Perkins three rows back, standing next to a uniformed officer, and went over. Perkins sighed and met me at the rope sectioning off the tee box.

"Where are Lisa and Darcy?" I said. "What happened?"

Perkins held up a hand. "Whoa, Jack. Hold on. It's not them."

"What's going on?"

Perkins shook his head, disgusted, and leaned close to me so a group of teens wouldn't hear. "It's O'Reilly," he said. "They found his body behind a TV satellite. He was beaten up and strangled." He motioned toward the back nine.

"Where's Pulchuck?" I said.

"We don't know. But Darcy and Lisa are fine. Lisa's in the TV tower with three cops, and Deirdre is with Darcy in the clubhouse with two more."

I nodded at the cops near the tee box. "You think Pulchuck might make a run at me?"

"I don't know what the hell he's going to do," he said. "I'm being safe. Now go make a birdie."

My wife and baby were under police protection. O'Reilly was dead. *Go make a birdie.* As simple as that. It was classic Perkins.

I shook my head and went back to Silver.

"What the hell's going on?" Silver said.

I didn't answer. The Faxon–Garcia group had hit to the green. I teed my ball, took two practice swings, and stepped up to hit, waggling the club. Sean O'Reilly was gone. He'd been a broken-down old man. He had sold me out and then repented. Six of us had been in Garrett, Maine, and had known what had taken place. One had died there. One was safely tucked away in Canada. One was Pulchuck. Now O'Reilly was dead. That left Perkins and me.

I squeezed the grip of the TaylorMade r7, still waggling the clubhead. Then I released my hands and felt the tension leave my shoulders. No three-wood here. No short, safe tee shot. A bomb over the bunker, then a wedge to the flagstick.

I brought the club back slowly, making a wide arc, then fired the club down and held the follow-through, my balance perfect. The ball carried 295 yards, leaving only 131, uphill, to get home.

Hayes followed suit—hitting his ball past mine. He would need to hole his approach to tie Woods. Unlikely. But he wasn't quitting, and I respected that.

At my ball, Silver was all business. He checked and rechecked the breeze. It was late afternoon, and the wind had picked up, but only slightly. There were probably 15,000 people lining the edges of the fairway and seated in the grandstand wrapped around the eighteenth green. Under different circumstances, this would have been what I lived for: I was at the center of the golf universe and, somewhere, golf royalty—Tiger Woods—was watching, eagerly awaiting my next shot.

But Jerome Pulchuck had been here. And now Sean O'Reilly was dead. I scanned the gallery, recalling Perkins's comments about golfers being targets and how the thousands of spectators could cause havoc while an assailant strolled casually away. I had always known that of all professional athletes, golfers were the most vulnerable. In fact, more than once, during professional tournaments, spectators (often streaking) had run onto a course and hugged a player or sought an autograph. Now, though, I realized how ugly those incidents could have been.

"Earth to Jack," Silver said.

I turned back. "I'm here," I said.

"One thirty-one. But there's a slight breeze at our back. Plus adrenaline. Hit the pitching wedge."

I nodded and took the wedge from Silver. Scanning the gallery was futile. Darcy and Lisa were safe. That was all I could ask for right now. So it had to be enough. I had 131 yards to the pin, for a chance at sudden death and the championship.

I stood behind the ball and looked at the flagstick, visualizing my wedge shot flying high and landing softly. The Titleist stopped six feet from the pin, six feet from forcing Tiger Woods to extra holes.

. . .

At the green, Hayes was first to putt, from twelve feet. He ran his birdie attempt a foot past and tapped in.

"Four inches, left to right," Silver said. "Don't give away the hole." He clapped me once on the back and then moved to the fringe.

The grandstand surrounding the green was shoulder to shoulder. In the television tower above the green, I could see the back of Lisa's head. She was seated next to her co-host, no doubt offering unbiased prospects regarding my must-make putt.

The shadows were growing long as the Texas day was ending. I crouched behind the ball to get one final read. Then there was nothing left to do. No more reads. No more practice strokes.

I stood, set the Bull's Eye gently behind the ball, and made my stroke.

The gallery erupted with anticipation the moment the ball left my putter. I looked up and watched the ball track toward the center of the cup, my fist starting to rise. It was center cut all the way. My right fist pumped overhead as the ball neared the cup.

But the Titleist stopped one revolution short.

My right arm fell limply to my side. I bent, hands on knees, and cursed for several seconds. Then I did what I had to do. I tapped the putt in and, smiling through clenched teeth, shook hands all around, and went off to sign my card for a tournament total of −10, one off Woods's winning score.

I kicked myself in the back of a police cruiser to the airport and all the way home, unable to forgive myself for leaving the tying putt short, although I had no idea things would only get worse.

Monday at 9:35 P.M. Darcy was asleep, Perkins and Lisa were in the kitchen, and I was sitting in my office, thinking. It was early fall now, but I wanted to smell the salty sea air, so the window was cracked. The scent was a rich earthy odor like mud and clams.

Cronjagger had given Perkins copies of Owen Henley's photos and they were spread across my desk. Perkins had used my office when we'd arrived, making calls, and apparently, reviewing the photos. He had brought the 9-mm back. It lay on the desk before me.

In the center of the desk, lay a picture of Nash standing on the pavement near a small kid. I had first seen the photo in Cronjagger's office. I picked it up now and looked at it closely. A large question mark was printed on the back, as had been the case with the original in Cronjagger's office. So they still did not know who the kid was. The photo was grainy and blurred, even more so than the original, but I realized something for the first time. It was fairly recent because Nash wore a shirt Lisa had gotten him last Christmas. I took out a notepad and jotted that down. I would call Cronjagger in the morning to let him know the photo had been take within the past year, unsure if that would help or not.

The picture had been shot from the side. Nash was striding

and looking straight ahead. The kid—I couldn't tell for sure if it was a boy or a girl because it was so blurred—had his or her head cocked at an angle, looking past Nash in the direction of the camera. Was the kid looking at Nash? I didn't think so. Was the kid looking at the photographer? Maybe just daydreaming. From the kid's height, I could tell the kid was two or three years older than Darcy and came up to Nash's waist.

There was a knock on the office door. I said, "Come in."

Nash walked into the office dressed in a purple and gold warmup jacket and blue jeans low enough to show his boxer shorts in the back. A white cord ran from headphones, which hung around his neck, to an iPod attached to his belt. His head was down, and he moved slowly and sat across the desk from me without a word.

"Hey, buddy," I said. "I'm glad to see you. Didn't know you were coming. Are you cutting class?"

He sat staring at the leg of the desk. He opened his mouth to speak, then closed it. He took a deep breath. His shoulders shook and tears began to fall. It was odd to see him cry. He was a twenty-year-old kid—in a professional athlete's body—but still a kid.

"My father," he said, "was no good." He still didn't look up, although his head shook, side to side.

There wasn't much to say to that. Everyone we had met verified it.

"You ever want something to be one way so bad that you . . ." His words trailed off. He leaned back and looked at me for the first time. His copper-colored cheeks were wet and shone beneath the ceiling lights. The skin under his eyes was swollen. He'd been crying a while. ". . . That you make it a certain way in your mind?"

I didn't say anything.

"I guess that makes me a little crazy," he said. "I mean, she told me. But I never let myself believe her."

"Nash, you're not crazy. Who told you what?"

I heard the heavy side door open and close. Through a window to my right, I saw Perkins. The garage was attached to our house like the long side of an "L," and spotlights illuminated the driveway. From where I sat, I could see the front of Lisa's Explorer and Perkins, his shoulder holster still on, toting a flashlight. He leaned through the Explorer's open passenger-side door to retrieve something.

Nash had his head down again. I was quiet. He had driven two hours, on a school night, to talk. The office door was closed, but on the other side of the living room, in the kitchen, the microwave's timer beeped three times. Lisa usually heated water for tea about this time each night.

"My mother told me about it," Nash said. "I guess things are the way they are, and you can't change them. And I guess people are who others say they are."

"What do you mean?"

"My mother hated him. I already told you that."

I nodded. Outside, Perkins shut the Explorer's door and turned toward the house but stopped and shone a flashlight beyond the Explorer, into the darkness.

"I used to ask her why. And finally she said . . ." Nash inhaled. His bottom lip trembled. "For a long time, she never told me. Then, before she died, she finally said why she hated him. She said"—his eyes fell to the floor again—"my father used to touch me, Jack, and made me touch him."

"Oh, Jesus, Nash." I started to get up, but he held up a hand.

"I thought if we could find him, he could tell me it wasn't true." He looked up at me. "And it wouldn't be true then, you know?"

I didn't comment.

"I don't remember anything," he said. "My mother said it happened."

"You were five when he left, right?"

Nash nodded. I thought about that. Five years old was old enough to remember sexual abuse. Maybe he had repressed it. I was no shrink.

"I wanted to meet him and to have him be . . ." He looked away again. "I don't want you to think this is silly."

"I won't."

"I wanted him to be like you. I wanted my father and me to be like you and your father. But then Cronjagger told us why he lost his job, and Claire told us about the other thing." He pushed his palms against his eyes. "I see you with Darcy and I wonder how anyone could . . . And to have it be me is just too much."

"Nash, we'll help you," I said.

But he wasn't listening. "After we saw Claire, I started having nightmares that I can't remember. But I tore my sheets the other night. I don't even know why I broke up with Michelle. We were fooling around, and I just got up and left."

My expression belied the horror I felt. *Nightmares he couldn't remember.* For the first time, I realized that even if Nash had met his father he wouldn't have had closure.

"I'll get you help," I said again.

"I'm alright. I can handle it."

I started to protest, but that was cut short by a tap on the window and Perkins motioning me outside.

"Stay here," I said to Nash. "I'll be right back."

Except, when I got outside, I knew that would not be the case.

There were four of us in the Ford Taurus, but unfortunately, only two people had guns. Perkins was in the back, on the driver's side, I was driving, and Pulchuck sat beside me. Marty Pike was next to Perkins and hadn't stopped glaring at him since I'd pulled the car out my long dirt driveway and headed to the interstate.

"Pretty fucking cute, Jerome," Perkins said. "I didn't see Pike come up behind me."

"Marty's an Indian," Pulchuck said. "They're used to sneaking."

"Fuck you, Jerome," Pike said. His voice rasped. "That's not funny."

I smelled alcohol. In the rearview mirror, I saw Pike lean close to Perkins.

"Think I'd miss out on this?" Pike said. "I owe you for my brother, asshole. When the time comes, I'll be the last one you see on earth."

"Or not," Perkins said.

Through the darkness, I could see Pike's hooked nose and beady dark eyes. He wore the Roots Canada porkpie hat again, blue jeans, and an open flannel shirt over a T-shirt. He had a 9-mm handgun, held loosely in his right hand, near the door and far from Perkins.

Pulchuck adjusted the defrost, turning on the heat. He wore chinos and a polo shirt. A stainless steel .357 with a black grip rested in his lap, his right hand gently holding it. It made me recall the gun I'd left on my desk. Good place for it. Perkins's shoulder holster was empty, so there was an extra gun somewhere.

"What are we doing?" I said to Pulchuck.

"Taking a trip. Part business, part pleasure. We'll even play a little golf."

"Golf, huh?" I said.

"Yeah. Just keep driving north, and keep it at seventy."

"Why seventy? What's in the back?"

"Just golf clubs, of course."

"Why did you kill O'Reilly?" I said. I knew the answer. There had been five people who knew of the golf-bag-exchange program at Garrett Golf Club. The remaining four sat in this car. I felt terrible knowing O'Reilly's apology led him straight to Pulchuck and a final resting place behind a TV satellite.

"That's an interesting question, Jack." Pulchuck turned in his seat and leaned his back against the door so he could face me. "I didn't want to take the time to find a place, then kill the old man in Maine. Because of you, Mr. Perkins, I had to get the hell out of there in a hurry. Figured I could catch up with O'Reilly back in Milton. But then he shows up in Texas." Jerome spread his hands and if to say, *Easy pickings.* "Actually, Jack, you, O'Reilly, and Mr. Perkins all have something in common."

"We know about your Garrett Golf Club scam, Jerome," Perkins said. "So cut the bullshit. A Massachusetts state cop knows all about it, too. And he probably already knows we're missing."

"Of course," Pulchuck said. "I figured as much."

We were quiet. The radio was off. The car had no cell phone that I could see. The only sound was road noise and the hum and whine of passing vehicles.

"O'Reilly and Owen Henley were broken-down people," I said. "You used them and then killed them."

"I gave them each a job," Pulchuck said. "Paid them both a lot more than they made anywhere else, too."

"You don't believe your own crap, do you?"

"Jack, like it or not, I'm a good guy to work for. In fact, I gave you a chance to find out. You could have named a reasonable price. Besides, both those guys came to me looking for work."

"Not looking to get killed," I said.

"I didn't kill Owen Henley," Pulchuck said. "Now everyone just sit back and relax. Things will work themselves out."

Pike snorted and grinned, still looking at Perkins.

We were on I-295, northbound, weaving through Portland. Traffic was light on a Monday at 10:55 P.M. We passed Hadlock Field, where the Portland Sea Dogs play. The high-rise library at the University of Southern Maine was on the left. The first time I had met Pulchuck, in the bar, he had offered money for Nash's photos. Later, in the hotel lobby, Pulchuck had said he came to "talk business," again a reference to money. It was then that he also mentioned having me "disappear" or suffer "an accident." Things had obviously reached that point. Negotiations were over.

"Things will work themselves out," Pulchuck said again, as he stared through the windshield.

"That what you told Owen Henley?" I said.

"Jack, why can't you believe that I didn't kill the guy?"

"Because your word's worth shit," I said.

He turned and looked at me for a long time. Then he nodded to himself as if he'd reached a decision.

. . .

Pulchuck kept telling me to drive. We had passed Bangor, and the muscles around my shoulders were stiff with tension. The air in the Taurus smelled of sweat and body odor. We had stopped once for gas, and Pulchuck had gotten coffee for himself and Pike. Perkins and I were running on tension and fear.

I was exhausted. The day's "downtime" had consisted of a conversation during which I had learned Nash was molested by the man we'd been asking about when all this had begun. Nash claimed he remembered none of it, but admitted to having disturbing dreams. Regardless of what he actually remembered, he needed help neither Lisa nor I could offer. I had planned to call Cronjagger about the shirt in the photo. My next call would have been to Dr. Denise Chavez, with whom I'd spent time in San Antonio. Those plans were now obviously nixed.

As I drove, I realized the abduction and trip to a destination unknown to me were parts of a thorough plan. Oddly, that knowledge put me a little at ease. After all, Pulchuck was not going to shoot me while I drove. He had somewhere to go.

I thought about what Pulchuck had said. He claimed not to have killed Owen Henley. Where ever we were headed, Pulchuck had no intention of allowing Perkins or me to return. So a lie seemed pointless. Additionally, Pulchuck never denied killing O'Reilly.

One player was noticeably absent in all this. Where did Terrell Smith fit? Did he know of the smuggling scam? He was Pulchuck's fall guy. Had he killed Owen? Why had he been partying at Curry College?

The digital clock on the dashboard read 3:44 A.M. now. I thought about home. I had to get back there. Darcy was surely sleeping peacefully, but Lisa was no doubt frantic. I hoped Nash had stepped up and consoled her. Perkins's wife, Linda, and five-year-old son, Jackie, had probably already arrived in Chandler. Cops were surely swarming my house and the grounds outside. Maybe they'd discover it had been Pulchuck who had lured Perkins to where Pike could sneak up behind him. Wishful thinking. While I was at it, maybe Pulchuck had dropped his wallet, or, better yet, left a note saying where they were taking us.

The radio was still off and the car was absolutely silent. Yet no one seemed ready to fall asleep, despite there being nothing to view beyond Bangor except dense Maine forest. I had a pretty good idea what, according to Pulchuck, Perkins and I had in common with Sean O'Reilly. And I figured it had to do with the guns.

We got off I-95 in Houlton, turned left, and went to Presque Isle. Then we drove northeast for another hour, crossed the Crystal View River, and turned right onto River's Edge Road. At 5:10 A.M. we were in Garrett, Maine. The fog rose off the river and enveloped the road. It was still a half-hour before sunrise, but Pulchuck seemed intent on getting somewhere.

"Why are you slowing down?" he said.

"Because I can't see anything. The fog is thick."

"Just drive," he said. Then to Pike: "Got it all set up?"

"Everything is ready," Pike said. "Everything will be where we said."

"No problems, right?" Pulchuck said. "I don't want problems."

"Jerome, I got my cell phone in my pocket. It hasn't rung."

"Does it work off the reservation?" Pulchuck grinned.

"You know, I'm getting fucking sick and tired of your Indian cracks. My brother hated that about you."

"Your brother was a punk," Perkins said. "He wouldn't have known a crack if it bit him in the ass."

In the rearview mirror, Pike looked like he'd swallowed a thumbtack. It was the first time Perkins had spoken in hours. I didn't know what he was up to, but he was certainly stirring the pot.

"My brother should have shot you," Pike said. "Now I'll do it for him."

"Your brother was slow and stupid. That's why he's dead. If you were even slightly smarter than him, you wouldn't be taking shit from Pulchuck."

Pike started to speak, but then paused. I now understood what Perkins was doing. Unfortunately, so did Pike.

"Say what you want," Pike said. "Just remember what I told you. I'll be the last one you see on this planet. I took less money this time to guarantee that."

"If you were smart, you'd keep your ass way the hell up in Canada," Perkins said, "because this golf-bag game won't last. They'll bust you at the border one of these times. They'll get Pulchuck, too, but it might take longer. This setup is perfect for him—no Customs on the U.S. side—but you have to pass Canadian Customs every time. That's too risky, Marty. They're on to you."

"No one's on to anything," Pike said, but he looked at Perkins a little longer than I expected.

"That's enough," Pulchuck said. Then to me, "Keep going. All the way to the golf course."

I drove into the parking lot at the border-straddling Garrett Golf Club. A dense layer of fog blanketed the course. No one would be able to play for at least another hour. As Perkins had said, there was no formal U.S. Border to cross. Americans and Canadians parked nose to nose, separated by a four-foot strip of tar and gravel. We were the only ones there. I didn't know what time the greenskeeping crew arrived, but I knew they parked near the back nine, off a dirt access road. The golf shop wasn't open yet; neither was the clubhouse, even though it was an hour ahead in New Brunswick.

I put the car in Park, and Pulchuck reached over, cut the engine, and put the keys under the passenger's seat.

"So you all set on what we're doing?" he said to Pike.

"Yeah. Like I told you, I left the bags near the target. The boat is there and that river is forty feet deep in the middle." Pike momentarily glanced at Perkins, then back at Pulchuck. "Afterwards, you can go back to Boston."

"And the river's not busy?"

"Not a soul on it the other day," Pike said. "I got rope and weights in the boat and a car on the other side. You got Terrell for sure?"

"Prints on the gun. Piece of cake."

I glanced at Perkins. He gave me a *keep-your-chin-up* look and a wink that said we'd be fine.

It didn't help me. Jerome Pulchuck had a detailed plan. And Marty Pike had cut a side deal of sorts, to kill Perkins. Popularity isn't always a good thing. Golf bags were in the back, Pulchuck had said. He was making another border run, except this trip included Perkins, me, guns, a river, rope, and weights. The combination did not sound hopeful.

Pike got out first. "Come on," he said, smiling at Perkins. "Showtime, asshole."

"Calm down, Marty," Pulchuck said. "Stick to the plan. Get the golf bags."

"No cart?" Pike said.

"These guys can carry the bags. Let's go."

The morning light was gray. To the east, I could see the first hint of sun. Ironically, the sun would rise, and the day would probably turn out nice. The thought made me think of Lisa and Darcy. There had to be a way to get back to them.

Pike tossed Perkins's handgun in the trunk and rechecked the load on his 9-mm. A round was in the chamber. Only three clubs were in each TaylorMade staff bag—driver, five-iron, and putter—although the bag I carried felt as heavy as my own did when loaded for a tournament. I tried to recall if Pulchuck, O'Reilly, and the Pike brothers had carried full sets the other time I'd seen them play.

"B. C. Budd in these bags?" I said to Pulchuck.

"Canadian money," Perkins said. "Right?"

"Of course," Pulchuck said.

"And the B. C. Budd is in the other bags," I said, "the ones we'll exchange them for."

"What makes you so sure it's drugs?" Pulchuck said. He walked in front and spoke over his shoulder. Perkins and I were behind him, walking side by side, and Pike, toting his 9-mm, followed.

"Because something just occurred to me," I said. "I know where Terrell Smith fits into this operation."

"Where's that, Jack?" Pulchuck sounded genuinely interested, even amused.

"He was at Curry College the other night, partying. He's your distributor."

"He's more than that now, but yeah."

"He's your fall guy, too," I said.

"We made the right choice, Marty. They have done their homework."

"So why is Terrell Smith worried about Wal-Mart?" I said.

"Maybe he wants a CD they carry," Pulchuck said.

Pike laughed.

"No," I said. "He came to us. Asked if Wal-Mart, where Owen Henley worked, had contacted us. He's nervous about something."

Pulchuck didn't speak. He cleared his throat once, though, and I sensed he was thinking. So was I. I looked around desperately, but saw only the gray outline of trees and fog-covered water hazards. The only sound was Pike's heavy breathing and the click and tinkle of golf clubs. Then Pulchuck cleared his throat again.

"Missing any money or pot, Jerome?" I said. "Maybe Owen Henley and Terrell had something going on the side. A skimming operation."

"Keep walking," Pulchuck said.

"Hey, wait," Pike said. "What did he just say? You accused me and Robert of taking some off the top, Jerome. What's he talking about? Your driver skimmed?"

"He's trying to distract us," Pulchuck said. "That's all. Keep walking."

We trudged around the water hazard on the first hole and moved up the fairway. The foliage had already peaked, but even in the gray light the leaves were vivid yellows, oranges, and reds. Neither Pulchuck nor Pike hit a golf shot. Pulchuck's stride was deliberate. We were going to a specific location. Pike had mentioned the bull's-eye on the fifth hole. Pressure on the golf course, even in the extreme, is never life and death. This was, and my mind raced. There had to be a way out of this. Again, I looked around. We were alone. We couldn't outrun handguns, and I had only a golf bag. I thought of my father's mantra—"If you can control your mind, you can control your actions." I exhaled slowly.

"How much money," Perkins said, "is in the bags?"

"Enough," Pulchuck said.

"What's the street value of the dope?"

"Four thousand a pound," Pulchuck said. "Fifty pounds, air packed, gets two hundred grand in Boston."

Perkins was nodding. "I didn't figure you for one big score."

"Nope. Steady business transactions."

I thought about that. The Garrett Golf Club, where U.S. residents could simply drive in, walk to Canada, supposedly play golf, then drive home, was the perfect venue for his "steady business transactions"—$200,000 a run was a steady business indeed. Deirdre had guessed at this operation. It seemed like a long time ago now. But guessing and proving were two different things. And now knowing and proving were miles apart. All four golf bags would be there. Somehow Perkins and I had to be the ones to walk out with them. But even that was secondary. They planned to kill us. Just walking out would be enough.

We had reached the fifth hole. It was a par five with a sharp dogleg and a fifty-yard pond, the hole with the bull's-eye target on the tree. We left the tee box and walked around the pond, toward the target.

"The river is down there," Pike said, "through the woods, at the bottom of the hill. The boat's waiting."

The sun's first rays cut through the morning fog. Beyond the bull's-eye, through the woods, I could see across the Crystal View River and further into Canada. Pulchuck was still leading, the .357 at his side, his back to us. He walked beneath the bull's-eye and kept going, his footsteps rustling the fallen leaves that covered the ground.

I knew we had arrived at the destination. They had put only three clubs in each bag for obvious reasons: The money took up most of the space, and fewer clubs meant fewer potential weapons for Perkins and me. But they needed at least a handful of clubs in case someone spotted them on the way back. Then they would drop a ball and play in.

I thought of Lisa, of Darcy, of Daryl Stingley's remark about being there to dance with your daughter on her wedding day. I pulled the bag closer to the middle of my chest and slowly slipped the head cover off the TaylorMade r7 driver. A golf club wasn't enough, but there was nothing else.

I looked at Perkins. The time had come. We'd driven six hours and were exactly where Jerome Pulchuck wanted us. Perkins and I had been through a lot together—childhood friends, college roommates, best man at each other's wedding, godfathers of each other's child. He had saved my life. But neither of us had ever been in a predicament this bleak.

"Now or never," I whispered.

"I don't care much for never," he said.

In front of us, Pulchuck stopped walking, his .357 at his side. As he turned to face us, Perkins charged him before the .357 was raised, ramming him in the chest with his huge shoulder, sending Pulchuck flying backward. They landed on the leave-covered ground, Perkins on top. Then they rolled over.

"He's mine, Jerome." Pike took two quick steps around me and stopped just beyond my left shoulder. He raised the 9-mm. "We had a deal. Leave him for me."

Perkins and Pulchuck rolled, struggling for control of the gun.

Pike bobbed and shuffle-stepped, trying to set the pistol's sight on Perkins. With one move, I pulled the r7 out, letting the bag fall to the ground. Pike heard it and turned, but I was already in mid-swing. The titanium head, traveling at all of my 120 miles an hour, caught him flush in the face.

As he fell backward, his right hand came up. I saw a flash and felt a hot poker sting my upper arm before I heard the sound. I spun to my left and fell back. Blood ran from the side of my left arm. I was momentarily stunned, then realized I'd been only grazed and scurried to Pike's motionless body. His face was bloodied, the bones around his eye socket badly disfigured. I grabbed the 9-mm beside his limp hand.

Perkins and Pulchuck were tossing, side to side, on the ground. Sunlight cut through the fog. I saw Pulchuck's handgun weave back and forth. They rolled once more, Perkins emerging on top, straddling Pulchuck, trying to grab his right arm and the gun. Coming from behind them, I moved to my right, away from Perkins, trying to point the 9-mm at Pulchuck. As I ran, I saw a flash from Pulchuck's right hand and heard the blast. Then I saw what I had not expected, what I had never expected—Perkins seemed to momentarily straighten, then he toppled over and lay face down, blood quickly darkening the colorful fall leaves beneath him.

Pulchuck turned the .357 toward me. I squeezed my finger three times, and he rolled away from me and lay still.

At 1:35 P.M., I stood with Nash in a corridor outside a waiting room at Cary Medical Center in Caribou, Maine. My arm was wrapped in gauze and in a sling. I had written a formal statement and signed it already. Garrett Police Chief Randy Miner, the big Maine State Trooper named Shirley, and Martin Cronjagger all stood across from us. Cronjagger had been at my house when the early morning call had come and had followed Lisa and Linda Perkins to Caribou.

"So, once more from the top," Cronjagger said, scratching his thick brown beard. "Just so I'm clear."

Miner held my statement out to him.

Cronjagger waved that off. "No. I want to hear it." His eyes were bloodshot. He had spent the night searching outside my home before driving north.

"Pulchuck paid Canadian money," I said, "I don't know how much, for the B. C. Budd. And Owen drove the shipments to Boston until he was killed."

"Worth two hundred grand, U.S. money, per trip?" Miner shook his head.

"Right," I said. "But something was up that I don't think Pulchuck ever fully figured out. When I said Terrell Smith, the young guy who distributed the dope for Pulchuck on the college scene in Boston, had come to us and asked if Wal-Mart contacted Nash, Pulchuck seemed caught off guard. When I asked if Terrell and Owen were skimming, Pike jumped down Jerome's throat about an accusation Jerome had made previously."

"And they were going to kill you and take the boat?" Cronjagger said.

A janitor pushed a cleaning cart past us. The hallway smelled of disinfectant, and ceiling lights reflected off the polished linoleum floor.

"I think they were going to shoot us and dump us in the river with weights," I said. "Then Pike was going to take the boat to Canada and Jerome was going to drive back to Boston."

"We found all four golf bags," Shirley said. "Two were full of dope. Two had Canadian money. But there was no Taurus in the parking lot when we got there."

"Maybe Pulchuck was going to stay in Canada a while and drive back later," I said, "and he had someone get the car."

"How's the arm?" Miner said.

I looked through the glass on the waiting-room door. "Insignificant."

We were all quiet.

"For what it's worth," Miner said, and pulled his hand out of his pocket and showed me a string of rosary beads. "I liked Perkins. He's in my prayers."

"Thanks," I said. "Pike and Pulchuck?"

"Pulchuck is gone. Pike is going to have problems—plastic surgery and they think he's going to lose his eye."

It made me think of Owen Henley and how he had been beaten before being shot. I didn't like how that made me feel.

"You think Pulchuck killed Owen Henley?" Cronjagger said.

"No," I said.

Nash looked at me. "No?"

"Pulchuck confessed to O'Reilly. We weren't supposed to be around right now. Seems like he'd have admitted to killing Owen Henley, too."

"Who then?" Nash said.

"I don't know." I looked at Cronjagger. "Where did the descriptions of the two guys Lea Griffin gave you lead?"

"Nowhere. Neither does the house O'Reilly mentioned."

"Lea called me and said you went to see her with a photo of Terrell Smith with Owen Henley," I said.

"It was from a roll of film Owen had developed before he died," Cronjagger said. "Makes your skimming theory seem likely. Terrell Smith said he didn't know Owen, that he was at a cookout and someone was taking pictures."

"Did you tell him Lea Griffin says he went to Wal-Mart several times to see Owen?"

"We didn't give him her name, but yeah, we mentioned it. He says a lot of people look like him."

"So it's a dead end?" I said.

"Hard to find a college kid in Boston who'll rat Terrell out. Probably even harder to find one who'll testify."

"If Owen was skimming and had something going with Terrell Smith, would Terrell kill his cash cow?"

Cronjagger crinkled his nose and shook his head. "I don't like him for that. He's smarter than that."

"So who?" I said.

"This is where you started," Miner said, "isn't it?"

Cronjagger blew out a long breath. Nash and I walked to the waiting room.

. . .

In the waiting room, Lisa was on a loveseat beside Perkins's wife, Linda, who cried quietly. Perkins's five-year-old son, Jackie, slept on a sofa. Darcy played with blocks on the floor. I sat beside Linda and held her hand.

Nash went to the far end of the room and sat alone. Only hours before, he had told me of nightmares that he said he couldn't remember. But their occurrence and his breakup with his girlfriend of a year seemed synchronized with his acceptance of what we learned about his father, as if a wall had been torn down, allowing a flood of realizations to manifest themselves into horrifying dreams and inexplicable actions. Nash now sat, elbows on thighs, head in his hands. He looked up at Linda several times, turning away each time they made eye contact.

"How long has he been in the operating room?" Linda said to me.

"Going on seven hours."

Lisa took Linda's hand and gave a gentle squeeze. Linda had been an elementary school teacher before being a stay-at-home mom. She was small next to Lisa, tiny beside Perkins. To others, her soothing voice seemed to go with Perkins's bull-in-a-china-shop demeanor like fire and ice, and the two were often humorous at parties—a housemother lecturing Hulk Hogan. Yet those people didn't know what they had overcome together, the loss of a child. They were rock solid together.

Linda stared blankly at the floor. "Seven hours is too long," she said, and looked up. "That's bad. I know it is. It's too long."

"Linda," I said, "he lost a lot of blood. I tied my shirt around his chest and ran for help, but it took a while to get him here."

Lisa shot me a look that screamed, *Be uplifting!* But I knew what I had seen in the woods.

"They told me a 30 percent chance," Linda said, and began to cry again—hard full sobs, as if releasing something she'd held back while Jackie was awake. "First Suzanne, now him."

I hugged her for a long time. I had been there when their first child, Suzanne, had passed after only three days.

"Not him, too," Linda said. "I can't lose him."

None of us can, I thought. *None of us can.*

"I'm so sorry, Linda," Nash said. He stood before us. "I'm just so sorry. This is my fault."

I let Linda go. She stood up in front of Nash. Lisa looked at me. I shook my head. We had to let it play out. Linda would say what she would.

"Don't apologize, Nash," Linda said. "He loved you like a son. He did what he did because he wanted to. You did nothing wrong."

I exhaled as a small man wearing a white lab coat over light blue medical scrubs walked into the waiting room. Linda froze. I sat motionless, trying to gauge the doctor's deadpan expression.

"The surgery went well," he said but didn't smile. "But he suffered a stroke. It will be touch and go for the next twenty-four

276

hours. If he survives," the doctor looked directly at Linda, "you should know he might not be the same."

Linda burst into long sobs then. I felt my face flush, my eyes blur. Childhood friends, college roommates, best friends. When we were seven, I had stepped on a rusted nail in the woods behind my house. Perkins had pulled the board from my foot and carried me home. It seemed he'd been saving me from rusted nails ever since.

Jackie stirred on the couch and woke to his mother's sobs. Lisa went over, lifted him, and walked to the window. She pointed at something outside and bounced him, trying to get him to laugh.

"I'm terribly sorry that I don't have better news," the doctor said. "But the road back will be difficult. He'll have to be patient and work awfully hard."

"He can work hard," I said. "He always has."

The doctor patted Linda's arm, nodded at Nash and me, and walked out.

I went to the window and stood beside Lisa. Outside, the sun burned brightly. Brilliant leaves dotted the skyline. I turned and looked at Jackie Perkins in Lisa's arms. I thought of Daryl Stingley's quote again.

"Nash and I are going back to Milton," I said.

"What?" Lisa said. She put Jackie down, and he went to his mother. "Your best friend is fighting for his life, Jack."

"That's the point," I said. "The first time I mentioned Owen Henley's death, Perkins told me he'd find the killer. He tried to save us both, but only I walked out of the woods today. And that won't go for naught. I'll start over, from square one."

. . .

Nash drove us to my house. I showered, changed into fresh pants and a button-down shirt, and got some things from my office. Then we drove toward Milton, Massachusetts. Nash had his CD collection, which didn't make my arm feel any better, but he was driving, and oddly, the shouting from the speakers seemed to help him concentrate. The trip was long and my arm ached, which made me think constantly of Perkins. I owed him and would start over now, where we had begun.

I was a little groggy from a painkiller but mostly just confused. I retraced my footsteps, mentally, as we drove under a bright afternoon sky. For a long time, I had leaned toward Jerome Pulchuck as Owen Henley's killer. Sean O'Reilly had told me Owen had first insulted Jerome by mentioning a "low-carb diet" to Pulchuck, then, in Garrett, Maine, I had heard Pulchuck call Owen a "freak" and tell the Pike brothers he was gone. But Pulchuck hadn't killed Owen Henley.

That left Terrell Smith and the two guys Lea Griffin saw at Wal-Mart the day Owen was killed. But I had Terrell Smith pegged as the brains in the skimming deal, so I didn't think he was the killer either. That left the two guys Lea had offered the sketch artist. Maybe I had spent too much time chasing the wrong pictures.

Lea Griffin got off work at 8 P.M. and agreed to meet us in the dinette.

"I need some more information," I said, and put a coffee in front of her.

Nash sat next me at the table in the café. Lea had, once again, declined the invitation for a meal and sat across from us. Two coffees in paper cups and a bottle of Gatorade were between us. The coffees smelled strong. A menu was on the wall behind the cash register, but Nash said he wasn't hungry. I had called Lisa at the hospital every two hours. No change. Perkins remained in critical condition.

"What happened to your arm?" Lea said. "I thought no one got hurt playing golf."

"Gunshot wound," I said.

"Jesus." She looked at the sling for several seconds, then at Nash. She sipped some coffee and glanced around the café. "What do you need from me?"

My arm didn't seem to interest her. That seemed odd. Or maybe I was just turning into one of those self-centered pro athletes. "What do you remember about the two guys who came to see you the day Owen was killed?"

"Nothing." She looked at Nash, and her expression softened.

"Nothing new, I mean. I said it all to the cops. How you doing, Nash?"

"Not very good," he said. His Gatorade bottle sat before him, half empty. "I've learned a lot about my father." He looked at the checkered floor.

"When you came here before," Lea said, "you were mad at him. You still mad?"

Nash looked up, tilted his head to the side, and stared at her.

"You said you were mad at him for leaving," she said. "Are you still?"

Nash leaned back and slid deeper into his chair. He had on his purple and gold warm-up jacket, which rode up a little when he slid lower in his seat and exposed a big belt buckle. He blew out a long breath. "No." He shook his head. "No, I'm not. I'm glad he left. He wasn't what I hoped he'd be."

Lea didn't speak, but she became very still. She was holding her coffee and set it down carefully. She folded her hands on the tabletop and sat looking at Nash, as if trying to gauge his thoughts. Then she became casual, picking the coffee cup up again and glancing toward the cash register. "Last time you were here, you told me you could hear it all." She turned back to Nash and shrugged. "What did you hear?"

Nash looked at her. I did, too. I sensed something going on between Lea and Nash and sat aside, watching it play out.

"Like I told you," she said, "you ain't missed much not having him around, Nash."

The last time we visited her, she had patted his hand, maternally. Her voice now reminded me of that.

"I found that out," Nash said. "Guess I had to find it out for myself."

"Any idea who those two guys were?" I said.

She was still looking at Nash, but managed, "The guys I gave the sketch artist? No. And you're wasting your time. They're long gone."

"You said that before. How can you be so sure?"

She turned toward me, smiled, and spread her hands. "Wouldn't you be?"

"What about Terrell Smith?" I said.

"What did the cops say about him?" she said.

"To us?" I said.

"Yeah. What are they saying about Terrell Smith? Do they think he did it?" She wasn't smiling or motherly now. Her voice was serious. There was a trace of eagerness in it. "They found a picture of Owen with Terrell Smith, you know."

"Yeah," I said. "They questioned Terrell about it."

"And?"

I leaned back in my seat a little bit and shrugged. I wanted to slow this conversation down. Something was going on with her. But she pushed forward.

"I hear he's a drug dealer." She nodded at me. "Yeah. And I think Owen was using. Or he could've been dealing. He was smarter than people gave him credit for. A smooth talker, too."

She had said that the night Perkins shot Robert Pike. It had bothered me then, but I had been distracted and things had spiraled afterward. It bothered me again.

"Lea," I said, "you told me Owen was a loner. An outcast. That doesn't fit a 'smooth talker.'"

"I know he's smooth-talked people, Jack." She looked at Nash. "What did you learn about Owen? Did anyone else say that?"

"No," Nash said and shook his head. "No one called him a smooth talker."

I leaned back a little farther and folded my arms. "Tell me what the two guys said to you."

"What two guys?"

"The ones you described for the sketch artist."

"They never talked to me, only to Owen."

I sat looking at her.

"You're wasting your time with them," she said. "Terrell Smith did it."

Nash and I both looked at her.

"How do you know that?" Nash said.

"Well, I bet he did."

"Is Leon here tonight?" I said.

"At work?"

"He was with you when I came here alone, remember?"

She shook her head.

"You mentioned your kids come once in a while so you can spend a little extra time with them."

"No. I never said that." She looked down at the tabletop, thinking. Then she looked straight at me. "Damn it all. Who did you tell that to?" Her voice was not eager now. Her words were urgent.

I didn't answer, but sat looking at her. Then I felt myself begin to nod. Owen Henley would've been able to smooth talk, but not adults. "Lea," I said. "Jesus Christ."

I leaned forward and took out what I'd gotten from my office and put it on the table between us. Lea stared at the photo of Nash with the kid in the parking lot.

"The blurred picture," I said, "is of your son, isn't it?"

She stared at the photo.

"We got it from Owen's collection. He was a pedophile, Lea. Wasn't he?"

Beside me, Nash stiffened. "Jesus, Jack. Not here. She's a stranger."

I shook my head. My eyes were locked on Lea's. "You know Owen Henley was a pedophile, don't you?"

"He deserved it. If you know that about him, then you know he deserved it."

"What?" Nash's eyes were wide. "You know about what he did to me?"

She looked at Nash. "You, too?" Her head shook back and forth, sadly, and her shoulders slumped. Her face turned maternal again. She covered his hand with her own.

"He did something terrible to my son, Nash. I caught him. I couldn't let him do that again, to anyone. Ever. Do you understand?"

"You beat him first, Lea," I said. "You tortured him."

"I didn't know what I was doing," she said. "I swear." Her eyes closed tightly and she grimaced. "I had the gun, so he did what I told him. He sat still and I tied him. Then I just . . . did it. I wasn't thinking." She looked at me. "You're a parent. Can't you understand that?"

I ran a hand through my hair. I didn't know what to say. Part of me did understand it.

"Your love is so pure," she said, "you love your kid so much. You want things to be a certain way." She was speaking to Nash now. "I didn't know he had a son, Nash. But I have a son, Nash, a little boy." She was crying now. No one was around. "I wanted things to always be a certain way for him. Do you understand?"

"Yeah," Nash said. "I do."

I watched as he nodded.

"I wanted my son to grow up not knowing about people like him. Now that can never happen. Owen took that from my son."

She stopped talking and cried. No one spoke. I realized I was sitting up straight now.

"Innocence," Nash said. He was crying now, too. "That's what he takes."

Lea sat staring at him, tears staining her cheeks. Nash looked back at her.

"What you did," Nash said, "was for your son." His eyes ran to me.

The long journey had been difficult, but it had been for Nash. So I didn't say anything.

Nash turned back to her. "Take care of your son," he said. "That's all I ever wanted from my father. And you can't do it from prison. Your secret's safe."

Lea looked at me. I sat staring back at her and thought about Perkins, about Daryl Stingley and dancing with your child on their wedding day. We had found out who Owen Henley had been and who had killed him. It had been a long journey to get a confession we wouldn't use. But life is only black and white on the golf course. I thought about what Linda had told Nash— Perkins, too, had done it all for him; we both had.

I looked at Nash and nodded. Then I stood, and we walked out.

EPLOGUE

L ess than four months later, on a Thursday afternoon in January, I was on the ninth hole at Waialae Country Club in Honolulu, Hawaii, for the season-launching Sony Open. I was relaxed and glad for the reprieve from Maine's harsh winter.

Lisa was covering the event for CBS, and Darcy, having just turned three, had spent her morning with me and was now at the day care. Nash was on Christmas break and had gone for a long run on the beach that morning. After receiving a letter from PGA Tour Commissioner Peter Barrett excusing me from further sessions with Dr. Denise Chavez, I had phoned her on behalf of Nash. He had been talking to someone for three months and was doing well.

I was on the green at the par-five, 510-yard ninth hole, standing over an eagle putt. I had been partnered with a Tour rookie I didn't know and a longtime friend, who was −2 on the first nine holes of the year.

Tim Silver and I read the twelve-foot putt from all sides. It would break eight inches left to right. An eagle would get me to −3.

"Give it hell, Jack," Padre Tarbuck said. He leaned on his belly putter and grinned.

"Plan to," I said. "You haven't shut up all day."

"Sorry," he said.

"Don't be. It's good to have a pain in the ass like you back."

"I knew you missed me," he said, his grin widening.

As I crouched over the putt, the Bull's Eye still felt like an old friend who had returned. My stroke was pendulumlike, and the

Titleist traveled down the line and clattered against the bottom of the cup.

I pumped a fist and looked toward Nash. He gave a fist pump back. Beside him, Perkins pushed himself up from a wheelchair and moved slowly three steps away from it and clapped. It was eighty-five and sunny in Hawaii, and the day felt like spring.

But that had little to do with the weather.